D0924568

## Advance Praise for
# WEEKEND FRIENDS

"Unflinching in its portrayal of modern-day parenting, *Weekend Friends* is a chilling debut that is as confronting as it is compelling. Unputdownable!"

—Nicola Moriarty, international bestselling author of novels including *The Fifth Letter, Those Other Women,* and *You Need to Know.*

"Ellwood-Clayton explores the uneasy path of modern parenting, adolescent angst, and the vast consequences of seemingly small choices, where a parent's best intentions are fraught with danger—and potentially deadly consequences. *Weekend Friends* is a deeply emotional tale that will make you laugh, cry, gasp, and ultimately leave you haunted with questions that have no easy answers."

—Annette Lyon, *USA Today* bestselling author of *Just One More*

"A razor-sharp read about the social pressures mothers and daughters face in their respective cliques and how those worlds can collide when more than one person has a secret."

—Georgina Cross, bestselling author of *Nanny Needed, The Stepdaughter*, and *One Night*

"Dark, enticing, and an incredibly poignant delve into modern motherhood."

—L. C. North, author of *The Ugly Truth*

# WEEKEND FRIENDS

# WEEKEND FRIENDS

*a novel*

BELLA ELLWOOD-CLAYTON

A POST HILL PRESS BOOK
ISBN: 979-8-88845-521-0
ISBN (eBook): 978-1-63758-973-1



Cover design by Conroy Accord
Interior design and composition by Alana Mills

Post Hill Press
New York • Nashville
posthillpress.com

Published in the United States of America
1 2 3 4 5 6 7 8 9 10

*For Matisse, my sunshine*

To err is human; to forgive, divine.

To parent—is to fuck up over and over again.

"The emotional system is immature in early adolescence, and small events can trigger enormous reactions. A negative comment about appearance or bad mark on a test can hurl a girl into despair which can last days or minutes, and a new pair of jeans or block of chocolate can elicit unparalleled bliss."

*Marise McConaghy, principal of Victoria's Strathcona Baptist Girls Grammar School*

Part 1

# BEFORE HIS FUNERAL

# Chapter 1

# OKAY, THÉO, I'M LISTENING

## —REBECCA—

### Anchorage, Alaska

What if the police figure out what happened? Will I go to jail? What will happen to Willow?

Another sob erupts. I cover my mouth to muffle the sound, close Willow's bedroom door, and hurry back to the living room. Leonard Cohen's "Anthem" is still playing on repeat.

Stop! I need quiet—to listen in case Willow comes out. With trembling hands, I shove the sleeping pills back in my pocket and turn off the music. Rain on the roof.

Théo is seated in the same spot. Of course he is. Slumped against the corner of the couch, eyes shut. It gives me so much comfort having him nearby; even though he's dead, he's still my husband.

*What should I do, Théo?*

His hands rest on his lap beside his phone. His wedding ring glints in the lamplight.

Clutching my abdomen, I breathe in and out, the faint scent of port in my nostrils.

*Think.*

Why would he send such an incriminating text? Had the drugs already affected his thinking? Or was it deliberate? He wanted me to cover it up.

Nothing Théo did was accidental. He thought everything through at least twice before speaking.

*Okay, Théo, I'm listening.*

The rain falls harder, pummeling the snow outside. A strange calm comes over me.

Théo is guiding me. We are partners united with the focus of protecting our family of three.

I list the evidence.

*The text Théo sent me.*

*Fingerprints on the blue Ziploc bag.*

*His search history.*

*Doctors' reports.*

*...His corpse.*

Outside, it's still dark. Another Alaskan morning. Short days. Sun rises after 9:00 a.m. Not much time. I have to call 911 soon. The wall clock reads 7:56 a.m. How? He's been dead for...hours? Adrenaline courses through my blood. They can't prove how long I waited before calling. Can they? Must get story straight. Willow.... Should I remove her from the house? The neighbors, an older married couple from Juneau, flash through my mind. Figure that out later.

I glance at Théo's phone. *Do it.* I scroll to his last sent message. Tap *Delete.* Rush to my room, grab my phone, and delete the text. A voice message from his mother, Yolanthe, blinks at the top of my screen. I'll deal with her later too. I rearrange the sheets so the bed doesn't look so torn apart.

Next: fingerprints.

Gloves? I find the oversized plastic ones in the kitchen. Ones that most nights I use for the hand-washing, while Théo loads the dishwasher and Willow plays on her iPad. A sob wells in my chest.

My family is gone.

My husband is dead.

He's never coming back.

"Shhh," I whisper as though to a child. And then, "Shut up, Rebecca."

Gloves on, I wipe down the Ziploc bag. He was terminally ill, what else is there to say? He'd talked about suicide many times before….

It's a good plan. Don't overthink it. Everything will be fine. They have no reason to doubt me.

I walk to Théo, my hands shaking violently as I reach for him. "Darling, let me move you, just a little." I hesitate. Will rigor mortis have set in? I touch his hand, a tight claw. Pry open his fingers. I slide the bag under his fingertips, wedge it into his palm. "Thank you, darling. That will help, that will—"

The doorbell rings.

A spasm of panic shoots up my spine. Who is it? How could the police already be here? They can't come in—his dead body, illegal drugs in the house. They could charge me with manslaughter. They could take Willow from me.

It rings again, a death knell. I check the time: 8:03 a.m.

"Théo!"

It's his mother.

*Fuck.* I press my body against the wall, not making a sound. Why's Yolanthe here? Usually, when she visits Anchorage from Montréal, she doesn't leave her Hilton hotel suite until after lunch. Is Gérard with her? Unlikely, since after two strokes, Théo's father rests most mornings.

More pounding on the door. "Théo! I know you're home!"

I have to answer it. Yolanthe will keep knocking and wake the neighbors.

I slip off my gloves and step into the hall. Do I look the part? A grieving widow who's tampered with evidence? Even before I've fully opened the door, cold air blasts my cheeks.

Darkness. As though it's the middle of the night. Framed by a landscape of piercing snow, Théo's mother, Yolanthe Fournier, stands before me, her stern eyes watching from beneath a fur-lined hood. Everything behind her is white: our garden, the hedges, the cars on the street, indistinguishable snow monsters. The rain, softer now, has turned the snow on the porch into slush.

I'm about to make an excuse about why she can't come in when she pushes past me.

"It's freezing," she says in her clipped French Canadian accent, stepping inside and shaking off her wet jacket to reveal the Chanel suit beneath. Crossing her wiry arms, she glares at me. "Where's Théo?"

"I…uh…"

"He sent a text message, a very strange one. I need to talk to him."

"You can't," I blurt. I should have listened to her voice message. I don't know how much she knows.

She looks me up and down. A jolt of fear unsteadies me. I've never challenged her directly. Then I realize I'm wearing my clothes from yesterday—jeans, a crinkled blouse, snow boots.

"Text? What did it say?" I ask calmly, despite wanting to scream and shake her and tell her how crucial it is. Every second we stand here talking threatens the rest of Willow's life. Another mistake: when I erased his last sent message, I should've checked to make sure he hadn't sent others.

Yolanthe fixes her gaze on my hands. "Why are you shaking?"

Why won't she tell me what the text said? If I ask again, it will give away how much I want to know, and she'll keep it from me. That's her style. Exclusion. Omission.

"It's terrible," I say. "Terrible." We can't keep standing at the door. "I'll tell you, but you must be quiet—Willow's sleeping. She can't come out."

"Where's Théo? Is he sleeping, too?"

I head for the kitchen, playing for time. Words are bombs. Whatever I tell her must match exactly what I tell the police.

"Sit—sit," I say shakily.

She remains standing.

"Please. It's important."

She perches herself on the edge of the chair, placing her Valentino purse on the table beside my camera and photo proofs.

"Tea…coffee?"

"I'd like to know why my son texted me late last night."

Two tea bags. Two mugs. I put the kettle on.

The longer I say nothing, the more suspicious I'll seem.

"He's gone, Yolanthe. He's passed."

"No." She grips the sides of her head. "No, that can't be right." Absolutely still, she stares at the wall, only her nostrils move, filling and exhaling. "I—I saw him on Tuesday—he was fine. He was talking about his new manuscript, moving away from the thriller genre…."

I open my mouth, then close it. *He wasn't fine. He was terminal.*

The spoon drops onto the counter. I flinch.

*I'm sorry I killed your son.* Is that what she wants to hear?

The kettle whistles. "Milk?"

"Théo asked me to—to—he had a female protagonist," Yolanthe says. "A…park ranger. He wanted me to read his newest chapter. He asked me to read it."

I take the tea bags out and drop them in the garbage like dead mice. I pass her the mug. "Drink. You're in shock."

She doesn't take it, just stares ahead, eyelids flickering. "I started reading the chapter. I have notes. I need to send them to him."

I touch her shoulder. We don't have time for denial. Willow could wake up any minute. "He was watching a movie…. He…" I steady my voice. "He died peacefully."

She looks at me unblinking, then she's up—moving with such speed that she knocks her purse, contents scattering as she screams, "Where is he?"

"Shush! Willow."

"Where's my boy?"

I gesture helplessly to the living room, and she's gone.

I find her kneeling at Théo's feet, moaning. Her head resting on his thigh, tears streaming down her wrinkled face.

"Please." I crouch beside her. "Please, for Willow's sake, be quiet."

She keeps moaning.

"We knew this would happen," I soothe, desperate to close the gaping hole of anguish so I don't fall in too. "He didn't want to suffer. This is what he—"

"Don't you dare! This is not what he wanted." Something between us shifts. Her eyes narrow and her jaw hinges open, as though she's just realized something. "I don't believe a word you say."

I stand, mind whirling. If I can't lie to her, how am I going to pull it off with the police?

"You never wanted to look after him," Yolanthe spits.

"Of course I wanted to look after him!"

She stands. "That night, you showing up at the hospital in that red dress. Disgraceful."

I knew it was a mistake to go to the Food and Hospitality Ball, but Théo thought I had spent too much time nursing him and insisted.

"Out partying while he's dying, weren't you?"

On the evening of the event, Théo was in terrible pain; we went to the hospital, and he assured me he'd be fine. I rushed back to his room afterward, slipping through the halls in my floor-length red dress, shocked to come face-to-face with his mother. "Yolanthe, Théo told me to go. I was there to network."

Her mouth twists. "Is that what you call it?"

I wipe my brow, sticky with sweat. My knees feel like they could give at any moment. What the hell am I going to do with her? I grab the arm of the couch and sit beside Théo, like some sick tableau of domestic bliss. Already, his jaw under his dark beard looks more prominent, the skin on his face sagging. My poor, beautiful Théo.

"It must have been the money," Yolanthe says. "It always is. Life insurance?"

Nausea hits me. Why won't she stop? The living room is sweltering, so hot it could melt all the snow covering Anchorage. The scent of popcorn rises from the bowls on the coffee table. I strip down to my tank top.

"How much is the payout, Rebecca?"

I clench my back teeth.

"How much?"

Nearly $2.5 million, but I won't tell her that.

"Was it the other man, then?"

"You can't be serious." If Théo was here, he'd say, *Watch out, Maman. If you keep talking like this, more dead bodies may well end up in the house.* It hits me like a shock wave—I will never hear him tell another joke.

Yolanthe needs to leave. Now. I have to call for the ambulance and coach Willow before they arrive.

"Nathaniel." Yolanthe's cheeks are scarlet. "Your friend from Instagram?"

Jesus. Was there anything Théo didn't tell his mother? I clutch the locket around my neck, ashamed for thinking ill of the dead. The flirtations I had with Nathaniel were well before Théo's diagnosis. They were harmless—even Théo agreed after I showed him the messages. Not that I had shown him all of them. "Nathaniel is just a work colleague."

"I know everything about your marriage," Yolanthe says in a low, hateful voice. "I even know about the intimacy issues."

*What?*

"Théo never had that problem with Claire."

His first wife. Trust Yolanthe to bring her up.

"Grand-mère?"

Willow stands at the entranceway to the living room in her flannelette pajamas, dark bed-hair sticking out in different directions. Two more steps toward us and she'll spot Théo.

"Stop!" I hold out my hand. "Darling, please."

"But—"

"Willow, listen to your mother." Yolanthe seems to have forgotten how rarely ten-year-old girls listen to their mothers.

"What's going on?" Willow yawns.

I can't understand why Willow is awake. The drugs I gave her a few hours before Yolanthe arrived must not have been enough. I should've given her a full dose.

"Why's Grand-mère here?" Willow asks.

"Because—because Yolanthe is going to take you out for…a special breakfast." I pray Yolanthe goes along with my improvised plan.

"But I've got school." Willow rubs her eyes. "We have our global warming presentations."

"Which I know you've worked hard on, but it's not every day your Grand-mère visits. Go to your room and get dressed. I'll be there in a moment."

If Yolanthe wasn't here, Willow would roll her eyes, but instead, she yawns and heads to her room.

A plan comes to me.

When Willow is out of earshot, I whisper, "I don't know what to do. I'm barely keeping it together. I don't want Willow to see his…corpse."

*Offer to take her.*

"*Mon Dieu.*" Yolanthe lifts a trembling hand to her mouth.

"I have to call 911 now. They're going to storm into the house…it's going to be awful."

"Well…should I take Willow all day?"

"Yes, yes," I say—quick, grateful. "I know it's a lot to ask, but please don't mention anything about Théo. I want to tell Willow myself, later, when she's back."

Yolanthe looks uncertain.

"Trust me," I say.

She stares at me coldly. But Willow has both our hearts, bridging our divided loyalties.

"We should tell Willow now," Yolanthe says.

"No. She can't speak to the authorities. It's too much for her. Please."

Yolanthe sighs. "You're her mother, not me." She heads to the kitchen and picks up her jacket and purse.

With Yolanthe off my back, I have to go into Willow's room, put on a happy face, and figure out what the fuck to tell the police.

Part 2

# BEFORE HER FUNERAL

# Chapter 2

# GHOST

## THIRTEEN MONTHS AFTER THÉO'S DEATH

### Boca Raton, Florida

Two kids race by, sneakers squeaking on the hallway floors, interrupting the nearby hum of lessons. Midmorning light filters through the windows.

"I'm not going in." Willow crosses her arms.

"Yes, you are."

"No, I'm not."

If we had pistols, it'd be a Western standoff. I want to whistle that gunslinger tune, but I know she won't laugh, and I don't blame her. If it was me entering a new classroom halfway through the first semester of sixth grade, I'd want to run the other way too. I need to convince her she's braver than she feels.

I bend down to her eye level and brush a piece of lint off the polo shirt that is part of her uniform. "Listen, Willow. It's school. Nonnegotiable until you're eighteen. I promise homeschooling would be worse. Me and algebra? Not fun. You can do this."

She shoots me a death glare, but her lower lip wobbles.

We've already had three fights on the way here, and I was supposed to have left fifteen minutes ago for a meeting with a potential lucrative client: The Bagel Guys. As a single mom, an identity I am still wrapping my head around, every lead counts.

"I hate this, Mom. I hate it. People are going to ask questions."

"Tell them what we rehearsed."

"No! I can't."

"Come on, deep breaths, like when you're teaching me yoga." I demonstrate inhaling through my nose and blowing out of my mouth like a puffer fish. The corridor smells like disinfectant, sunscreen, and metallic lockers. "And remember, if anyone brings up—"

"Hello?" A woman in her mid-twenties, presumably Ms. Naseer, stands in the hallway, one hand on her open classroom door, the other on her hip. Everything about her is colorful—the fabric of her maroon skirt, the glittery bangles around her wrist, and the small gold ring in her nose.

"Hi, we're new. I'm Rebecca. This is my daughter, Willow." I push Willow gently toward the teacher. "The woman at the desk escorted us here but, ah, I asked if she'd give us a few minutes alone as we've had some... *resistance*."

Willow scowls.

"How old are you, Willow?" Ms. Naseer tilts her head.

"Twelve. Almost."

Preteen. The word itself is frightening, the brink of so much change. Her body shows all the signs: her chest has formed little buds, there's a fine dusting of hair under her arms, and her moods? A Florida hurricane is less turbulent. But given everything, that's more than understandable.

"And your favorite subjects?"

"Gymnastics."

"I said *subjects*. Not pastimes." Ms. Naseer is stricter than she looks.

Willow glances at me. "I guess, art?"

Schoolwork isn't Willow's strong suit. She loves to move her long-limbed body, to leap on a balance beam, to tumble, high, off the mat, or somersault on a trampoline—she's not for the earth; she belongs in midair.

Fittingly, Théo named her after Alaska's state bird, the willow ptarmigan. It suits her. Gracefulness and agility.

"Okay, this is where I leave you." I bend down and kiss her cheek, noticing that her breath smells faintly of the almond milk she had on her oatmeal. I once made the mistake of taking her to visit a dairy farm when she was younger and inadvertently turned her into an activist. Hell hath no fury if I try to buy animal milk. "See you at 3:30."

Her big brown eyes plead with me.

"You have to admit, it's not as bad as camping at Chinitna Bay." Our last family holiday, Théo's idea, was on the shore of Cook Inlet. When we woke up in the morning, our tent was encircled with giant grizzly paw marks.

A tiny smile appears on her face, revealing her crooked front tooth, which the orthodontist warned me is a month away from needing braces. I smile back. After everything she's been through—everything we, as a team, have endured—this is our fresh start.

It's not as though we didn't try staying in Alaska. Each day, we waited for it to get easier. It didn't.

After a year, I made the decision. A break from Alaska's harsh winters to the other side of the country to heal. Palm trees and endless sunny afternoons.

Although I never lived in Florida, Mom was raised here. Most summers during high school she brought me and my younger brother, J.J., down from New York, and we rented a beach house in the northern part of the state—in "Jax," Jacksonville.

Willow takes a step toward the door, then pauses. "You packed my iPad, right?" Students need to bring their personal devices so the teachers can set tasks and email homework assignments.

"You've got everything you need."

She frowns, expression grim, and I can't help wincing. *Not everything.*

"Love you," I mouth.

She cups her left hand into a half heart. I do the same with my right. To anyone else, it just looks like a wave.

She trails after Ms. Naseer into the classroom. The door shuts. Umbilical cord snipped.

My eyes are still itchy from the paint fumes in our new house. Digging in my purse, I find my eyedrops, and flood my eyeballs.

Although Willow doesn't know it yet, she's got everything to look forward to. Maybe I do too. Théo used to tell Willow, "The beginning is always today." Although I liked the sentiment of each day being full of opportunity, sometimes it annoyed me, especially when I was picking up his belongings from the day before off the floor.

Now, I'd give anything to find his snow boots beside the TV in the living room. His half-open novels all over the house. Those discarded Post-it notes with illegible scrawl, scene ideas for his manuscript. His fleece jacket draped over the couch, smelling of trees and wind from his daily walks.

I hurry down the school hall, and barely notice the woman blocking my way.

"I know you!" she says in a slightly accusatory voice.

I do my best not to show my irritation. If I don't leave soon, I'll be late for my meeting. The woman's close to my age, perhaps a few years older, mid-forties. Tanned, wearing a low-cut dress, red hair in loose curls around her chin.

"I definitely know you. Pilates?"

I shake my head. I'm a jogger and prefer to exercise outside. Green space or "blue space," the term psychologists now use for time spent being by the ocean or lake.

"Wine Society?" she offers.

"Sorry, not me." Something about her does seem familiar, though.

"Rebecca Grimly!" She claps her hands together; the sound echoes off the lockers around us.

A passing teacher turns and glares as if she's going to send us to detention.

"That was my maiden name." It clicks. "Odelle Rackark?"

Instead of answering, she envelops me in a tight hug. Her perfume, jasmine with an undertone of green tea, is overwhelming. When we were teenagers, she smelled of tennis balls and coconut suntanning lotion, and her hair wasn't red but a shade of brown she always complained about, wishing it was anything but mousey. She also used to be chubby with a milky complexion.

She steps back, eying me. "It's Odelle Wragge now. How long has it been?"

"God. Forever. We were girls!"

"It was"—she holds up her fingers, calculating—"shit, twenty-two years ago."

I met Odelle at the annual tennis camp in Jax. As teens, we were highly competitive and well-matched, although her backhand always let her down. Why did she move to Boca? How strange we both ended up in the same southern town.

She gestures out the window. "Should we grab a coffee, and you can tell me every sordid detail of your life?"

Some things don't change. She always enjoyed putting others on the spot: cute guys, overbearing coaches, catty girls. With the skill of a caricaturist, she could reduce any person into one true, but vicious, line. It used to make me laugh, but I'd instantly be ashamed for going along with it.

"I'd love a drink, but I have a meeting." Besides, catching up with Odelle would lead to conversations I wasn't ready to have. The whole point of moving to Boca, rather than Jax, was to avoid bumping into ghosts from my past.

We head outside, enveloped in the Florida double whammy of sun and blue skies. As we cross the manicured grounds of Aqua Vista Academy toward the parking lot, I can't help but think the campus resembles an upscale bed-and-breakfast, with cream and black cottages surrounding the main building. Yolanthe insisted that Willow attend the best private school in Boca, and here we are.

The air is humid, unlike the glacial wind in Anchorage, and I immediately break into a sweat, thighs damp. I take out my car keys and mentally plan my route. Hopefully I-95 won't be congested.

Odelle raises her chin and looks at me from under her eyebrows. "What do you do?"

Something makes me hesitate; it's as though she's waiting to hear what I'm going to say so she can outshine me with her own achievements.

Or maybe I'm imagining things. I never used to be defensive. Then again, a lot has changed in the last year.

"I'm a food photographer."

"With what magazine?"

"I freelance." I don't add that I have connections with Miami's top chefs and best restaurants. That I cornered the Alaskan market as a niche food stylist of big game, moose, bear, and aquatic delicacies. Alaska is home to forty-eight species of fish. I don't need to prove anything. I don't.

"Is that why you're at the school—to take pictures?"

It's strange. I don't want to tell her about Willow. I don't want her to know anything too personal about my life. I shake the feelings off. "My daughter's starting here."

"Oh wow." She waits a moment before pouncing. "Why's she starting mid-semester?"

"It's just how it worked out." I try to sound breezy. The Odelle I remembered was wildly fun, but her bullshit radar should not be underestimated. "How about you? Did you pursue criminal law?"

"The opposite." Odelle laughs. "Party planner. Instead of locking them up, I let them loose."

I laugh along, hiding my surprise. She used to talk about justice. About the necessity for getting drug lords off the street and drug users out of jail. Her father, Peter Rackark, was a judge—a big name in Jax. I never imagined she'd leave a community where she was so entrenched. Then again, once I made the decision not to stay in Anchorage with its painful memories, to take Willow back to the place where I spent my teenage summers, it only took us a few weeks to pack everything we owned and disappear.

As we near the row of parked cars, Odelle's fast pace and swinging arms remind me of her formidable serve. A diamond on her left finger catches the light, a marquise solitaire, at least four carats—unlike the simple gold band I used to wear. *Pour tous jours* was engraved within: "For all days," an endearment Théo would whisper to me in the early years when we were first in love, and nothing was more erotic than him speaking to me in his native tongue. Once the honeymoon period was over, a few years into our marriage, there was less *honey* and more *moon*: cold, cratered, rough circular depressions on our surface.

"So, who's the lucky guy?" I ask Odelle. "Don't tell me you married Jimmy 'Kiss-Me-Now-Or-I'll-Die'?" That was her crush, a playboy, who "coached" older ladies at the tennis club. We were thrilled to have our very own Johnny Castle from *Dirty Dancing*, the same bad-boy windblown hair and attitude. We used to cruise by his house, spying on him through his windows, leaving anonymous love letters that we'd sign off, "Nobody puts Baby in the corner."

Odelle smiles, the wrinkles adding depth and beauty to her face. "Yup, husband number one. He turned out to be a class-A douchebag, but he gave me the best presents in my life. My daughters, Lucy and Stella." Before I get a chance to ask, Odelle says, "Lucy's twenty, she lives in Illinois."

"And Stella?"

"She goes to Aqua Vista. She's twelve."

"Oh…" Our girls are in the same year. How peculiar, like galaxies colliding.

Odelle stops in front of a silver Mercedes. "If you can't have a drink now, let's get the girls together after school." She gives me a knowing look. "I'm sure they'll be the best of friends."

My instinct tells me to stay away, but then I think of Willow. If anyone needs a friend right now, it's her.

Mistaking my silence as acceptance, Odelle says, "Great! It's a plan. See you at pickup."

# *Chapter 3*

# THE LION'S CLASSROOM

—WILLOW—

*The beginning is always today*? Papa is wrong. First days suck. You never know what jerks are going to be around. Usually, there are a lot.

When I enter the classroom, a few people look up, but most keep talking to their friends, too busy to notice. That's okay. I don't want the attention.

Ms. Naseer says, "Willow will be joining our class. She's come all the way from Alaska. Willow, why don't you tell us a little about yourself?"

*Kill me now!*

I shuffle on my feet and say I'm from Anchorage. I want to say that my papa is—I mean, was—a famous writer. Famous might not be entirely true but his books *are* at bookstores, and he's been on podcasts and stuff, so he's kinda famous. But Mom says we shouldn't talk about him. So, I tell them I like gymnastics. And *Harry Potter*. And that in the northernmost town in Alaska, they don't see the sun for sixty-seven days of winter.

Dark days. They made Papa's depression worse, at least that's what I heard my mom tell her friend, Jane, anyway.

"You'll enjoy the sunshine here then," Ms. Naseer says. "We're one of the sunniest states in the nation. Class, I'm trusting you to make Willow feel welcome. Willow, there's a seat at the table at the right."

As I move toward the table, everyone's eyes are on me, judging. It only takes a split second to figure out whether someone's cool or a loser. Some days, I feel like both.

*I don't care. I don't care. I don't care.*

I walk like I'm at a gymnastics meet, shoulders back, eyes ahead, like a "lioness surveying her kingdom." Coach's words, not mine. Gymnastics. Another thing I miss about Alaska. Even though my mom said I could join the team here, gymnastics makes me happy, and after what happened with Papa, I don't deserve to be happy ever again.

I didn't listen to him the night he died.

Would he still be alive if I had?

I sit at the only empty seat—between two boys, across from three girls—and drop my bag at my feet.

A boy beside me has messy hair with curls falling in his eyes. I can feel him looking at me, and eventually he says, "Hey. I'm Alek."

My face heats up. "Hi, I'm Willow. Oh, wait. You already know that." I try to laugh it off as a few heads turn.

Bending, I pull out my pencil bag and try not to fiddle with the zipper. Mom should've let me stay home for another week. I place my basic black pen—didn't want to risk being uncool—eraser, and pencils on my desk.

The boys have the same uniform as me, polo shirts and khaki shorts, but I'm wearing a pleated skirt. Even though there are some other cute boys in the class, *if* I had to pick, I'd chose Alek.

I've never had a boyfriend. Never been kissed. Never *wanted* to be kissed. But some boys are cuter than others.

Once everyone has settled down, Ms. Naseer says, "Only three weeks until camp, kids. Willow, we'll have to get your forms sorted out right away."

*Three weeks?* No way. I'm not going to camp friendless.

"The Everglades National Park is a wonderful camp location…1.5 million acres…made up of coastal mangroves, sawgrass marshes, pine flatwoods…"

Barely listening, I peer around at the girls. Normal girls and rich-looking girls—clones without a hair out of place. Professional blowouts by the same hairdresser. In Anchorage, nobody cares about stuff like that. Long hair's only good because it stops the windchill in winter.

Ms. Naseer drones on. "Low-oxygen soil…slow-moving waters… sediments…"

You can tell the girl seated across from me is popular. She just has this aura or something. Blonde hair, shaved underneath on one side, and giant cat-shaped eyes. She's wearing a red pendant necklace with matching acrylic nails. She catches me staring and I quickly look away.

The school policy says no nail polish or jewelry. Won't she get in trouble?

I check the wall clock. It's gonna be a long day of pretending everything's alright. Good thing I have plenty of practice.

At the front of the room, Ms. Naseer scratches her head. "Where did those forms disappear to? Give me a minute."

As she searches in her desk, the girls at the table beside us gossip, and I can't help eavesdropping.

"Where's Sarah?" one of them asks.

"She faked being suicidal to get attention," a girl says. "Now she gets to stay home from school for a week."

"Well, if Megan Markle faked it, right?"

"Yeah, mention you want to die, and you never have to do homework again."

They both laugh, like death is a joke, and I feel I'm walking in deep snow, my legs stuck, unable to move.

"Here they are." Ms. Naseer pops up from her desk and comes over and passes me some papers. "Make sure your parents sign the forms."

*Yeah, right. I'll be ripping those up.*

As Ms. Naseer walks away, I swipe my hair off my face and accidently knock my pencil bag to the ground. *Nooo.* My *snowman* eraser—and *penguin* pencils—and other embarrassing Alaskan animal stuff skitters to the floor.

The popular girl picks each one up.

My stomach flips, all nervous and bubbly. She'll think they're baby-ish. She passes them back and whispers, "Cute. So aesthetic," in not a sarcastic way.

"Uh, thanks."

Ms. Naseer bangs on and on about the Everglades essay we need to write. I prop my chin on my hand, gazing out the window at a tree with white flowers. On the top branch, two birds look like they're cuddling, wings pressed up close to each other. Then one kinda jumps on top of the other and flutters its wings. I wonder how birds actually *do* it?

I chew my lip and let my eyes go out of focus, slipping into dreamworld—Papa used to call it that, anyway, whenever I spaced out. I clench my fists, digging my nails into my palm until it hurts, leaving angry moon marks.

I miss him.... It's weird; I don't just miss the good things. I'd be so happy to have him lecture me about homework or get angry because me and my friends were being too noisy when he was trying to write. The funny face he'd make when he farted. Those cringy French songs he'd sing in the shower. How much salt he'd put on his food because he couldn't taste things well.

Sitting up straighter, I force myself to concentrate on what Ms. Naseer is writing on the whiteboard. That's what he'd want me to do.

*See, Papa.* I'm listening now...even though I didn't listen when it mattered the most.

*I hate myself I hate myself I hate myself.*

## Chapter 4

# MAKE NICE

### –REBECCA–

The sun glistens on Aqua Vista Academy, as though blessing all of its pupils. I follow the blooming magnolia pathway, stopping for a moment to squeeze eyedrops into my irritated eyes and psych myself up for the first school pickup. My heart races. I'm not sure if it's because of the white-knuckle drive to get here on time after my Bagel Guys meeting—I-95, the main highway, has five lanes in each direction filled with aggressive drivers—or because the first day of school for Willow is also the first day of school for me.

I cut around to the back of the school where moms, nannies, and a few dads congregate near the classrooms or huddle in smaller groups beside the play equipment. A freshly mowed lawn stretches out behind them. The scent of eternal summer, grass, and blue skies. New terrain. Yes, Willow deserves this.

Even though I try to slip into the waiting area unnoticed, Odelle spots me. She comes right over, lifts her Gucci sunglasses onto the top of her head, and says with a sly smile, "Hello, Blast-From-My-Past. I still can't believe you're here!"

We spend a few minutes catching up, and she learns my address—*renting a house on Glendale Drive*—asks for an update about my family—*Dad passed six years ago, heart attack, mercifully quick, Mom's still in New York, J.J.'s married, no kids*—and introduces me to her friends.

Most look like they're in their early forties. After forty, it seems like no one cares exactly how old you are. You're just not young anymore.

I plaster on my best meeting-new-people face.

Unlike the moms of Anchorage in their Kathmandu fleeces and all-terrain shoes, these mothers scream Florida—sun, sex, surf. They're trim, dressed like tropical birds in fuchsia, lime, and turquoise, wearing beaded sandals or espadrilles. Unabashedly girly. Feminism, in Alaska, has desexualized us, banning figure-hugging clothes, low-cut tops, anything that will stop us from being taken seriously. Which is the way I like it. But now, makeup-less, in my linen beige suit and brown flats, I feel stuffy, uptight. A crone among goddesses.

"Fiona is a nurse." Odelle touches the tanned shoulder of a blonde woman with a round, kind face. "Call her for all your emergencies."

Fiona rolls her eyes good-naturedly. "Please don't. My training has lapsed, so officially I'm not practicing. Other duties," she says with a shrug. "You know, kids. And call me Fi."

"And this is Paulita. Guard your husband."

When Paulita laughs, her whole body moves. She is stunning, with her dark glossy hair and bright fitted dress.

I don't tell Odelle she needn't worry. My husband is no longer with the living, and he preferred the librarian look. Glasses, pencil skirts, buns.

Paulita tsks. "Odelle forgot to mention I'm running for mayor next year. *Vota por mi*!" Impressive. "And that I'm happily married. So no need to guard your husband."

"Paulita and I go way back," Odelle says. "Our eldest daughters were besties."

"Where are they now?"

"Lucy is a dancer, lyrical. She's at Columbia in Chicago," Odelle says.

"And Giavanna's at the University of Florida." Paulita lifts her bracelet-laden wrist in a dismissive wave.

"Modest much?" Odelle punches her shoulder. "Paulita's eldest is a former Miss Florida and studies medicine now."

Being a high achiever must run in their blood.

In my periphery, something moves behind one of the trees. My pulse quickens. I shade my forehead against the glare, but there's nothing out of place. No person in the shadows.

*Get a grip, Rebecca.*

Too many months of insomnia is the problem. I'm jittery. Unfortunately, sleeping pills aren't an option, not with Willow's night terrors. I need to hear her if she screams for Théo during the night.

I thought moving across the country would stop my paranoia, but it appears my guilty conscience follows me wherever I go.

It started in the weeks following Théo's funeral. I'd be doing something—buying groceries, picking up Willow from a playdate, dining at a restaurant with my friend Jane—then I'd feel it: the uncanny sensation of being watched. As the months passed and we tried to resume a normal life, the feeling came and went.

At first, I thought it was someone from the insurance company.

I'd been granted Théo's insurance money, a "death benefit payout" of $2.5 million.

Everyone believed he died of natural causes—the EMTs, the doctors, the insurance company, our family, and friends. There was no investigation. Only I knew I committed a fraud. Afterwards, I invested most of the insurance money and set some aside for Willow's college fund.

In Alaska, there is no Death with Dignity Act. Terminally ill adults can't end their life with lethal doses of medication from physicians. Based on the archaic clause in our state's penal code, if a person intentionally aids another person to commit suicide, they can be charged with manslaughter.

Of course, when Théo was diagnosed with cancer, we could've moved to Oregon or California or any state that does have a DWD law, but the timeframe was too tight and Théo refused to uproot Willow from school.

"Have you met the head of school yet?" Fi asks me, pulling me back into the present.

"No, he wasn't here when I did the school tour," I reply.

"Wait until you hear him play. He's a musician, and *hawt*."

The bell rings, and Fi and Paulita head off in different directions.

The school doors fly open, and the students rush outside in groups, voices raised in boisterous conversations.

I use mommy vision to locate my child—a skill I've fine-tuned after years of looking for her at amusement parks, zoos, and kindergarten sandpits.

Obviously trying to disguise her aloneness, Willow hides her gangly frame amongst a group of boys. My heart aches as though it's me and I'm the one wishing not to stand out, to blend into a sea of anonymity.

I wave vigorously, showing too much emotion for the protocol of a school pickup.

Willow quickens her step, embarrassed.

I give her a quick hug, and she whispers into my ear, "I'm not going to camp. That's all everyone talked about."

Camp? I didn't realize this was coming up. I should've thought to ask for the events calendar when I did the school tour.

"Aren't you cute," Odelle says to Willow.

Willow flinches and pulls away. She hates being called cute and skipped the entire stage of collecting fluffy toys, drawing pictures of rainbows, and seeking affirmation from anybody other than her papa.

"Willow, this is my old friend Odelle," I say, transferring her heavy school bag from her shoulder onto mine.

"Old soul, twenty-year-old figure!" Odelle quips, which is true and kind of hilarious, but I keep a straight face.

"Hi," Willow replies politely. Her eyes say something else: *This better not mean I'm going to be forced to stand around while you two gossip.*

"Willow, you're a mini-Rebecca," Odelle says.

Although we both have black hair and pale skin, that's where the comparison ends. She's long and lean and has a mysterious, delicate beauty. I'm compact and athletic. Théo used to say I was the splitting image of Jennifer Connelly in *A Beautiful Mind*. I'd laugh and reply, "Sure, a more dowdy sister."

Willow catches my gaze and jerks her head toward the parking area.

"So, are we still on?" Odelle asks me.

Mmm. It's safer to make an excuse and take Willow home, but perhaps I shouldn't look a gift horse in the mouth. I have the ability to hand my daughter a friend on a platter, an insta-companion. Having someone she knows at school will give her what I can't—a support line—and it will also make camp a possibility rather than a public hanging.

I turn to Willow. "Actually, honey, change of plans. We were thinking of going out with Odelle and her daughter."

"She's right over there." Odelle points to a group of girls hanging out near the climbing bars. "Stella? Stella! Come here!"

After being called a few more times, a girl with brunette braids reluctantly picks up her bag and walks over. She has a confident gait and a necklace with a red pendant. In her hand, she clutches a few sticks of twisty licorice. Red acrylic nails, filed into lethal weapons.

"Stella, this is Willow," Odelle says.

Stella takes out her AirPods. "Hi," she says, her smile accompanied by matching dimples. Everything about her is soft, curved, sealed, and pleated at the edges like a dumpling. Her mother, on the other hand, would be the spicy dipping sauce, splashy and complex, chili oil, soy sauce, vinegar.

"Hi," Willow mumbles.

Odelle addresses the girls, "Willow's mom and I used to rule our town and we need to plot our comeback." Odelle giggles and I do too, the sound of my laughter surprising me. Back in the day, when we arrived at any party the mood immediately shifted. We *were* the party.

"We'll pick up some snacks," Odelle says to Stella, "and meet them at a park for a picnic. Then you and Willow can get to know each other."

I can't help but smile. Odelle plans playdates now with the same vigor she once arranged house parties. *I'll pick up some beer and we'll meet at the jetty before we hit the party.* Then, the scope out. Who was there? Who wasn't? Who did we want to kiss? We'd knock back our drinks, talking nonstop in our two-person bubble, where no one mattered but us, then sway in the living room or the backyard, wherever the bass was pounding, undulating our hips, singing along to the music, and belting out the chorus with abandon—aware, but not caring, that we had an audience. In the end, it was always each other's reflection that gave us the biggest high.

Until it didn't.

Does Odelle remember the incident, the strange thing that happened at the end of that last summer?

"Which park are we going to?" Stella asks her mom.

I stare at her eyelashes as she speaks. They're not fake, are they? Odelle lets her daughter have acrylic nails and fake eyelashes at *twelve*?

"The one between our houses. Fort Park."

"No way, it's haunted. I'm not going there."

"It's not haunted." Odelle makes *Angry Mom in Public Face*, which is basically a normal face, but the eyes are big and crazy and mean business.

"Fine," Stella says, although it's obvious she isn't happy about it. Luckily, the girls are still at the age where we have some measure of control, but soon, when they cross into teen territory, we'll be at their mercy. If they turn out to be anything like us, we're in trouble.

"See you in fifteen minutes," Odelle says to me. "I'll bring *adult* refreshments." She grins, all mischievous.

They wave goodbye. Just as we head toward our car, a man too handsome to be wandering around the mother-populated school grounds approaches us.

"Mom!" Willow elbows me. "It's *Mr. Brady*."

"Who?"

"The head of school."

Surely not. He's far too young for the job. Too tanned and relaxed. My mouth twists and I fight the sensation to laugh.

Only in Boca.

# Chapter 5

# MR. BRADY

As the head of school gets closer, Willow and I both grind to a halt as though he's a government official about to check our passports. A ripped government official who moonlights as an exotic dancer.

"New student alert." He grins at Willow.

He's tall with wavy brown hair and a friendly face. Instead of wearing a jacket and tie, he's in a button-down shirt, sleeves rolled up. His arms are muscular, and I imagine he spends a lot of time on a rowing machine or doing the breaststroke at South Beach.

"Most first days of school are no fun," he tells Willow, "but they're especially not fun when you start mid-semester. Don't feel bad if today wasn't great."

"Thanks." Willow shifts on her feet.

"I hope everything's all right so far?" His concerned eyes wrinkle at the corner. And their color—the stylist in me can't help pitch them as though for an editorial—*Alaskan green, forest leaves touched by raindrops.*

"I'm Mr. Brady. Welcome to Aqua Vista Academy." He offers me his hand.

"Thanks. Rebecca Fournier." I shake his hand and notice he's not wearing a ring. Maybe he has a girlfriend. Maybe he has a few.

Brady gives Willow a formal handshake. "And you are—besides my newest and brightest student?"

"Willow."

"Great name. One of my favorite characters has it," Mr. Brady says.

"Who?" I can tell Willow likes him.

"In the movie *Willow*, directed by Ron Howard, Willow is a young farmer chosen to undertake a perilous journey in order to protect a special baby from an evil queen. Fabulous fantasy adventure story. You'll have to see it."

Willow nods happily.

"Where did you move from?" Mr. Brady asks me. "Come far?"

He has no idea how far. We've traveled from death to life, from brokenness to a new, shattered whole. But here in Florida, the sun always shines, and the sea is only five minutes away, welcoming, ready to cleanse us. "We're from Alaska."

"Really? Wow, wouldn't have guessed. I always think Alaska is just dog-sledding and glaciers."

"Ha, no. Anchorage is big. We sit at tables. We even eat with cutlery."

"We do sometimes catch our own dinner, though," Willow says.

"Wild polar bear on a bed of orca?" Mr. Brady asks, deadpan.

"More like fresh salmon," I say.

"There's reindeer dogs, too, which are yummy," Willow adds.

"Rudolph dogs?" Mr. Brady makes a horrified face.

"They're just hot dogs made of reindeer," Willow says.

"Don't forget Inuit ice cream, *Aqutak*: seal oil, reindeer fat, snow, and berries." I smile.

"Mom styles food photos," Willow says. "Her berry pics are in *Food & Wine*."

My hype girl. It's sweet she's proud of me. My ode to Alaskan berries—cloudberries, highbush cranberries, crowberries—recently gained a lot of attention.

He turns to me. "You're a photographer?"

When I nod, he says, "So was my mom. She studied under Clyde Butcher. He does enormous black-and-white landscapes."

"I know of him. Florida's Ansel Adams, I hear."

"Well. We're lucky to have you."

Is he flirting with me?

He clears his throat. "A new family to add to our community."

"No gatekeeper?" *Shit. I'm definitely flirting back.*

His smile widens. "That would be me. Consider yourself in."

"There's that saying, 'I don't want to belong to any club that would accept me as one of its members'?"

"Ha! Groucho Marx!" He laughs. "I'm going to enjoy you."

The innuendo. Now I'm the one feeling like a schoolgirl. The sun is getting hotter by the second—where's a water fountain? Are the other moms watching? I don't need a flirting-with-the-head-of-school target on my back.

As Mr. Brady talks with Willow for another few moments, I observe them. His demeanor is playful, energetic, and warm. The students are lucky to have such an engaged leader.

I catch him checking out my left hand. Inappropriate considering A) this is about Willow, and B) I'm a-too-recent-to-be-feeling-this widow. But I think I like it.

Even though I'm not wearing a wedding ring, for all he knows I'm happily partnered.

"If you don't have any other questions?" Mr. Brady says to me, and there it is—an undeniable exchange of sexual energy.

Another feeling surges through me, obliterating it: guilt.

How can I be reacting like this to someone other than Théo?

Even though Théo hasn't been dead for long, our sex life had become like arctic tundra. We were a team, like-minded, respectful, committed, but we hadn't had sex in years. I've always liked sex; actually, I loved it.

I missed the intimacy, the physicality.

Shortly after Willow was born, Théo's low sex drive became impossible to ignore. I thought it was me, that our relationship had reached a sexual flatline like so many of my other friends with kids: sensuality transferred to the adoration of offspring. Only later I came to understand that not only was depression dampening his desire—so was the cancer. How long had it been poisoning him before he was diagnosed?

But I didn't know this then. All I knew was my husband didn't want me. He didn't want to be near my naked body curled up against him in bed. He didn't want my kisses that started at his neck and ended when he pulled away, returning to whatever novel he was reading. A literary chastity belt.

"By the way," I say to Mr. Brady, "I didn't realize camp was coming up so soon. Given Willow is new, it might be too much for her to attend."

"You could always volunteer to join, keep an eye on her yourself."

Willow lifts her shoulders in a shrug. An okay from her?

"I'll be there too," Mr. Brady adds like an afterthought, but we both seem to grasp his true intentions—an invitation. He glances at the ground.

I give him a wary look. *I've been around the block. I've met your kind. Even if I could take your interest seriously, I'm off-limits.* Of course, I am. I'm a mom at the school, a widow, and too old. He must be thirty or so, at least ten years younger than I am. Although, if the tables were turned, no one would think twice. I'm no longer the girl I was when Odelle and I were young and full of confidence. That part of me is gone and never coming back. Might as well have a sign across my pelvis: *Out of order.*

He half-smiles as though he can read my mind. "What do you think, Willow? Should your mom come? I make great s'mores."

They're both staring at me, waiting for a "yes."

"As fun as that sounds, I'm afraid I have to work."

"As usual," Willow mutters.

I shoot her a disapproving look.

"Aw, that's too bad," Mr. Brady says with an exaggerated frown.

"Mr. Brady?" A mom struggling to carry a helmet, a basketball, two school bags, and a scooter pops up from behind him. Some other moms, who must have been waiting for a break in our conversation, nearly topple him over, accosting him with questions.

"Sammy was sent to the nurse again. Why weren't we informed?"

"Are you attending Paulita's fundraising dinner?"

"Mrs. Richardson keeps calling Molly a..."

I didn't quite catch the last bit, but it was either a "lesbian" or "thespian."

Before getting dragged off, Mr. Brady glances over his shoulder with a half-formed wave. A busy man with his adoring flock. I'll do my best to avoid him. But my younger self pushes up through the ice like a milky-white snowdrop burning through snow. What would happen if I didn't?

# Chapter 6

# THE LOST GIRLS OF BOCA

"I don't want to hang out with someone because her mom's making her," Willow complains as we get into our car.

"Maybe Stella will turn out to be your best friend." I turn on the engine, blasting the AC.

"Or not. Her mom's weird."

Goosebumps prickle my skin. I adjust the air vents. Willow's intuitive. "How so?"

"She's fake and loves attention. She's had so much plastic surgery."

"She hasn't had plastic surgery." Has she? Maybe Botox? Odelle's skin seemed flawless, her eyebrows sculpted, giving her a monied, polished look. Admittedly, my skin care routine is a handful of warm water before brushing my teeth.

"How was school?"

A long pause.

"Like, in *Harry Potter* terms?" I ask.

"Ms. Naseer was like Professor McGonagall—strict but nice. And the recess duty teachers are worse than Snape."

"Uh-huh." At least she's talking. Lately, I've been finding it hard to get into her head.

I reverse our navy BMW out of the parking lot. It was Théo's "midlife crisis" gift from his mom. Yolanthe spoiled him in a way I never could; I suppose that's what happens when you're ultra-rich and only have one son.

My car was old, requiring too much time in the shop, which gave me the perfect excuse to sell it before we left Alaska.

For a man who prided himself on being anti-materialistic, Théo loved this car. The back seat was always covered in books. He couldn't pass a bookstore, thrift store, or garage sale without saying, "Just five minutes." One of the hazards of being married to a writer. At home, he considered every flat surface in our house a bookshelf. Most books, though, stayed unread. I used to tease him as I passed him in the hall, murmuring *tsundoku*; the Japanese term for the art of buying books and never reading them. It had broken my heart to box up every one, save those he wrote himself—a crime series set in our stunning Kenai Peninsula—and leave them at a thrift shop in Anchorage.

Another hazard of being married to a writer was his love of silence, which at the beginning of our relationship, I found endearing. (*Such a serious artist!*) But, over time, it came to include total resistance to even discussing the possibility of baby number two. Each year as Willow got older, the gap between our first child and our potential second child grew until it felt infeasible.

I signal and move into the next lane. Even driving around Boca is pleasing: the flat roads lined with palm trees, everything domed by the ever-blue sky. I put on the stereo. Willow sings along to the song under her breath, *The young ones will never die....*

I run my hand over the leather steering wheel. Mr. Brady, youthful and charming, larger than life. Théo would be intrigued by him, possibly considering him for one of his characters. Peter Pan in charge of the Lost Boys and Girls, or, in this case, the tweens of Boca. I wish I knew if he was single or not. Purely out of curiosity, obviously. Was it Paulita or Fi who mentioned he played music? Folk songs on the guitar, jazz riffs on the sax, or maybe he was the singer, front man for the adoring fans. I could ask Odelle. No. I shouldn't be thinking about him. But I am....

A man hasn't given me that kind of *buzz* for years.

That's fine. Mr. Brady can be my guilty pleasure—eye candy at school. There's nothing wrong with a little healthy objectification, is there?

Willow yawns. "I want to go home and sleep."

That's her way of dealing with stress and sadness: blackout sleep. For the first six months after Théo's death, besides school, she barely left her bed.

My grief was different, a numbness that covered everything like a blanket of snow. No pleasure from life. Food without flavor. Conversations with friends, colleagues, family—all bland. Meaningless. Nothing made me *feel* anything except being with Willow.

It didn't help, the lies.

After letting Willow know Théo had died and comforting her, I said it was important she tells no one, not even our family members, what happened at our house the night he passed away. "The police might question you," I warned her. "If they do, you have to tell them you went to bed early, that it was just a normal, regular night. Do you understand?"

She'd looked at me confused and said, "But you taught me never to lie. Honesty, always."

"Some things are private," I explained. *And much too dangerous.*

If the truth came out about that night, the psychological damage to Willow would last a lifetime.

As I near the park, my phone rings. My dear friend, Nathaniel. He called twice last week, and I never got back to him. I bite the bullet.

"Nathaniel, how are you?" I put him on speaker.

"Good, good."

He always doubles things for emphasis; it's as annoying now as it was when we dated during my first year of college. What he lacks in grace, he does make up for in fabulous foodie conversation.

"Are you well?" he asks. "I tried calling before...."

"Sorry, with the relocation, there's been a lot on my plate."

"Well, that's a good place for things to be."

I laugh.

"How's the Sunshine State?"

"Sunshine-y."

"I always thought you might move back here." He doesn't hide his disappointment. "What's better than New York, New York?"

"Nothing." *Nothing*, I echo silently. "The food keeps calling to me: the baked pretzels, the Italian ice, the eggrolls. I'm going through withdrawal."

"You should come up soon. Your mom would love a visit."

"I will."

"Let me know and we'll grab dinner. I remember you were very fond of seafood. Oysters, I believe. The most romantic seafood. Casanova himself was said to have gulped down fifty for breakfast every day."

I glance at Willow, who's putting a finger down her throat.

Dinner, yes. A date, no. When Théo was alive, dinner with a male friend was just dinner, but as a single woman—is it ever?

I pull up to the park set between two quiet residential streets, hidden from houses.

"Are you making friends down there?" he asks.

"We are."

"I know things must be tough without Théo. When I was at the funeral—"

Willow stiffens and it all comes back.

*...Approaching the Alaskan Heritage Memorial Chapel, the sunshine and snow too bright, Willow crying, "I can't, I can't," her mittenless hand pulling my arm....*

"Sorry, Nathaniel, gotta go."

That was our tragedy. We knew Théo was sick. We knew the end was coming. But we didn't get to say goodbye.

# Chapter 7

# MILKWEED

Large oak trees border the circumference of Fort Park, providing dreamy patches of shade. In the middle of the park stands a grouping of four wooden castles with bridges and interconnected walkways, hidey places, and metal climbing bars. A swing set has one seat missing.

I spot Odelle and Stella lounging on the grass.

As we approach, we pass a man on a bench reading the newspaper and two moms camped out with strollers and a Noah's ark assortment of plush animals. Odelle hovers beside a picnic blanket. There's wine, grapes, and brownies, white plates, and linen napkins. But Odelle's brought plastic straws. I glance at Willow. Thankfully, I don't think Willow has seen the straws yet.

We join them on the picnic blanket and Odelle holds out the tray of brownies. "Help yourself. Stella's creation."

The color of the plaid picnic blanket reminds me of Théo's favorite blanket, which I now keep on the arm of the couch in our new home.

Willow bites into the gooey square. "Mmm, so good."

"The secret is marshmallows," Stella says. "And not overbeating the eggs."

"You're good at baking," Willow says to her.

"I should be. Mom makes me do most of the cooking. Like, she puts in requests for dinner."

"For real?"

"Every night. Quinoa, kale, quinoa, yams. There's only so much I can do."

Willow giggles.

"Why should I do all the cooking?" Odelle says, sitting with her knees tucked under her. "Have your cake and eat it, too? Pfft. Moms buy the groceries, bake the cake, clean the dishes afterwards, serve the cake, and if we dare to eat a slice, well, weigh yourself in the morning."

I would laugh, but the weight comment makes me uneasy. To encourage body positivity, I've made a point to never complain about my appearance, mention calories, or use the word "fat" in front of Willow.

I scan the park. Is the man on the bench watching us? From here I can't tell, but come to think of it, the fact he was reading the newspaper is suspicious in itself—who does that anymore?

As the girls chat, Odelle offers me wine, pouring a full glass.

"Mom!" Stella takes an iPhone out of her pocket. "Take pics for my Insta."

The girls stand side-by-side, their heads tilted toward each other. They're almost the same size, their hair a similar length and color, but Willow's is a few shades darker brunette. Stella's an inch taller, with more meat on her bones. Odelle snaps a few pictures as they pose. Stella lifts her face, pouts, angles her cleavage. She sticks out her tongue. Willow copies.

"Why are they doing that?" I ask Odelle, *sotto voce.*

"Doing what?"

"The tongue thing."

"It's a trend on social media."

"It looks…sexual."

"Don't be such a prude! It's cute."

I slip off my shoes and try to get comfortable on the blanket. "When did Stella get an Instagram account? Not to be judge-y"—although I am judging—"but aren't they supposed to be over thirteen?"

"Whatever." Odelle joins me on the blanket. "All the girls are on Instagram, TikTok, Snapchat. You don't want Willow to feel excluded."

"Did you hear that, Mom?" Willow calls out, grinning. "It's social suicide."

"Your friends in Anchorage weren't on Instagram." I slap an ant off my ankle.

"Ahh." Odelle tosses her hair back. "So, that's where you've been."

The wine tastes incredible, a sharp edge to the sweet floral. Each sip relaxes my posture, my head slightly heavy.

We devour the food—the moist brownies, the crisp grapes, and the warm chicken-and-mushroom pies that Odelle miraculously produced from another basket.

The girls run across the park, near where the trees grow thick.

"All right, Rebecca, quit the small talk. I want to hear about your life. Sex, politics, race, religion?"

"Ha. Let's start with our careers. What made you stop pursuing law?"

Odelle picks a blade of grass. "I made it through the first two years of college, and, I don't know. I met this guy, Antonio, from Brazil, and I dropped out. If you saw Antonio do the "Lambada," you would've done the same. But, in all seriousness, law wasn't for me. I was only doing it to please my father."

"Your dad must've been furious when you quit."

"He got over it. Anyway, it turns out running your own business is more demanding than criminal law."

"Tell me about it."

"Photography, right?"

"I'm a food stylist."

Odelle screws up her mouth, her tongue protruding at the corner, and then licks her lips, and I remember how she used to make the same expression when the referee sided with the opposing tennis player and she was about to blast him. She lived for confrontation. "What does that even mean?"

Awakening my competitive side, I grab my iPhone. "Here, take a picture of our picnic."

Odelle gives a firm smile, rising to the challenge, and takes a few pictures before passing me back the phone.

"Nice," I reply, looking over the images. I walk barefoot to the closest tree, wondering how long it's been since I felt grass between my toes, since I spent an afternoon hanging out at a park with someone who used to know me better than my high school boyfriends. After breaking off a small branch from the silver maple, I collect a sprig of Milkweed, bright orange, and yellow flowers, and return to the picnic blanket. Scooping up a handful of grapes, I drop them in clusters onto the blanket from above, scatter the maple leaves and place the flowers, just so, beside the brownies. I angle myself above, aligning the shadows to replicate the lazy afternoon.

When I'm finished, Odelle cups my phone in her hands and studies the picture. "It's beautiful—so artistic."

"Thanks." I smile, genuinely pleased.

On the bench, the man appears to still be reading. Not a figment of my sleep-deprived imagination.

"Did you go to art school?" Odelle asks.

"Self-taught. There's lots of courses online. Anyone can do it."

"Pfft, false modesty. Same as when we played tennis. It'd be 6–2, 6–0, and you'd be all, 'Anyone could have won.'"

She's got me there.

"No wedding ring?" she says.

"None." It's in my mother's safety deposit box in New York, a gift for Willow when she turns twenty-one. I gave it to my mom before we moved to Boca because I didn't want to be branded as the poor widow or judged for moving on too soon. My grief is private, not to be shared.

"Ugly divorce?" she presses. "How do you even co-parent from Alaska?"

"No, it's not like that. He…passed." I avoid her gaze and reach for my locket. "I'd rather not talk about it right now, if you don't mind. I'm still processing."

"Oh God. Of course. I'm so sorry. Was it recent?"

I give her a look and instead say, "What's your husband like?" A big shot, no doubt, with killer sex appeal. I know her type.

"Ron Wragge." She says his name as though trying it on for size. "He's brilliant. A senior partner with Ernst & Young. Travels a lot. Asia mostly. He's in Bangkok this month."

"Is it difficult with him away so often?" I serve the question hard, extra spin. If she keeps prying into my life, I'll pry into hers.

She smiles mysteriously. "Pluses and minuses. He rents an apartment there."

"And this is husband number…" I hold up two fingers and when she shakes her head, I hold up another.

We both laugh. Given Jimmy-Kiss-Me-Now-Before-I-Die is Stella's and her older sister's, Lucy's, father, I wonder if Ron wanted biological children of his own.

I take another gulp of wine.

Odelle leans back on her elbows, stretching out tanned legs. "So, after high school, then what?"

"I worked at my parents' pharmacy for a while. Then traveled, got into photography."

"Love affairs?"

"A few intense relationships, nothing like what I had with…Théo. My husband."

"How'd you meet?" she asks gently.

"I was in New York in my experimental art stage. I had this idea to do a study of a street corner—show up at the same place for three months and capture the subtle changes."

"Fascinating."

"There was a coffee shop on the corner. Two, actually, kitty-corner from each other. Each day, the same man sat at the window table of one of them. He was scruffy, with a beard, hunched over a laptop. I imagined he wrote screenplays about lofty ideals. Then, one day, as autumn was changing the colors of my photographs, he came up from behind and said he wanted to name a character after me."

"Romantic!" Odelle coos. "But I bet it was his go-to pickup line."

"Be nice." Somehow, I invariably end up laughing at her insults, even when I'm the punchline. It's always been hard for me to hold a grudge with her. After all, she saved my brother, J.J., from drowning. A bunch of us were out on boats on Lake Underhill one summer; no one knew he was in the water. J.J. had done all the wrong things: He was drunk. He didn't have a life jacket on. Only Odelle noticed him sinking.

She helped me too—helped me out of my shell and to stand up to my parents. If it wasn't for her, I might've followed in their footsteps and become a pharmacist.

"How did you meet Ron?" I ask.

"He was a colleague of my father's if you can believe it. Gah. Should've seen the signs."

"Ouch."

"Don't look at me like that. Don't you dare think for one second that my life is bad. The truth is, I like him being away."

"Really?"

"When the cat's away, the mice will play. And I know where the tastiest Camembert is."

We cackle so loudly that we don't hear the girls approach. They stand before us, arms crossed. The fun police.

"What?" we ask, Mom Faces back on. For a short while, it had been like I was somebody else.

"We're thirsty."

Odelle hands them old-fashioned lemonade bottles with striped straws.

Willow does a double take.

Oh no, here she goes.

Ever since she watched some Netflix eco documentary, she's become a Nature Warrior.

"Um, did you know that five hundred million straws are used every day," Willow says, "and get thrown away? Plastic never breaks down and turtles swallow straws."

"Huh." Odelle frowns and it's hard to tell whether she's offended or not.

"Some people don't know about the turtles," Willow says. "It's messed up."

"Wow, yeah, I buy loads of straws as a party planner. Cocktails with straws are fun...but maybe not if it's hurting animals?"

"Definitely not." The two girls seem to agree.

"Tell you what, do some research about the most eco-friendly straws, then come to my office—which is often poolside"—Odelle trills gaily—"and put forth your case. If you want to save the world, you need good presentation skills."

Willow smiles, and the girls sit on the blanket, chugging the lemonade.

"I like your necklace," Willow tells Stella.

The silver chain reaches below the neckline of her T-shirt. The pendant, I can see now, is small red kissing lips, like the emoji.

"Thanks. Me and my friends all have one. It's because of our names—*KISS*—Katia, Issy, me, and Sherice."

"Cool," Willow says. "I think one of your friends might be in my class. She has the same necklace. Blonde hair."

"Yeah, that's Issy. She's into music and cheer. And she's pan."

"Pan?" Willow asks.

"You know, gender blind. Gender doesn't determine who she likes."

Willow still looks confused. Twelve-year-olds in Anchorage don't talk like this.

"Issy's Fi's daughter," Odelle tells me.

"Mom, don't eavesdrop!" Stella says. "C'mon, Willow, let's relocate."

They do cartwheels on the grass, one after another, legs spinning like windmills. Willow does some tricky flips, running fast, before diving headfirst into the air. Then she walks on her hands.

"She's great," Odelle says. "Have you signed her up for cheer?"

"No, Willow does gymnastics." Or she used to. Ever since Théo's death, she won't allow herself to do the activities that brought her the most pleasure; she's punishing herself.

"Well, in Boca, it's all about cheer."

The girls are on the raised wooden platform positioned on the second-largest castle. Willow wraps her knees around the high bar, hanging upside down. Beside her, Stella yawns and scrolls on her phone. Although they're the same age, it feels like there are years between them.

"Cheer practice is after school on Mondays, Wednesdays, and Fridays," Odelle says. "I'll see if I can get Willow a tryout. I hold some sway with the higher-ups at the school."

Without thinking, I reach out and touch Odelle's knee, and say, "Thank you," my voice thick with emotion. Maybe bumping into her was a blessing. She's been nothing but welcoming.

A crackle, like a branch being stepped on in the nearby bushes.

My head snaps around. "What was that?'

"Birds? They never shut up." She flicks a red curl from her eye. "Another thing—you should come to Paulita's party. Ostensibly, it's to celebrate the work of the Aqua Vista Fund volunteers. We just got a new turf lawn for the school. Hello…? Earth to Rebecca?"

"Sorry." Cold despite the warm temperature, I rub my arms.

"Anyway, the school council will be at the party. The main fundraising core, the principal Mr. Brady."

Oh. I feel a surge of excitement—or is it apprehension?

"Our girls are having a mini party at Paulita's, too. In the wing, upstairs."

Their own wing? We're not in Anchorage anymore.

"Mom! Mom!" Willow yells, her voice barely reaching me. "Help!"

Odelle and I jump up and all I can think of is last year. *The same scream. Willow over my bed, shaking me. "It's Papa, it's Papa! Wake up!"*

Odelle grabs her purse and we run toward Willow's voice, deep in the wooden castle that's closest to the bushes. Crouching, we enter, smelling sawdust as we climb up the small, cramped space.

Willow is against the wall, clutching her hand. Blood drips down her finger.

"Owww. I cut myself!"

"On what?" I ask.

"A nail. It's bad."

Odelle takes her hand, and before I know what's happening, Odelle slips Willow's finger into her mouth and starts sucking nosily like she's slurping a slushie.

My stomach flips. What is she doing? I want to pull Willow's hand away, but I can't move.

"There you go," Odelle says, a few moments later. The blood has stopped, and, like a magic trick, she got a Band-Aid from her purse, applying it to Willow's finger, quicker than I ever could.

"Uh, thanks." Willow takes a step away, wiping her hand on her jean shorts.

On the wall, someone has written in white chalk:

**Little girls suck big dicks for free**

I share a look with Odelle. God knows why someone would write that. The kind of person you fear at a mall when your child wanders off and, for a few horrific minutes, you can't see them. The kind of person you're warned to watch for in movie theaters and public bathrooms. But, ultimately, we know what children don't: it's the people closest to us we need to worry about.

"If anything bad or uncomfortable ever happens with a man, you always tell us," I say. "Okay? Willow?"

"Can you not," she snaps.

I lead the way out. She's tired. Since Théo's death, being in public for too long puts us on edge.

"C'mon," I say. "It's time to go home."

The man reading the newspaper is gone.

# Chapter 8

# ROCKET SHIP

## Two weeks later

The ceiling fan spins, a lulling rhythm. I could turn on the AC but prefer the tropical feel. The oriental lilies I used for my shoot add to this, filling the kitchen with a heady scent. Our rental is unremarkable, a two-bedroom, white stucco, single-family home at the end of a cul-de-sac. What sold me on the house was the open-plan kitchen. Those windows overlooking the lime-green palm trees offer more than excellent light. They offer abundance—optimism.

The front door lock clicks.

"Hungry?" I call out to Willow.

"Starving," she says, entering the room.

"Green or red?"

"Green."

I toss her an apple, then assemble a plate of crackers and peanut butter. As I hand her the plate, I can't hold back a groan.

"Bad back?" she asks.

"Just a lot of overhead shots today." I suspect I've pinched a nerve, but I don't want her to worry. She already does enough of that for a nearly twelve-year-old.

Willow's in her practice cheer uniform—the colors of Aqua Vista, blue and silver. I'm thrilled she's started a team sport again. She sets her phone and schoolbooks on the counter.

In the two weeks since Willow started school, Stella has included her in her group of friends. Ms. Naseer said Willow is adjusting to her new class, and, most tellingly, her night terrors are retreating. Since Théo's death, they come at least once a week. She wakes, body coated in sweat, calling for him.

"How was cheer?" I fold the reflector from today's shoot and take the sheet off the counter.

"Good." She sits on the stool and stuffs a few crackers into her mouth.

"Any competition?"

"Not really. Stella's good at tumbling. And everyone says Katia's an awesome flyer, but she's been sick." She takes a bite of apple. "So, this thing happened. Coach took me aside."

"And?"

"She wants me to be a flyer." She shrugs, my humble little gymnast. In Anchorage, she was the top of her team and had a bedroom full of trophies.

"Congratulations, but…"

"But what?"

"It's a dangerous position." During the stunts, flyers are at the top, or thrown in the air, at risk of concussions, especially if dropped. I open the fridge and pour us kombucha.

On the counter, her phone buzzes. I read the text upside down, rubbing my sore back.

Sender: Katia: **400 c**

Huh. I'm about to ask Willow what that means when she says, "Come do some yoga."

"Can't, someone has to cook and tidy." *And do hours and hours of editing.* But I know better than to bring that up. After she goes to sleep, I'll be at my desk until midnight, reviewing the pictures I took earlier today, selecting the best, then editing them forever.

Once Willow has finished her snack, she persuades me otherwise.

She's my yoga buddy. Blame her boho upbringing, her baby yoga classes, followed by *Cosmic Kids Yoga* on YouTube, or a natural calling to teach, but she is, and always has been, my guru—my 4'7" personal trainer. When she was little and I took her to the park, rather than playing, she'd run me through strenuous Sun Salutations, making me balance on one foot, counting out loud as I shook like an ancient flamingo with a compromised pelvic floor.

"Take off your dress before we start, Mom." She unrolls two yoga mats.

I'm usually straight into shorts and a tank top the minute I walk in the door, but my silk sheath is so soft and breezy against my skin. I undo the buttons, slip it off, and hang it over a chair, then lay on the yoga mat in my underwear and bra.

Mr. Brady enters my mind. His golden biceps and silly jokes about Alaska.

"Best part of the day, worst part of the day?" I ask, turning onto my side. Usually, we play this at bedtime, but lately, I feel the need to check in earlier.

"Best was hanging out with KISS at lunch. We came up with this dance routine because we're doing a talent show at camp."

She wants to go? "Could be fun," I say, trying to hide my hope.

"Maybe."

"Worst part of the day?"

"...Missing Dad."

This is her usual answer. I nod.

"You?" she asks.

"Best: landing a new client, Raz-Pops. And my worst was—" *The pain in my lower back. Crippling loneliness. The sensation of being watched.* "Missing Dad."

She leans over and opens my locket.

A wedding picture of Théo and me—Alaskan wildflowers in my hair, mountain forget-me-not and arctic sandwort—Théo, eyes shut, kissing my cheek. Whenever we went for a walk or a hike, he'd collect wildflowers for me. A romantic.

"Let's start," Willow says. "Breathe in, deep from your tummy. Hold it! One...two...three.... Downward-facing dog.... Plank...."

Théo used to tease me that with three creatives in the house, a writer, a photographer, and a miniature yoga teacher, it's a surprise we managed to pay the rent. That made me uncomfortable in the early days before my business took off. How could he joke about financial straits? Come the end of the month, we often wouldn't be able to pay the bills. Théo would make a quiet phone call to his mother, standing in the hall, speaking in a hushed voice, and the next time I'd open our bank balance, voilà, money appeared. Of course, I was grateful, but Yolanthe isn't the kind of person you want to owe a blood debt to.

After twenty minutes, Willow moves on to my favorite part of her class.

"Now close your eyes. We're going to go on a journey. Imagine you're in the sky, zooming through the galaxy. Lift your arms, point your toes. You are a rocket ship. Stars are everywhere, planets, Venus, Mars, Jupiter—"

My phone rings, and I flinch.

"I'll get it." Willow jumps up. "It's Granny, on FaceTime."

Before I get a chance to collect myself, my mother's New York accent dominates our space.

"Willow, your granny misses you!"

"You, too," Willow says.

"Goodness, Rebecca," Mom says, "what are you doing sitting around in your underwear, which"—she tsks, as though it's a greater oddity—"doesn't even match."

I feel like telling her widows don't need nice lingerie. But Mom gets her hair set every two weeks and never leaves the house without lipstick and kitten heels, so she'd be the last to empathize. Always the undisputed leader of our family, she has been "the popular girl" her entire life. Some women, even from a young age, have the X factor and reign at the top of the social hierarchy without even trying.

I grab my dress and slip it over my head. "Willow was putting me through my paces. I'm about to start cooking dinner."

"Gotta do homework. Bye, Gran." Willow waves.

"Wait," I call as she heads down the hall. "Your diary."

Willow grabs her bird-covered journal and keeps on.

In the kitchen, I prop my mother's face against the apple bowl and begin dicing tomatoes for my bouillabaisse.

"How are you?" I ask.

"I'd be better if my hip wasn't giving me trouble. You look…" she trails off.

"What, Mom?" *Tormented? Grief-stricken?*

"Darling, the dark shadows under your eyes are simply morbid."

"I'm not getting enough sleep. I need to get out more, jog or swim. You remember how beautiful the ocean is?" I use the flat side of my knife to squash the garlic cloves.

"Mmm." She breathes in deeply as though she can smell the saltwater, and I can tell in her mind she's back in Jax, sitting on her beach chair, her hair tied in a scarf like a 1950s pinup, Dad at her side asking if she'd like a drink, more sun lotion, a dip in paradise. He always catered to her.

And now both of us are husbandless.

I presume the conversation will glide to familiar topics. The bitchy things said at her bridge group. J.J.'s glowing achievements as a leading osteopath in Manhattan. The competition in her neighborhood over Frank, the retired carpenter who all the women over seventy have designs on (and subsequently have many critical furniture matters—"Broken bedside table! Unhinged kitchen door cabinet! Hurry, come quick!"). Instead, she stares at me, injured, with the perfectly made-up eyes of a film star. Angry Bette Davis.

"Why won't you talk to me? Why won't you tell me what's going on?"

"What do you mean?" I reach for a frying pan.

"Ever since Théo's diagnosis, you've cut me out."

She's not wrong. The afternoon we found out comes back to me in a rush.

*Stage 4 colon cancer. Not localized but distant, meaning the cancer has spread to far parts of the body, his liver, his lungs.*

*"What's the prognosis?" I whispered to the doctor when Théo refused to ask.*

*There was much beating around the bush, comparing studies, recounting positive recovery stories.*

*"How long do we have?" I said. "Give us a number, please."*

*A 14 percent chance of living in the next five years. Give or take.*

*"I'm out, Rebecca," Théo had said afterward. "Some people can handle the hospital visits, the chemo, the solemn conversations, while each day they get weaker and have to shit in a bag. Not me. I'm ending it."*

*"You are not ending it!" I raced beside him down the sidewalk, waiting until a couple walked by us before grabbing his arm, forcing him to meet my eyes. "Théo! Think about Willow—think about me."*

*"What I'm thinking is it's a damn shame those suicide 3-D coffins aren't available yet."*

*"Stop it!" I shouted, blood pounding in my ears. "Stop talking like that."*

*My throat hoarse, my heart breaking, we walked home silently against the biting Anchorage wind.*

"Rebecca?" My mother is waiting for me to respond.

"Dammit." The oil in the frying pan sizzles; the temperature is too high.

I wish I could tell her everything, but given that both my parents were pharmacists, the less my mom knows, the better. After all, people would suspect she gave me the drug.

"It's just hard. Trying to move on…." I take the carrots and celery out of the fridge.

What I don't want to remember is the arguments Théo and I had leading up to his death. Why wouldn't he listen to me? If only he'd seen my point of view, then I wouldn't have been forced to do what I did.

It's not like we didn't fight before cancer came along. All those issues that seemed so important. Théo was a master moper. He would be cordial during the actual argument, showing no indication he was upset. Then, the Arctic Sulk: days—even weeks—of cold shoulders, one-word answers. He'd never come around on his own. I'd have to cajole him, outlining my part, what I did wrong. His part? No, he was unimpeachable.

Then, the fight we always returned to: He didn't want to have another child. And he *certainly* didn't want to practice making one….

"Mom, I better go."

"Talk soon, darling."

When I hang up, I have two missed calls. I listen to the voice messages.

The first is from Nathaniel, checking to see how I'm doing. The second message sends a warm, unexpected shiver through my body.

"Hello, Rebecca. This is Mr. Brady from Aqua Vista Academy." A brief rustling. "It was a pleasure to meet you and Willow." [Pause.] "Could you come into the office? There are a few things I'd like to discuss with you. Ah..." [Clears throat]. "Looking forward to seeing you, and, er, hope you're settling in well. Bye."

I step away from the stove. Why would he summon me to his office? I thought the dean of students dealt with new kids, troubled kids, the bullies, and the bullied. Did Willow do something wrong? Oh, shit. Did she say something incriminating?

# *Chapter 9*

# DARE

The school run. We drive along North Canary Palm Drive, all white houses, palm trees, and manicured lawns. Willow rests her head against the car window, cheerleading bag at her feet, the morning light ethereal.

Then the feeling comes. It starts like a chill, a temperature drop. The hair stands up on my arms. I jerk my head and look over my shoulder.

Nothing out of the ordinary. Steady traffic. A gray Mazda on my left, a 4WD with kids' bikes attached to the back to my right, a yellow Porsche behind me.

I feel hunted. But I can't see the hunter, only sense him. Earlier this morning, when I went for a run, I had the same sensation.

Christ, I need a therapist. But, after doing yoga with Willow yesterday, at least my back feels better. Small blessings.

Not for the first time, I wonder if someone could be following me from the insurance company. In cases of suspected insurance fraud, sometimes insurance companies hire police to gather evidence. But—a year after Théo's death? All the way across the country? Highly unlikely.

I make a sharp right. The Porsche turns, too, and moments later, zooms past. The driver appears to be in his fifties; he has combed-back blond hair and pale eyes. And he's picking his nose.

Willow yawns.

"Didn't you sleep well last night, honey?"

She grunts. Charming conversationalist.

On her lap, her phone pings. The screen shows a text message, numbers followed by the letter "c."

"What's that about?" I ask.

"Nothing. Just Katia sending a math answer."

The traffic picks up on East Palmetto Park Road, cyclists pass by in groups, cars honk.

*Théo, have I been imagining things? Am I losing my mind? Or is this part of grief, fragments, delusions? Was bringing Willow here the right thing to do? She seems okay, doesn't she? But me…*

I take a diaphragmatic breath, sucking air into my lungs, and turn on the radio. What with my imaginary stalker, having a conversation with my dead husband, and this morning's meeting with Mr. Brady, I'm a jumble of nerves.

Although I questioned Willow last night about why Mr. Brady might want to see me, she assured me there was no reason she could think of. So, the meeting today must be a "get to know you" chat.

Cutting it fine, I pull up to the school parking lot at 8:54 a.m.

"Bye, Mom." Without hesitation, Willow runs to the KISS girls.

Every time I see them together, I silently name them by the acronym:

K–Katia. Latina. Petite. The unquestionable queen bee and star flyer. Paulita's daughter, the woman running for mayor next year.

I–Issy. Caucasian. Blonde undercut. Pan. Loves cheer and acting. Willow told me she gets the starring role in the school play every year and has been in a few TV commercials. Daughter of Fi, the nurse.

S–Sherice. Black, with Beyoncé good looks. According to Willow, she's the smartest kid in her class, which isn't surprising, given both her parents, who I haven't yet met, are surgeons.

S–Stella. Caucasian. Effortlessly cool. Good cook. Candy addict.

KISS. Bonded by popularity, their years of shared elementary school, and their marketing dream name. I wonder if Willow will ever be one of them, wearing a pendant around her neck. How would "W" for Willow fit? KWISS—not great.

The school bell rings.

After seeing Willow off, I planned to slip into the bathroom and touch up my hair, but Odelle catches me in the hallway.

"Hey, pretty lady. Why are you so dressed up?"

Admittedly, my dress is shorter than normal, my lipstick a few shades darker than I'd typically start the day with, and my perfume, which I rarely wear, is Jo Malone's Mimosa and Cardamom, carefully dotted at my pulse points, the inner wrist and base of my throat.

"Time for coffee?" She grins. "Spiked with, I don't know, Ozempic?"

"Tempting, but I have an appointment."

"Oh?"

I shouldn't have said anything. That woman has the nose of a bloodhound.

"Anything interesting? Give me the tea."

"Nothing, I hope. A meeting with Mr. Brady." I refrain from saying he made the call himself, that I replayed the message more than once, listening to the cadence of his voice: a mixture of warmth, authority, and… something else? Dare.

Odelle hooks her arm through mine. "The least I can do is walk you there. We should have dinner soon. Get all the moms together with their hubbies."

Impossible. Unless she's also inviting a medium.

She stops walking. "Foot in farking mouth. Sorry!"

Nice. My husband's death is so forgettable.

"I thought Ron was in Bangkok."

"Flew home last night." Her expression turns hard as we continue down the hall toward the school office. "Complaining he's jet lagged. Such a baby."

"All the travel must be hard on him, being on his own."

"He finds company."

I shoot her a glance. Female company?

"There's a big crew of senior consultants," Odelle explains. "They dine together most nights. Have maids, chefs, drivers. Lonely he isn't."

"That's good, I guess? Well…." I nod toward the office.

"Talk soon, Becks."

I still. "No one calls me that anymore."

Odelle embraces me, holding a moment too long, before whispering, "I do."

I pull back. The incident when we were teenagers floods my memory. The smell of her coconut sun-tanning lotion. Our misunderstanding. One too many Jell-O shots.

"You never forget your first," she laughs. "Have a good day. Don't take me too seriously. No one else does."

Baffled, I approach the school secretary, Mrs. Funicella, "Mrs. Fun," a woman who's rumored by the students to be over a hundred years old. Kids are so nasty. I doubt she's a day over seventy.

"You're here because?" Mrs. Fun frowns from behind her thick glasses. Her hair appears permed and she's wearing a matronly floral dress, which adds decades. No wonder the kids age her up.

"Appointment with Mr. Brady." Saying his name, my voice wavers. How juvenile. I straighten my lilac dress. This is about Willow. Nothing else.

Mrs. Fun leads me to his office, limping, one hip higher than the other. The door is half-open, but before I get a chance to ask her if I should go in, she shuffles away with surprising speed.

Am I ready to be alone with a man who makes me tingle? The first since Théo?

## Chapter 10

# HEAD OF SCHOOL

"Hello?" I call out.

Greeted only by silence, I take a step closer to the door. "Mr. Brady?"

There's no answer but I sense a presence on the other side—is someone breathing? Unable to help myself, I poke my head around.

A boy, maybe a year older than Willow, sits at the head of school's desk with an open laptop.

"Little young for the job?"

The boy startles, and I fear I've made him uncomfortable. His buzz cut is shaved close to the scalp and his uniform is too small, ratty, and stained.

"Sorry," I say. "I'm looking for—"

A voice comes from behind me: "Ah, I see you've met Head of School Angus."

I spin around. Mr. Brady looks even more appealing than when we first met. His hair is damp, as though he recently showered, reaching just past his ears in dark waves. He's wearing brown pants—fitted in all the right places—and a white button-up shirt that could do with another iron.

I readjust my purse on my shoulder, conscious that I may have been staring.

"Head of School Angus has won the highly coveted prize of being me for the day, on a Monday. Unfortunate, because if it was Sunday, he'd be out surfing right about now."

I laugh, charmed, despite my misgivings.

"Finish off your paragraph," Mr. Brady says to Angus. "Let the words flow, deal with spelling and grammar afterward. What you want in your first draft is feeling."

Mr. Brady's eyes meet mine and I smile nervously, feeling utterly too much.

"He's crafting the intro to the school newsletter. Others might consider this a dry task, but Angus is opening with a few jokes and then letting the community know what's happened during the last month. Doing a stellar job." He pats Angus on the back and stands beside him at the desk.

Angus beams.

Positive male role model. That box is ticked.

Mr. Brady and I share a glance. *Bang*! It's like an electric shock. I look away. I'm way too old for this.

"Please, take a seat," Mr. Brady says to me. "Angus, you've done a mighty fine job. Why don't you go ask Mrs. Fun to add it to our file. You can spellcheck together."

I sink into a squishy armchair.

"I don't like Mrs. Fun," the boy mutters, avoiding eye contact.

"Angus! Between you and me, the word that best describes Mrs. Fun is 'surly,' on a good day. But that's only because you don't know the secret to winning her heart."

Angus cringes. Clearly, the last thing he wants to do is win Mrs. Fun's heart.

"Everyone has a weakness. Something they'll do anything for. Guess what hers is? Jellybeans." Mr. Brady walks over to the bookcase and opens an old hardcover book, but instead of pages, there's a secret compartment inside. Angus's face lights up. "I gotta hide the goods or every kid at Aqua Vista would be visiting my office for a sugar fix. Take this baggie here, give it to Mrs. Fun—she likes the green ones. She'll melt in your hands."

Suddenly, Mr. Brady's focus is back on me. I swear he's checking out my legs. Théo used to say they were the sexiest legs in Alaska, which always made me laugh.

"What kind of jellybeans are your favorite, Mrs. Fournier?"

"Um. Sour ones. Lemon, lime." *Tart,* the word plays on my lips.

Angus gathers his things and walks to the door, his long arms dangling by his sides.

"Hit the music room later?" Mr. Brady calls after him. "The girls will swoon when they hear you on the drums."

Angus shrugs, trying to hide a grin.

The room seems different once we're alone. Mr. Brady sits across from me at his desk. It's almost like a date without candles or wine, but strangely more intimate, raw—fluorescent lights, scars, and all. Plus, the naughtiness of being in the head of school's office with its associated role-play, isn't lost on me. *Have you been a bad girl? Do you need detention?*

He watches as I take in his office. Movie DVDs stacked on his desk. A guitar in the corner. Ah, that answers that question. And mugs, everywhere, on the shelves, piled on the bookcase, spilling out of boxes. I read a few:

> *I'm a principal. What's YOUR superpower?*
>
> *Instant head of school—Just add coffee.*
>
> *If at first you don't succeed, try doing what your head of school said in the first place.*

"Quite a collection," I say. "You could make a killing on eBay."

"Oh yeah?"

"When my business was first up and running, I sold my prints on eBay." There's no reason to go on about it, but I can't stop talking. "It was impossible to keep up with the orders. Every morning, I'd wake up and there'd be more. It gives you a real sense of customer demand. Although there are a lot of wacky people sending odd messages. How did your mug collection start?"

He leans forward. "I swear, it started off with one. I made the mistake of always using it—occasionally walked around the school grounds with it. From there," he grins and shakes his head, "every Christmas, every Hanukkah, every end-of-year present. Mugs." He lowers his voice. "Secret? I regularly drop boxes of them off at the thrift store. Who needs hundreds of mugs? Trust me, the teachers don't want to carry principal mugs."

I laugh, deep from my belly, my face warm despite the buzzing AC.

"Have you settled into Boca?"

"Yes. Although we haven't seen all the sights yet."

"Lot of places to explore," he says. "Sugar Sand Park, Gumbo Limbo Nature Center, the FAU Stadium. Plus, all the water sports. Anyway, I wanted to check how Willow's finding school. And to ask you a favor."

Thank goodness nothing is wrong, a routine new child checkup. What kind of favor does he have in mind?

"*Insomnia* with Al Pacino," he says. "*Into the Wild*, a fine job by Emile Hirsch."

I bite my lip. He's speaking in riddles.

"*The Edge* with a young Alec Baldwin and Sir Anthony Hopkins," he continues.

All movies set in Alaska. "Movie buff?"

"Absolutely," he says. "It's storytelling that fascinates me. Brain scans have found that when we read a story and something expected happens, our brains produce a little dopamine, but when something surprising happens, well, the shot of dopamine is much more intense."

"Interesting." Is he an adrenaline junkie? "So, Mr. Brady, about Willow—"

"Call me Brady." He moves a pile of papers on his desk. "Socially, Willow seems to be fitting in well."

I nod. The relocation is going better than I could have imagined. Moving to Boca was the right thing to do; in a sea of mistakes, I've made one good choice.

"Academically, her math is above average, but she's behind with English."

"I know. It's the strangest thing because…" Because her father was a writer and read to her every night, either epics—I'm talking Dostoyevsky—or from his own work in process, the way radio stations used to broadcast novels, doled out chapter by chapter. Ever since he died, she hasn't picked up a single book. It's as though she hates everything he loved.

"I have a recommendation," Brady says. "Games such as Hangman or Scrabble, and apps like Rocket Speller and Word Wizard."

"That could help, thanks." I cross my legs. His eyes follow the movement. "As for camp, I'm still not sure if she's ready to go."

"Don't underestimate her. Besides, you could join us. We always appreciate parents' help. You'll have to sign up by..." He checks the wall calendar. "Last week."

Crap.

"But for you, I'll make an exception."

"Thanks."

We don't speak for a moment. Is the meeting over?

I study the office for other signs of his personal life, of a girlfriend. He has a massive corkboard with pictures tacked to it: laughing faces of Aqua Vista Academy students, Christmas concerts, groups of men and kids on boats, the shimmering Atlantic Ocean. I can't look away from the last pictures.

"Dad's Weekend," Brady says. "We do it at the end of every year with Palm Breeze charters. Sail up and down the bay. It's also a fundraising initiative for my project."

"What project?"

"Autism Awesome. I'm raising funds to help kids in Florida with autism find and develop their spark, then get extra tutoring or experiences so they can excel in that area. The goal is long-term mentorship."

"Impressive."

"Nah, not impressive. Although it is important." He shifts in his seat before speaking in a confidential tone. "Someone very special to me has autism. I've seen firsthand the challenges he's faced. Once kids find out what they're great at, even if other things in their life don't go their way, they have a foundation, something they love."

"We're all lucky if we can find that." Both Théo and I were fortunate enough to pursue our passions. Every day at 5:30 a.m., even on weekends, Théo climbed out of bed, made a full cafetière of coffee, and entered his study not to be seen again until midafternoon or later.

My gaze moves back to the sailing photos.

"Let Willow's dad know about Dad's Weekend. We often start with fishing lessons and—"

"Oh." I must have made a strange sound because Brady snaps his head toward me. "That's not necessary." It comes out stiff, formal, the tremble in my voice gives too much away.

Brady folds his hands on the desk, waiting patiently. His eyes shine with dark anticipation.

"There is…none. Willow's father." I sniff. "Colon cancer."

Brady blows air out of his mouth. "I'm sorry. For you and Willow."

Pain, black and sickening, surges up my chest like vomit. I rise from my seat. "Actually, I forgot, I have a meeting…."

"Are you sure? I could make you some tea? Lots of mugs to choose from."

I smile through my tears. He passes me a tissue, which I take without looking at him. How could I let myself fall apart like this? He disarmed me in less than half an hour. I blame it on the mugs.

Moving quickly toward the door, I step into the hall.

Brady walks past me, brushing his arm against my shoulder.

"Hello," he says to the man walking by. "Are you a new janitor?"

"Tim," the man in a cap and a blue worker uniform answers. "I'm filling in for Ryan this week. He's visiting family in Texas."

The two men shake hands, and the janitor walks away.

I'm about to leave, too, when I remember. Turning back, I say, "There's one other thing."

"Do you want to come back inside?"

In his office, I remain standing. "I was meaning to ask if I could book an appointment for Willow with the school counselor?" I'm a full believer in therapy; the trouble is, I feel equally as strong about protecting our secrets. In Anchorage, Willow had a few sessions with a grief counselor, although I'd coached her about what she could and couldn't talk about.

"Consider it done. Jan Boroskwi has been working here for a decade. Very experienced, a mother of four."

"Thank you. You didn't say what the favor was."

"We don't need to talk about it now."

"Go on." The sooner we get back to neutral territory where I'm not crying in his office and talking about my dead husband, the better.

"I've found out something about you."

My heart jumps out of my chest, and I look over my shoulder, as though the police are about to storm in and cuff me.

"You're a great photographer."

I smooth my dress down, relieved.

"Every year the fundraising committee comes up with events to get parents in a generous mood," Brady says. "Art Synergy is at the beginning of the second semester. It's an art auction, dinner, dancing, and celebrating the children's work. Would you consider photographing the student's artwork for the preview? We use the images for the school calendar."

"Sure. Glad to help."

"Great. If you could get in touch with Odelle Wragge, she's in charge of that event. I'll ask Mrs. Fun to send you her contact details."

"No need, Odelle and I are good friends. From high school, actually."

A look of concern crosses his face, or maybe I only imagined it.

"Oh, uh, I see," he says. "Odelle's husband is a philanthropist. One of the key donors of Autism Awesome."

"That's lucky," I answer, but Aqua Vista Academy is starting to feel incestuous.

# Chapter 11

# SNOW WHITE

"Does this look okay?"

When I turn around, I have to do a double take. In those strange few seconds, my child seems unfamiliar. Willow stands in the kitchen entranceway, a proud, defiant tilt to her chin.

"Gosh, you look beautiful, so…grown-up. What happened to your bathing suit?"

"What do you mean?" she asks, straight-faced.

I press my tongue against my teeth. "I didn't know you are a budding fashion designer."

Her pink one-piece bathing suit is shorn in horizontal slices, exposing her skin.

"Hey, come here." I pull her onto my lap where I've been sitting at the kitchen table reviewing my Raz-Pops spread. Regardless if it's Sunday morning or not, a new client requires extra attention. Normally I'd be cross she destroyed something that could've been donated to the thrift store, but the bathing suit had already lost its stretch.

"In my day, they called this look punk rock," I tell Willow as I sip my iced coffee. "DIY clothes were all about antiestablishment and self-expression. Do you want me to get some safety pins? We can pin them across here." I run my hand along the edge of the fabric near her collarbone.

She pulls away, but I hold her, not wanting to let go.

"I love you," I say. *Don't grow up too fast.*

This is the first time she's shown any interest in fashion. Or her appearance, for that matter.

Willow lifts up her arm and groans. "Why won't you let me shave, Mom? I'm so hairy."

"The hair comes back thicker if you shave. Right now, there is hardly any hair. When you grow more, we can look into waxing or electrolysis."

"But we're swimming *today*!"

"It's natural. You'll be fine."

She shifts on my lap, digging her tailbone into my thigh. "My tummy hurts."

"Did you eat anything funny?"

She shakes her head.

"Cramps?" She got her first period three months before her twelfth birthday.

"No."

"When are we leaving?" Willow asks—every question in a tween's repertoire contains a built-in moan.

We're due at Odelle's soon for a swimming date with the KISS girls. "After we've done a few rounds of Hangman and you've tidied your room." Following Brady's advice, to boost Willow's literacy, we've been playing word games, and I've hired an English tutor named Hannah, recommended by Fi. I take out a blank piece of paper, thinking of a word before drawing five horizontal lines across the bottom of the page.

"M?" Willow moves off my lap to sit beside me, leaving her phone face up on the table. There's an incoming text.

Sender: Katia: **350 c**

"More math?" I ask. "It's strange how often you two text math answers to each other."

"Oh my God, Mom. That's what you're worried about?"

"What's the 'c' stand for?"

"Stop, you're so annoying."

I drink my coffee and draw the post the man hangs from. Last night, in bed, I succumbed to temptation and googled Mr. Brady, starting with his bio on the school website and then moving down different rabbit holes.

Mr. Brady, it turns out, is thirty-three. Nine years younger than me. I picture his tanned hands. His warm face, those silly mugs, the playful banter. But not only that: his attentiveness, the way he listened to every word I said, the passion with which he runs his charity.

*Off-limits.*

"A?"

"Yes." I fill in the second line with the letter A. From what I could determine, Brady was once a semiprofessional swimmer. Those gorgeous arms put to good use. And his first name is Clint; I can see why he doesn't use it.

It takes Willow a few minutes to get the first word: "party." My next word will have to be more challenging. I draw eight blank lines.

"S?"

"No." I add the post. Evidently, Brady's band—aptly, if not unsurprisingly, named The Brady Bunch—has gigs around South Florida and occasionally in Boca. There were pictures of them in dark bars. Although they were recent pictures, in a nod to the era of the TV show, the band was wearing seventies clothing—tight pants flared at the bottom, lurid, open-necked shirts, sideburns, gold necklaces. Standing center stage was Brady, guitar strung across his body, shoulders slightly slumped as he embraced the microphone.

Willow's next two guesses are wrong, and the page fills with the hangman's head and body.

Afraid of being found out, I didn't listen to any of Brady's songs. Would he be able to tell if I viewed them? *Caught: forty-plus-year-old mother perving on daughter's principal.* But still, I wondered, what does Brady sound like when he sings? I lay in bed afterward, twisting and turning, unable to sleep, shocked by how badly I wanted to hear it.

"T?"

I fill in a letter of the word.

The hangman's arms, then legs, are drawn as she makes more incorrect guesses.

"P?"

"Sorry, Willow." I connect the head to the post with a noose. "He's dead!"

A sudden burst of chirps from her phone distracts her.

"The word was midnight," I say pointlessly. Willow is already immersed in her phone.

"My friends want to group chat. Pleeease?"

"Okay." When you give your child technology, they treat you like you're Santa Claus. When you try to take it away, they treat you like an enemy of the state.

Within seconds, our living room fills with the squealing sound of twelve-year-old girls. I catch a glimpse of their boxed-out faces on the screen.

K–Katia, the soon-to-be running mayor's daughter, the loudest and undeniable ringleader, in spite of her diminutive size.

I–Issy, the actress.

S–Sherice, STEM queen, obsessed with robotics, who's currently laughing at something Katia said.

S–Stella, in braids, her dimples on show.

And the other girls who, like Willow, are trying to join the KISS ranks. Apparently, they've been nicknamed "the Drew Barrymores." When I asked Willow how they got the name, she said, "The movie *Never Been Kissed* with Drew Barrymore."

Right. These girls had never been *in* KISS. Clever. Nasty.

At the same time as Willow runs out of the room, my phone rings—

Damn, Théo's mom, Yolanthe. It's been weeks since I had Willow call her. I must put a reminder in my iCalendar. With the relocation, building Florida clients, and taking care of Willow, I feel like I'm always a day behind. Scratch that, a month.

I jump up, spilling my drink on the table. I lunge for my Raz-Pops spread, reaching it just in time.

Dashing to the kitchen for a dishcloth, I answer the phone.

"Hello, Rebecca." She's pissed; her Québécois accent always seems stronger when she's angry. "I'd like to speak to my *petite fille*."

"Sorry, Yolanthe, Willow's getting ready to go to a friend's house. She's on a video chat."

"A what?"

"Never mind. I'll get her to call you when she can have a good conversation. I'm sorry we haven't been in touch. Are you available this evening?"

A long pause. Since our first meeting in the hotel lobby of the Ritz-Carlton, my mother-in-law has despised me. She sensed, it seemed, as I stood beside Théo pre our "getting to know you" dinner at the hotel's restaurant, that I was to be his next, second, wife. Fueled by some weird Oedipal complex, her goal ever since had been to clock each of my missteps, slowly building her case against me. Didn't she know not being his first wife was already a burden, one of the three chinks in our otherwise solid marriage? As our relationship progressed, not only was I haunted by the ghost of Théo's ex, but the ghost of our former sex life and the second baby that he didn't want to give me.

She sniffs into the phone. "This evening is fine."

"How's Gérard?"

"As well as to be expected. Thank you."

There is no chitchat, no asking how I'm doing, only the screaming accusation: Not only did I take her son, now I've taken her only grandchild. And therefore, I'm the *diable*. The devil.

I suppose I'm partly to blame. There was talk before Théo died about the possibility of Willow and me moving to New York, close to both grandmothers since Montréal was less than an hour and a half flight away. Yolanthe had pinned her heart on it. But Florida beckoned. You'd think Yolanthe would be happy we were now at least in the same time zone.

We say goodbye and hang up.

Théo always liked a good debate, unlike Yolanthe and I, who are both guilty of avoiding uncomfortable topics.

Honestly, at the end of the day, I'd rather listen to an audiobook of the dictionary than spend hours shooting down someone's point to win an argument.

The minute cancer entered our house, the most gruesome unwanted visitor, the debate never ended. Not only did Théo refuse treatment—and that was a *fait accompli*, not open to discussion—he wanted to end his life on his terms.

His points:

A—His favorite uncle, Edouard, died from colon cancer. Théo saw him through it and was adamant not to go the same way. Also, after two strokes, Théo's dad, Gérard, considered himself "a cripple." Someone who had to be cared for. "It's not going to happen to me, Rebecca. No way." Slow or rapid disintegration.

B—He'd done his research. Nembutal, referred to as "the peaceful pill" or "the death pill" was the pro-euthanasia people's drug of choice. It worked quickly, painlessly. Mix the powder with water, drink it, and fall into an endless sleep.

But…Nembutal could only be purchased online from overseas. It was illegal to import a class C drug into the country, and a person could be fined and get a prison sentence if caught with it. Insurance didn't cover it—obviously.

C—Ultimately, people have an explicit right to die. Death was a private matter. If there was no harm to others, the state had no right to interfere. We're more humane to animals than to people in that way.

My points?

Live for us. Cancer can be overcome, miracles happen, don't take away that chance.

And…insurance didn't cover suicide.

And…anyone involved in assisted suicide could receive manslaughter charges. Alaska wasn't California.

Night after night, I begged him.

But if nothing else, Théo was a realist. A mommy's boy realist. A small caveat: His parents were Catholic, and he insisted I didn't tell them his intentions. It would break their hearts to think of their son in hell. When the time came, I should tell them he died of natural causes.

*Oh, Théo. What happened broke their hearts much more.*

So even from then, I lied to his mother. And Yolanthe could tell. Not what I was lying about, per se, but that every word out of my mouth was bullshit.

"Mom!" Willow stands before me. "Let's go."

"Right." I get up, dazed. "Did you change into another bathing suit?"

"Yep."

Our swimming bags are already packed. I pick them up from the hall. Where are my keys? I grab them from the basket on the side table and put on a wide-brimmed white hat. The mirror reflects the false me, the lie: a tanned woman in a sundress, without a care in the world. Willow follows me outside into the blinding light.

# Chapter 12

# CREAM

When Willow and I arrive at Odelle's, I knock on the door, and a man in his fifties answers.

"Oh. You must be…"

"Ron Wragge." A firm handshake. He's wearing a linen shirt tucked into khaki shorts, showcasing his protruding belly. Blond, gelled hair, a Roman nose, light blue eyes, vintage Rolex. Old money, I presume.

I can't stop staring. He looks exactly like the man picking his nose in the yellow Porsche.

"I'm Rebecca. This is Willow."

He smiles at Willow with genuine interest. His cologne, gosh, it's divine. Peppercorn, wood, and…mandarin. "Stella's told me about you. It's great she's got a new friend." He gestures inside. "Come this way."

We follow him through the house, or "mansion," as Willow had called it when we'd arrived. A beautiful, over-the-top, white-columned, I-have-succeeded middle finger to anyone who might have dared think otherwise.

In the hall, a thin woman dressed in beige approaches.

"Sorry, I didn't answer the door, Mr. Wragge. I was otherwise engaged."

"That's fine, Cynthia."

The rooms are full of modern furniture in challenging abstract shapes, chandeliers resembling ski equipment, and floor-to-ceiling windows providing the kind of lighting photographers dream of. We pass a home cinema, his-and-her offices, guest rooms…. In the kitchen, a hovercraft-sized cement island is lined with platters of appetizers, shrimp, coriander, mango, lime. With the art and perfectly arranged flowers, Odelle's home feels like it's ready for a real estate viewing. Any minute, interested buyers will burst in demanding to know the square footage. You'd never guess in a million years that a tween lived here.

"Willow!" The girls squeal as we step outside into the entertaining area, gold light glistening on the pool filled with bright inflatables, the heat of the midafternoon diffused by palm trees and large sun umbrellas.

KISS are decked out in identical, sleek, red bikinis, bandeaus tops and bottoms that barely cover their bottoms. Some "Drew Barrymores" are also here, introduced as Natalie and Esrif. They're all too young to look so beautiful, with round faces, dewy skin, flat stomachs, and long legs. Their hairstyles are meticulously waved and probably need a Sephora-store of product to keep it that way. They'll steal the hearts of Boca in a few years, but for now they're probably riddled with self-consciousness. What a shame; when we are young and utterly breathtaking, we are often our most insecure.

"You're here," Odelle says to me with a nervous laugh.

"And I've met your better half."

Her face pales. "Let's get you a drink."

Where did Ron disappear to?

Hmm. Odelle, who always had to have the hottest man in the room—bad boys who drove motorcycles and whose only job was seduction—has ended up with this guy. Power is an aphrodisiac, but still. Ron seems as stiff as a surfboard, but perhaps he's acrobatic in bed or so brilliant he sees through Odelle's mind games.

"Quick question," I ask. "Does your husband have a yellow Porsche?"

"One of his many cliché overindulgences. Why?"

"I saw him driving near my house."

"No mystery there. His colleague lives on the same street."

"Oh." I glance at Willow. There's bathing suit drama. She's smiling, but from the way she's standing, shoulders stooped, in her floral one-piece (our only alternative after she slashed her pink one), I can tell she feels excluded.

Seeing them all together, realization hits: Willow *is* a Drew Barrymore—a girl vying for a spot.

A flare inside of…hope…that she gets included. How immature of me. But I know how it feels to wish you were popular.

I was the tomboy, the tennis player, with a gym bag and flat chest, never part of any girl group save the unnamed sporting one: *Make Athletics Take Us Seriously.*

In my family, J.J., my brother, was the sought-after one. Mr. Personality versus studious Rebecca. My parents loved J.J.'s gregariousness, his humor, while I was celebrated for academic achievements, spelling tests, my tunnel vision with tennis. I wanted to impress them and was going to follow their footsteps—become a pharmacist, until Odelle Rackark rocked my world.

"Before you jump in," Stella says to Willow, "look at what we got you."

Is it a "KISS" pendant?

Stella hands Willow a gift bag.

Willow pulls out a red bikini. "Whaaat? Oh my God. I'm putting it on right now.'

"Yay! Bathroom is inside, Cynthia will show you," Stella says.

"Who's Cynthia?"

"Our butler. She works here on the weekends."

I turn to Odelle. "Are there any other parents coming?"

"Of course not," she says. "I want you to myself."

***

The afternoon approaches dinnertime and the girls are lined up in a row, tanning on towels, slathered in oil, phones in hand. I'm onto my second glass of Sauvignon Blanc, tween pop blaring from speakers. It would appear like Willow and I have landed on our feet. In a fancy garden in Boca with my old frenemy. Who'd have thought?

Odelle turns on her sunbed to face me. Her bathing suit is cut in a deep V, ample cleavage on show. She is wearing a straw hat, aviator sunglasses, and different length gold necklaces, charms catching the light. I'm in my navy, hide-my-stretch-marks "mom suit."

"So…why Alaska?" Odelle smirks. "From East Coast city girl to igloos?"

"Ha." I sip my water through a straw, which I notice is metal. Willow said her meeting with Odelle was a success. Clearly so. I'm surprised; I never pegged Odelle for a conservationist.

"At least tell me why you left New York."

"Théo was as French as you can get." I lean back in the chair, the wine loosening my tongue. "After we met in New York on that street corner, it was a whirlwind romance. We barely slept. Talked all night, had sex constantly, being with him was…everything."

"It's always the best in the beginning. Before you find out how god-awful they are."

Wow. How bad were things between her and Ron? But…relationships do change. Théo couldn't get enough of me at first. Later he tensed whenever I reached to touch him.

"Anyway, more details," Odelle says. "You know I like picturing you hot and wet."

My swinging foot stills. I guess we'd have to discuss the incident soon, what happened between Odelle and I that summer. The soccer guy who asked for a threesome. For now, I keep talking to cover my discomfort.

"Well, it turned out Théo was only in New York for a two-month writing trip. He was going back to Anchorage. He'd been married before, to an Alaskan, and even though their marriage didn't last, his love affair with the state had." Not to mention his reverence for this first wife, Claire, a graphic designer. Luckily, she lived in Juneau, and we never met. Although, I could tell by what he *didn't* say that she still held a place in his heart and from what Yolanthe *did* say that she held a place in hers too. Yolanthe kept a picture of Claire on display in her house, for goodness' sake. "Théo liked to have intense writing periods, then camp in the summer. During the winter, he'd go on soul-searching treks to Flute Glacier or Crow Pass Trail. The hero's journey."

Odelle is listening intently, collagen-injected lips parted.

"I was happy to move to Alaska. I wanted new landscapes to photograph…."

"You were always the lucky one."

"I'm not fucking lucky." My voice is shrill. "He had cancer, Odelle. One day he was fine…then months later, gone."

"Oh, baby, I'm sorry." Odelle looks taken aback. "I meant you were lucky that you had true love. I can be such a selfish narcissist sometimes."

"It's okay." I sigh. "You're brutally honest too. I appreciate that."

She leans over and wraps her arms around me. I rest my head on her freckled shoulder, smelling the familiar scent of her skin. Her hand trails over my lower back.

"You're tougher than you think," she says. "Remember when we finally got on the court and faced off with the Rabbinawitz twins? Everyone thought they'd cream us, but you, you made us train harder; you didn't let us think, even for a minute, that we wouldn't dominate."

I draw back. "But…we didn't win."

"Not my point." She studies me carefully, eyes laser-focused. After all this time, I can still read her. She makes that expression, tongue protruding from the corner of her mouth. She's about to launch an onslaught of questions. "So, with Théo—"

"Odelle, I'm not ready to go into to all." Suddenly, I wish I were anywhere else. The two glasses of wine I had mean I shouldn't drive home anytime soon. How long would it take to walk? Fifteen minutes?

She's not going to let me off the hook that easily. "It's healthy to talk about your problems. At least, that's what *all* my psychologists say. Especially my most expensive one."

"Like everyone's, our marriage had problems…."

"Oh?"

"Théo was melancholic, had low-level depression. His mother has the same disposition, but unlike her, Théo never used antidepressants. Well, he tried them for about six months and said they dulled his artistic core." They also dulled his sex drive.

"With Willow and her moods, sometimes"—I can't meet Odelle's gaze—"I'm afraid she has it, too…."

"Time will tell. Kids are resilient. You'll know what to do. Mother knows best."

Yeah, right. That premise only sets us up to fail. Having a child doesn't mean we also have the answers.

When Willow was born—passed to me and placed on my chest, shrieking—I didn't know what to do when she wouldn't latch. I lay there, her tiny body squirming in my arms, feeling inadequate. And during the first three years of her life, when she wailed throughout the night, I didn't know whether to let her cry or to bring her into bed with Théo and me.

Once she got older and went to school, I thought it'd get easier, but not a single day goes by without making a mistake. Sometimes we're blinded, and every decision we make only pushes our child closer to the edge.

"Life's been hard on you, babe. And death…" Odelle says, stroking my arm near my wrist, "is natural. It shouldn't be shrouded in secrets."

Maybe, if it's straightforward.

If each of us, in our small family of three, weren't equally fucking culpable.

Pulling my hand away, I curl my knees to my chest. A terrible feeling rises from my stomach like whiplash. It moves to my neck, choking me, squeezing my vocal cords.

"Becks? What is it?"

"It must be the heat." I feel like I'm dying, scorching, but I'm ready to surrender to the sun. For it to burn me whole. Like Théo, cremated into dust.

My preference would have been to scatter his ashes at Cook Inlet, near our house, where Théo, Willow, and I used to walk along Bootleggers Cove on Sunday mornings, but Yolanthe insisted I follow the Vatican's orders which said remains should not be scattered, nor kept in urns, or preserved in mementos. Cremated remains should only be kept in a "sacred place," such as a church cemetery. And that was where Théo was now: the Notre-Dame-des-Neiges Cemetery in Montréal, a country away from Willow and me, but, of course, close to his grieving mother.

"Here." Odelle offers me water, putting the glass to my lips. I gulp it back. "Don't worry, you've got me now. And if anyone gives you any trouble, I'm one badass boss bitch."

I'm moved by her kindness, her formidable force.

She puts her arm over my shoulder. "I'll look after you, Becks, and your little girl too."

"You sound like the witch in the *Wizard of Oz*."

"The good witch—Glinda. Maybe I'll put a spell on you."

*What would it be?* I wonder as I gaze at the aqua sky.

As though reading my mind, Odelle says, "Boca is your home now. You don't need to look for it anywhere else."

# Chapter 13

# GIRLS JUST WANT TO BE MEAN

"Serve it!" Katia yells.

The girls are in the water, finishing a game of volleyball, KISS versus the Drew Barrymores.

Meanwhile, the only exercise Odelle and I have had in the last hour is repositioning ourselves on our sunbeds.

Cynthia comes out balancing a pitcher of mojitos on a tray. "Ladies, some refreshments."

"You're a lifesaver," Odelle says.

When Cynthia goes to pour me a glass, I hold up my hand. "No, thank you."

"Poor sport." Odelle sulks as Cynthia picks up the empty glasses and departs.

"I have a meeting in the morning. I need to be on my game."

Willow spikes the ball and hits Issy on the head. "Gotcha!" she screams.

I flinch. What has gotten into her?

"Nice aim," Katia cackles.

The other girls laugh as Issy pulls herself up and sits on the side of the pool.

"Apologize, Willow," I call out.

"Sorry," Willow says to Issy.

"Let's suntan," Katia says a few minutes later, and all the rest of the girls comply—the only acceptable response to a Katia suggestion. They jump out of the water, mermaids emerging from the chlorine sea.

My phone beeps. I can't see in the glare, so I cup the screen.

It's an unknown number; I open the message.

**I have another favor. Brady**

A shock of pleasure shoots up my body. Odd, though. Texting me on the weekend.

"It's a joke, isn't it?" Odelle says.

"What is?" I cover the screen. Did she see his message?

"The way we portray our lives, versus the actual truth."

"Oh. Do you mean with Ron?"

"Ha!" She snorts. "Our love story died a long time ago."

"I'm sorry."

"I'm not. I have my freedom, he has his, and"—she gestures to her house—"we have this 'totally sick' lifestyle, as Stella would say."

"Are you going to stay with him?"

"Not sure."

"Forgive my ignorance," I say and pause, aware I'm treading on dangerous ground. I don't know how long Ron has been in the picture. "Might separation be less difficult because he's not the biological father of the girls?"

"Full of the hard questions today, huh?"

"Did Ron ever want children?"

"Passion-killers that they are? That's a hard no." Odelle swigs her cocktail, and I glance at the girls who are huddled around Katia's phone.

"Anyway, if my plan succeeds, by the end of middle school, Ron and I will be through, and Mr. X and I will be on."

"Mr. X?" I glance around, wary of Ron sneaking up on us.

"Oh, yes, Becks. When you find a man so incredibly hot and skilled, particularly with his mouth, you never look back. Unless you find a woman who's even better."

A laugh erupts from my belly. She's such a flirt.

But here I am with my own secret flirtations. What favor does Brady want?

"Who's Mr. X?" I ask. "And why wait until the end of middle school?"

"All I'm going to say, sweet pea, is that he's a dad from school. A married dad. Don't look at me like that, he's virtually separated from his wife."

"Oh...." I can't disguise the disapproval in my voice.

"Judge all you like, but following the rules doesn't promise a better life."

"Gross!" Katia points at her phone screen. "She looks so trash."

"Totally," the girls chorus.

It's impossible for me not to think of Odelle's affair from the wife's perspective. Jane—my closest friend back in Anchorage—was the unfortunate victim of a "nanny situation."

No one saw it coming, even though we probably should have, considering the nanny was very Swiss, very blonde, and very twenty-four. Jane's husband, a firefighter, was a hands-on dad and loyal to a fault. The deception shook us all. "How would you like that happening to you?"

"It wouldn't." Odelle caresses her breasts. "Once men get *the rack*, they never go back."

"You're ridiculous." We laugh. Odelle's last name, Rackark, lent too easily to the high school nickname.

When the laughter fades, she says, "Why do I always get myself into such messed-up situations?"

"I don't know. But you always get yourself out of them."

My phone beeps. Brady again?

"I feel like dancing." Odelle downs her glass. "Girls!" She calls them over.

I scan the message. Nathaniel is in Miami for work and wants to meet on Saturday for lunch. I text him a time, the place I'll leave up to him. He loves discovering new restaurants.

"Dance-off! I'm the DJ." Odelle flicks through a playlist. "We'll start with a classic."

The first bars of "Girls Just Want to Have Fun" begin. Odelle starts dancing, arms in the air as she sings the opening lines. "Stella and the rest of you—over here." She stops the track. "Who's doing this with me?"

The only response is birdcall.

She turns to me, hand outstretched. "Becks, let's show them how it's done."

"I'm good."

Odelle restarts the song and drags me off the sunbed with surprising strength.

"Mom! Are you drunk?" Stella yells.

"I wish," Odelle replies wickedly. "I just wanna boogie!"

Stella groans and the girls laugh.

The rhythm pulsates as Odelle dances me around the pool. Cyndi Lauper sings about boys taking beautiful girls and hiding them away from the world.

The girls make goofy faces, like this is all so stupid and cheesy and "aren't the moms lame," but there's a shared sense of fun in the air.

Odelle picks up the bouquet from the table and I grab a pink pool ring inflatable. Laughing, we spin in each other's arms.

As Odelle sings out the chorus, she shakes the bouquet over the top of us, the white flowers falling like confetti.

I parrot the next line.

We dance some more and sing the last lyrics of the song at full volume.

The next song from Odelle's playlist starts, Salt-N-Pepa's "Push It."

Odelle excuses herself to the bathroom and I keep dancing. Wait—the feeling is strong. Primal. Is someone watching me?

"Popcorn anyone?" Ron asks from the open sliding door.

My eyes dart to Willow. She looks queasy. It happens to me, too, when I smell popcorn: an olfactory trigger from that terrible night.

The rest of the girls grab handfuls of popcorn, stuffing it into their mouths.

"Guys," Katia says, "let's practice our dance routine for camp."

"Should I film it?" Ron asks. "So you can replay it and spot your mistakes?"

"Good idea," Sherice says. "Make sure you get footage of all of us. I'll edit it later before I post it."

Within minutes, Sherice puts on their chosen song, and they begin their choreography, dancing as though they are in a raunchy hip-hop video.

Willow has a huge wedgie, exposing half of her white bum.

I call her name so I can tell her to pull her bathing suit down, but she doesn't hear me.

"Eat your dust," they sing in unison.

Standing side on, they slap their asses at the same time. "You ain't seen nothing yet! You ain't seen nothing yet!"

*Dear God. Why does it have to be so sexualized?*

They do different cheerleading formations, kicking their legs high, KISS in front, the Drew Barrymores—none who are on the cheer squad except Willow, so they're completely clumsy and out of time—behind.

"We're so good we can do it backward." In unison, all the girls turn around, their backsides facing us, and chant, "Backward! Backward! We can do it backwards!"

Odelle comes out, fresh towels clutched in her hands. "Stop!"

Sherice turns off the music.

"Dry off," Odelle says. "Come inside! Cynthia has set up snacks in the movie room. Don't keep her waiting."

"Are you okay?" I ask her. "You seem…"

"I'm fine," she says, all the intimacy of before vanished.

We move to the movie room, and the girls settle down to watch some teen flick. Stella gets up, saying she'll get the video of their dance routine so Sherice can start editing it.

A few minutes later, Stella comes back empty-handed.

Odelle looks up. "Well, where is it?"

"Dad's office door was locked," Stella says with a frown. "I knocked, but he wouldn't answer."

"That's strange." Odelle rises and opens the door. "I think I can hear the shower running upstairs now. Ron must be out of the office. Get his phone. Go." She turns to me with a tight smile. "Can I get you another drink?"

"I might, ah, take Willow home. I think it's good if we have an early night."

"Sure," Odelle says.

I reach for my keys, then stop myself. "I probably shouldn't drive."

"No problem, I'll get Ron to run you home."

"Thanks, but it's a beautiful night. A walk will do us good."

Getting away from Ron Wragge will do us even better.

# Chapter 14

# THE FAVOR

I drive down Dixie Highway toward Palm Beach Records, which, according to Google, is a high-end recording studio. A strange place for Mr. Brady to ask to meet, especially on a Sunday, but he said the favor was school-related. The early afternoon traffic is light. The sky is a vivid blue, with cauliflower-shaped clouds that look like they were drawn by a kindergartener on a sugar high.

Already, the day has been fantastic. I went for a morning run, lasting twenty minutes longer than yesterday's, and returned home, my body slick with sweat; toxins released. Willow woke up in a cheerful mood, looking forward to shopping with Issy.

When I texted Mr. Brady and asked what the favor was, he replied that he needed me for my brilliant mind—and would I please bring my camera.

A wiser woman might have declined. Spending time with someone, especially someone who makes my temperature skyrocket on sight, is dangerous.

Yet here I am, pulling into the parking lot in front of Palm Beach Records, a two-storied, Spanish-styled building that looks like the kind of places senior citizens go for dance lessons.

Once I'm out of the car, nerves hit me, as strongly as the heat.

I text Mr. Brady that I've arrived.

A few moments later, he replies: **Great. Studio A.**

Inside, a group of guys in baggy clothes, gold chains, and cherubic smiles are spread out on two leather couches, laughing about something. Moving past them, I weave between a bunch of rockers with mullets and guitars who reek of pot. I should've worn something cooler than my capris, V-neck, and sandals. I need a placard: Mom on the loose! Last seen at the grocery store/school pickup/laundry room.

A sign with an arrow indicates Studio A is on the second floor.

My sandals slap the linoleum as I walk up the stairs.

Down the hallway, Studio B is to the left and Studio C is to the right, but where is—

"Mrs. Fournier."

Matronly. I want to be seen as a woman, not a mother. As a single entity, not a dead man's wife. I turn to face the ridiculously handsome Mr. Brady. "I prefer Rebecca."

"Good of you to come, Rebecca." His face looks different, lit up from inside, as though his aura is jacked up. "I know it's an unusual place to meet. Really appreciate it."

"You've got me curious." More than that. You've kicked my libido into gear. After years of lying dormant, it's awakening. Whether I want it to or not.

He grins. "Charities are returning to old school bartering, matching what skills one person has with how they can benefit someone else. Thanks for lending us your expertise."

"My pleasure."

Now why did I have to pick that word?

His eyes dance and we stare at each other a second too long.

"The studio's just down the hall. Follow me."

He's wearing shiny, red basketball shorts and a T-shirt with rips on the shoulder. Flip-flops. His calves are muscular and tanned, just like the rest of his lithe, athletic body.

"Wow," I say as we enter the studio. The mixing area is huge, with two couches and a round coffee table covered in notepads, sheet music, and a laptop. It smells like leather and potato chips. "If you're renting this by the hour, we should get to work."

"No problem. I'm sure you've got other plans today. On my end, there's no rush. I have a year pass."

"Oh. Okay." Expensive. My friend in New York is a musician and I'm aware studios can cost hundreds per hour—how can he afford it? Maybe he comes from money or someone else foots the bill. A sugar momma?

"I know that look," Brady says. "I managed to get corporate sponsorship. It's multipurpose. Lots of kids in Autism Awesome have musical inclinations. Either a certain instrument, song-writing skills, or an interest in mixing or producing. And I'm in a band. The Brady Bunch."

This I know, having Google-stalked him. "Catchy name."

"Would you like to take a seat?"

I choose the softer looking couch and place my camera on the coffee table. Slipping off my sandals, I tuck my feet under my legs, trying to appear nonchalant. Just chillin' in the studio.

Brady sits across from me, legs wide. "Secretly, I occasionally use the studio for other things."

Seducing Aqua Vista mothers?

"I may or may not have a solo career I'm trying to, ah, kickstart."

"Oh? How's that going?"

"Laughably. But that's what I try to teach the kids—perseverance. How are you supposed to get okay at something—or great at something—if you don't give it a go? There aren't any shortcuts. Only practice."

I nod. It's a sentiment we share. "So, I'm here to take pictures of up-and-coming Autism Awesome musicians or…?"

"I need your help with something." He looks at me with a straight face, as though he's about to say something deadly serious. "Pokémon."

I wrinkle my nose. The kids' Japanese trading card game?

"Angus—I think you met him in my office—should be here any minute. He has a formidable Pokémon collection, tons of Mega EX and EX and GX's."

I nod, having a vague idea of what they are.

"Money in his family is tight, so Angus wants to sell his collection on eBay. I need some help photographing and setting up an eBay account, and," he shrugs shyly, "I thought of you. I know it's below your paygrade, but… anyway, Angus will lay some tracks on the drums afterwards, if you've got time to take a few shots of that, that'd be great."

"No problem," I reply.

"I've been thinking about y-you."

Blood rushes to my cheeks.

"Sorry, sorry, I shouldn't have said that." His cheeks color, too. "I mean—ever since you came to my office, and were upset, I've been wondering if you're all r-right. Concerned, is all. Far out. I haven't stuttered in years. I used to do it when I was nervous."

I made him nervous?

"When I was a kid, I got teased…a lot. Which made me stutter…a lot. Ancient history."

"Kids can be the worst," I say.

"And the best."

A shared look of understanding passes between us.

"By the way, I had dinner with my mom the other day. I said there was a beautiful new mom at the school who took amazing photos." The tips of his ears are bright red. "She agreed about the photos. She likes your Alaskan berries series."

"Thanks." I'm stunned that he was talking to his mother about me.

He eyes me. "How's Willow?"

I picture the girls suntanning by Odelle's pool in red bikinis. "She's doing great, building a social life."

"For her age group, it's usually a time of transitions and contradictions. She's the center of her universe, but she chooses to spend time with friends. She's developing her identity, but desperate to fit in."

"Exactly."

"Girls often start being rebellious at this age. But they're also better at problem-solving and logic."

"Thank goodness for that." I wait a beat. "Unless they use their logic to be more rebellious."

He laughs, a warm, natural sound. "Let me set something up." Brady grabs his laptop and places it on his lap.

As he types, I can't ignore my reaction to him; just being in close proximity, I have palpitations in my chest, my hands are sweaty. How long has it been since I felt sensations like this?

Many years.

Although the physical bond with Théo lessened over time, he found other ways to show his love. He recognized me for my mind, my artistic side. He used to always say, *How can you make art if you don't feel it?* He complimented the way I mothered Willow, and there were still the wild Alaskan flowers, poems, but the sex…I craved it. The rejections hurt.

"You look deep in thought…." Brady hesitates, then sets aside the laptop. "What's up?'

"Nothing, nothing, hey—" I pick up my camera. A distraction. "While I'm here, why don't I get that cover shot for your bestselling album?"

A broad smile.

"Keep talking." I sit back, peering through the camera lens, more comfortable like this, with a barrier between us.

"So, as I was so eloquently trying to say before, you've been on my mind. Are things okay?" He speaks simply, a man comfortable talking about emotions, facing awkward situations others would swim away from.

*Snap.*

"Sometimes it's a lot," I answer, shifting angles. "Willow and I are on our own in Boca."

*Snap.*

"Can you rest your arm on the edge of the couch and lean forward?"

He follows my directions. "Has anyone ever told you that you look like the actress, Jennifer Connelly?"

"A few people. I think it's just the dark hair."

"I think you're just humble."

"Realistic."

"Where's your family?" he asks.

"My mom's in New York. I have a few aunts and uncles there. One brother." I answer his next question before he asks it. "I didn't want to raise Willow in a bustling city. We moved here because, as a teenager, I used to do tennis camp in Jax. I loved the ocean. The palm trees."

"Nothing beats SoFlo."

*Snap.*

"Is your family here?" I'm curious about how relaxed and confident he is, with charisma and good looks, while at the same time, he seems fragile underneath, especially now that I know he stutters when he's nervous and was teased as a kid.

"Orlando."

"Do you miss them?"

"Paddy, mostly, my little bro. He has autism."

Now Brady's foundation makes sense. My last picture has just the right amount of emotion. Sex symbol with a heart of gold.

"Moving down here was the right thing to do," he says. "I needed a change. New beaches, new restaurants. Shit, that's not the real reason."

I wait.

"I got my heart broken. Shattered."

I place my camera on my lap.

"I've been in love twice. My high school sweetheart, who I went out with for five years, and Chana, my ex-fiancée."

"What happened?"

He folds his hands on his lap, seeming pensive. "She was religious, I wasn't, it was complicated, but ultimately simple: we were never going to work. Because she was older, more mature, perhaps she had a better insight into our futures than me. I've been single for about a year."

A knock on the door.

Angus pokes his head inside the studio.

"Er, hi, Mr. Brady." His voice breaks from high-pitched to deep, puberty in full effect. He clutches two shoeboxes which, I presume, are the Pokémon cards. "I took the bus myself."

"Well done," Brady says with a brilliant smile. "Look at me, surrounded by the most promising people in Boca." He catches my eye.

Angus puts the shoeboxes on the table before glancing expectantly at Mr. Brady.

"Once we've done Pokémon, Angus, I've booked you for an hour on drums."

"Cool." Angus straightens up.

"I think Mrs. Fournier will be impressed by your sick beats."

"I'm afraid I won't be able to stay too long," I say. "I have lunch plans. We better get on with it."

"What a shame," Brady says.

Spending time together outside of school was a one-off. I won't be alone with him again.

Too much chemistry.

# Chapter 15

# OYSTERS

Always displaying the utmost of manners, Nathaniel stands as I approach his table at Oceans 24.

"I hope you don't mind," he says, dressed for the occasion in a blue and white linen shirt and chinos, "I ordered appetizers." As usual, he's managed to score the best table in the restaurant. Sea-facing. Prime real estate.

"I wouldn't expect anything less." After being in close quarters with Brady, I need a drink and a good chat with a dear friend who's been there for me through ups and downs. I sit and reach for the wine bottle.

"Allow me." Nathaniel takes the bottle from my hands. "I know you like a generous pour."

It's an old joke, one I wish he'd stop using. I swallow the wine; it yields a beautiful light acidity with a hint of pear. "What is this?"

"Avocado wine." Nathaniel puffs up his chest. "Made from the oil's separation during fermentation."

"Unusual flavor."

"Well"—he smooths his thinning hair—"I didn't want to bore you with muscadine, although the Rosa Fiorelli Winery is quite impressive. Impressive, indeed."

Food talk is our currency. It's how we met, how we ended up in bed together, and why we stay in touch.

My phone pings. "Sorry, might be Willow." I check the text message. It's from Odelle:

**Seeing Mr X today. Planning seduction. At lingerie store figuring out if I should go crotchless...baby doll...or full leather...**

I text her, **ur crazy**, and put my phone away.

The waiter approaches and places a dozen raw oysters, lobster tails, and flame-grilled artichokes with creole dipping sauce on the table.

"Thank you." Nathaniel dismisses him with a formal nod.

I go straight for the lobster. "How's work?" Pulling away the shell, I lift out the meat and dip it into butter. *Delicious.*

"The never-ending battle against sugar," he says.

"Kids' breakfast cereals are the worst. It's like they're *trying* to give them diabetes."

He squeezes a lemon wedge. "Too true. Maybe there's a campaign in that."

Nathaniel is a food anthropologist who studies the role food plays in communities and societies. When I met him, he spent half his time traveling, comparing beliefs about food and how those ideas relate to predominant religious beliefs throughout Southeast Asia. Now he's corporate New York, fighting the good fight: hidden sugar in kids' food.

"Nice place you chose," I say, glancing around the busy restaurant. Sometimes, when we see each other, it's crisp white tablecloths. Other times we sit on the curb beside food trucks, salsa dripping down our fingers. Wherever the location, we feast.

He fixes his tidal blue eyes on mine. "You look great...younger."

I arch an eyebrow.

"Not that you ever looked old. But what's different?"

"Running, sunshine, a sea change." *A sexy head of school.*

Nathaniel raises his glass. "Cheers. To the view." He nods at the Atlantic, then in my direction. "And the even more spectacular one before me."

Please don't tell me that's why we're here. This is his big move? Swoop in after Théo's death and reclaim his woman?

Théo would laugh if he were looking down on us. *There's your lovesick friend pulling all the tricks. Lobster. Compliments. What's next?*

What Théo never understood is Nathaniel and I enjoy each other's company because we truly love food. Théo's diminished sensitivity to taste reduced his ability to appreciate sweet, sour, bitter, and salty. Every time I enjoyed a meal in front of him, I felt guilty.

Years before Théo entered my life, Nathaniel and I met in New York at Murray's Cheese on Bleecker Street. Our eyes met across the crowded room, wild with desire—not for each other—but for the smoked mozzarella, the Brillat-Savarin, the Boerenkaas gouda. Nathaniel kept asking the cheesemonger questions—which cheese would complement different wines or dishes. I sidled up beside him, and said, "That must be some dinner party you're planning."

He replied, "It'll be even better if you join me."

The next night, he took me out for the best meal of my life, I drank too much, then we went back to his apartment and had sex. Full-bellied, lazy, comfortable sex. I never planned to be in a relationship with him. We just repeated this routine—food, drink, sex, sleep—until somehow, we were dating. After about four months, not only was I fattening up, but I felt weighed down by the predictability, and the fact that I never wanted to kiss him when I was sober. Luckily, he was off to Thailand to continue his PhD research, saving me from having an awkward breakup conversation.

As Nathaniel interrogates the waiter about which farm the produce comes from and what kind of relationship the restaurant has with the farmer, my mind wanders. Brady sitting across from me, *I've been thinking about you.*

When the waiter leaves, Nathaniel spreads his napkin over his lap. "You haven't seen your mom in a while." It's an obvious reprimand, but since it's on behalf of one of my favorite people, I let it slide.

"We'll come up once Willow's more settled."

"Where are you living?"

"A house; it's ordinary, but the light's amazing. I often work from home." I serve myself more asparagus.

We fall back to our regular topics: chefs we both admire, exercise, mutual friends. I tell him what I like about Boca.

Afterwards, he says, "So it seems your relocation has been a success."

“Except for the fact I might have a stalker.”

“A stalker?” He looks alarmed.

I explain the feelings I’ve had, the sense of being followed.

“Please take all the necessary precautions,” he says. “You’re my closest friend. I’ll do anything for you.”

As we finish our mains, I ask, “What business do you have in Miami?”

“Winery visits, mostly. I’m here for another day. I was hoping”—his Adam’s apple bobs up and down—“I was hoping I could take you out for dinner tomorrow night.’

*Damn.* Lunch is one thing, dinner has connotations.

“No can do. Early business meeting the next morning.”

“That’s too bad.” He nods into his wine glass. “Too bad, indeed.”

Bracing myself, I say, “You know, Nathaniel, I may have the wrong idea here, but…I’m not looking for anything romantic with anyone.” As I say it, I realize it’s true: I don’t want a love affair, an entwining of souls. I want to honor the sexual part of myself that’s been shot down year after year. To be in my body, not my head. In the present, with no ties to the past or future. I want sex. But not with Nathaniel.

He leans back in his chair with an uneasy smile. “I would never pressure you. I’m here for you, as a good friend. We’ve known each other for a long time. When I met you, I didn’t even have this.” He pats his full stomach, and I laugh, grateful that it’s not uncomfortable between us. “We’ll meet and eat. You let me know if you ever want more than that.”

A cluster of pentas are in a vase on the table, bright pink stars. Although I still buy flowers for work, I never buy them for myself anymore. The petals wilt, the stems get moldy, the vase of water becomes rancid, filling the whole house with the awful stench. It’s the same with love: what’s the point if it’s only followed by death? Food, on the other hand, is meant to be devoured, savored; everything lives and dies within the meal.

“I’m still a little hungry,” Nathaniel says. “Can I tempt you with dessert?”

I reach for my wallet, hoping he gets the message. “Rain check?”

# Chapter 16

# JOEY BOY

*Mosquito repellent, flashlight, batteries, M&Ms, sunscreen…*

Having run through the list in my head, I park my car and stroll along Boca's main shopping strip. The town center cafés are full of the after-lunch crowds enjoying the public holiday. My favorite café is on the corner, and it's just two blocks away is the place I purchase all my camera supplies. It's hard to believe that after only a month, Boca already feels like home.

I swing my purse over my shoulder and head to the corner store. It should have everything.

Camp is only four days away. I signed up to go along and it turns out Odelle, Fi, and Paulita are also volunteering. Last week, we all went out for dinner, with Sherice's mom, Deisha, too, at Las Fajitas, and through nachos and margaritas, enchiladas, and churros dipped in chocolate, the conversation never stopped—covering topics such as travel, juggling demanding careers, and raising tweens. We laughed a lot. Fi is also a jogger, and we've started running twice a week. Paulita said she wanted to introduce me to some potential clients. And, if it was appropriate, some potential bachelors.

Clients, yes. Bachelors, no thanks.

After visiting Brady's studio, we've interacted a few more times: once, after assembly, we had a brief conversation; another time, at school pickup, he asked if I could take some candid shots of the teachers in the staff room. I agreed—after all, we weren't going to be alone—and the next day spent an hour with him and the rest of Aqua Vista Academy. (Mrs. Fun turned out to be the most photogenic.)

I catch a glimpse of myself in a mirrored storefront. A middle-aged woman in a white, short-sleeved blouse, yellow skirt, pretty sandals, dark hair blown out. *Boca*-ized.

Hey, you know what? I look pretty damn good. Maybe flouncy suits me. Running every morning is making me stronger, leaner, and boosting me with endorphins.

As I reach the corner store, something makes me pause. A Range Rover approaches…slows down…. Is the driver watching me? No. Phew. He's checking out the younger woman behind me.

Inside, I grab a basket from the front of the store. Candy aisle first. Three packets of Willow's favorite M&Ms as well as some chocolate bars—

*Shit.* Mr. Brady—I mean Brady—is walking toward me.

Head down, he's speaking softly to himself as though reciting a grocery list. I glance from left to right. Do I have time to leave?

Before I get a chance to analyze my desire to flee—which most certainly has something to do with *the fantasies*! I've been having about him—he looks up.

"You," he says with a warm smile.

We're standing only an arm's distance apart.

"Buddy, you need to be more careful," I tease.

"Of…alligators? Tiger moms?"

"Don't think I didn't notice you muttering to yourself in public. Not a great look." Though in his faded jeans, T-shirt, and leather slides, he looks mouth-watering.

He laughs. "I always do that. I never remember what I came in for."

"Maybe you should write a list." What a lame "mom idea."

"I know I needed beer…chips, worms, and…the last thing I can't remember."

"Going fishing?"

"Boat's ready to set sail." He gives me a funny look. "What are you doing?"

"Grabbing last-minute things for camp—" It's only then that I notice where we're standing. *Extra-large and ribbed. Trojan Pleasure Pack. Magnum Bareskin.* Oh hell. I jump away and gesture for him to follow me to the less salacious sunscreen section. He rubs his mouth, seemingly trying not to laugh. Could I be any less composed?

"What are you doing after this?" he asks.

"A few errands."

"Where's Willow?"

"At Issy's, Fiona Larsen's house." I fumble with my basket. "A few of the girls are having a sleepover."

"That settles it, then." His smile widens. "You're coming for a boat ride with me."

"Uh…no."

"You gotta see *Joey Boy*. Beautiful vessel."

As the older, more experienced one, I call the game. "You're the head of school at my daughter's school. Should we be seen together?"

"Who says we have to be seen?"

"DIE!" a child yells.

I swivel around.

An elderly woman shuffles by with a small boy, maybe her grandson, who has a Fortnite figurine in one hand and a plastic semiautomatic in the other. He points the gun at me. "DIE! DIE!"

I wait for the grandmother to scold the boy. She only smiles.

"C'mon, Rebecca," Brady says quietly. "A boat ride would be fun. You can educate me about how to build an igloo. Skin a grizzly. Have you been fishing before?"

"Ah…yes…with my…"

"Husband?"

I clear my throat. "I haven't been fishing since he got sick. He liked to fly fish. Honestly, I hated having to be quiet the whole time so I didn't scare off the fish."

"You don't have to be quiet with me," Brady says. "In fact, I think the sound of an intelligent food photographer from the Alaskan wilds will lure the fish closer."

The *click* of heels. A woman in her twenties comes up from behind me and gives us a double take.

Brady steps out of my personal space.

What am I doing? Even contemplating his invitation is unwise.

Once the woman exits the aisle, Brady says, "It would be good to show you the sights. You're new here. It's the chivalrous thing to do. Tell you what, I'll let you know what dock I'm on, describe the boat, and if you want to show up in"—he glances at his sports watch—"exactly twenty-two minutes, we can set sail."

"That's not a good idea."

"The best ideas never are."

He gives me the details and I tap them into my phone.

"See you soon, I hope," Brady says.

Maybe in another lifetime, in another town.

With a wave, he walks away.

Dear God, from behind, his worn-in blue jeans hug a tight, round ass. Those tanned arms.

*Get a grip, Rebecca.*

I don't get a grip, because twenty minutes later I'm standing on the dock, hair flying in my eyes despite my wide-brimmed hat, searching for *Joey Boy.*

# Chapter 17

# PINCH!

## —WILLOW—

"That's hilarious," Katia laughs. "Alek is so funny."

"I know," I say. "He always tells good jokes."

I wriggle Issy's red dress over my head and look in the mirror. The dress is too tight and too short. My mom would hate it. And *I* hated changing in front of Katia, but when the head of KISS offers to give you a makeover, you say yes. She's been doing my makeup in Issy's bathroom, while the rest of KISS watch a horror movie in Issy's room.

The bathroom is massive. Beside the sink are old-fashioned silver brushes, fancy perfume bottles, and a basket of hair accessories.

"Alek is cute, too," Katia says. "Don't you think so?"

"I guess."

The KISS girls and I talk about the boys at Aqua Vista all the time, especially Alek Horvat, Maxwell Zimmerman, and Jay Yoshida. Depending on which KISS girl you ask, they're either a friend or an enemy.

"Okay, pucker up." Katia leans in, outlining my lip with a pink lipliner, the makeover's finishing touch.

I hope my breath isn't bad.

In the next room, the girls screech, and Sherice yells, "Use the knife."

Katia is staring at me. "Oh my gosh, look."

"What?"

"Pinch your thigh," she says with a weird squinty look on her face.

"Why?"

"Just do it." She smiles like it's all a joke, but I know she wants me to do it for real.

I look at us in the gold lit-up mirror and lift my dress. Then I study my thigh. I've never looked at it before and thought, *thigh*, as one single thing cut off from the rest of my body. There's hair on it and veins and a purple bruise. I pinch the upper bit and squeeze.

"Gross, right?" Katia says.

"Um, I guess." I didn't realize I had fat like that on my thigh. So squishy. Katia's right, it's gross.

"Stella's is disgusting, too," Katia says. "She doesn't follow my diet. Her BMI is bad."

I don't know what BMI is, but I'm not going to ask.

Katia raises her leg, propping her foot on the counter ledge. She runs her hand over her own thigh, tanned, tiny, perfect-looking. "You want to be part of KISS, right?"

I nod. Me and every other girl at Aqua Vista wants to join and she knows it.

"When you pinch your thigh, there can't be any fat." She demonstrates.

"Oh. Okay." I fidget with the hem of the dress.

"I'm trying to help you. That's why I have you send me your calories for everything you eat."

It's been annoying doing that. And weird. But Katia said it was stage one. I wish I could get out of this stupid dress and put my T-shirt and shorts back on.

"It's time for the next stage," Katia says. "So, we look hot in our bikinis, right? So, from now on, you need to ask permission before eating anything."

Ummm, is she serious? I focus all my attention on the patterned tiled floor.

"Text me whenever you want to eat. Like, 'Can I have 350 calories?' And remember, keep using 'c's,' in case someone reads our texts."

I must look unsure, because she says, "It's stage two. All of us do it. Stella messes up, though. She's weak." Katia grabs a brush, stands behind me, so we're both facing the mirror. She begins brushing my hair.

"Willow, you're close to getting into our group. We see lots of potential."

The praise feels good, like the bristles of the brush against my scalp. I breathe in her cotton candy body spray. If I get in, I'll never have to sit on my own at lunch anymore. Katia plays stupid games like that. Excluding one of the Drew Barrymores from the group for no reason. Should I trust what she says? Maybe it's another game.

"You're an awesome flyer." Katia keeps brushing my hair. "And you're pretty. Even Alek thinks so. I talked to him about you." She sets down the brush and starts braiding my hair.

Oh no. What did she say to him? Me thinking he's cute and having him *know* I think he's cute are completely different things.

"I know how to get him to like you," she says.

I don't want him to like me! I don't want anything to happen!

"I'll tell you at camp."

Camp. Is it weird to look forward to something and dread it at the same time?

A tug at my roots. "Before I tell you anything"—Katia weaves strands of hair from my temples into a French braid—"I need to make sure you're worthy of my secrets. You have to do something to prove how much you trust me. Stage three."

I pick at my cuticle. "I'm not sure...."

"Don't freak out. It'll be fun."

When Katia tells me what I have to do, it doesn't seem like such a big deal, and even if it was something worse, I'd probably go along with it. That's how bad I want to be in KISS.

# Chapter 18

# ROW-MANTIC

## —REBECCA—

"You're here," Brady says, raising his palm to the sky as I approach the boat.

I step on board, which, to my unseaworthy eyes, looks like a mini yacht. Once I find my balance, I pass him the bag from the general store. "I come bearing gifts."

"Aw, you shouldn't have." He takes out a box from the bag, unwraps it, then throws his head back, laughing.

It's a mug that reads *YODA BEST PRINCIPAL*, with a picture of Yoda.

"You're hilarious," he says.

"I'm scared."

"Of what?"

*You. This.* "Floridian reptiles. Sharks. Things that get you when you least expect it."

"You've got nothing to worry about. Take a seat. Would you like a motion sickness pill?"

"Thanks." I accept the pill, knock it back with some water and join him in the cockpit.

Sitting side by side, the glistening water around us, it's painfully obvious: we're about to go off on an adventure, alone, for no other reason than we want to spend time together.

"What's the itinerary, captain?"

"Up the Intracoastal."

"Sounds great." I keep my tone jaunty. Platonic.

He turns on the engine. We start slow, then the speed picks up slightly, wind whipping my hair back. Although we're exposed to the elements, an overhead awning provides shade.

For the second time, I wonder how Brady affords such expensive hobbies on a head of school's salary.

"This beauty is a Parker 750 cabin cruiser with 150 HP engine." That doesn't mean anything to me, but I can tell—from the reverence in his voice, the spotless deck, the care in its maintenance—that Brady loves it. Over my shoulder, I notice a small cabin with a sink, porthole windows, and a cozy-looking couch covered with a woven, brightly colored blanket.

A flash of Brady and me, half-dressed, entwined on the couch.

*Stop it! Thank goodness he can't read my mind.*

As we cruise along the Intracoastal, I focus on the scenery. The waterway runs parallel to luxury homes and rows of palm trees interspersed with dark mangroves. Occasionally the peace is disturbed by rowdy groups on fishing tours or people on Jet Skis breaking the no-wake rule.

As the last boat fades into the distance, I'm lulled by the steady slapping of waves against the hull and the distant high-pitched cries of seagulls. Along the foreshore, I can make out blue herons, great egrets, ibises.

Half an hour later, we reach a quiet inlet. Brady stops the engine and pours us beers. He drinks from his gift, and I pick a mug from his boat collection, captioned *DON'T MAKE ME USE MY PRINCIPAL VOICE.*

The paranoid side of me is glad we're somewhere private. Over the last year, there have been many times I've thought I need a psychologist to deal with my grief over Théo and my feelings of being followed. But maybe my therapy needs to be more of the physical variety. Sexual healing.

"You okay?" Brady asks. "You seem tense."

"I'm fine. Enjoying being away from it all." *Away from my role as mother. And grieving widow.*

He opens a bag of salt and vinegar chips. "Haute cuisine?"

"Ha." I munch on a few handfuls, briefly thinking of Nathaniel and his abhorrence of junk food.

"Tell me three things about you I'd never guess," Brady says.

"Is this a drinking game?"

He meets my gaze, his voice serious. "It's whatever you want it to be." He doesn't sound like he's talking about the game anymore.

"Right, three things. In my twenties, I liked doing art experiments. I'd take a photograph and then leave it in the backyard for six calendar moons, exposed to sun, rain, damp. I loved seeing the effects, and then I'd name it something like *182 Days of Weather*."

He whistles. "Cool." The sincerity in his voice catches me off guard.

"Um, I spent a year as a Peace Corps volunteer in the Philippines. And… third thing…" For some reason, Odelle pops into my head. "I used to have this insane tennis rivalry with Odelle Wragge—her last name was Rackark then. We did tennis camp, four years running."

"Is that so? Huh."

"What are three things about you?"

"There's the *Brady Bunch*." He opens his tackle box. "When I was a kid, I desperately wanted to be Greg Brady, the eldest brother. He surfed, played football and guitar. He stood up for the other kids and had a real sense of fair play. Not to mention the prettiest girlfriends."

Girlfriends…plural?

"What else?" I ask.

He takes out his fishing rod. "My family are high achievers. When I was young, they were too busy to do normal family things. Not around much."

He was neglected. My admissions feel flimsy now. Superficial. "Who raised you then?"

"My grandma. Man, she'd forgive me for a million sins. I have two older sisters and one younger brother." He selects a shrimp from a small Styrofoam container.

"Still, it must've been hard without your parents' support."

"It's nothing. Water under the bridge." Touchy subject noted. He inserts the fishhook through the shrimp's body. "Do you want to fish?"

"That's a hard pass. Third thing?"

He casts his rod into the water. "Don't ask me about my middle name."

"Well now I have to know your middle name." Clint *something* Brady.

He smiles. "Swimming was a big deal for me. I was semiprofessional before I got into teaching. That's my third thing."

We discuss the early morning trainings when he was a child, his later wins, his losses, then his pivot into education.

"How did you become head of school given"—*you're too-young-for-me-what-am-I-doing-here*—"your age?"

"Lucky, I guess. I won lots of teaching awards. Became associate dean of students quickly."

"How'd that work?"

"I was teaching at Boca Raton High School and finished a part-time master's degree in educational leadership. Did pretty well, so that got me the private school gig, associate dean of students. Then I was dean of students. Two years later, the Aqua Vista Academy head of school retired. The assistant head of school wanted a big lifestyle change and resigned. They needed someone quick. I applied. It was a case of right time, right place."

*Like now? Or is this wrong time, wrong place…wrong man?*

He sits close, studying the water. Part of me wants to jump overboard, swim to shore, as far away as possible from a man who could make or break my daughter's school experience. I shouldn't be here alone with him. Should I? Maybe not everything's meant to be planned. Years of being a mother, juggling my business and the household, catering to everyone's needs, there was no time to ask, "What do *I* need?"

*Put your child first,* that's what Yolanthe often says.

Mothers do that for so long, through sleepless nights and tantrum-filled days. Negotiating screen time, bedtime, biting our tongues when we want to scream so loud we'll break their eardrums. Holidays, Easter egg hunts, trick-or-treating, Christmas, birthday parties, each cake more lavish than the last, every moment captured on the iCloud.

Then, miraculously, they start school. We think—we did it. We presented them to the world, alive, well-groomed, with rudimentary manners. Give us our Nobel Peace Prize. Isn't it "me time?"

But then why, when we do finally grant it to ourselves, do we feel so guilty?

Now, salty spray on my face, a cloudless blue sky above, desire circulates through me with a voice of its own, telling me to do reckless things.

What would it be like to kiss Brady? How can I even think that?

I close my eyes, the sun on my shoulders, swayed by the gently rocking boat.

After catching two fish, Brady sets his rod aside. "There's another place I'd like to take you to. You up for it?"

"Yes."

With the engine back on, we continue up the Intercostal.

Curious about his younger brother, I ask, "What does Paddy love? You said before you help kids find their spark. What's his?"

"Well, about ten percent of boys with autism spectrum disorder have an outstanding skill well beyond their peer level. It often shows up in math, music, art, and memory for dates, places, routes, or facts. Paddy's skill is frogs. Correction—frogs and toads. He can tell you everything there is to know about the southern chorus frog, the pig frog, the eastern spadefoot. Last year he got a part-time job at the Back to Nature Wildlife Refuge."

"Wow, how perfect."

"It's great. Maybe one day you'll meet him."

"Maybe." I feel like I can't breathe. "Does working with kids make you more or less likely to want your own?"

"I want kids, for sure. But I'd prefer to adopt."

"Really?"

"I can see myself with a few boys."

A sandy stretch of beach comes into view, full of sunbathers. A picturesque pier. Boats moored.

"Boynton Inlet," Brady says.

"It's gorgeous."

"I'll go a little further where it's more private." He steers the boat north.

"Got any jokes?" he asks.

I think about it. "No, sorry." *Except the one about the widow and school principal.*

"Why do oars fall in love?" he asks.

"I don't know."

"Because they're row-mantic."

"Very cute," I reply.

"Why did the girl boat have problems sailing?" He waits. "She didn't have boy-ancy!"

I snort, but not at the joke—at my sudden disbelief that I'm in this unimaginable situation. Then I'm really laughing, a stomach-clenched, tears-in-my-eyes, cackle.

"I've got another one." Brady elbows me, egging me on. "What causes some boats to become party boats?" After a beat, he says, "Pier pressure. P-I-E-R."

I keep laughing. I want to stop, but I can't. Clutching my ribs, my whole body starts heaving. I don't know why I'm laughing so hard. I don't have control over my body. Even worse, I start hiccupping.

"You okay? It wasn't *that* funny."

"I know." I hiccup again, which makes me laugh all the harder.

"We're here," he says.

The sandy beach is deserted.

Once I calm down, I catch him watching me.

"Sorry…uh…it's hot." I readjust my hat, sitting straight.

"You're fucking beautiful."

I'm stunned. My body warms all over. No one has talked to me like that…ever.

"Swim?" he asks.

"I—ah—don't have my bathing suit."

"You don't need one."

# Chapter 19

# THE PACT

Speechless, I bring a hand to my hip.

"Ah, yes, Mr. Brady, I do need a bathing suit."

"The water looks amazing," he tempts. "Refreshing." As though daring me, Brady takes off his top, revealing the full trifecta: an exquisite, tanned chest, wide shoulders, ripped arms. Then he gives me a look. *Are you game, old woman? Or are you going to let fear rule you?*

I feel a flutter in my chest, a rigid smile on my face.

*Mind*: Hell no.

*Body*: Please, yes.

The words spring from my mouth: "Sure. Sounds fun."

Maybe a swim is exactly what I need. Hat off. I unbutton my blouse, button by button. Brady watches me, only his eyes moving.

The blouse drops to the deck.

Skirt next. I stand up on the bow, unzip the side, and step out, letting it pool at my feet.

"Wow," he murmurs.

Exposed and unashamed, I'm grateful that Yasmine Eslami makes some of the best lingerie in the world—French, skin-toned lace.

I pull back my shoulders; his eyes devour me.

"Rebecca." He says my name like it's a drug. Feverish.

*Thank you, Yasmine*. My stretch marks disappear. The fine lines around my eyes and forehead—vanish. I feel like a goddess, more beautiful, because

I've survived between life and death, loved fully, lost, and learned how to rise again.

"C'mon, champ." I grasp the rail. "Let's swim. Show me what you got those gold medals for."

He grins and I'm struck by his raw sex appeal. It's not only his looks, but his life force, his vitality. The sun melting icicles.

His jean shorts land in a lump beside my skirt.

Black boxers that I could pull off, feel how hard he is beneath.

I clench my legs, stung by the swollen feeling down below.

"Let's do it," he says. "Don't wimp out on me now." He dives into the turquoise water, his body slicing into the sea.

*One, two, three,* I count, before jumping off the deck. I don't think about Théo. I don't think about Willow. All I think about is the water enveloping me, the taste of salt in my mouth, Brady swimming closer, the ocean his most perfect backdrop.

I want his lips on mine. I want him inside me. I want nothing else. But as a sexually experienced woman, one thing I know is to prolong the foreplay—anticipation is the best aphrodisiac. The longer I can keep Brady desiring me, the longer I can guarantee his full attention.

"Mr. Brady, you shouldn't be in the water with me," I singsong, playing to the taboo. "A mom from school."

His eyelids grow heavy. "Maybe I need you to survive."

"Huh?"

His eyes fall to my breasts. "For your boy-ancy," he jokes, playing on the earlier punchline. "Better than a lifejacket."

"Goof." I splash him. I'm no "The Rack," like Odelle, but I have B-cups that haven't yet given away to gravity.

He bares his teeth. "Oh no, you don't. I'm gonna get ya." He chases me in the water, grabbing for my legs. I kick, and swim away, before he seizes my hips, pulling me to him.

He brings his face close to mine, and I swear he's about to kiss me. I shut my eyes, then—

*Splash*! Saltwater in my face.

"You're naughty," I say. "Pretending you're such a good guy in front of the kids and their families, but underneath, total jerk."

Something changes in his expression. He looks away. I didn't mean to hurt his feelings.

"I don't think you're a jerk." I kick my legs to stay afloat.

"What do you think of m-me?"

"Remains to be seen." I tilt my head, endeared by his stutter, his nervousness. With that, I take a gulp of air and dive underneath the water, the deep blue, gliding between the sun rays, then lower, to where the water is colder, murkier.

We swim for a while, then climb back on the boat.

"Well, that was fun," I say, dripping onto the deck.

He glances at me, his eyes following the lines of my body as I stand there in see-through lingerie. "I have, ah, some towels in the cabin."

I follow him inside, each step more dangerous, more forbidden. Once we touch, there's no going back.

He picks up a towel and faces me. "Turn around."

I shiver, waiting to see what he'll do next—waiting to see what *I'll* do next.

Using the towel, he dries my shoulders, then my hair. An intimate gesture, something a parent does for a child. Waves rhythmically lap against the boat and birds circle in the air, crying as they soar higher. He towels my arms and back; the rough material scratches my skin, causing a ricochet of fine sensations.

"So, you said you were single, right?" I need this confirmed because any second I might pounce on him and one thing I'll never be is a cheater—a cougar, on the other hand, was not out of the question.

"I haven't had a serious relationship since Chana."

I remember him mentioning he was younger than her. Why does he like older women? Reenacting a childhood script. Mommy issues. "Are you seeing anyone?" I push.

"No. Now that I've met you."

"Oh?" I turn around and face him. "Are you devoted already?"

I watch the small movements change on his face: his pupils enlarging, eyes bright and glossy, the rise of his Adam's apple. "If I'm with you, I won't be with anyone else."

"*If*?" I ask coquettishly.

He grins, lips tight. "When."

"Mmm. You better take me out for dinner then."

"Ahh." He nods, in silent understanding. "Not that kind of girl?"

"That's right. I'm not that kind of girl. But I am that kind of woman." The words shock me.

His mouth parts.

I grab his arm, staring him in the eyes. "I want you. Right now, Brady. Fuck me. I can't take it a minute longer."

"Who needs dinner?" he growls. His lips land on mine, hot, warm, tasting of summer, and salt and vinegar chips, and sex. Within seconds, his hand cups my ass. Our kisses grow deeper.

"Christ you smell good," he says. "I could have you right here."

"Have me anywhere," I whisper, grabbing his dick over the top of his boxers. It's big, erect.

He half moans, half laughs. "I didn't expect this."

"Yeah, well. Moms have a lot of pent-up aggression. We get shit done. And I want you to do me."

Why am I being so alpha? Talking like I'm in a porno? There's no time to question anything as we fall onto the couch, me on top, kissing each other's necks, shoulders, eyelids, hands in each other's hair, lips to lips. He skillfully takes off my bra.

*Death of the wife, return to the teenager.*

*Oxygen. Life. Sunshine.*

It's as though I'm reviving the person I used to be when Odelle and I spent our summers together, when we recognized our sexual power, when we knew that we *were* the party.

Right now, this is the best party of my life, of flesh, of desire.

A tugging sensation, deep in my stomach. My bare toes push against the edge of the couch. Oh my God—I couldn't be—am I about to—?

When did I last have an orgasm? Five, maybe, six years ago.... Sex with Théo was tender, solidifying our commitment, but it wasn't exciting. Each year his sex drive dwindled until it was a small flame that took *a lot* of fancy handiwork to get going....

Brady stops and kisses me slowly, his tongue teasing my mouth.

That tugging sensation is back—building...whoa!

"We can slow down if you want." Brady touches my face. "You need to be sure. I know things have been difficult for you and your family, maybe—"

"Stop talking, Brady. You on top." I wriggle underneath him. "Hard as you can." I'm burning up, lust and pain clashing together. And grief too. I blink back tears, pooling under my eyelids.

No. This is hot. This is my forty-year-old-plus woman ruling the goddamn world moment. I'm not going to cry.

Brady wipes the tears from my eyes. "We've got time. We don't need to rush."

"I want to rush—I don't want to think. I don't want to do the right thing."

He sits up. "So, I'm your mistake?"

Laughter peals out of my mouth; it sounds heartless, cruel. "Yeah, I guess you are. All my other mistakes are so...permanent. You have no idea." I wipe the tears off my cheeks.

He looks at me cautiously, eyes filled with concern.

"Ah! The moment's ruined." I grab the blanket and cover my breasts. "This is not sexy."

"You're wrong. You're sexy as hell, even when you're a hot mess. But I'm not doing this when you're upset."

"I want to. Please." I lunge toward him for another kiss in an attempt to be seductive.

He holds me away at arm's length.

Mortified, I turn away so he can't see my face. Why am I acting out like this? I've been celibate for too long. "We should go back," I stammer. *Where I can lick my wounds in private.*

"Uh-uh. Come here." Brady shifts on the couch and lifts the blanket over us. He runs his hands through my hair.

Snuggling closer, I match his breathing. After a few minutes, my body relaxes against his.

"What are you thinking?" he asks.

"I don't know. That…that this kinda feels like cheating on Théo, my husband…." The tears come now, full force. I hide my face against his chest. Brady holds me tighter as I keep crying, releasing the pain. The door of our marriage is closing. I can feel the shift, separating the Alaskan winters from this warm, tropical place.

"It's natural to be sad," Brady says. "I can see how much you miss him."

"I miss our family. I miss Willow having a dad. Someone who loves her as much as I do."

"That's understandable," he soothes. "I get it."

I keep crying, warmed by his gentle voice that keeps murmuring kind things.

Outside on the deck, my phone rings.

I stiffen. "I better check that." A mother can never ignore a ringing phone. Half-relieved to get out of his close quarters, I jump up, wrapping the blanket around me.

My heart drops when I read Fi's message:

**Hi. Unfortunately the girls have had a disagreement. Willow's crying. She wants u to come and get her right away.**

Christ. I hope she's okay. This is punishment, isn't it, for putting my needs before Willow's? Karmic whipping.

I rush back into the cabin and explain the situation to Brady.

"I'll take you back right away. I'm sure it'll work out. These things can get blown out of proportion." He gives me a reassuring nod. "For girls in this age group, their friendships are as intense as love affairs."

Love affairs, huh? I have the feeling he has experience with those.

Everything feels awkward: reaching for my bra from the ground, realizing it's too wet, and I'll have to go braless; angling my body away so I have privacy to step into my skirt.

As we cruise back, I keep my distance, stunned by what happened—especially my role as initiator.

The silence between us grows more uncomfortable. Does he regret what happened? Do I? I'm analyzing this when Brady says, "I want to do this again."

Oh…"That doesn't seem possible. Not without the whole Aqua Vista community finding out."

He pauses. "We'd have to make some sort of agreement."

"Like?"

"Because of my position at the school, we could see each other but keep it on the down-low."

I'm too old to be involved in anything on "the down-low," or to not speak directly. "Is this arrangement something you have with other women?"

"Hell, after I've seen how amorous you get on *Joey Boy*, how could I want anybody else?"

I smile and he says, "Do you want to be weekend friends?"

"Explain."

"You know, after dark friends, not nine to five ones. Deal?"

I look over the side of the boat at the waves, nausea rising in my stomach, remembering the last deal I made.

*It only took a few weeks.*

*I came home from the blistering cold, my hands numb, and took off my scarf, beanie, coat, and gloves. From the look on Théo's face, I knew something had happened.*

*"What's wrong?" I asked.*

*"It arrived."*

*A punch to my stomach. "Where is it? You can't have a death drug in the house! Willow might find it!"*

*Théo showed it to me. It had been delivered from China in a flat-pack—in clear plastic. To my naked eyes, it looked like cocaine. "I'll keep it safe from Willow," he promised.*

*Not good enough. "At least put it in something obvious so it can't be mistaken and, God, end up as an ingredient in a birthday cake."*

*I found a blue Ziploc bag in the cabinet. Transferred the Nembutal into it. Put it in a canister which I hid at the top of the linen closest.*

*Then we made a pact.*

*It was to be solely under Théo's care, put in a locked box, for which only he had the key.*

*He couldn't drink it without warning me first.*

*Obviously, when he decided to do it, Willow couldn't be at home.*

*That was our pact, as sacred and more serious than our wedding vows.*

*Neither of us expected I'd go back on my word.*

"Rebecca? Are you okay?" Brady asks from beside me.

I nod and for the rest of the boat ride, conflicting emotions war inside of me, and I barely manage small talk. There's one thing I'm not confused about, though—something I've been waiting to do, seeking a meaningful spot in nature, where I could leave it for the elements, as I left my photographs when I was a student. Willow will have the ring when she's twenty-one, but the locket is mine to do with it what I wish. When Brady's not looking, I unlatch my necklace. I don't need a physical reminder of Théo strapped to my body. We had a life. And now there's more life for me ahead. *Au revoir, mon amour.* I drop the locket into the sea, watching as it's swallowed whole into the water's depth.

Once we reach the dock, Brady touches my arm, his expression thoughtful. "Call if you need anything. Conversation. Another boat ride."

I smile, too confused—and embarrassed—by what happened to know how to respond.

"See you for camp Monday morning," he says.

Maybe sooner. "Are you going to Paulita's party?" Apparently, it's celebrating the efforts of the school fundraising team, but surely it's also for her political run.

He nods.

"Well, see you Saturday night."

"Until then, Rebecca."

I step onto the platform and turn around. "I'm not going to use Rebecca anymore. From now on…call me Bec."

# Chapter 20

# WARNING

"You better come in," Fi says when she answers the door.

She wipes her hands on her apron, a blush coloring her cheeks, the epitome of a perfect blonde Stepford wife, not too tall, not too curvy. You'd hate her for it, but she always says it like it is. No pretense.

Fi leads me to her cheerful, open-plan kitchen painted a Mediterranean blue, with terra-cotta tiles, numerous plants, stacks of cookbooks, and something heavenly-smelling—beef, tomatoes, thyme—simmering on the stove.

It's only now I realize I've had nothing to eat or drink but potato chips and a mug of beer. That crazy Brady boat ride....

"Iced tea? Coffee?"

I shake my head. Honestly, I'd like a cup of Truth with a side of Hurry-the-Fuck-Up. "Is Willow okay?"

"Yes. They're all watching a movie in Issy's room." She stops and gives me an apologetic look. "I'm sorry to alarm you. Maybe I shouldn't have called...."

*But you did. You cockblocked me from having sex with my daughter's middle school principal, which is probably a very good thing, but still.*

A ridiculous smile teases my lips. *Did I just use the term cockblock?*

"I better go and check on her," I say. "What happened?"

"I'll tell you everything after you check she's okay." Fi waves her arm toward the hall. "Third room on the left."

When I reach the room, the door is ajar, laughter coming from inside.

I knock and when Issy calls out, "come in," I step inside.

The girls are on top of Issy's four-poster bed, tanned legs poking out in different directions, comfortable, having fun.

Willow smiles at me—she's wearing so much makeup it's cartoonish. Are those fake lashes? I'm sure she left the house this morning in shorts and a T-shirt, but now she's in a skimpy red dress.

"Everything good or…?" I ask.

"Mom!" She grits her teeth. "We're trying to watch a movie."

"When does it finish?" I attempt to gauge the situation.

"Probably twenty minutes," Issy answers in her best please-the-adult-so-they-leave voice.

Does Willow want to go home or stay for the sleepover? I'll have to ask her after the movie.

Back in the kitchen, Fi pours us two glasses of mineral water, slices of lime on the rim, and we sit at her cluttered farmer's style kitchen table. Behind her, a split-level lawn leads to a garden of lush, overgrown flowers—blue daze as groundcover, orange and yellow coreopsis, purple gerberas. Farther to the right, there's a half-court basketball ring and a giant trampoline. Lucky kids.

"I was giving them space," Fi begins, her bright blue eyes wide. "I didn't want to be a lawnmower mom, you know, 'mow down' a path so all obstacles and struggles are removed. It's hard to keep up with all the parent terms, isn't it?" She holds up her fingers and lists them. "Helicopter, free-range, tiger, elephant—and now, of course, everyone wants to be dolphin parents. Parents who value play, downtime, and flexibility."

"Right, well. What happened with Willow?"

"They were doing streaks on Snapchat."

"Streaking?" I picture a nude man running across the tennis court at Wimbledon.

"Similar to likes on Facebook or hearts on Instagram. Streaks count how many consecutive days two people have been sending Snaps to each other. Every day they send a Snap, their streak gets longer."

"Okay?"

"Well, Katia and Stella have the longest streak." Fi glances over her shoulder before continuing. "But Stella broke it."

"What does this have to do with Willow?"

"Stella started a new streak with Willow. Katia wasn't happy."

Why are we talking about Katia as though she's an A-list celebrity? She's prepubescent, five-foot, and has the voice of a mouse.

Fi glances at me from under her eyebrows. "Apparently, Willow's a really good flyer too."

"And that's a problem because…?"

"Not a problem." Fi's mouth twitches. "It's just that before Willow joined, Katia was the best."

I square my shoulders. "So, Willow's ruffling feathers?"

"Which normally isn't a bad thing. We want our daughters to excel…. Maybe I shouldn't be telling you this…."

"No, please." I lean forward, grateful for her candor. "Tell me."

A soccer ball flies across the kitchen floor. Then a teenager races past me, followed by his doppelganger, a quarter of his size.

"Balls. Outside!" Fi points to the backyard.

Her sons laugh. One seizes a mega box of chocolate chip cookies from the butler's pantry, the other snatches two cans of Squirt from the fridge, and in a blur of green-and-white stripes and scruffy blond hair, they roughhouse, colliding into the wall, and then out the backdoor.

"Enter and exit Sven and Benjie," Fi says. "Charming, huh?"

I can't help but think of Brady wanting to adopt boys, of Brady as a father. "You were saying?"

"That boys are a lot easier?" Fi taps her finger against the rim of her glass. "Don't tell the other moms what I'm about to say, okay?"

Uneasiness lodges in my chest. I force myself to sound cavalier. "Sure."

Fi edges her chair a little closer and lowers her voice. "You know about KISS and the Drew Barrymores?"

I nod.

"For some of the Drew Barrymores who got close to KISS but didn't make it, well, let's say the fallout has been serious."

"As in?"

"Two girls left the school. Psychologists were involved. One ended up at an eating disorder clinic."

"What happened?"

"It's the 'three girls thing,' isn't it, but intensified? Someone's always left out. KISS gets their power from exclusion. They've been friends since grade one. They only know being popular."

Imagine being insulated with power and acceptance. Willow had two friendship groups in Anchorage: the girls that did gymnastics, and the quiet kids at school that drew or played in nature during lunchtime.

I put my elbows on the table. "So, KISS has been a stable clique for years, with no one else allowed in? Drew Barrymores never become part of KISS?"

"Oh, some girls get in for a while. Sherice used to be a Drew Barrymore. Katia's always been the leader. Even as a little girl."

"Why? Because of her parents?" The soon-to-be-running-mayor and the head of Florida's biggest car dealership have clout.

"Yes, of course. All of it," Fi says. "Money, prestige, good looks. Katia's older sister, Giavanna, was Miss South Florida. But it's something else, that X factor, I suppose. Anyway, Katia's best friends with Stella. Issy and Sherice are best friends too, but they're definitely second rung. It's awful, I know. I worry about how entrenched Issy is, but moms can't control who their kids are friends with."

"True," I say.

"Anyway, the Drew Barrymores compete to hang out with KISS and that's what allows KISS to treat them in shitty ways. Whoever's at the bottom of the ladder gets it worse."

"The queen bee syndrome."

"Right. The girls who want to fit in end up being bystanders—silencing themselves—knowing their place in the group could always be taken if they don't go along with the pack. Then there are the girls at the bottom of their friendship pyramid. They're allowed to hang out with the queen bee group for the sole purpose of eventually being excluded. Or sometimes they're just weekend friends."

"Meaning?"

"Fine to hang out with on the weekend or when no one from school is around. But that's it."

Well, I guess "weekend friend" has different meanings depending on whether you're a tween or an adult.

"And today?" Cut to the chase. What happened to Willow?

"I found Willow in the hall by herself crying. I asked what was wrong, but she wouldn't tell me. That's when I texted you. I took Issy out of her room and she told me that Katia was pissed about the streak thing and said something privately to Willow. That's all I know."

*Spoiled brat.* My anger toward Katia shocks me. I tell myself to rein it in. She's only a child.

"Ten minutes later, they were all laughing and playing on the trampoline. Katia and Willow were holding hands and jumping." Fi rolls her eyes. "You know what's the biggest challenge facing twelve-year-old girls?"

"Um, hormones?"

"Other twelve-year-old girls," Fi says.

"Touché. Well, thanks for telling me everything. I know it's complicated...we're all friends and our daughters are too, which makes things awkward."

"It's all right," Fi says with a nervous laugh. "You're part of the family now."

Are we? It's hard to believe that five weeks have already passed since we arrived in Boca—a mix of dinner parties, pool parties, cheer practice, chatting at school pickup. Did Willow and I let down our guards too quickly?

"It's a fine line, isn't it?" Fi says. "Parents have to be open with each other, but at the same time, they can't blame each other for the things our kids do."

"Tricky."

Fi glances at the back window where her boys are shooting hoops. "I mean, try telling another mom that when her eleven-year-old son was over, you caught them looking at porn on their iPads. Now that's awkward! And don't ask what they were looking at because it'd horrify you!"

"Not asking." I laugh, deep from my belly. I love how frank she is, how unpretentious; I think we'll grow to be great friends. "Actually, asking."

"*Harry Potter* porn."

"What?" I nearly spit out my mineral water.

"As in, *Harry is sitting in the library studying potions when busty Hermione distracts him in the most pleasant way....*"

"Oh, no."

Fi gets up and checks her pot. "Kids are kids. They make mistakes. It's called growing up, right?"

I try to match her relaxed attitude. But what mistake did Katia make? What did she tell Willow privately?

"The problem is that everything they do leaves a cyber footprint," I say. "Ten years from now, they'll show up at a job interview, and the woman will just shake her head and show them the door because of some stupid comment online."

"It's a different world, all right," Fi says.

Whatever she's cooking smells delicious. "What are you making?"

"Couscous-stuffed beef tomatoes."

"Hell, I need a wife."

"Can I get you something to eat?"

I check my watch; it's been at least twenty minutes. "No, thanks. I better get Willow."

"If you'll excuse me, I'm going to call the boys in to do their chores. Their future wives will thank me."

As I walk down the hall to Issy's room, my phone buzzes.

Brady.

With a crushing, breathless feeling, I read his text: **Gotta love fishing. Best. Catch. Ever.**

I laugh out loud and then quickly cover my mouth.

He's hilarious and so forward, and everything in me is telling me being with him is a bad idea, but nothing in me believes it's going to stop. All I know is I need to touch his body again, be kissed by him again.

Not the smartest idea. I slip my phone back into my pocket.

I talk privately to Willow, and she insists she wants to sleep over.

Before I leave, Fi gives me a big hug and tells me to drop by whenever I like. "I'm sure there won't be any more drama between the girls."

I can only hope she's right, but something tells me she's way off.

## Chapter 21

# DON'T PLAY WITH WILLOW

Don't ask too many questions. Trust she has the maturity to deal with it herself.

Said no tween mother ever.

The next day, Willow and I are at the Fort Park, and no matter how hard I try, she won't tell me what happened with Katia.

"C'mon, just give me a summary."

"It doesn't matter, Mom. We sorted it out."

"Then you shouldn't have a problem telling me *what* you sorted out. Why do you only hang out with KISS? Make some other friendships. You're welcome to invite any other girls over from school."

"But KISS are nice. Sherice's smart, and Issy has the best ideas. Stella's so funny when we're alone. And Katia, I don't know…everyone just wants to be around her. She's fun."

"It's time to have fun with other people."

Willow throws her arms up in the air. "It's my life!" With that, she jogs away toward the forts.

"And don't think for one minute we're not going to discuss why you have a Snapchat account without my permission," I call out after her. "Or fake lashes."

As Willow climbs the equipment, I sit at the picnic table and respond to some work emails. Then I review the site of a new client who asked for a dummy spread about their squeeze-bottle herbs. I jot down brainstorming notes: *medicinal herbs, time-honored therapies, pagan images? Lavender, St. John's wort. Culinary herbs, fennel, cilantro. Wok image? Steam rising, ginger, garlic, star anise—*

My phone pings with a message from Nathaniel:

**How are you?**

**Juggling. Are u still in Miami?**

**Back in NY**, he texts back. **When u visit next, we must go to Hinata. Let me know ur potential dates & I'll book a table. Need to book well in advance. Sashimi to die for.**

I swat a fly away from my face—the kind that bites.

Everyone who read the recent issue of *Bon Appétit* knows about Hinata. Apparently, to find the *izakaya*, the Japanese tavern, you walk through the lobby of a normal office building in Midtown, pass a security guard, then head down a flight of stairs. But I'm sure I read that you can't book in advance. Maybe that's changed.

Oh, shoot. Willow is swinging upside down, way too high on the bars.

"Willow, get off!" I yell.

I text Nathaniel: **Sorry, gotta go.**

Looping my purse over my shoulder, I run to the platform on the fort. "Get down! What are you trying to do, kill yourself?"

"I have to practice my Around the Worlds and Death Drops."

"It's not safe."

"At least let me do The Genie—"

I'm in the midst of arguing with her when my phone rings. Yolanthe. How could I have forgotten to get Willow to call her?

"Hello," I answer. *Down*, I mouth to Willow, thankful when she cooperates.

On the other line there is a pause, followed by three stern syllables. "Rebecca."

"I'm sorry about not calling. I have Willow with me here now."

"That's fine." Then, in a quieter voice, "I didn't expect you to keep your word."

Is open hostility necessary? Ignoring the bait, I beckon Willow. "Come here."

Yolanthe is a bitter woman. I made the mistake of once sharing this opinion with Théo. Oh, he argued otherwise. I respected that she saw a regular therapist (weekly, if she wasn't traveling), but that didn't take away the fact that she acted like Théo was *her* husband (the analyst must have a field day with that one). From the day Yolanthe and I met, whenever the three of us were together, she treated me like I wasn't in the room. When I spoke, she wouldn't grant me eye contact; at best, she'd sniff. And she never let me forget that if it wasn't for Théo's first wife, Claire's, fertility issues, there would've been no need for a second wife.

Her granddaughter, however, she loves as ferociously as she adored her son. I pass Willow my phone. As they chitchat, I half listen, half daydream.

"Yeah, lots of friends," Willow says into the phone. "Mm-hmm. Camp soon."

The heat of the day is softer now, lulling, and I massage the back of my neck, thoughts flowing through my mind—herbs, basil, and mint—Fi saying, *You're family now*, which felt like both a warning and an invitation—Brady's salty lips, his tanned hands cupping my breasts. Best catch ever, huh? What was I thinking? First, even agreeing to go on the boat ride, then on the boat, the things I said, just thinking about it sends a full-bodied cringe through me. It felt right in the moment, fated, but now I can't help feeling foolish and—

"Why Grand-mère? Our dance isn't too risqué."

How does Yolanthe know about her dance for camp? I must have missed that part of the conversation.

"Fine. I'll get a different bathing suit," Willow tells Yolanthe. "Maybe you can visit and bring me some French ones. Red's my favorite color now." She laughs and turns to me. "Mom, do you want to say goodbye to Grand-mère?"

"That's okay. You say goodbye for me."

"Yeah," Willow says to Yolanthe. "I miss him too. He always did that, didn't he?"

Willow is set to inherit a great deal of money when Yolanthe and Gérard pass. Currently, and surely to Yolanthe's disgust, I'm appointed guardian of the money until Willow is twenty-one. Knowing Yolanthe, she's made a deal with the devil to live until then, so I don't get a chance to do what her older sister, Valeriane, did to her all those years ago. Apparently, Yolanthe was screwed out of millions.

Once Willow gets off the phone, she cuddles up to me, burying her head under my neck.

"Is this about what Katia said?" I ask, resting my hand on her thin red dress, which she borrowed from Issy.

"No."

"About Papa?"

"I…I can't even remember his voice or what he smells like."

I stroke her hair. "It's okay, baby. He loved you so much."

"I want the memories to feel real again."

"Me too." If only I could help her…. An idea strikes.

Before we leave the park, I try one last time. "Can you please tell me what Katia said?"

"Fine. Katia's mad about what a good flyer I am. She called me a bitch, but she was just joking."

"That's the whole story?"

"You're driving me crazy!"

"I want to know what's happening in your life."

"Well, now you know. Let's go. I have homework."

"What? Am I hearing things?" I playfully bang my head.

As we walk toward the car, I can't help but think that Willow left something out of her account. Her diary flashes in my mind, the bird on its cover, the key to its lock hidden in the porcelain heart jar on her bedside table. That would be an invasion of her privacy, her trust. Although, we have made an agreement that I may occasionally check her iPad to make sure the kind of things she's looking at are age appropriate.

A few hours later, when Willow comes out of her room, after finishing her homework, I surprise her with dinner.

"What's that smell?" she asks.

I smile and nod toward the dining room table.

"Oh my God." She covers her mouth.

I've set the table with wildflowers, a habit I had in Anchorage during the Alaskan summers, something Théo always loved, and instead of water glasses, there are two cans of Coke, and in the middle of the table, rather than a healthy dish with steamed vegetables, there's a heaping plate of *poutine.*

"Yummy!" Willow squeals.

The Québécois dish, French fries and cheese curds topped with brown gravy, was Théo's most beloved comfort food—not a dish his mother made, but one he had countless times during the brutal Montréal winters.

"I was thinking we could make a special dinner every so often, something he loved, and we'll share a memory, okay?"

"Yes," she says.

"That's how you keep people alive. Through memories."

Willow stuffs a few French fries into her mouth. "Oh, Mom. So good!"

"I couldn't get proper cheese curds, so I used halloumi."

We sit together and devour the poutine, sipping Coke. Halfway through, she stops eating mid-chew and says, "Oh, no, I should text…"

"Text who?"

"Um, no one. It doesn't matter. It's just a school thing."

"Okay. Favorite memory?"

"Mmm." Her eyes light up. "The Coke. Papa always got it for me."

"Did he now?" Our house had a zero-soft-drink policy.

"Yeah, like, every time we went camping or hiking, he'd stop at the gas station and get a six pack of Coke."

"A six pack?"

"Ah-huh." She grins. "And candy. Much as I wanted."

"That sneaky devil," I say fondly.

And just like that, the poutine doesn't taste good anymore. I wipe my greasy fingers, ashamed for thinking of any other man, for touching any other man, for craving any other man.

Being with Brady is a betrayal.

*Théo, do you want me to stop?*

# Chapter 22

# WHO SHOULD I KISS?

KISS and Willow work the room of thirty or so guests at Paulita's party with trays of scrumptious hors d'oeuvres. They're wearing Converse sneakers, white T-shirts, and black miniskirts. "Too short," I said earlier to Willow.

"But it's our uniform!"

It must be a Boca thing. Throw an extravagant party at your gated lakefront mega-mansion and have your tweens play minimum wager. *See, we're instilling work ethic.*

When did I get so cynical? Maybe I'm just in a bad mood because Brady isn't here. Not that I should want to see him, especially with everyone around.

"It's nice to meet you," I say to Deisha's husband, Wendell Turner, who is standing beside Deisha. They're a handsome couple, both tall, fit, impeccably groomed. I wonder what it's like for two surgeons to marry each other. Imagine the pillow talk.

We're chatting by an indoor vertical plant wall. Classical music plays over the hum of adult conversations. The water feature outside, six fountains circling the pool, babbles.

"I've heard all about Willow," Deisha says, accepting a flute of champagne from a passing adult server. "The girls are doing a great job tonight."

I nod and Wendall says, "Nice place for a party."

"You can say that again." The Le Lac enclave consists of a select number of private estates within landscaped surroundings. Each home boasts spiral staircases, marble kitchens, and lavish inside–outside entertaining areas with lake views.

The party, celebrating the school moms' fundraising efforts, is also a schmoozefest pre Paulita's run for mayor.

"Is Sherice looking forward to camp?" I ask, eyeing the front door. Brady said he was coming, but it's nearly half-past seven already.

"Very much so." Deisha's long earrings jingle as she talks, highlighting her cornrows. "Particularly the science elements on the itinerary."

I stop myself from asking if they're volunteering to come along. Given I've never seen either one of them at pickup or drop-off, I'm guessing they haven't scheduled the week off. No judgment.

"Ladies, don't you look gorgeous!" Odelle sideswipes me and a few drops of champagne spill onto my wrist.

"This old thing?" I touch my silver sheath, a special dress, which I paired with pointy white heels. What I'm wearing underneath, though, is truly exquisite. Another lace creation by Yasmine Eslami: a corset-style bralette and G-string, in ivory. I also put my hair in rollers. At age thirteen, my mother taught me the secret art of the perfect curl with the reverence usually reserved for things less secular.

Paulita, in a striped pantsuit, comes over with her husband, greeting us with kisses. "*Bienvenido*. Glad you could make it. This is John."

The introduction to the owner of the state's top car dealership is unnecessary. Posters and TV ads feature the friendly face of John Clark—bald, warm brown eyes, and a smile that says, *Forget everything you've ever heard about car salesmen. Trust me.*

"Hi everyone!" Fi joins us, her blondness more pronounced by her all black outfit: a silk blouse, shorts, and stilettos. Erik, her husband, gives off a Norse Viking vibe, bearded and broad-chested.

Within minutes, Wendell, John, and Erik excuse themselves to join the other dads playing billiards in the adjoining den.

The school's receptionist, Mrs. Fun, and a few other teachers stand together across the room, scarfing down crab cakes.

"Who's that?" I ask Odelle, pointing to a young, knockout brunette in a peach dress, with hair to her waist.

"Paulita's eldest, Giavanna. Former Miss South Florida."

Katia shares a resemblance to Giavanna, but it's obvious who holds the crown. It would be hard growing up in her shadow as the younger, less beautiful sister.

"Cheers," Paulita says to the moms. "We deserve a reward for all our fundraising work."

We clink flutes.

"Great party," Odelle says, her sequined green dress sparkling under the lights, "but where's the boy candy?" She drops her voice to a conspiratorial whisper. "Fuckboys."

A moment of awkward silence.

"Isn't Ron coming?" Fi asks softly.

"He's back in Bangkok. Where everything's cheap. I'm surprised he doesn't live there full time. Oh, look, there's—"

Brady walks through the door. I force myself to focus on Odelle, who's now laughing at something Paulita said. Her laughter sounds on edge, maniacal.

I touch her arm. Poor Odelle. She seems to be having a rough time. Is it because of Ron, or are other factors at play? It doesn't take much for Odelle to go ballistic. When she was younger, she'd keep everything to herself and then have an angry meltdown in public. It happened more times than I could count. Once when we were at a store and she discovered they discontinued her foundation, she screamed at the manager. Another time, at the tennis club, a boy turned her down and she went into this dramatic, Oscar-worthy public performance that ended with her smashing a glass.

"Thanks for having the girls stay over," Fi says to Paulita. "Do they not have the best life?"

"The best," I echo, and all the moms release a smug sigh. After an hour of serving and collecting plates, the girls are having their own catered dinner in Katia's wing, followed by a slumber party. After the drama with Katia, I wasn't for it, but Willow persuaded me. Being left out was not an option.

Surreptitiously, I watch Brady enter the foyer. He casually glances left and right. My heart beats faster. Is he looking for me? He's wearing fitted black slacks and a white button-down shirt, his hair gelled back. Underdressed, but sexy "AF," as the tweens say.

"What are you guys doing for the long weekend?" Paulita asks. "Because I was thinking…girls' trip!"

"With kids?" I ask, knocking back my drink.

"Absolutely *not* fabulous," Odelle plays on the name of the classic English TV show. "Fall break—mommy style."

Fi giggles. "The way you say it makes it sound pornographic."

Odelle grins. "Well, it could be. Depending on what we want."

"I was thinking we could go to St. Augustine," Paulita says. "It's only a four-and-a-half-hour drive north."

"That's where we honeymooned," Deisha says. "Ponce de León discovered the Fountain of Youth there."

A fountain of youth is precisely what I need when dating the very definition.

"Quaint place," Paulita says. "There's a Spanish fort, cobblestone roads, and, of course, Michael's Tasting Room." Paulita screws up her face (which, note, doesn't wrinkle). "I thought we'd stay at the Casa Monica Resort and Spa—treatments during the day—"

"—and debauchery during the night," Odelle finishes, batting her false eyelashes. "There's a porn mall nearby too, in case you're wondering."

Fi shakes her head. "Not gonna ask."

I glance at Brady, who's surrounded by the teachers and Mrs. Fun.

"I'm in," says Fi.

"Me too." Deisha nods.

"Would I miss a party?" Odelle says.

Which leaves me. "Thanks for the invite, but I'm not sure. I have too much work on." And I won't be allowing Willow to spend a full weekend with KISS. Although, I guess I could find a babysitter.

"Well, at least think about it," Paulita says.

"Becks?" Odelle is in my ear. She drags me away from the other women. En route, we grab new glasses of bubbly from one of the adult servers. "Tell me I look hot."

"You do, babe. Always. Any special reason why?" It's not like her to need reassurance.

"Mr. X is here and I'm DTF."

"Meaning?"

"Down. To. Fuck."

Oh Lord. "Then why did you mention the boy toys?"

"Red herring, sweet pea." Her dark eyes twinkle. "Don't you read crime novels?"

"So, if I was playing detective…" I pause and look around the party. Most of the dads are standing beside their partners or they're lounging around the billiard table in the next room, glasses of amber liquid in hand. "I'd question all the dads here to find out which poor man succumbed to your charms."

"Pfft. *Lucky* man."

"Is his wife here, too?" I can't hide the harshness in my voice. "Is she lucky?"

"Shh, she's nearby."

"Right now?"

Odelle nods.

"Shady," I reply.

She shrugs. "You're dying to know who he is. Should I give you anoth -er hint?"

Odelle knows me too well. It was one of our teenage party games, a merging of that children's board game *Who Am I?* with a slightly X-rated *Who Should I Kiss?*

"Is he…wearing glasses?" I ask.

"Nope."

"Is he…holding a drink?"

"Nope."

"Is he…bald?"

"Bingo!" She laughs. "Awww, did I make it too easy for you?"

By all accounts, there are only three bald men at the party. By the end of the night, I'll figure out which one is Odelle's cheating lover.

"Come on." Odelle grabs my arm. "I need food. I've only eaten egg whites today."

We find Willow and Stella in the hallway standing side-by-side, empty platters on the ground. They're giggling, without a care in the world. They seem to grow closer with each passing day.

"Slackers," Odelle greets them.

"Mom!" Stella says.

"You're no good to me," Odelle says to Stella. "I'm after carbs. Becks, follow."

I give them a goofy smile and play along. "Ruff ruff."

The girls return to their private conversation. When I turn back, Katia, the queen bee of KISS, approaches them. She looks formidable in her home environment. She must have learned that strut from her beauty-queen sister, Giavanna, whose presence feels magnified given the countless framed photographs of her throughout the house. Is it my imagination or does Katia's skirt look shorter than the other girls'? She says something to Stella and then both girls walk off, leaving Willow on her own.

Oh crap. "Odelle, I'll talk to you later."

"Bye, bae. Mingle time."

Why does Stella always do this? If Katia isn't around, Willow and she get on like a house on fire, but the second Katia appears, Stella drops Willow.

I'm about to go back and check that Willow's okay when Sherice walks over and whispers something to Willow, who laughs as they skip off.

There! I pull a curl off my damp forehead. No problem. I'm acting like a helicopter mom. I need to be more elephant. Or was it porpoise?

"Bec."

God, just hearing him I melt. The nickname only he uses.

I turn around. "Hello, Mr. Brady."

There's no one else in the hall but us.

He clocks me from the top of my head down to the tip of my toes, and says, "It's going to be hard to be low-key tonight."

"Oh?"

"When I wanna rip off that dress. Right. Now."

My mouth goes dry, a contrast to what his voice inspires further south. "A bit risky talking like that in public, don't you think?"

"When I'm with you, I can't think straight."

A smile builds.

"I haven't been able to get you out of my head," he says.

"That's understandable. It was a nice boat ride."

"*Nice*?" He brings a hand to his chest, appearing crushed. "I thought you might say meaningful…or X-rated."

"Hm-mmm." I smile pleasantly, my body warm and primed.

"I hear the girls are having a sleepover here tonight," he says.

"Yes, they are."

"Might you want to come over to my house?"

"Not tonight. Patience, headmaster. Enjoy the party." With that, I rush off, chest pounding. There is no way in hell I'm going to be caught flirting with the head of school. We're in Boca to make a new life—not to have it destroyed by gossip. But now there's a new voice in my head, the younger me that I thought was buried. Unfortunately, she's only interested in one thing: *Brady*.

# *Chapter 23*

# APPETIZER

Paulita's party is in full swing. I spend some time chatting with Sherice's mom, Deisha, who was also raised in New York. Then, drawn to Fi's warmth and honesty, for the next half an hour, I stay mostly by her side. We discuss her boys' sports schedules—her youngest plays tennis—and I question her about local delicacies, as one of my new clients is looking for fresh ways to advertise their Boca Raton classics.

I watch Brady from my periphery. He's speaking to Giavanna by the table of appetizers. Not that I'm insecure; she's much too young, and her flesh-colored dress much too tight. Then again, if I had a derrière like that....

After sharing a few words, they go their separate ways.

I swallow my champagne, the bubbles tingling on my tongue, while Brady does the rounds, chatting with each person he encounters like he's got all the time in the world. Throughout the evening, I overhear him have deep and meaningful exchanges, "good ol' boy" joshing and back-slapping banter with dads and private discussions with concerned mothers about their worrisome tweens. He switches styles of communication, his body language, the range of his smile.

Confidante, buddy, confessor. An intimacy expert.

Not one person he talks to looks bored or uncomfortable, and afterward, without fail, the person appears noticeably happier, as though a weight has lifted from their shoulders.

*Who are you, Brady?*

Another mystery amuses me. Mr. X could only be one of three people. Paulita's husband, John, which seems highly unlikely or—there.

"Excuse me, Fi. I need a refill."

"Sure," she says.

After getting a top-up from a passing server, I walk to the outside deck overlooking the pool. The night air is scented with exotic flowers.

I introduce myself to Bald Man #1 (short, large birthmark covering half his face) and his wife. Born and raised in Boca, the couple is lovely, but they're also dead boring. Knowing Odelle, there's no chance, no matter how much money or prestige are involved, that Bald Man #1 is her fuckboy. Crossed off the list, I excuse myself and scan the party for Bald Man #2. I find him standing inside, beside the edgy Cristina Lei Rodriguez sculpture. He's tanned and has an intricately groomed goatee.

As I head his way, I'm cut off by Fi, Paulita, Deisha, and Odelle, who want to discuss the ins and outs of traveling to camp on Monday.

Paulita clutches her chest. "Five o'clock a.m. is a cruel departure."

"It'll be fun," Fi says. "I'll bring thermoses of espresso."

"Mixed with whiskey?" Odelle asks.

"For you? Anything," Fi says.

Brady enters our circle, arm-in-arm with Mrs. Fun. Her limp seems worse, and she leans on him for support. She's wearing a mauve sack and her strands of mismatched necklaces almost look punk rock under the dazzling chandelier lights.

"Hello, fundraising queens," Brady says. "You all deserve my gratitude."

Being so close to him in public, my inner thermostat skyrockets into overdrive. Can people see my reaction? The color in my face? The unsteadiness of my legs?

Brady says, "Thanks to you all, we've put in a turf field and the kids are out there every day, getting much-needed exercise."

Why couldn't they just use the grass? *Private schools.*

"Like they need it," Odelle scoffs. "They're naturally thin and gorgeous. Us? We're working against gravity."

Mrs. Fun puts a hand on her hip. "And commercial-based propaganda that says the aging body is unsexy." She adds, deadpan, "You have no idea how many seniors want to date me. I think it's the hair."

We all laugh. Who knew? It's not a misnomer: Mrs. Fun is funny.

Odelle's laughter doesn't die down. She bends over, wiping her forehead. All night, she's been acting unhinged.

"Everything alright?" Brady asks her.

"Peachy."

What's gotten under her skin? Is there more going on with her and Ron than she's letting on? Is it because Mr. X's wife is at the party?

"Thanks for hosting tonight," Brady says to Paulita.

"It's no bother," she replies, her posture rigid.

"Everyone at Aqua Vista appreciates it."

Paulita doesn't smile. There's obvious tension between them—some kind of history? She sighs. "There's only ten minutes until dinner and I need to speak with the caterers."

Frankly, it's odd hearing Paulita talk about food when I've never seen anything that can't be sucked through a straw pass through her lips.

Brady steps closer to Paulita. "Mrs. Clark, Mrs. Fournier has kindly agreed to photograph all the kids' art for Art Synergy. Do you happen to have a calendar of last year's artwork that I can show her?"

"Of course. I always keep those types of things."

"Where, if you don't mind? I don't want to pull you away from your guests."

Paulita points down the hallway. "You know the room. Second library, third door on the left. School shelf."

Why is the head of school familiar with her house layout? Unless, of course, he's familiar with her daughter, Giavanna. Here I go again. Théo used to accuse me of being jealous of his first wife. Why is it when you throw a stunner into the mix, women get paranoid that men will lose their minds? Because men lose their minds! Just think of poor Jane back in Anchorage and her husband, who fell in love with their nanny. But Brady is an honorable man who's won awards for teaching. Although our exchanges aren't standard mother and head of school protocol, the heart (or in this case, body?) wants what it wants.

"Thanks." Brady nods. "Mrs. Fournier, do you have any image ideas that might correspond to the seasons, which, of course, in South Florida are generally only two seasons, summer and winter? Excuse us, ladies."

Brady and I walk together down the hall.

I feel the eyes of my three friends, and Mrs. Fun, burning my back.

"What are you doing?" I hiss.

"The way I see it, we've got six minutes, maybe seven."

"For…?"

"I can't be this close to you and not taste you."

Oh hell. He's stealing me away to kiss me! It's romantic, no doubt, but reckless, and I really shouldn't go along with him, even though every single particle of my body wants to be alone and—

He makes a sharp turn into the third room. I follow him and move to close the door behind us.

"Uh-uh," he says. "Now that would be obvious. Keep it open."

"But—"

"Five precious minutes." He walks to the floor-to-ceiling bookshelf, climbs onto a moving ladder, and slides to the right until he comes to the desired shelf.

The room smells like old books, leather, and orange-scented furniture cleaner. A grandfather clock ticks in the corner.

"Here it is," Brady says, taking out the calendar. "Magicians pull off tricks in front of everybody's noses. It's all about sleight of hand."

I don't care what it's about. I just want his lips on mine and his tush in my hot little hands.

He swings off the ladder and walks to the leather Chesterfield couch.

"Bec, stand here."

"So bossy." I join him behind the couch, my back to the entrance door, and face him. "I like it."

He passes me the calendar. "Hold this and talk photography. Don't stop. I'll keep my eye on the door…and you."

Why? What's he planning?

"Open your legs," he says.

"*What?*"

Everything below our waists is blocked by the couch, so if anyone walked past, all they could see would be a man and a woman discussing a calendar.

"Please, baby."

"Um." I can barely process what he's saying. And no one's called me baby since I was in my twenties.

He smiles at me with ease and familiarity.

Maybe women his age are into this kind of stuff?

*C'mon, old-timer. Don't be so uptight.* I can do this.

Smiling nervously, I flex my right foot out of my high heel and fractionally open my thigh.

This is so bad, it's good.

"Okay, so..." I flip the calendar open to January. "Here we have a wintery picture, almost Frozen-esque. I would suggest something warmer. More Florida."

"Warmer sounds good." Brady stands before me, adjusting my position. "Are you okay with this?" he whispers.

I nod, licking my lips. I'm game for whatever he wants. He seems awfully good at being secretive. Why is he so well-practiced?

He places his hands on either side of my thighs. His fingers are rough, calloused, probably from playing the guitar. Goosebumps dance all over my skin. As his hands roam higher, my dress rises. He pushes it up to my waist.

"Bec, God." His jaw drops open at the white lace.

Precisely the effect I was going for.

His hands cup my bare behind, the G-string tight against my sex.

"Move it," he says, staring me in the eyes.

I stretch the fabric to the right.

Without warning, he slips his finger inside of me.

Oh—my—my gosh.

Instinctively, I arch my back, a ricochet of sensations scorching me. I shut my eyes, disoriented. Every second intensifying.

"Keep talking," Brady says.

I flick open my eyes and focus on the calendar. "Well—uh—um—February, Valentine's Day art. Maybe we could—could do something old fashioned with cut-out doilies and hearts. Oooh…" A moan escapes my lips as he rubs my clit, skillfully flicking it with his forefinger.

"You're so wet, Bec."

What I am is freaking insane. I glance over my shoulder at the door.

"Don't worry, I'm keeping watch." He shifts the weight on his feet, a bulge straining under his pants.

"I need to taste you," he says.

Leaning toward him, I lift my chin, ready to be kissed. To hell with the consequences.

"Too dangerous," he says. "Anyone could walk by. But…" Standing far enough away that nobody would be the wiser, he dips his finger into my pussy, slowly, purposefully, then without breaking eye contact, he pulls his finger out and sucks it. "Mmm…three minutes."

Zappy sensations shoot through my body. "Wait"—I grip his shoulder—"Listen!"

Someone's coming.

Footsteps nearing the door.

I yank down my dress, and Brady steps away, just as Odelle pops her head inside the library.

"There you two are. Dinner's about to be served."

"Great." I turn to Brady, who's taken his phone out and is typing a very important fake text.

"Do you think Paulita will mind if I borrow this?" I ask Brady. "The themes are sorted."

Odelle eyes the Art Synergy calendar in my hand before studying Brady. Does she have a clue what we were doing?

"For God's sake, can we cut this bullshit?" she says.

The muscles in my eye throb. No. No. She can't know. "Pardon?"

"Talking about school and children," she says. "If I have one more conversation about what to pack in their lunchbox, I'm going to slit my throat. Alison McCafferty spends her nights watching YouTube clips about how to put smiley faces into vegetables. I wanted to strangle her and tell her to get a life."

Brady laughs. "Mrs. Wragge, I'm trusting you to lead all the dinner conversations."

"Oh, you're trusting me," she trills. "Should I trust you? In my book, no man should be believed."

I step into the hallway. "Odelle, will you save me a place at the table? I'm going to check on the girls before we sit down to eat."

Face flushed, I rush away, all but leaving my damn glass slipper.

Then again, Cinderella wouldn't let a guy finger her on a second date.

# Chapter 24

# RAT'S MOUTH

I knock on Katia's bedroom door.

"Shhh!" comes from inside.

A scattering of footsteps.

Nearly a minute later, someone unlocks the door.

"Hi, Stella."

"Hi-iii," she answers, keeping the door partly shut.

Behind her, the girls lounge on the couches. Issy is half-buried in a beanbag.

The girls' wing is almost identical to the adult one, but instead of subtle colors and conversation-starter light fixtures, it's a mix of nightclub LED lights–slash–messy girl's room.

"What are you guys up to?"

Collectively, they chorus, "Nothing."

They're all on their phones—couldn't they just talk to each other?

"What is it?" Willow asks sharply.

"I just want to know what you're doing. Then I'm gone. *Poof.* Like magic."

"We're putting stories on Snapchat, Mrs. Fournier," Issy says. "Don't worry, they disappear after twenty-four hours."

"You still need to be careful," I say. "People can take screenshots of your posts. Pictures exist forever." They pretend to look interested, but their expressions are unilateral: *Go away.*

"Okay." I wave. "Be good."

Yeah, yeah, how ironic.

"Be smart," I correct myself. "That's all I ask."

Good girls and bad girls are outdated concepts and exploration is important, sexually and otherwise. But no parent wants their daughter exploring her sexuality on the World Wide Web.

I'm tempted to join the girls, to collapse onto one of the beanbags and not return to the party and face what I've done.

Getting fingered in a public place.

*Am I insane?*

Apparently, yes.

Everything between Brady and me is moving too fast. Could Odelle tell what we were doing? What would the other moms think if they knew?

Back in the adult wing, the table is exquisite: crystal, china, orchid-arrangement centerpieces. I take my place, gulping the wine, an Australian shiraz.

Brady is at the end of the table, almost opposite from me, seated by Mrs. Fun.

Fi's husband, Erik, laughs at my right and says to Wendell, "That's what I said."

"Absolutely." Wendell helps himself to some conch fritters. "I'm surprised they don't have a *Real Wives of Boca Raton.*"

"They so should," Odelle pipes up. "Starring us. Don't they know Boca is the Beverly Hills of Florida?"

"Pity the name," a man with a New York accent says.

"Why's that?" I ask.

"In Spanish, *boca raton* means rat's mouth," Paulita replies. Her plate, I notice, is gleamingly stark. Three cherry tomatoes and a tiny heap of microgreens.

"The meaning of the city's name has been disputed for years," Paulita's husband, John, says with his car salesman authority. "'*Boca*' also means 'inlet' and '*raton*' was an old navigator's way to describe jagged rocks that could be like a rodent eating away at the bottom of a ship." At the end of the table, Giavanna yawns, managing to look pretty even while exposing her molars.

Odelle glances in my direction. "Once a name sticks, it's hard to get away from it."

Same as my reputation.

"More wine?" a waiter asks.

Well, that went down fast. "Yes, please." I was tipsy earlier, but now I'm veering toward drunk. *Slow down.*

I peek at Brady. He's buttering Mrs. Fun's bread roll. Could he be more adorable? There are so many appealing sides to him: the way he treats Mrs. Fun, Angus, and me, the way he interacts with the school parents, always deeply engaged.

"A toast," Brady says, using the edge of his knife to tap the crystal glass. "To our wonderful hosts, Paulita and John. Thanks for throwing a great party. I really enjoyed the appetizers"—here he gives me the briefest eye contact—"and I'm looking forward to the main course."

I bet he is. If that was starters, bring on dessert.

"Community participation is one of the standout things about Aqua Vista," Brady continues. "We're known as a school that works together—"

"And parties together," Odelle interjects, and everyone laughs.

"So, thanks, all," Brady says.

Odelle addresses the room, "By the way, Ron's disappointed he couldn't make it, but he wanted me to announce that his company has chosen Mr. Brady's Autism Awesome as their main charity to support this year."

Claps, cheers, and thank yous follow.

Over grilled spiny lobster and risotto arancini with a Florida citrus sauce, the conversation at the table covers politics—schoolground to statewide—to the men, inevitably, debating the merits of the Jacksonville Jaguars versus Miami Dolphins versus Tampa Bay Buccaneers.

I let my mind wander, all the while, not allowing myself to look in Brady's direction.

Sometime later, Odelle's throaty laughter floats across the table.

Aha! Mystery solved. Sitting a few seats away from Odelle is Bald Man #3. He's wearing a fancy suit and has an outlandish twisted mustache, his wife, a meek ash blonde, to his right.

It was Odelle's laugh that gave it away, and her batting her eyelashes. I can read her like one of Théo's short stories. Ever since I've known her, she's craved her father's attention. Unfortunately for her, she never got it. That is until she figured out that breaking the rules was the one thing that guaranteed he'd take notice.

Hindsight hits me. I picture her naked in the shower, the steamy bathroom, her pink skin. Was I one of the rules she broke?

A creamy flan topped with caramel syrup is served. Fi's husband, Erik—who really does look like a Viking, especially if he grew out his golden locks—and I chat about our work. He asks, "And your husband?"

"Théo Fournier, a writer."

"The Alaskan series?"

"Yes." I flush with a vicarious sense of achievement.

"What book is he working on now?"

"He's..." I falter. "I'm a widow."

"I'm sorry."

"It's okay." Holding my spoon midair, I realize that to a certain degree it's true: I am okay; I'm starting to move on. Acting like a horny teenager is taking me away from my identity of a bereaved single mother.

I don't expect anything with Brady, nothing serious or permanent, but being in my body, focusing on the physical, is pulling me back into life. As ridiculous as it sounds, he's healing me. "It's funny, the more you embrace life, the less death eats away at you."

Erik covers his mouth with his napkin and coughs.

"Sorry, I shouldn't be talking like this at a party."

"That's fine. My mom passed recently. It was a long process. She was eighty-two, dementia, but we lost her a long time ago. When their mind isn't right, the loss is as great as their death."

"Very true." I down the rest of my wine. "Life isn't all parties and falling in love."

He nods slowly and I fear I've given away too much.

But I can't stop talking. "At this stage, it's about growing old gracefully, and if we're lucky, looking after our loved ones when they can't look after themselves." My eyes tear. Erik nods, so decent and caring, reminding me of what it's like to have a husband, a trusted companion. "But then…sometimes you're not given the opportunity to look after the person who needs you the most." Dammit, I'm falling apart. Too much alcohol. I drop my head.

"There's no shame in grieving."

There's shame when you make a pact with the love of your life and then break it. Add to that, only half an hour ago I was drunk in lust in the library with another man.

"If it was legal in Florida, I would've helped my mother," Erik says quietly. "It's the compassionate thing to do. The Right to Die movement."

"Yes—yes, I agree." I grip the neck of my wine glass, and, deflecting, say, "Would you mind passing me the plate of chocolate truffles?" I feel like I'm sinking in my seat, my toes touching sand, submersed in saltwater.

If only we could go back to Bootleggers Cove on Sunday mornings, Théo and I walking ahead, holding hands, the scent of seaweed, Willow running back and forth along the water's edge, stopping to look at shells or find flat stones to skip with Papa. We didn't know how perfect those moments were or that there would never be better moments ahead. That our family of three was already dying.

After dinner, I say goodbye to Willow, thank Paulita and John for hosting, and order my rideshare. With one final glance around the party, unable to spot Brady, I sidle up to Odelle and tell her I'm heading home.

I need to be alone to clear my head. I don't know if my thoughts about moving on are a way to trick myself, a hall pass to be with Brady when I should be focusing on my daughter, on my business, on patching up my gaping soul.

"Okay, sweet pea," Odelle says. "I'll see you out. Although if you stay, I'll make it worth your while." She touches the sleeve of my dress as we walk down the hall. "You smell just like you used to, honey and musk."

I step away and tilt my head. "I think you might've had too much to drink." My throat is dry, and my high heels pinch my toes, blisters forming.

Her eyes narrow into slits. "Going to refuse me again, are you? Leave me at the party alone?" She tilts her head, mimicking me. "I think you might be a clit tease."

For Christ's sake. She needs to get over what happened between us a hundred years ago. "Look, if you mean—"

"I don't mean anything. Go home, Becks. Sleep tight. See you bright and early for camp. We'll sit at the back of the bus, won't we? Where the bad girls belong."

She's hammered. If she wants to talk about what happened all those years ago, we can do it another time. When we're both sober and thinking straight.

Odelle pushes open the door, and we walk out into the balmy night.

"There's your ride," she slurs.

In between the Mercedes and Teslas, the Honda Civic stands out.

I wave to the driver and say goodnight to Odelle.

# Chapter 25

# TAKE ME HOME

I flop into the backseat of the rideshare, my legs wobblier than I care to admit.

"Uh, hi," the driver says.

"Hi." I slip off my high heels and press the pads of my toes against the floor mat. Ouch, my blisters sting. "I can't wait to get home," I say out loud. The state of this car is shocking. The seat is covered in dog hair and from the smell of things, the driver just finished an onion burger.

"I'm ending my shift," he says. "I'd prefer not to drive to your side of town." His face is obscured by a baseball cap, any distinguishing features impossible to make out. The alcohol-induced blurriness doesn't help either. "Book another driver."

I can't put those damn shoes on again. "I'd appreciate if you took my ride. It's not far."

A reluctant nod, then he reverses out of the driveway.

What a strange evening, full of surprises. Did that even happen in the library?

Psychically in tune, my cell pings.

**Where did u go, Cinderella? Did ur pumpkin coach arrive?**

**Ha!** I text Brady back. **More like a driver who snacks on raw onions.**

A laughing emoji. **Why did u leave?**

**Early night was in order.**

What I don't add: *I had to flee. To save myself from being naughty with you.*

**When will I see u again?** he texts.

**Isn't that a song?**

**The Three Degrees, incredible female vocal group from Philly. U didn't answer my question. It's not too late to change route.... Adult sleepovers are fun too.**

**See you at camp.**

**Looking forward to it.**

**Me too.**

Oh, that man is trouble. Sexy, delightful, trouble.

The driver turns left along eighteenth street, and we head down West Hillsboro. A silvery moon poses in the sky, a seductress who knows how to work her curves.

This is Willow's first sleepover since Théo's death. Of course, I have reservations about her spending more time with KISS, but despite my best efforts, I couldn't talk her out of it, and she promised she'd text if anything happens.

The driver changes lanes. His sleeves are rolled up and I can make out a tattoo of an anchor on his wrist.

My body sways gently in time with the movement of the car.

*What would you do, Théo? Would you insist she come home?*

What I've never told anybody, what I never want to let enter my mind, is how Théo and I spent our last few hours together.

Tears sting my eyes, the alcohol making me mentally weak.

*Don't think about it.*

A blubbery sound comes out of my mouth. Then another.

"Do you want the radio on?" the driver asks, no doubt used to driving women home in tears.

"Thanks."

As we pass mansion after mansion, I do think about it—how perplexing it is that after such a loving relationship, from our first conversation on that street corner in New York to his dance around our favorite Italian restaurant when I told him I was pregnant, through sickness and health, it could all end in one vicious argument.

Those horrible things I said.

I swallow, my throat thick with saliva, and reach for my locket, realizing with a start that it isn't there. It's at the bottom of the Intracoastal, an act which felt poetic at the time, but now seems pitiful—the dramatic move of a middle-aged woman who should've been home in bed rather than boating with a young guitar-playing Adonis.

Tightness builds in my chest, a feeling I know all too well, something I wear every day as though clothing, something I wish I could throw into the sea, but like a message in a bottle, the waves would wash it back to me. *Guilt*, a fragrance by Rebecca—a touch of resentment mixed with base notes of regret.

It would be such a relief to tell someone what happened that last night.

I check the time on my cell. Almost eleven; not too late.

Glimpsing at the driver, I imagine all the things he's overheard in the backseat of his Honda.

Mom answers on the third ring. "Rebecca. What's wrong?"

"I…." Am I really going to do this? My stomach gurgles. The conch fritters I had earlier, clashing with everything else I consumed. "How're you?"

"Good, dear." The TV blares in the background, and I can picture her in the recliner, hair in rollers, pink fluffy slippers, a sugar-free treat on her lap.

"How did Willow's cheer practice go this week?"

"Oh, good, yes…they're changing her practice schedule. No more Mondays."

My phone pings with a message. Probably Brady. Lost for words, I cradle my head in my hand. "I've been thinking about Théo."

"Naturally, darling." She pauses. "Have you been drinking? You're slurring."

"I was at a party. You know you said you thought I was holding something back?"

"Yes?" She breathes heavily.

"There are things I haven't told anybody…."

"It's not good to keep secrets. I've been telling you that since you were a little girl."

My eyes are wet. "It has to do with our last night together."

"Tell me." Her voice is soft, full of love.

"I yelled at him, Mom. We fought. I called him an asshole." Tears slide down my cheeks. "I said he was selfish. I knew he wanted to die, but I wouldn't let him. I needed him—for Willow."

"It's okay, it's okay," Mom repeats, but her words of comfort can't reach the darkest place in my heart, the place that's broken, that can never be fixed. "Mothers and daughters, husbands and wives, partners, we see the worst of each other, and that's what makes our love the real deal. What is love? Forgiving each other and trying again."

"I know. But Théo and I never got *our* again."

She makes a noise as though she's about to say something, then hesitates, probably thinking about my dad: twenty-two years of partnership, then…gone.

"I want to go back and do it differently," I say. "Not just how I responded to his cancer and our last year, but who I became in our marriage."

"I understand."

"We were content, it's just—" I press a fist against my mouth, wanting to stop the terrible words. Jazz plays on the radio, the trumpet, jarring. "The person he married, full of life and art, disappeared. It's not that we stopped loving each other, we always loved each other, we were committed to our family…."

"What changed?"

The dark palm trees blur outside the window. "Me. Being a mother, taking care of the house, my business. Our relationship became less about passion and more about organization—who's doing this, *why* didn't you do that."

"That's marriage. Mothers have too much on their plate. Feminism lied to us: We can't have it all. Be a perfect mom, wife, career woman, keep the house spotless, cook nutritious meals, stay fit, and look gorgeous at the same time." She coughs. "Théo never expected you to be perfect."

"I know. It's just, somehow, I ended up giving the other things more attention and him less…. He was right in front of me, my loving husband,

and I put him down for not being able to pay the bills or not wanting to be intimate with me."

Behind us, a car beeps, assaulting my ears.

"You have to focus on the now. You're still grieving. Prioritize what brings you pleasure, what makes you happy."

Maybe she's right. Maybe Brady is exactly the medicine I need.

"I miss you, Mom." With the chasm open, I consider telling her what happened after our fight. I was responsible for ending Théo's life. But—no—I shouldn't, not smart. Even though she's not practicing pharmacy, she has a reputation to uphold; people seek her advice. It could taint her. Still, I could ask her to keep a secret….

I glance at the driver. *I've said enough for now.* Prying ears.

"Nathaniel stopped by recently," Mom says.

"Nathaniel? Why?"

"Just a casual visit. He brought me the most divine quiche Lorraine."

I can't hide my annoyance. "Why won't he get the drift?"

"Haven't you ever wondered, darling, you have so much in common…."

"What happened between Nathaniel and me is ancient history." As I'm speaking, we pass the Islamic Center. Nowhere near home. We're heading in the opposite direction.

My throat tightens. *What's going on?*

"Rebecca?" my mom says.

With my left hand, I pretend to scratch my thigh, then quickly check the door handle. Locked.

I have to get out of the car.

# Chapter 26

# EMOJI

*Act calm.*

*Don't let the driver know you sense anything.*

I grip my cell, try to sound casual. "Ah, wait a sec, Mom. Excuse me, driver, we're supposed to be heading northeast, but we're on 5th Avenue and 35th Street"—I blurt out the closest street names—*victim's last known coordinates.* In case the gods are against me, punishing me for my sins.

The headlines: *Boozed-up Boca mom kidnapped by rideshare driver post party. Her last intimate moment was in the host's library doing inappropriate things with the head of school.*

The driver doesn't answer.

Are there any cameras in the car? Can't see any. What's to stop him from turning off the road and—oh God.

My brain kicks into gear. Should I tell Mom to call 911?

A metallic taste fills my mouth.

"What did you say?" the driver asks.

With each word, something becomes more obvious—his voice, I've heard it before. At a work meeting in Miami? At Aqua Vista Academy? In his thirties, he's ordinary-looking, with brown hair and stubble, wearing a flannel shirt, jeans, and a baseball cap. I don't dare stare at his face.

"We're going the wrong way," I repeat to the driver.

"Rebecca?" my mom says again.

My body starts shaking. Is he the person who's been following me all these months? The man on the park bench, the noises in the bushes.

Christ! How long has he been planning this?

I'm seconds away from telling Mom to call the police, when the driver says, "Sorry, ma'am, I was taking a shortcut and got lost. Let's get back on the main road."

*Okay. Okay. I might be okay.*

But how could he get lost when he's following the GPS?

The driver does a U-turn and retypes my address into his navigation app.

My body sags with relief as the little screen lights up the path home.

"You're worrying me," Mom says. "Is everything all right?"

I find my voice. "So, um, how's—J.J.?" For the next ten minutes, she fills me in about the recent accomplishments of my brother.

The driver pulls up to my white stucco single-family home at the end of the cul-de-sac. I don't want him to think I live here—alone, manless—so, still holding the phone to my ear, I say to him, "Thanks. My sister's been unwell, and I always check on her before her husband drives me home."

"Rebecca? Your sister? What's going on?" Mom asks.

When I get out of the car, he screeches off; all I can get from his license plate is "L" and "3."

"Hold on, Mom." I check my phone.

Eight minutes ago, a missed notification from the rideshare company: my ride was canceled.

I search for the driver's details—a totally different driver, different car.

*Eight minutes ago, I was chatting to my mom, clueless about his bad intentions.*

"Everything's fine, Mom." *Shit! Who was he?* "Talk later. Okay?"

Inside, I yank the blinds shut and double-check all the doors and windows are locked before pouring myself a stiff drink, adrenaline shuddering through me. I stand at the cluttered kitchen counter. I'm never letting Willow take a rideshare alone. What kind of world is this—of predator and prey? What would've happened if I hadn't been on my cell and told Mom my location?

With shaky fingers, I call the Boca Raton Police Services.

A woman answers.

"I think I've been—I was nearly—kidnapped." Saying it aloud, a wave of fresh terror grips me.

"Where are you now? What are you doing?"

"At home drinking Bombay gin."

There is a pause. "Where did this incident take place?"

"Ah, um." I swipe my brow. "I was at a party for our fundraising team, not that I've done any yet…but they've, that's the Boca moms at school, they've included me. I called a rideshare. I went outside with my friend, Odelle, who was acting ridiculous, and I got into the car."

"Did you check the registration?" the officer asks in a monotone voice.

"I…I…no, I should've done. The car smelled like onions, but I was too busy thinking about…oh, never mind. The driver told me to order another car, but I convinced him." My ring rattles against the crystal tumbler.

"Did you consume alcohol?"

"Yes, yes, too much." I lower my head. Lust. Gluttony. Greed. "If you were there, you'd have done the same. Their wine list was impressive. Nathaniel would've…"

"Who's Nathaniel?"

"I'm sorry. I think I'm in shock."

After I recount everything that happened, and then some, the police officer says, "From a legal perspective, no crime has occurred."

"But someone's been following me. Just last week in the bushes…." I can hear the craziness babbling out of my mouth, but I can't stay silent. "I keep having this creepy feeling that someone's watching my movements."

A longer pause this time. "How long have you felt that way?"

"Since my"—*husband's death.* "On and off over the last year."

"To rephrase," the officer says, "inebriated, you got into a car without checking if it was your rideshare. He told you he didn't want to take your ride, but you persuaded him otherwise. You didn't see his face. There was no use of force or any act to restrain you during the ride. When you asked about the location, he took you straight home. Plus, occasionally, you hear strange noises in nature and have a 'creepy feeling' you're being followed."

She waits for me to say something, but there's nothing to add; I'm already damned. Without proof, I seem hysterical.

"Okay, Ms. Fournier. I've logged your report. If anything else occurs, please let us know."

"Thank you."

M-o-r-t-i-f-i-e-d. How could I just hop into his car? Odelle practically pushed me inside that Honda. For a strange second, I wonder—no—she wasn't in on it, was she? Could she have hired someone to track me? Absurd. Besides, I started feeling like I was being followed prior to moving to Boca.

Everything in my life is a mess—including the house. I survey the living room. Before Willow and I left for the party, there were many outfit changes. Earlier in the day, we started a big craft project, ribbons and glitter are all over the dining room table, sheets of paper, paints, both acrylic and watercolor, buckets of muddy water.

Willow's left her iPad out.

Without thinking, I flip it open and glance at the screen.

Three new messages.

They're from a group of senders with handles I don't recognize. They've sent emojis…like a code. I shove the pencils and felt pens off the table, clattering as they hit the floor, and sit down, a siren in my brain.

I stare at the first emoji.

> —a girl with dark hair.
>
> —an equals sign.
>
> —a brown curvy triangle with eyes.… Shit, feces.

Then…a pig. A cow.

My pulse races as I read the last message Willow received: **You'll never be one of us.**

Those little bitches.

I scan the rest of the messages. Chains, group messages, shared memes.

One message exchange stands out. Willow sending numerous requests to a person with an unknown handle.

**Can I have 250 c?**

**I would like 500 c pls?**

**Not sure if it's 120 or 170 cs, but can I have just 1 more?**

I perch on the edge of the chair. *What on earth are cs?* When I'd asked Willow about them before, she'd said she and Katia were doing math homework together.

More messages between Willow and who I must assume is Katia.

**Pls can I have extra 120 c? Craving chocolate so bad.**

*Cs*...calories.

Why the hell is Willow asking Katia for permission to eat?

## Chapter 27

# THE EVERGLADES

The sky is still dark as we congregate around Paulita's Benz in the school parking lot. All the KISS girls are in tank tops and shorts, ready for the early morning bus ride to the Everglades. The rest of the sixth graders, Ms. Naseer, and Brady mill about the two school buses, along with parents waiting to see their children off. Kids clutch their pillows, a feeling of anticipation in the air, of adventure. Camp is always a highlight of the year.

But not for us.

When we first arrived, Willow stuck by my side, but now, she's sitting on the curb, scrolling through something on her phone, consciously appearing busy—not alone.

"Did you bring the special coffee?" Odelle asks, winking at Fi.

The KISS moms are in leisure gear, the designer variety. YSL and Gucci with gaudy red and green stripes.

"Espresso and cream thermoses to go around." Fi opens her backpack.

"You dreamboat." Odelle accepts a thermos. "If I wasn't already married, you'd so be on my radar."

Fi and Paulita laugh, and we all take a thermos.

Can Odelle stop herself? Insatiable for attention, she turns every exchange into innuendo. Maybe I'm being harsh because I suspect her daughter might have been responsible for sending the nasty emojis or, at the very least, was a silent bystander. I presume it was Katia's idea, but she's too shrewd to catch the blame herself. She needs a fall guy. Or in this case, a fall girl.

"So, what's the plan for Art Synergy?" Fi asks Paulita.

"We'll have a meeting soon, maybe make a long lunch out of it," Paulita suggests. "Rebecca, didn't Mr. Brady say you were doing the calendar?"

"Uh, yes." I clear my throat, not used to hearing "Brady" and my name used in the same sentence. He's currently talking to a group of teachers, and I'm avoiding looking in his direction, which is surprisingly difficult. My eyes are drawn to him with a force that's unsettling.

"And we need to plan our St. Augustine trip," Paulita says.

Fi cups her thermos and takes a sip of coffee. "Have you all cleared the dates?"

Everyone nods, except me. Given the emojis sent by one (or all) of their daughters, it seems unlikely we'll soon be traveling together on a moms-only pampering weekend. The optimist in me hopes once we determine who sent the messages, apologies will be made, and we can work toward the girls having less toxic relationships. But before talking to the group of moms, I need to have a heart-to-heart with Odelle. She's the person I know best, and we have shared history. Then I'll decide where to go from there. I gulp the strong cream coffee, wondering if it's possible to be friends with women whose children are unkind to yours.

Paulita says, "I'll go ahead and make the spa bookings for Saturday. Are we thinking massages or facials?"

"Both," Fi and Odelle say in unison.

As they debate the weekend itinerary, I think back to discovering the emojis. I immediately called and checked on Willow. She said she was fine and wanted to stay at the sleepover.

When I picked Willow up in the morning, she appeared to be her normal self. We drove home without event. Maybe nothing had happened while she was there. Once inside, we sat on the couch, and, knowing I was going to destroy all trust, I told her what I found on her iPad.

Her face screwed up, eyes blazing. "You looked in *my* iPad? At *my* messages?"

"Honey, I'm sorry. You know our deal. Every so often, I can have a quick scan of your iPad, just to make sure everything's okay."

"It's not *our* deal." Her cheeks turned red, fists clenched. "It's you—looking at my private stuff."

"The emojis the girls sent…."

"They were just joking, Mom."

"*Who* was joking? Which girl sent it?"

"I don't know." Her voice breaks. "Show me the messages."

"Look, see—unknown numbers." I explained I'd called the numbers the night before, and when they'd rung out, texted: **This is my daughter's iPad. Stop sending hurtful messages.**

But I knew, and Willow knew, that KISS were behind it.

Willow stood up. "I freaking hate you," she screamed, shoving my novel off the coffee table.

"I'm sorry, I'm going to have to say something to their mothers."

"No! You can't. It's all your fault!"

Every choice I made since I touched Théo's cold, lifeless body, was for her. Except, of course, Brady. That rare, crazy indulgence was for me.

It's then I noticed her legs: shiny and hairless. "What have you done?"

"It's called a razor." She glared at me. "I want to get my arm hair lasered. I can't walk around looking like a primate. Don't tell anyone about the emojis. No parents or teachers. If you do, you'll ruin my life. Promise."

"I'm sorry, I can't promise that." I leave the hardest subject to the end. "What about those calories messages between you and…?"

She half turns away.

"Who, Willow?"

"…Katia," she admitted, her high emotions of before seemingly contained now, battle-scarred acceptance.

"But—how did—I don't understand. You ask her if you can *eat*?"

"No, Katia was helping me."

"Helping you starve?"

"Helping me lose some weight. I asked her to. She knows all the calorie stuff because of her sister."

*The beauty queen.* Both sisters had surely learned diet tips from Paulita. A mother's body hang-ups are passed on to their daughters as surely as DNA.

Willow and I went on to have a big talk about body acceptance, healthy weight for her age, and she assured me she'd stop dieting.

"Bags in the bus," the portly driver calls out. His white hair is pulled back in a long braid and he's wearing a suede vest. "We've got a two-hour drive ahead, but we'll make some stops along the way, maybe even…somewhere over the rainbow." He sings the melody.

A few boys snicker.

Willow's still sitting on the curb, my sweet little outcast, putting on a brave face.

"Line up, folks," the driver says. "Time to get…on the road again." He starts humming the tune.

I walk to Willow. Out of habit, I scan the area for the man who pretended he was a rideshare driver. Everywhere I go, I look for him. Last night, I scoured the internet rereading and taking notes from articles about what to do when you think you're being stalked. Change your patterns. Take different routes home from work. The camp trip is fortuitous timing; it's doubtful he'd follow me to the Everglades.

Willow rises and puts her duffle bag in the cargo hold of the bus. Then we head toward the lineup.

My heart drops. Who is she going to sit with?

"Stella!" Odelle cries, joining me. "Stella! Come here." Under her breath, she grumbles, "That girl lives in a dream world. Those AirPods. I swear I spend most of my life yelling at her only to realize she hasn't heard a thing. I may as well get a degree in fucking mime."

I laugh. As usual, Odelle has an uncanny ability to lift my bad moods.

"Good morning, ladies." Brady passes by, throwing a friendly smile in our direction. He's wearing khaki shorts and a yellow T-shirt that says "May the Forest Be with You" in *Star Wars* font.

Being near him, I break into a light sweat. Volunteering to come along was a mistake. Willow and I should've stayed home, far away from KISS and my internal Brady drama.

"Hi," Odelle sings back. "Nice day for it." The joviality leaves her voice replaced with disdain. "At least the weather in South Florida never lets us down."

Why is she acting so odd?

"It's going to be a great trip," Brady says before hurrying away.

Alternatively, it could crack like an Alaskan glacier. Especially if I accuse my new friends about their daughters bullying Willow.

Stella finally notices Odelle waving to her; she takes off her AirPods and walks toward us.

"Hey, Willow," Stella says with a sweet-dimpled smile. Face of an angel, soul of something more troubled?

"Hi." Willow shifts her backpack. Definitely uncomfortable. Does she suspect Stella of sending the emojis?

Odelle puts a hand on her hip. "Took you long enough, Stella. I wanted to make sure you packed my mosquito repellent. You know I'm allergic to bites."

"Yeah, I packed it. And your fancy face cream and silk pillowcase.... Did I miss anything, *Mom*?" she adds, all sarcasm.

While the girls talk together, I overhear Stella say to Willow, "Too bad you weren't assigned to my tent."

Odelle grabs my arm. "I'm going to do something." Her pupils are dilated, voice breathy. "Lord give me the balls to pull it off."

I barely register what she's saying as she rushes away. My focus is on Willow and Stella lining up at the bus together. I press my palm to my heart. *Bless you, Stella*. Hopefully, she wasn't involved in sending the emojis. Willow isn't going to have to sit alone on the bus after all. Oh—

Spoke too soon.

Katia approaches Stella, Sherice and Issy trailing behind. They talk animatedly, arms over each other's shoulders, while Willow stands to the side.

There's no way Willow's going to get a spot on the bus with one of them—and I shouldn't want her to. Even though they're only twelve-year-old girls, they have the power to destroy self-esteem with long-ranging effects. How much adult pathos can be pinned directly back to those early schoolyard traumas?

Fi touches my elbow. "Still recovering from Saturday night?" Her hat frames her snub nose, and her bright blue eyes are coated in thick mascara. "Hangovers are worse in your forties, right?"

"Sure are," I reply.

She gestures to her phone screen. "Somehow, we both ended up on the boys' bus. I must warn you, having two of my own, it's going to smell. The socks. The farts. The armpits. We should've packed gas masks."

I pull a face. "Why are the buses segregated?"

"The kids won a contest with Mr. Brady. They surpassed their weekly reading challenge, so they had three camp wishes granted. One of them was to have segregated buses."

I frown. "How 1950s."

"Well, kids who don't identify as male or female can go on either bus."

"What were the other wishes?"

"Later bedtime and dessert after lunch and dinner."

I look back to where Willow was last standing; she must have already gotten on the girls' bus. With one final glance, I follow Fi into the noisy bus where Brady is sitting in the front seat with Angus.

"Where should we sit?" Fi asks Brady.

"Anywhere you like." He shrugs good-naturedly. "There may just be two seats free across from me."

For a fraction of a second, he meets my eyes.

Whoa! A bullet of intensity.

The front half of the bus is entirely packed except the seats he obviously saved for us.

I scoot to the window seat, letting Fi take the aisle seat closest to Brady. Although I'm flattered about the VIP seating assignment, a small part of me prickles. Brady planned this. He knew Willow would want to be on the same bus as me. Were his own needs more important? Then I dismiss it. Surely a lot of kids are going through a difficult time right now—it's called early adolescence. Plus, most kids want space from their parents, not the other way around.

Flustered, I fasten my seatbelt.

"Rebecca," Fi says, "you know you can talk to me, right?"

"Ah, sure." I smile brightly into her concerned face. Can she be trusted? She's always been direct and whenever I'm around her, I feel like I can breathe more deeply and be myself. Should I confide in her about the cyberbullying? After all, she's the one who told me some Drew Barrymores had to leave the school because of their fallout with KISS. Didn't she say one of them ended up in the hospital? But no. I need to talk to Odelle first and stick to my plan.

"Did you volunteer for this same camp with your eldest son?" I turn the conversation to neutral ground.

"Yup. Glutton for punishment, aren't I?"

"What are the sleeping arrangements?" I picture Brady's tent, and I don't know whether I want to be close to it or miles away.

"Four per tent for the kids," she answers.

"Pretty big tents, then."

"You should see the adults'. They're more like glamping rooms. Big green canvas tarps over cot beds. I think they fit eight, from memory."

"Single-sex?"

As the word "sex" leaves my mouth, the noise in the bus quiets.

Out of the corner of my eye, I catch Brady turn toward me, mouth agape.

Geez, it's not as if I'm blathering on about fornication purposely.

Fi looks at me and wrinkles her nose. "Of course."

"The Everglades is North America's largest subtropical wetland ecosystems," the driver says into the microphone in a deep smoker's voice. "Often compared to a grassy, slow-moving river, it's home to hundreds of animal species. Sit back, enjoy the ride. But don't act like animals yourselves."

Despite my friend sitting beside me, and sexy Brady flashing me warm, secret looks, I can't enjoy anything without knowing if Willow is okay.

Besides, I may have a stalker on my hands.

Who was the rideshare driver? Had I seen him before? What next steps were necessary? Clearly, the police weren't going to do anything.

As the bus bumps along the uneven road, I grip my armrest and review my plan for when I get back to Boca.

Step 1: Up my workout game; I need to be able to run faster.

Step 2: Buy a gun.

Step 3: Refresh my shooting skills.

# Chapter 28

# CAMPFIRE

It appears to be the perfect night at Hidden Lake Camp. In front of the fire pit, Brady plays a folk song on the guitar, Angus beats a handheld African drum, and two girls harmonize in accompaniment, the rest of the sixth graders listening on. As the fire crackles and cicadas sing their insect chorus, I shift on my feet, because no matter how beautiful the music, how sweet the scent of roasting marshmallows, or how handsome Brady looks holding the guitar in his arms as though it were a child, I can't shake the feeling that something is very wrong.

Around the circle, orange and deep-blue flames paint the children's faces like villains in a comic book. Which girl sent messages to my daughter telling her she was shit, that she would never belong? Was it Katia, standing beside Stella, both girls holding long sticks into the fire, their marshmallows burnt black? Or did Issy and Sherice do her dirty work? Sitting together in camp chairs, total concentration on assembling their s'mores.

When I checked on Willow twenty minutes ago, she was fast asleep. She's sharing a tent with two girls from the school orchestra. During the day, she had a stomachache, real or imagined, I couldn't be sure. After dinner—mac and cheese, corn on the cob, followed by ice cream—she said she needed to lie down, and she's slept ever since. That's her way of dealing with sadness: blackout sleep for days, if need be; then, like a butterfly, she emerges from her cocoon with her grievances behind her, warred and won during battles with the subconscious.

"Sinful, aren't they?" Odelle says to me, drawing a marshmallow apart, the gooey center stretching like gum, before smooshing it onto a graham cracker.

"I prefer chocolate on its own."

"Any requests?" Brady calls out when the song finishes. He looks handsome in his jean shorts and hiking boots, the flames from the fire casting him in a golden hue.

"Fleetwood Mac?" Odelle suggests.

"Mom! Get out of the seventies," Stella says, and a few kids laugh. "Some Bieber, though, now *that* would be awesome."

"Stella! Don't embarrass yourself," Katia reprimands her. Then she turns to Brady. "Can you rap, Mr. Brady?"

That, I'd pay to hear. But I have other things on my mind: all day, through setting up our tents, archery, and an afternoon hike, I've been waiting for an opportunity to speak privately with Odelle.

When the next song finishes, I touch her wrist. "Can we talk?"

She raises her eyebrows. "Sounds ominous."

We walk down to the riverside, following the dirt path around its edge until we get some distance from all the kids. The moon, center stage in the sky, glows bright, aware of her earthly audience.

Far from the fire, all I can hear are the cicadas, a slight breeze rippling through the tall grass, and my own shallow breathing.

"So. I don't know everything, but there's been an incident."

"Oh?" Odelle crosses her arms, already on the defensive.

"The night of Paulita's party, somebody sent Willow these terrible messages."

"Threatening her?"

"No, no. They were emojis."

Odelle's mouth twists like she's trying to stop herself from laughing. "Was it a cry face?"

Hot anger sears through me. "An emoji of shit, a pig, and a cow."

"Oh, I get it."

"Get what?" I ask.

"The theme, farmyard."

Why isn't she taking it seriously?

"C'mon, Becks, why are we out here in the friggin' forest, when I could take an Ambien and be curled up in my sleeping bag?"

"The messages ended with *You'll never be one of us.*"

"You're blaming the girls? Emoji warfare is a very serious accusation." Odelle fights just like she did when she was a teenager: an impassive face paired with undermining words.

"I'm just letting you know what happened. The messages came from unknown numbers."

"Mmm. Very damning evidence."

"And Willow's being pressured to lose weight."

Silence stretches between us.

"Fine. I'll ask Stella about it."

"Can you please be subtle when you talk to her?" Willow would be devastated if she knew I mentioned anything. I soften my voice. "This isn't something I feel comfortable bringing up with the other moms yet." Although, I'm still considering speaking with Paulita about the girls' calorie messages. "I don't want to make it worse or blow it out of proportion."

Odelle gives me a look that says, *You already have.*

"If it was your daughter—"

"Calm down, they're twelve."

"As mothers, we want to protect our children, but it's important not to overprotect them, either, and—"

Odelle slaps my arm.

"Hey!"

"Mosquito," she says. "A fatty that's sucked lots of blood."

I flick its smeared body off my forearm. "Look, I'm trying to say kids learn from adversity, but…."

"But what?" Odelle says.

"Don't you ever wonder about Katia? Why she holds so much power over them? If anyone had the idea to send those emojis, it would be her."

"Now we're demonizing Paulita's daughter? Nice." Odelle glances back toward the fire. "Are we over the melodrama? Some of us have serious shit going on in their lives. Some of us found out something they thought was real…is over."

"Are you all right?"

Tears glisten in Odelle's red-rimmed eyes. Is it about Ron and her marriage?

"Yes, I'm all right," Odelle snaps. "I'm always fucking all right."

"Well, I'm here if you want to talk."

"Why would I do that? So you can bail on me? History repeating itself?"

Gritting my teeth, I look her in the eye. "Is this personal?"

"What do you mean, Becks?" Each syllable out of her mouth grows harsher.

"You still seem upset about what happened when we were teenagers."

"All this petty stuff," Odelle waves her hand, gesturing to the river, the long dark grass. "First world problems. I don't care about any of it."

"What do you care about? Mr. X? Being with a married man?" The words slip out before I can stop them.

She sucks in her cheekbones and raises her chin. "Oooh, Miss High and Mighty. Always doing everything right, looking down on the rest of us."

"That's not true. I'm messed up like everyone else."

"So what is true? What do you remember about that night?"

I think back to our last summer in Jax. "We'd trained all day because the match was coming up. And there was a party at…."

"The McMillions," Odelle fills in. "That's what we called them because they were so loaded."

"It was the last party, at the end of the summer, before our final match. We had too much to drink and were dancing in the backyard under those big Chinese lanterns. My shoulder was sore all that week and every time I did a backhand, it pinched." Instinctively, I rub my shoulder. To this day, it gives me trouble.

Odelle sighs impatiently. "And?"

"We were dancing. You took me aside, near the bar, and kissed me." I look at her now, half in shadow, blue-black light coloring her strong nose and full lips.

"You kissed me back," she says accusingly.

"I know.... I'd never kissed a girl. I was shocked that it didn't feel different from kissing a guy. We kissed for a few minutes, some soccer guy interrupted us and asked to join in for a threesome. Then, half an hour later, all the shit went down."

"The shit! As in me expressing my feelings?"

"I...I can't recall everything. Too many Jell-O shots." The night was a series of flashes, disconnected, but I'll never forget her yelling at me, grabbing the glass of beer from my hand and smashing it onto the floor.

"Let me fill in the blanks," she spits. "I liked you all that summer. The whole school year before, I waited for you to come back to Jax when we'd see each other again. Did you forget I sent you those letters?"

"I thought they were friendly."

"Then you and your mom arrived, and our tennis was on fire, we were set to win first place, and I'd waited all summer to tell you how I felt...but I chickened out and thought—I'll *show* you how I feel. I kissed you, and you kissed me back with so much passion, I knew you felt it too."

I stand still, waiting for her to continue.

"When we were back inside afterward, I came up to you and said, 'About that kiss,' and I was seconds away from confessing I had a huge crush on you, but you know what you did? You laughed in my face. You said, 'Now that I've had my warm-up, let's play *Who Should We Kiss?* and do it for real.'"

"I'm sorry. I don't remember that."

"Well, I do!" Odelle cries. "And so did half the party, because after you left Jax, everybody called me lesbo for years. They didn't get it—I wasn't a dyke, I didn't like *girls*—I liked you."

I take it all in, trying to make sense of our time together. "After that summer, did you have other experiences with girls or—"

"No! Weren't you listening? I'm not bi." She smacks her lips. "I wish I was, it would make my life a hell of a lot more interesting. I was into *you*."

"You could've told me." My voice rises. "You could've shown up for the match and then it wouldn't have been forfeited. Not only did we lose our friendship, we lost our trophy."

"And what was more important to you?"

She's got me there. After all, I had my friends back in New York, and my mom in my ear all summer saying Odelle was a bad influence.

She turns toward the lake, makes a whimpering sound.

"Don't cry." I pat her back. "I'm sorry you felt rejected. I was young and stupid."

"Ha!" She laughs. "You're not young anymore but you're still stupid. I'm not crying about that. I'm crying about *him*."

"Mr. X?"

"Same. Old. Story. The love of my life doesn't want me. You'd think after years of therapy I wouldn't still be chasing unhealthy relationships. Guess that's ten thousand dollars down the drain."

"Oh, Odelle."

"No matter how much you pay someone, daddy issues don't go away." Odelle shrugs my arm away. "Whatever. I'm going to bed." She stomps off toward the campfire.

For a minute, I consider following her. But the last thing I want to do is go back and sing "Kumbaya" or be stuck in a tent with Odelle.

Bending, I retie my shoelaces. The whole Odelle situation shows my lack of perception. Is my intuition sharper now? Am I better at reading people and situations—or I am still floundering? I get up, stretch my arms, trying to shake off the bad energy.

Was I insensitive all those years ago? Acting holier-than-thou? Do I still come across like that? It's certainly not how I feel. Behaving formally was the way I was raised, my mother's fondness for etiquette was legendary. But was it also a way to hide my true self? Maybe it's time to let go of the mask altogether. By our forties, we've damn well earned the right to not care what people think.

The silvery lake beckons. A night stroll might help me sort through my thoughts.

I've only been on the path for a few minutes when my cell pings with a text from Brady: **Where are u?**

There is no internal debate, no guilt, no fear. Without an ounce of hesitation, I tap out my reply: **In the woods…. Come find me.**

# Chapter 29

# HERE, NOW, US

In the darkness, every sound is magnified—the night birds, the crackling branches, the rattle-song of crickets.

It feels poetic, waiting for Brady like this, under the moon, in a hidden location, a clearing along the walkway, with logs to the right, and overhanging trees veiled in Spanish moss. Or I could be tricking myself, maybe it's tawdry: lust dressed up as something else.

How long will he be?

I rub my hands together, guilty already with the knowledge that he will touch me soon. That I won't be alone anymore. Since Théo's death, I've faced everything on my own, protecting Willow, hiding our secrets, handling it all. With Brady, it's the opposite, I lose control. That could be the attraction; with him, I'm not a grieving widow, a worried single mother—I'm a body desperate for another body, for connection and escape. What's more human than that?

Sensing something, I still.

A noise, far off in the distance; a tiny beam of light.

I'm as flighty as a teenager. He'll be here shortly, probably within minutes.

Combing my hair with my fingers, I search my pockets for gum—spearmint—then chew quickly, appraising my outfit: shorts, a fitted T-shirt, sneakers. Not sexy. But, when showering this morning, I used a body wash scented with cloves and cinnamon, and afterward, I washed and blow-dried my hair, and applied a new perfume, carefully dotting my wrists and décolletage. Basically, I smell like a chai latte.

Yeah, yeah. Because this is what everyone who is going camping does. Where did I think we were going? The Ritz-Carlton woods?

Of course, I dressed for him, imagined him, and now I'm waiting for him, as though I conjured all this through dark magic.

Footsteps draw near.

Whistling—he's humming a tune. I cock my ear, trying to place it.

Squishing my gum in the wrapper, I do my best to appear casual, no big deal, as though waiting in the woods for my lover is an everyday occurrence.

The whistling gets louder.

A spike of adrenaline nearly knocks me off my feet. God help me. Should I be doing this? Is it too late to call it to a stop? Why is it so hard for women to know what they want? To claim their desire?

"Boo," Brady says, stepping out of the darkness, a flashlight in his hands.

Loose curls, fractionally longer than when I touched them last, frame his face. In the moonlight, his green eyes are animal-like, intense.

"Hi." I grin.

"Hey." His voice is gruff.

I start to say something at the same time he does. We both stop, so the other can go first.

Awkward. It's as though neither of us knows what to do because it's *so* obvious what we're about to do.

"What did you tell everyone?" I breathe in the damp scent of the forest.

"That I needed to check the canoes, get things set up for tomorrow."

I push my hand against his chest. "Liar."

"I'd do anything for you." After a beat, he adds, "Please don't ask me to rob a bank."

"Your crimes have nothing to do with money."

"Ah." He nods, playing along. "Am I stealing your heart?"

"Idiot." I chuckle. "The way I see it, we need to build trust. Tell me your middle name."

"No way."

"Okay, then maybe we should head back...."

"Bec," he groans.

"Out with it."

"You can't tell anyone."

"Promise."

He lets out a long-suffering sigh. "Eastwood."

"Clint *Eastwood*! No! Your mother didn't..."

"Yeah, she did. She loves movie stars; especially him. *Dirty Harry. Escape from Alcatraz.*"

"Don't worry, I won't tell anybody your secret."

Stepping closer, Brady embraces me in a tight hug. "I'll hold you to it." He smells of campfire, of smoke, and the outdoors. I can't form words, it's overwhelming—his pheromones, the night air on my skin, my need to be touched, kissed, to do anything he wants me to do.

"I missed you," he says.

"Me too," I whisper, not wanting to let go.

...It's too much...the intensity of him being here, the heated words with Odelle, the worry and fear over Willow. My emotions messily collide.

"What's wrong?" He touches my chin softly, his thumb under my jawline.

I step back, snapping a stick underfoot. "It's Willow."

"What's going on?"

"Ah, well..." I'm wondering whether or not to tell him what's going on—he *is* head of school. "I don't want to get anyone into trouble. But I need some advice."

Brady gives me an encouraging nod.

I take a moment to collect myself. "Willow's having some difficulties with her friends."

"That's right. The text you got when we were on *Joey Boy*."

"The girls seem to be at war one day, then best friends the next. It's hard to know how to respond as a parent."

He nods. "For girls, middle school is practically *The Hunger Games*."

"It's as though they're purposely trying to undermine her. They're aware of their own power and get off on it."

"There's a subtle type of bullying used by girls against other girls. Psychologists call it relational aggression. It can range from being left out of invitations to parties, or not being allowed to eat lunch with a group of girls, to being completely shunned."

"Right, but then later the same group can turn around and include the girl."

"Exactly. That's why it's painful. They're friends, but they're not. There's another term for it." He pauses. "Intimate enemies."

How fitting. Sadly, it also reflects my own life. Wasn't Odelle, my closest friend in Boca, reliving her decades-long grudge less than an hour ago?

"Usually, one or two girls are at the top of the hierarchy—the rest are terrified they'll get demoted or frozen out if they don't go along with the top girls. I'll look into what's happening, speak to their teachers. It's unacceptable."

"Thanks."

"How's Willow going with the school counselor?"

"Well, I think."

"What's most important is that you build Willow's resilience and self-esteem. I'll shoot you some good resources."

We breathe silently together, the woods alive with strange sounds.

That spurs on another thought, something I've been meaning to discuss.

"Brady, it seems you have a thing for older women."

"That was blunt."

"I'm curious." I angle my body to face him.

"I like people who are themselves, who've lived, who have gravitas. Older women are sexier."

"Who was your first older woman?"

"Er, I lost my virginity to my buddy's older sister. Who was the first guy you were with?"

"Adrian Kowalski. Tall, smart. His parents went away for the weekend; I told my mom I was going to my friend's birthday party. It hurt, then it didn't. It seems so long ago now. I was a teenager. Now my daughter's a preteen."

"Wish there was a pause button on life sometimes, huh?" Brady strokes my hair, rhythmically, drawing it back from my temple. I shut my eyes and rest my head against his shoulder.

When I'm with him, I feel like there's a merging, a union of the free-spirited side of me with the wiser woman I've become. I am more than my pain; it doesn't define me.

"Look at that moon," Brady says.

I glance at the silver crescent, half-hidden by translucent cloud, then stand and face him. "I'd rather look at you."

No more pussyfooting around. We're not children. We both know why we're here.

## Chapter 30

# KARMA IS A _ITCH

My pulse races as I straddle Brady's lap and lean in for a deep, slow kiss. He tastes of marshmallows, of autumn, of unformed dreams. My hands are in his hair, his dark curls. My lips are kissing his cheeks, his shut eyes, his guitar-strumming fingers. Every part of my body is alert, wanting more, wanting him. He kisses my neck, sucking hard, then moves his mouth lower along my breastbone.

God, yes.

Underneath me, I can feel his cock straining under his jean shorts. I rub my hand against the denim.

He moans as I grind against him; desire whiplashes through me, frightening in its force.

I can't keep track of his hands, they're everywhere at once; at my back, on my hips, squeezing my breasts through my shirt, unbuttoning my jeans.

"I can't keep kissing you," he says, between small hard nips, "and not be inside you."

"Well, what are you waiting for?" I barely recognize my wanton voice.

The sky darkens, the moon covered in silvery haze, as Brady takes my hand and leads me into the heavy brush. It smells like pine trees. He stops at a clearing, and sighs.

"What is it?" I ask.

"If you don't want to do this here, we could always—"

"I can handle some outdoor action," I say with bravado, pulling off his belt. "Inside me, now. I need to be as close to you as possible."

With a wry smile, he takes off his shirt, and then mine, before laying his on the forest floor like a blanket. "My lady."

I grin nervously. *Snakes, alligators, mosquitos, oh my.*

"Lie down, sweetheart."

For a moment, I pause.

*Don't be so squeamish! So grandmotherish!*

Once I've laid down (trying to ignore the sharp rock under my hip, and something that feels like a branch digging into my shoulder blades), he climbs on top of me, the weight of his body pressing me against the earth.

"Are you sure about this?" He kisses my inner wrist. "We only get one chance to have our first time."

"Um, I think there might be some rocks underneath me."

He rises and pats the ground beside us, clearing the space, before relaying his shirt. We return to our "man woman in the wilds" position.

Mmm, much more comfortable.

Shutting my eyes, I pull him closer to me, no reservations, only sensations, and trust.

It feels like a dream, a past life, a time where people made love in the woods. He kisses me tenderly. Being with another man after so long, after nearly fifteen years, I would've thought I would be shy or afraid, but I'm neither.

Our kisses grow harder, feverish. I wrap my legs around his waist, needy, clawing at his back, losing my sense of self. Within minutes, we've taken off the rest of our clothes, throwing them aside on a nearby bush, until we're naked—skin-on-skin, slick with sweat.

At some point, he stops touching me.

"Come back," I plead, desperate for body contact.

The ripping of the condom wrapper.

*Hurry.* I can't wait another second.

"Ready?" he asks, brushing my hair off my face.

Entirely, without any doubt.

He enters me, shocking my body by his width, by how right it feels.

I arch to meet him as he pumps into me, directly to my deepest self, shattering my walls of protection. My carefully presented self. Now I'm free again, without armor. Free, and falling.

My breathing changes, I'm moaning, making sounds I've never made before. Is this death or rebirth? Something painful, beautiful, total.

He stops a few minutes later when I keep whimpering. "Is it too rough for you on the ground?"

I meet his gaze, half-drugged. "Couldn't be better." I feel all the cliché things…cosmic, meant to be, out of this world. I feel like I'm levitating. That this is a spiritual connection, soul-to-soul, firing me up, like dark voodoo.

"You couldn't taste better," he says. "Look better. Feel better."

"Charmer," I say huskily. "Don't stop."

Brady rocks me, pounding my core. Each collision brings me closer. An orgasm overtakes, every part of my body clenched, vibrating, his mouth on my ear, "You're am-m-mazing."

His stutter unlocks me: the sweet, shy boy hidden inside the man.

"I want to go on top." We switch positions, half-rolling together into the bush, which is decorated with our undergarments like a Christmas tree.

A few moments later, his orgasm follows. He plows into me, face buried at my neck, his pleasure, my pleasure.

The moon emerges from the clouds, shining down on us.

A deep breath of release, then—

"What the hell?" Brady pulls back.

"What is it?"

"Shit! Poison ivy!" He yanks me up and drags me to a flat patch of ground. "We just rolled onto a bed of it."

"You're not serious!" I try to identify the leaves in the darkness.

"It gets worse."

I fold my arms across my bare breasts. "How's that even possible?"

"Our clothes." He points to our abandoned underwear, shorts, and socks, glowing in the moonlight, all on the damn poison ivy plants. "They're contaminated."

*"What?"*

"The oily resin, urushiol, is invisible, but it's all over our clothes. There's no way we can put them back on."

"Is this some kind of trick?"

He blows air out of his mouth. "Afraid not."

"Oh hell…." Suddenly embarrassed by my nakedness, I use one hand to hold up my breasts, and the other to cover my vajayjay. "What should we do?"

He raises his eyebrows and gives me a you're-not-going-to-like-it look.

"Brady, if you think for one minute I'm running back to camp bare-assed, you've got another thing coming."

"Aw, man." He walks on the spot. "This is just like that movie, when—"

"Shut up!"

He scratches his ear, seemingly entirely comfortable wandering around in the nude in front of me. "I know washing off the oil reduces your chances of getting a rash, but there's only a fifteen-minute window for that to work. Which means we've got, thirteen, maybe fourteen minutes."

"Well, hello, Mr. Boy Scout—where were you earlier? If you knew so much about poison ivy, you think you wouldn't do me over a bed of it."

He laughs so loud I'm worried the whole camp can hear us.

"Shh!" I scold him.

"I wasn't thinking. The moon was covered in clouds. I couldn't see a thing. Plus," he leans over and gives me a deliciously soft peck on the lips, "your beauty is blinding."

"Think!" I pinch his arm. "We need a plan."

"Your call. What's worse? Option A? Wear clothes that guarantee hundreds of blisters, hives, and itchiness that can last for up to ten weeks—possibly targeting our private parts. Option B? Wash off the poison in the lake and maybe come close with an alligator. Or option C? Leave our clothes here, book it to camp, grab fresh clothes and have showers. I'm guessing we've got twelve minutes left."

"Oooh! None of those options are good, but I place too much importance on my life to swim in alligator-infested water." What have I got myself into? Is this punishment for being a floozy? Mother dares to have public sex with head of school.

"I value my job," Brady says. "My career." He wrings his hands together, avoiding my eyes. "This on top of what happened in the past…it'd be a nail in my coffin."

His past? What does he mean?

"I'm thinking the lake," he says.

"No way. I'm not dying tonight."

"Okay. To be clear, we're running back to the camp nude? Eleven minutes."

Unbelievably, it seems the best option. "There's no one out in the woods. If there is, well, we'll hear them before they see us."

Something like fear flashes across his face, his mouth set in a grim line. "This is my job we're talking about, Bec."

"I have an idea. I'll call Fi, tell her I fell in a patch of poison ivy, and I've left my clothes in the woods and I need her to leave me a new outfit in a bag near the canoes, asap. Once I'm dressed, I'll get your clothes, and bring them to you. After your shower, you retrieve our clothes. What do you think?"

"Absolutely crazy," Brady says. "Let's do it."

I make the call to Fi, then glance longingly at our clothes strewn over the poison ivy.

Nodding, Brady kicks them into a nearby patch of tall grass.

Wearing nothing but our birthday suits, and clutching our cells, we hurry along the path, lit by Brady's flashlight, listening for voices.

"Who even are you?" Brady says. "You said you were a photographer, but now I've seen you in action, I'm guessing you're an undercover cop? A spy?"

"I'm just a mom." *Who may have had a little practice tampering with evidence, lying to the police and my own family.* Now I guess I can add public indecency to my rap sheet.

We race down the path, careful not to trip on sticks or uneven ground. It isn't long before we're able to pick up the babble of distant voices and the light from the campfire comes into view.

"Slow down," I say. "We need to be really careful now. "Urg. I'm starting to feel itchy." I scratch my legs. "The back of my thighs sting."

"Your mind is playing tricks on you, babe. It usually takes twelve hours to get itchy. Once we're back at camp, we need to wash everything, ideally in a washing machine. Our shoes, shoelaces. The resin can remain potent for years."

"All this information…too late."

"And lotion, any cream you have, lather it on your skin." His white teeth gleam in the darkness. "Obviously, I wish that was my job."

"Stop flirting and—oops, watch out for that rock." I lead him around it and then we pick up our pace. "What if we show up at breakfast tomorrow with matching rashes all over our bodies?"

"Damn, I don't know. What would Clint Eastwood do?"

"Please don't tell me you ask yourself that in lots of different situations."

His lopsided grin is all the answer I need.

"Did you pack any long-sleeved tops?" he asks.

"Nope."

"Me either."

"Try to find something to cover yourself tomorrow," he says. "Then, partner in crime, we'll have to hope for the best. Do you think the gods are looking out for us?"

"Maybe for you. They'd like to see me burn in hell."

"Why?"

I grimace. "Keep moving."

Five minutes later, we approach the canoe area close to camp. The sound of kids is louder.

Terrified someone might spot us, we hide for a moment behind a tree.

"Do you see a bag anywhere?" Brady asks.

*Thank you, Fi.* "Sure do." A plastic bag glows near the foreshore. My new outfit.

Half relieved, half scared shitless, I state the obvious, "Christ, I have to get from here to there, without anyone seeing me."

"Go, girl," Brady whispers, "run like the wind. I'll look out for your… behind."

# Chapter 31

# SALTY

Willow is awake when I check on her.

"Where were you?" she says with the outraged accusation of every child when their mother isn't available at the precise moment they need them.

*Oh, come on.* The last time I saw her she asked me to leave her alone.

The sound of wrappers being opened momentarily captures my attention. The other girls sharing her tent are munching on snacks packed by well-meaning parents.

I crouch beside Willow's sleeping bag. What should I tell her? *I had savage, yet meaningful, sex with your head of school until we realized we were lying in a bed of poison ivy and then ran, stark naked, back to camp....* "I went for a night walk."

"Your hair's wet," she says accusingly.

"And then I had a shower. Are you feeling better?"

"I had the best dream. We were in Anchorage, hiking with Papa."

"Sounds wonderful. Did he seem happy?"

"Yeah, he was holding a walking stick and talking about the different shapes of the clouds." Sighing, she rolls onto her back, her dark hair fanning her cat-printed pillow from home. We picked out the sheet set when we first arrived in Boca as part of our "fresh start." It's a cute pattern of Siamese, tabbies, Persians, and black cats.

"My stomach hurts," Willow says.

"Hopefully, you'll feel better in the morning. Maybe it's all that junk food you had earlier." I check my watch. "It's almost ten. You need a good sleep."

We talk for another few minutes before I kiss her on the cheek goodnight.

Once in my own "tent"—as Fi described, a makeshift room covered in a green tarp—I wave hello to the parents and two female teachers, hoping no one noticed my long absence. The tent has the aroma of mosquito repellent, expensive perfume, and faintly, but pervasive enough for it to seep into every particle of air, mud. *Eau de dirt.*

Maneuvering past everyone, most of whom are lying in their sleeping bags, chatting, I head to the corner of the room where Odelle and I had set up earlier in the day. Thankfully, she's already passed out. Lying on her side, her hands tucked in a prayer position under her chin. An Ambien coma. Kneeling over my bag, I search frantically for body lotion. Brady had said I'd need it. I should count my lucky stars Odelle is asleep and I don't have to face an interrogation about my whereabouts.

I was never good at keeping secrets.

Mom used to always say, *You'll get in less trouble if you tell the truth.* So, I told her everything. She was my 1950s-attired priestess, my absolver, operating from a moving confession booth—in the car, while I munched on peanut butter crackers, at the library as we returned thirty-plus books, in bed at night when she tucked me in. Throughout the years, my sins varied: *I snuck cookies while you were folding clothes in the laundry room*; *I lied to my friends and told them I'd been to the Grand Canyon because most of my class had already been*; then later, *I did drink at the party, I'm sorry, will you forgive me?* And she always did. Our pact was honesty. We didn't leave things out. We didn't mislead each other. There was safety in a truthful world because you knew what was real and who you could trust. We couldn't have had a stronger mother-daughter bond, but since the night of Théo's death, that's changed.

Now, I have two secrets.

What happened to my husband. And the identity of my current lover.

Grabbing my body lotion from the bottom of my bag, I uncap it and layer my skin.

Lie upon lie. It's sickening. Did I tell anyone the truth? Not my mother. Not Willow. Not my friends. Was I honest with myself?

*Stop this. Why am I being so harsh?* It was Mom who said I should focus on what brings me pleasure, resuscitation. Who's to judge what gives me oxygen? What brings me back to life?

Two of the parents start giggling. They are mothers of boys so, as is the way, throughout the school term, we've barely interacted.

Heads stooped, they fumble with the tarp door, trying to find the zipper.

"I need my glasses," one of them says. "Why is it that the day after you turn forty, your eyes stop working?"

"And your back. Slipped discs are a bitch."

"Nothing's reparable. Your spine, your gums, your knees. They're just old."

"Wait until you hit sixty," a teacher joins in the conversation. "It gets as dry as the Sahara down there."

I smile in the darkness. Personally, I never felt so young all my life. What was that saying? *You're only as old as the man that you feel*; guess that makes me thirty-three.

I scoot over and open the door for them, careful to quickly zipper it up afterward to prevent the mosquitoes from getting in.

Time for bed. Once I'm in my sleeping bag, I shut my eyes, ready to savor, like the last piece of dark chocolate, the last fork of gnocchi dripping in butter, the last juicy blackberry on the bush, every single moment that passed between Brady and me, each touch, each kiss, each ridiculous second of our mad dash back to camp.

Running my hands over my body, I check my torso for bumps. No rash—yet. Nevertheless, throughout the night I keep squirming in my sleeping bag, riddled with itchiness, which, probably, is all in my mind. For all I know, I could have dozens of mosquito bites or spider bites from my sex-in-the-woods caper. And my tush! The forest floor is certainly a far cry from my plush king size. Either way, it was worth it.

He was worth it.

***

Breakfast, the following morning, is when I next see Brady.

I'm walking back from the bathroom with Willow when his voice causes me to stop and look up.

Two steps away, he's standing with Angus, wearing a long-sleeved shirt and jeans, his hair messy, as though he didn't bother giving it a comb. I wonder where he got the shirt; perhaps he borrowed it from one of the dads or a male teacher. Other students mill around, most still in their pajamas. Did Brady get a rash? It's hard to tell because of the clothes he's wearing and the dark stubble on his cheeks. In one hand, he cups a steaming mug with a picture of a screaming face, captioned, *The students are coming!* In the other hand, a folded piece of paper.

"Hi," he says with a relaxed smile when I approach him.

Doesn't this subterfuge unnerve him? From the twinkle in his eye, maybe he likes it. The cat-and-mouse game.

"Hi," I say, aware that I should disguise the effect he has on me. The reasons are twofold: we have an audience, and this is the first time we've seen each other since being intimate; I need to play it cool. Which is hard given what I'm wearing. Not having packed any long shirts, I've resorted to orange leggings, a T-shirt, and a sarong draped over my shoulders.

"Did you have a good sleep?" he asks.

If we were alone, I'd answer, *Pornographic.* "Fine, thanks. Beautiful campsite."

"Is it ever." Keeping a straight face, he adds, "You should check out the path along the river. Real nice."

Speechless, I bite my lip.

Now that we've crossed the physical barrier, and therefore will be likely to do it again—and soon!—the exchange feels more weighted, significant. Technically, we're not doing anything wrong, two consenting adults, but it's…taboo. Does the head of school have the right to sleep with a parent from their school? Is it a moral question? Neither of us is partnered. Even still, the social ramifications, not to mention Willow finding out, and, of course, the ripple effect on Brady's career.

But that doesn't stop my heart from feeling happy, or stop me from saying under my breath, "Later, Clint Eastwood."

"What do you want for breakfast, Willow?" I ask, moving past him and weaving between the crowd of hungry kids. I don't want to cause trouble for Brady or make Willow aware of anything. Being at camp is about building memories with her; she's my priority. The best tactic is to keep my distance.

"Do you think they'll have pancakes?" Willow asks. Bright-eyed and full of energy, she's in much better spirits than yesterday. She looks cute in thin, white cotton shorts, a red T-shirt, and a high ponytail.

"Fingers crossed. Something sure smells good."

From behind us, Stella says, "I'm so hungry I could die."

"Me too," Willow says.

At the breakfast area, we wait in a line behind a boisterous group of boys talking about their YouTube channels. Once our turn comes, we pile our plates with crispy bacon, scrambled eggs and, to Willow's delight, fat pancakes with Canadian maple syrup. Sitting outside at one of the empty picnic tables, I knock back some coffee. Kids talking, laughter and birdsong fill the air. With the backdrop of the Hidden Lake, almost purple in the morning light, and the lush greenery, I'm tempted to take a photo, captioned, *Camp Delicious: Food tastes better outside.*

You know what else tastes better? Sex.

I take another sip of coffee, a burst of equal parts euphoria and fear spreading through me. As hot as our sex was last night, it was like warfare, tearing down my walls, his lips on my wrist, stopping to whisper, *We only get one chance to have our first time.*

Absently, I scratch my neck.

"Busted." Odelle sits beside me, placing her bowl of fruit salad in front of her. "What are you smiling about? I thought you'd be salty, analyzing every detail of our beef."

Salty? Why does she act like she's her daughter's age? "Hilarious. You think you know me so well. You have no idea."

"Oh really?" She grins. "Please tell me you're doing something disgustingly inappropriate?"

"Pft. How unlikely would that be?"

"Exactly, that's my domain. Why are you wearing that…outfit?"

"Why not? We're in the wilderness." I sop up the syrup on my plate with a forkful of pancake. "So, everything's okay between us?"

She frowns. "I'll take that as a very lame fauxpology."

"Odelle, I told you. I am sorry."

"Consider it squashed."

And? Is she going to apologize for her insensitivity about Willow being sent those nasty emojis?

Odelle takes a bite of eggs and then stops mid-chew. "What's on your neck?"

"Huh?"

"There's red bumps all over the left side."

"Camping, right?" I cover my neck with my hand. "So. Many. Bugs." Friggin poison ivy. I glance at Willow's plate. "You've barely eaten anything." Five minutes ago, she'd said she was starving.

"My stomach. I told you."

"I hope you're not coming down with something." That anxiety is getting the best of her. Or it's the damn calorie thing.

Just as we're finishing breakfast, Brady calls for everyone's attention and informs the kids it's time for the sporting competition.

Most of them groan, but not Willow—if anything, that's her strong suit. Finally, she can have a chance to shine.

# Chapter 32

# ROPE BURN

## –WILLOW–

Our class stomps through the trail in the woods. We're supposed to be "listening for wildlife." Yeah, right. All I can hear is Mr. Brady at the front of the line talking about camp movies and Alek Horvat, Jay Yoshida, Maxwell Zimmermann, and the other boys behind us going on about some basketball game and Shaquille O'Neal's size twenty-two shoes.

My mom and the other parent volunteers stayed back at camp to get things ready for the talent show tonight.

I walk with Stella, Katia, Issy, and Sherice. They're wearing skirts, tank tops, and their KISS necklaces, plus black Converses. You'd think it'd be weird that they're all dressed alike, but it's not. They look cool, and they know it.

What *is* weird is KISS and The Drew Barrymores were supposed to be wearing our talent contest clothes. That's what Issy told me, anyway. I'm the only one wearing our red-and-white outfit. Issy said we were going to wear them and practice our dance routine in between all the boring sporty stuff. Well, someone forgot to inform me the plan changed. As usual.

"It sucks we're not in the same tent," Issy says.

"And after I specifically asked Ms. Naseer to put at least two of us in each tent," Katia says. She glances at me like she forgot I was there. "Sorry, Willow. Five's an uneven number."

Whenever we take a bus trip or choose a partner in class, I'm the odd one out. I hate it. It's embarrassing. I guess they've known each other longer than they've known me, and I still have to prove myself, like Katia said... but it really sucks.

Even though it's morning, the air is muggy and smells like a frog tank. My arms swing as I walk, my body warming up. Everywhere you look, it's green, green, green. Cute little birds chirp in the trees.

In my dream last night, Papa and I were hiking on Flattop Mountain. We used to go there. He always carried bear spray in his backpack, and I had bear bells attached to my boots and around my wrists. There was even a lake called Bear Lake. Papa would tell me to sing because it's good to be noisy in bear territory. It's the only time I'd ever sing in public, something really cringy like "Yellow Submarine" or "You Are My Sunshine."

"Urgh! I hate sports!" Issy moans.

"Totally," I say. I love PE. Anytime I get to run and leap. I hide my competitive streak from KISS. I only want them to see my good side.

"Sports dominate our curriculum," Sherice says. She's so smart, she always talks like that. And don't get her started on robotics, her fave topic. "There are more important things to do than being able to sprint."

"Unless there's, like, a zombie apocalypse," Katia says, and we all laugh.

"I can't wait for the talent contest," says Issy, who loves to perform. "We need to practice later."

I feel like saying, *I thought the plan was we were going to do that now*, but I keep my mouth shut. I don't want to make them mad.

Stella comes to my side and whispers, "Did you see Maxwell checking me out during breakfast?" She's been in love with Maxwell Zimmermann since first grade. In her diaries, every page, literally, is his name, line after line. Or just his initials: MZ, MZ, MZ, MZ...

"I think so...." Honestly, all I saw was *her*, staring at him. Could she be more obvious? I don't know how to feel about her right now. She probably sent those emojis.

Stella says, "But look at him. How can I help myself...."

So what? He's a jock, blond, muscly, with the tiniest resemblance to Justin Bieber, which is probably why she loves him.

Finally, we come to a clearing. The teachers must have been here earlier because ropes hang high from trees, and there are buckets full of bean bags and a bunch of sticks with flags.

"Hey, Willow, come here for a sec."

I follow Katia over to a log.

"Sit here."

I plant myself to her right.

"This is where you're going to meet tonight. You and Alek."

*Whaaat*? I'm not meeting a boy alone in the middle of the woods. If this is what she meant by knowing a way to get Alek to like me, she's crazy.

"Maybe I should show him that special video you made then."

"Please, Katia. Don't!" She can't. I press my hand against my cheek, dizzy. "You promised it was only for you. *Please*."

"Everyone over here," Mr. Brady calls out.

"Katia, don't show anyone."

She skips ahead.

Mr. Brady tells us our team colors and divides us into groups. I'm with Issy.

For some reason, Issy stands super close to me, almost behind me, and keeps saying, "I've got your back." Does she mean about meeting Alek—because *I'm not doing that.*

Mr. Brady claps his hands together. "Attention brave warriors of the Everglades. Before we give this a go, I'll talk you through the different activities and choose a lucky guinea pig to demonstrate. Running relay?"

Jay puts up his hand.

"Pick Jay! Pick Jay!" his friends cheer.

As the official fastest boy in the class, Jay takes every opportunity to show off. I don't blame him.

He runs the course, his knees high, slicing through the air.

Someone else demonstrates the flag activity.

When it comes to the ropes, Mr. Brady, says, "We haven't had any girls. Who wants to demonstrate?"

All the girls look around to see who's going to volunteer. Like, who'd want to climb up there and have the whole class judging if they have a good butt or not?

Mr. Brady says, "Where are the boss girls who are going to show the boys how it's done? C'mon, future Olympians."

Katia raises her hand.

"Excellent," Mr. Brady says. "We have our volunteer."

"Um, no," Katia says. "Willow said she'd do it."

*Why would she say that?* My whole body is hot. Beneath the cypress tree, Alek and his friends watch me.

I look at Katia, hoping she'll laugh it off and it's all a joke.

"Stage three," Katia mouths. Then, slowly, deliberately, she touches her necklace.

If I do it, I'll be part of KISS? So worth it. I can almost feel the pendant around my neck.

I nod at Mr. Brady. After doing gymnastics for a thousand years, the rope is nothing. It'll take me a minute to get to the top.

The noise of the crowd disappears. My muscles tighten, ready to spring.

*Go!* I grab the ropes, moving quickly, one hand in front of the other. In my head, Papa's voice says, "Fly, Willow, fly," the way he used to call out when I was running along Bootleggers Cove. I'm nearly at the top. The air feels fresher, and sunlight touches my face. I like that everyone's watching, that I'm showing them my skills, and—

"Oh my God!" a girl cries out.

"Gross," a boy snickers.

What are they talking about? I look down. Everyone's gazing up at me. It's weirdly in slow motion. Boys shield their eyes.

"Eww! Is that blood?" Esrif, one of the Drew Barrymores, says.

*My white shorts! Noooo! Did I get my period? But—but—I couldn't have. I finished it last week.*

Everyone's yelling and pointing. I slide down the rope, my hands burning because I'm not gripping the rope properly. Tears roll down my face, but I don't even care that I'm crying in front of my entire class, all I care about is getting away.

A terrible feeling, a hundred times worse than embarrassment, fills my body. Who is going to want to hang out with me again? Or have sleepovers? Or, one day, kiss me? I'm disgusting—now everyone knows it.

Once my feet hit the ground, Ms. Naseer hurries over and pulls me away from the group, passing me her own long-sleeved shirt. "Let's tie this around your waist, sweetie." She knots it firmly, her gold earrings jingling. I close my eyes, focusing on the jingling sound. It's like…bear bells. If I squeeze my eyes shut hard enough, I can pretend I'm back in Flattop Mountain, and soon Papa and I will find a place to stop, and we'll eat the picnic Mom packed. Ham and cheese sandwiches with the crust cut off, peanuts, fizzy apple kombucha, M&Ms, and—

"Willow?" Ms. Naseer touches my arm.

I open my eyes and stare at her gold nose ring.

*Don't cry. Don't cry. Don't cry.*

Holding back tears, I check behind me. Stella and Issy and Sherice and Esrif and some other Drew Barrymores are huddled around Katia, and Katia—she's laughing, she looks happy. My social suicide is so hilarious.

My stomach drops, like when you know you're about to be sick, and you start running toward the toilet to barf.

"Willow, it's going to be okay," Ms. Naseer says.

*No. You're so wrong.*

I don't even bother going over to KISS, and they don't bother coming over to me. I knew Issy and Sherice were closer to Katia than to me, but Stella? For her to stand there with them. Not even to come over and see if I'm okay? That's just….

The rest of the class is whispering, and Mr. Brady is talking in his serious voice, which never happens, and it's all like a movie, like I'm not really here, and everything would be better without me.

I sit out during relays and capture the flag. When no one's looking, I touch the fabric in-between my legs, then sniff my finger.

A familiar smell…ketchup.

*Ketchup, fucking ketchup!*

Katia—we were sitting on the log…then after—Issy—kind of covering my butt. They set me up. They never liked me. They hate me!

"Time to head back to camp," Mr. Brady calls out.

Hands fisted, so mad I could kill someone, I walk with Ms. Naseer. A total loser move. But none of that matters anymore.

Ms. Nasser stops for a moment and disappears into the bush to examine a bunch of mushrooms or maybe they're toadstools. Two Drew Barrymores, Esrif and Natalie, come over.

Thank God. Not everyone's ignoring me.

"Hey, Tampon!" Natalie says quietly enough that Ms. Naseer probably can't hear her. "Why don't you buy one?"

They both laugh like they've never heard anything funnier in their entire lives.

My knees feel wobbly. I, literally, might vomit.

"Go on, Tampon, stop gushing blood everywhere," Esrif says.

My body goes all tight, the air is being squeezed out of my chest. I want to kick her in the shins or pull her hair as hard as I can. "Shut up, you…bitch!"

"Willow!" Ms. Naseer is at my right, holding three big, spotted mushrooms. "That's a deplorable way to speak to someone. What on earth are you thinking?"

The words threaten to fly out. Katia—she—she put ketchup on my shorts. She humiliated me *on purpose*. If I tell, KISS will hate me even more. I kick the dirt, wishing I could disappear. Why are the girls so mean? Were KISS just pretending they'd let me join this whole time? Who sent the Drew Barrymores over to say those mean things? Direct orders from Katia? Everyone at Aqua Vista does what she says. Why did she turn against me? Maybe Katia secretly likes Alek, or—

Oh my God! Did my mom accuse them of sending the emojis and this is, like, payback?

And Katia has that video.

*Why am I so stupid?* My heart hurts, a weight pressing down on it. Spots in my vision. Can't breathe very well.

One foot in front of the other, I follow the path back. Every so often I look up at Ms. Naseer, but she has a frown on her face and her arms are stiff at her side.

*Fine. She hates me too.*

# Chapter 33

# AFTERSHOCK

## —BEC—

"So," I sigh into the phone, "That's what happened." It's been three days since we returned from camp, and I'm giving my mom all the gory details.

"Horrible," she says. "And after everything Willow's been through."

"Why can't she catch a break?" I scan the front yard for the rideshare driver impersonator before flopping onto the couch. Now that I'm back in Boca, my paranoia has tripled. But at least I've done something about it.

As soon as we got back from the Everglades, I drove to Miami, walked into a gun shop, filled out a 4473 for the NICS check, and paid $300 for a police trade-in 9mm Beretta Nano. Florida has a statewide three-day waiting period. On Friday afternoon, I picked up the 9mm. Now I'm armed.

To get my concealed carry permit, I'd have to take CCW classes, and the paperwork alone could take months to process. Not gonna fly. I've signed up, but in the meantime, I'll have to carry illegally. I've booked a refresher session on Thursday; I need to be able to protect myself—and Willow—in case he comes for me again.

When Willow got home from school an hour ago, she said she had a headache and went upstairs to sleep. I'd been for a jog and was about to have a shower when Mom called.

"Did you stay at camp after that?"

"We had to." I knot my hands together, fighting the sensation to scratch my wrist where a tiny lashing of blisters has appeared. I'm officially the victim of poison ivy and it's even worse than Brady predicted. It's like having a yeast infection *everywhere*. "I can't teach Willow to run from her problems. Thankfully, we have a long weekend coming up."

"Did Willow get teased when she went back to school?

"She told me a few girls called her Tampon again—lots of looks and whispering. She knew everywhere she went, people were talking."

"Aw, poor kid," Mom says. "Did you find out who was responsible for sending the emojis?"

"Turns out it was the Drew Barrymores—sorry, the girls who want to be in the popular group. Odelle did a little digging and found out. I let the school know." Odelle had also apologized to me for being insensitive about the emojis.

"What was the school's reaction?"

"The next day at camp, the teachers oversaw a group discussion about bullying. They talked about puberty too, how it's important not to period-shame, that everyone's bodies are changing, and they're all going through the same changes. So I guess that's something."

What I leave out is the tense talk I had with Brady. Although he agreed Katia was probably behind the rope-climbing incident, he didn't want to take it further. It made me wonder if he was worried about the ramifications of upsetting her influential parents, the ones who were rumored to be bankrolling the school's science program. How else to explain it? Not standing up for kids was completely out of character.

I tell my mother, "Katia is the problem. The girl who volunteered Willow to climb the rope."

"Is she a bully? Lonely kid, antisocial?"

"The opposite." The desire to scratch is overwhelming. I pick up the pink calamine lotion from the coffee table, squeeze it into my palm and lather my arms. "She's popular, excellent social skills. Actually, they're friends."

"They're friends but they don't like each other? Frenemies?"

"Exactly. One of the other moms thought Katia felt threatened by Willow's flying skills at cheer, which is a bit of a long shot. Or her friendship with another girl, Odelle's daughter."

"It's strange you're friends with Odelle again. I never thought things with her would end well," Mom says.

I stop rubbing the lotion into my skin. "Why's that?"

"Call it sixth sense."

Willow's intuitiveness seems to have come from my mom; it certainly skipped me.

"This Katia girl, why do you think she's trying to hurt Willow?"

"Because she can." Brady came good on his word. We met yesterday and he gave me a printout of recommended articles, and a stack of books, including "the bible on the topic," *Queen Bees and Wannabes.*

I readjust myself on the couch. "Apparently, bullies usually have high self-esteem, the cute popular girls. Outcasting. That's what it's called when kids are ditched from their friendship group."

"I see," Mom says.

"There's something I want to read to you about relational aggression. Which book was it from…? Right, Rachel Simmons." I grab it from the coffee table, flipping to the bookmarked page. "So, it says: 'Unlike boys, who tend to bully acquaintances or strangers, girls frequently attack within tightly knit friendship networks, making aggression harder to identify and intensifying the damage to the victims.'"

"Goodness," Mom says.

I carry on, reading, "'Within the hidden culture of aggression, girls fight with body language and relationships instead of fists and knives. In this world, friendship is a weapon, and the sting of a shout pales in comparison to a day of someone's silence. There is no gesture more devastating than the back turning away.'"

"Have you spoken to the girls' mothers?"

"I sent a group text."

"Rebecca." She tsks. "Having a civilized conversation would have been wiser."

"A text is casual. Getting them on the defensive isn't going to help Willow long-term or help keep our lines of dialogue open."

"What did you text?"

"Something like, 'just to let you know, Willow's been going through a hard time. People sent her emojis of shit and a pig and said, *You'll never be one of us*. At camp, she was volunteered to rope climb, after being set up to sit on ketchup.'"

"And their reaction?"

"Polite. I'm planning to talk to Katia's mom."

"Hang on, darling, I just need to add drumsticks to my sauce for the *coq au vin*."

I lock my hands together. *Scratching will only make it worse.*

Although the plan was to go away during the long weekend with Paulita and the other moms, it still feels like a bad idea. On the one hand, being friends with the girls' mothers feels like a betrayal to Willow. But isn't it important to keep adult relationships separate from our children's? Maybe I would be helping Willow by befriending the moms of her friends. Plus, I could gather KISS intel. I adore Fi, am impressed by Paulita, as for Deisha, I'd like to know her better, and despite the tension between Odelle and me, I'll always have a soft spot for her.

At any rate, it looks like the decision might not be up to me. When I was talking to Odelle earlier, she let it slip that all the moms went out for dinner on Thursday. Somehow, I also wasn't in the loop about the rescheduling of our Art Synergy meeting and missed it.

Willow, too, has been excluded. Not invited out for snacks after cheer or to Issy's house yesterday with KISS.

How flimsy were our friendships if one incident could crush them? I hug my elbows, feeling the sting of rejection. Do we ever grow out of wanting to be part of the "in" group?

The irony isn't lost on me. My experience with the moms mirrors my daughter's experience being excluded. It pisses me off that Willow, the victim of the situation, is being pathologized as the problem. Once you're not fun anymore, bye-bye. Is that how it works?

My cell vibrates with a text. Brady, probably. Not a day goes by without him sending messages, which I've come to take more pleasure from than I care to admit. And the phone calls—we talk most nights after Willow goes to bed, spending hours covering everything, his years of competitive swimming, his ex, Chana, Théo's illness, Brady's hopes for Paddy, my fears about Willow, our work aspirations, which countries we want to travel to.

My willpower is lessening. I need to see him again, not in the corridors, not during school assemblies, but alone. What worries me most is that I'm no longer afraid of the consequences.

Brady and I need to let things play out at a natural pace, rather than the full-throttle speed we're currently going. There's a chance things could work out between us. Willow will probably freak out, but she'd do that about anyone who isn't her dad. At her age, she'd know it has to happen sometime, and at least she likes Brady. School parents and staff would just have to deal with it—consenting adults should be allowed to be together.

I check the text. Nathaniel has sent a review of a new vegan restaurant in New York.

"I'm back," Mom says. "Why don't you and Willow come and visit? It would do you both good."

For one thing, I look like a circus freak. *Come one, come all, see the wondrous Blister Woman*. "Maybe next month."

"I can't help feeling you're trying to avoid me."

"We've just been busy."

Another attack. The sensation of a hundred little bugs on my neck, knees, inner elbows. *Don't scratch!*

I remember when I was little, the buildup of telling her one of my secrets, the knot in my stomach as I confessed what I'd done, watching the subtle change of expression on her face as she listened to each word, and the feeling of release that came afterward. Our pinkies entwined, *Honesty always*. I wish it were so easy now. I wish her granddaughter wasn't involved. A pact between two people is hard enough, but when you add someone else into the equation, someone you would give your life for, the original pact is as good as dead.

"Is Willow having a birthday party?"

"She doesn't want one." Ooooh—a spot on my knee. *Don't scratch.* "I can't get her out of her bad mood. I've tried everything, making her favorite food, asking her to do yoga with me, but she always wants to be by herself. She won't talk to me about how she feels. Twice this month, I couldn't even find her."

"Where was she?"

"Fort Park, about a fifteen-minute walk from here."

"You shouldn't let her go to the park by herself."

"I know," I snap. Giving in to temptation, I scratch my knees, hard.

"Things will work out. Talk soon, darling. Take care of Willow." Her voice drops. "Be careful. It's hurricane season in Florida; you need to take care of yourself, too."

I'm planning on it. But it's not the weather I'm worried about.

# Chapter 34

# WEEKEND FRIEND

The next day, I'm leaning over the kitchen counter, paying bills, when Brady texts.

**Home from swimming. Making my famous Bolognese. Come over?**

The pattern is consistent: He keeps asking, I keep declining. After what happened with Willow, I need to be here for her.

Right now, Willow is upstairs in her room nursing a headache.

**Wish I could**, I text Brady back. **Momma duties.**

**Moms have needs too….**

**Agreed!**

**Well, u know the address.** He'd given it to me before when we'd discussed me coming over, then aborted plans because Willow's cheer practice got canceled.

He texts: **Very itchy.**

**Me too. The poison ivy is killing me. Need scratching post….**

**I can think of the perfect thing….**

**Whatever do u have in mind?** I type back, a silly grin on my face.

How can everything be going to hell and be so fantastic at the same time? More to the point, why can't Willow have an amazing friend texting her things that lift her up from the darkness?

*Ping*. Another message.

**I miss you, Bec. Badly.**

I hold the phone to my chest, warring emotions inside me. When did this end up being a romance? Why is he with me when he could be with any number of collagen-faced, perky-breasted younger women with multi-egged ovaries who are ready to embrace life? Not someone who's been worn out and nearly destroyed by it.

My fingers betray me, tapping, **I miss you too. I miss your body....**

This damn itchiness makes it hard to think.

A shower might help. I strip off my shorts, tank top, and sports bra, chuck them in the laundry hamper and am about to walk upstairs when I realize I've left the gun.

Although I may not be carrying legally, I am carrying stylishly. I grab my Prada purse from the table and jump up the stairs two at a time.

Clearly, taking care of things isn't my forte. Poison, guns, or husbands.

And, yeah, keeping a gun in my purse with a child in the house is irresponsible. It's also the only protection we have.

Alaska is well-known for its open gun laws. No firearms registration, no permit required to purchase firearms, and no background check to buy a handgun from a private individual. Open carry is legal. So, Théo made sure we could shoot. But he taught me a long time ago. I hope I remember what to do if it ever comes down to it.

After my shower, I slip into a cotton T-shirt and colorful silk shorts with white lace trim and review my calendar for the week ahead. On Friday, Willow's scheduled to get braces (bad timing, undoubtedly) and I have a proposal due the same afternoon.

The doorbell rings.

Is it Brady, in the flesh, here to check up on me? He wouldn't dare. Far too risky.

I dash down the hall and open the door.

Stella stands before me, holding her AirPods. Her bike is lying on the lawn, and she looks like she was crying, eyes red and puffy. She seems to have lost weight even in the short time since I've seen her. And her hair is black, the same shade as Willow's.

"Your hair looks nice."

"It's a semipermanent," she says, not meeting my gaze. The sky, behind, steals my attention, so blue and vast, no sign of the heavy rain that was forecasted. "For Halloween next month. So, I, ah...." She opens her backpack and takes out a Tupperware container. "Brownies for Willow."

Well, that's a little rich. Showing up six days later, when Willow needed an ally the day of the rope debacle. But I can't pretend to know or understand what's going on between all the girls, and, most importantly, Willow would want to see her. "Come in. She's asleep. I'll just get her."

It takes me longer than I expected to rouse Willow. By the time we get downstairs, Stella's curled up on the couch, a sad frown on her face, Théo's plaid blanket covering her legs. She looks like a lost kitten, in need of a good cuddle.

Stella jumps up when she sees us and grabs the brownies. "Um, here. I made these. Lots of M&Ms in them. I know you hate walnuts, so I didn't add any."

"Thanks," Willow says.

"After you eat some, do you want to come over?"

Willow looks at me.

*Say no. There's no reason to hang out with someone who treats you so badly.*

"Please, Mom? I really want to."

"You have homework."

"I finished the stuff that's due this week."

The sixth-grade teachers have given the students a social media assignment where, for one week, they have to log in their notebooks every time they receive an email, text, phone call, notification, or DM on Facebook, Snapchat, or Instagram, then classify type of message.

"Pleeeease," they chorus.

Knowing Willow is desperate for company, for friendship, I nod.

While Willow scarfs down the brownies, I pour myself mineral water and pretend not to eavesdrop.

"Mmmsogood," Willow mumbles, mouth full.

"I know, right?" Stella says. "Mom asks me to make them for her whenever she's PMSing. It's my secret recipe. They have a zillion calories, though. Katia said I can't...."

Unable to hear the rest of her sentence, I nearly choke on my drink. Is Katia calorie-shaming Stella, too?

I busy myself with salad prep, straining my ears.

"I feel really bad about the emojis," Stella says to Willow. "Even though *I* didn't send them, I was there. Sorry."

"Did you know about the ketchup?" Willow asks her.

"No, I swear. The girls can be, like, evil. Don't worry, they'll include you in KISS again. Someone's always out."

Willow and Stella grab their belongings, and we head outside. A change is coming. The blue skies of earlier have vanished, the sky gray.

I walk them to the sidewalk. "Are you going to be okay?" I bend to hug Willow.

"Yeah." She grimaces.

Why do I always coddle her in public? I must stop that.

"I'll pick you up at seven, okay?"

"Too early!" they both chime.

"We need to spend time together," Stella says, linking her arm through Willow's. "We haven't seen each other for ages." *Excuse me?* A flash of anger rips through me, followed by a wallop of remorse for feeling outrage toward a twelve-year-old girl.

How do they do this? Flip from non-friends to best friends depending on who's around?

"It's a school night." I glance at Stella, her disloyal, fair-weather friend. *I can't trust that you're in safe hands.* Where was she when Willow was ridiculed, called Tampon, ditched from KISS?

"Please!" Willow begs.

"Fine, eight," I succumb, a weakness for anything that puts a smile back on her face.

Willow flicks her kickstand. "What will you do?"

"Oh, work stuff." Nervy, riled-up anticipation zings through me. "Glue myself to my desk. Boring!"

I know I should feel guilty about lying—the minute she disappears from sight, I'm heading to Brady's to surprise him—but the truth is, the only thing I feel is unadulterated excitement. Poison ivy be damned.

# Chapter 35

# DEATH WISH

I approach Brady's porch, my heart racing.

Sure, I could've warned him I was coming, but that wouldn't have been as much fun. I have a hall pass and I'd be a fool not to maximize it.

The risk is being seen. I took precautions—large hat, sunglasses, parking a block away—but even so, standing on Brady's porch, the sky looking like it's going to burst any moment and drench all of Boca Raton, I'm a ball of stress. What if someone from school sees us?

Or someone else.

On the drive over, I had the feeling I was being tailed. I noted the different makes of cars, but none of the drivers looked overly suspicious. The gun in my purse gave me some sense of security. Hopefully, I'll never have to use it.

Brady's house is art deco, painted tan, a surfboard leaning to the right of the door. The grass needs a mow and the plants, mostly native, could do with a good prune.

But I'm not here to grade his gardening skills.

*Woman up.* Taking a raspy breath, I knock on the door.

Silence.

I flex my foot, sliding my toes in and out of my high-heeled sandal.

A minute later, I knock again. That's strange, maybe he's—

Steps coming!

The door opens, and there he is in sweatpants, a wooden spoon in his hand.

Shirtless.

Oh, I'm a goner.

"Bec?"

"Hi. I…."

"This is a surprise." He grins. "A really good one. Come in."

Reggae plays from inside. I follow him down the hall and am hit by the smell: tomato sauce, basil, and him—fresh salty ocean.

Once we reach the kitchen, he stands beside me.

I could kiss him now, that plump mouth, but I hold back, enjoying the anticipation, the desire that grips me with such force my ribs feel like they'll crack.

"Nice place," I say stupidly, the words buzzing on my lips.

His house is similar to his office: cluttered, but clean. A basic white kitchen with a rice cooker and coffee maker on the counter, a few dishes in the sink, a spider plant that needs watering. Chopped tomatoes and sprigs of basil on a cutting board. The living room consists of two brown couches, bookcases jammed with hardbacks, a huge music collection, a guitar leaning against the wall. Photographs on the mantle.

Drawn to them, I take off my hat and walk over to get a closer look at the black-and-white picture of his band. Then I pick up a framed family photograph. Young Brady and another boy, half his size, who must be his little brother, Paddy, gazing up at him adoringly. I study another picture, drawing my finger along the silver frame: teenage Brady in a bathing suit and holding a trophy, his equally handsome parents on either side of him, his mother, captivating, with the same dark hair and wolfish eyes, and his stocky father, somehow less formidable than his wife. These are the people that hurt him, that never had enough time for him? Or maybe they only made time for him on special occasions like when he had a trophy in his hand.

"Red or white?" Brady asks from behind me. I place the picture down and turn around.

"I prefer—"

He leans in and kisses me on the mouth. He tastes like pasta sauce, spicy and hot. I run my hands down his back, over his ripped muscles and spine, my knees weak, the sensation of falling, fast and deep, into a glacial crevasse.

"Do you have gin?" Or a rope to pull me up.

"Mm-hmm," he murmurs, kissing me again, his tongue flicking the corner of my mouth.

"With tonic, please, if you have it."

"You smell so good."

I step out of our embrace.

"And those shorts," he says. "Hot."

"Leg guy?"

"You know it."

As he prepares drinks in the kitchen, I ask, "What do you do when you visit Orlando?"

"Paddy and I fish every day. And catch frogs. And he makes me cook for him. Mac and cheese for lunch and dinner."

I smile at the obvious affection in Brady's voice and accept my G&T, taking a satisfying sip. "Does Paddy have many friends?"

"He's a homebody. Like lots of kids with Autism."

"What was that like when you two were growing up?"

He crosses his arms. "If my mother didn't want me, imagine her reaction to a boy that needed her all the time, who was dependent on her to communicate. She ended up having to be a full-time caretaker whether she liked it or not."

"Did she grow to like it?" When he doesn't answer, I ask, "What did she want to do when she was younger?"

He swigs his beer. "She had a flair for acting. Loved movies. She met a casting director by chance, and he gave her his card and said if she was ever in California, look him up."

"Did she?"

"Nah, she got knocked up." He points to his chest. "I stood in the way of an Oscar. Indirectly, she never let me forget that."

I reach to stroke his forearm, but he moves away.

"Hungry?" he asks.

"Itchy more than anything."

A flash of a smile. "Sorry about that."

"It wasn't your fault. I asked you to meet me in the woods. I kinda knew what was coming." He laughs—a sound that delights me. I resolve to make him laugh again. "How's your rash?"

"Worst spot is my right knee."

"That makes sense, given our, er, position."

The pleasing sound of his laughter washes over me, the next words out of his mouth greater still: "Let me feed you."

I sit on a stool at the counter and watch him slice a pineapple into segments for our dessert, whip cream with a whisk, his body swaying to the reggae beat. "You know, Brady, this is my perfect date."

"Good to hear it." He puts a pot of water on to boil. "How'd you find your get-out-of-jail-free card? Please tell me it's a sleepover?"

"'Fraid not. I have to pick up Willow in a few hours."

"We better make the most of it then."

I shake my head. "You. Are. Such. A. Flirt."

"Nah, a romantic. I'm glad you came." He stops what he's doing and looks at me. "Not glad."

"No?" The air shifts.

"Fucking ecstatic."

Oh, I know that look. It comes before he undresses me, before his mouth is on mine, before he's whispering delicious things, and it's too late for me to think straight.

"I'm terrified." The words slip out of my mouth, unplanned.

"Why?"

"Because…." *I have a gun in my purse that I'm not confident to use and an unidentified man following me and, crazily, what scares me more is the feelings I'm having for you.* "Things between us are moving quickly."

"I'll keep going at your pace. You call the shots."

I glance away and take another sip of gin. "Dinner smells great."

"Family recipe," Brady says.

"Can you share the ingredients?"

"Never."

"So many things you can't tell me, huh?" I think back to what he said when we were in the woods. Things about his past…things he wasn't proud of.

"You've got it the other way around," Brady says.

He's right, how hypocritical; I want everyone to trust me when I'm the one who isn't trustworthy.

My phone beeps. "Excuse me, I better check that."

Nathaniel's texted: **I have a card for the birthday girl. What's your mailing address?**

"Who's that?" Brady asks.

I slide my phone back into my purse. "An old friend."

Twenty minutes later, Brady and I sit side-by-side on the couch, twirling spaghetti into mouthfuls, our legs intertwined. The pasta is al dente, and the sauce is seasoned perfectly.

Good cook? Tick.

Good lover? Tick.

Good man? His devotion to Paddy, his way with kids, his commitment to his charity. Well…tick.

My eyes travel to the picture of his band, to Brady, curls falling in his eyes, open-mouthed, crooning into the microphone.

"Will you sing for me?"

"Sure. Later."

"Promise?" It's my fantasy to hear him sing. No bar, no band members, no kids around a campfire. A solo performance.

He raises his eyebrows. "Have I ever let you down?"

So far, his main detractors are his age and job title, everything else is stellar. Except…I face him and lift my chin. "To tell you the truth, I don't understand why you didn't pursue the ketchup incident with Katia. Is there something going on that I don't know about?" Paulita's party comes to mind. How intimately Brady knew the layout of her house—and her residual coldness. Giavanna in her peach dress, looking more tantalizing than the summer fruit.

"I spoke with Katia when we got back to school," he says. "I'm afraid, at this point, it's one girl's word against the other." He holds his glass in front of his chest. "I know how awful and embarrassing that was for Willow. I've talked to all the staff about it—teachers are watching, hypervigilant."

I picture Stella at our doorstep, holding out the Tupperware container full of brownies.

"Give it some time," he says gently. "When parents interfere in kids' battles, it can escalate. Let the school handle it."

I knock back the rest of my G&T. A little late for that advice, buddy.

"I've planned an assembly after the long weekend," he says. "An expert to discuss bullying, with a focus on the role of bystanders and relational aggression between girls."

"Good." The students need to be educated.

"Willow's going to be okay. I'll make sure of it."

After we talk about our weeks ahead, he sets our plates on the counter. "Dessert?"

"I'm too full." I rise and follow him to the kitchen.

"Mmm." He puts his arms around me, bringing me closer. "Not hungry for anything else?" He kisses my neck, softly at first, with growing bite.

I pull back. "Urg, sorry, this rash makes me feel so unsexy."

"Is the itching bad?"

"Real bad. How about you?"

"God-awful." He scratches his arm. "And it's hard not to scratch because you're here."

I grin. "You can go ahead and scratch."

"I have a better idea. Come upstairs. It's time to finally be alone."

# Chapter 36

# SING TO ME, GUNSLINGER

Brady leads me upstairs, but instead of bringing me into the bedroom, he takes me into the bathroom. Leaning his arm against the doorway, he says, "We're going to do something really hot. Up for it?"

I shake my head. *I'm middle-aged and inflexible. Just being here is wild for me.* "Go gentle on me."

"That's the plan." He runs the bath—almost spa-size, taking up a corner of the room—and puts this nylon stocking ball into it.

"What's that?"

"An oatmeal bath. Helps take away the itch." He adjusts the tap, adding more hot water.

I cross my arms. "I don't know…I have rashes everywhere." And stretch marks and other things women my age—

"You're beautiful."

Out the window, the sky is darkening, a rich mauve. The rain starts pattering the roof.

"Do you have any candles?" I ask.

He retrieves two candles from the kitchen and with the flick of a match, the room fills with a honey-yellow light. We undress and curl up together in the bath, my head on his chest, the warm water cocooning us. I shut my eyes, listening, his heartbeat, the train horn in the distance, the running water, and the outside downpour. He draws a washcloth over me, washing my hands, arms, breasts, stomach, legs, and toes. It soothes the itch better than any calamine lotion.

He kisses me. I touch him, everywhere, his tight stomach, his rock-solid pecs and the dark hair on his chest, his soft earlobes, and sweet-tasting mouth, and then lower, his hard penis. We move together, the water splashing. I get on top. He grips my hips, guiding me. The tip of his penis slaps against my sex. Then it's gone. Then it's touching me again.

Oh, God.

"You're very good at this," I whisper.

He teases me until I can't stand it, until I force him to stay still, using my body weight to lock him in place.

"Don't hold out on me, Brady."

Yes, he fills me. I clench down on him, taking him in as deep as I can.

Before I know what's happening, he's standing, offering me his hand as I climb out of the bathtub, lifting me in the air, cradling my body. "Baby," he says, his voice low.

Without bothering to grab towels, he carries me, dripping, down the hall. Opens a door.

We must be in his room. It's pitch black. The rain, louder now. He lowers me onto the bed. I let my body relax against the mattress, my knees bent at the edge of the bed.

"I need to taste you." He pulls my thighs apart and kisses my center, his warm tongue speaking to me in another language altogether.

My body becomes wild, bucking. Not my own. Not myself.

"Ahh, God! Please!" An orgasm gains speed, building too fast. My body seizes up, legs clenched. A spasm ricochets through me.

"Wow," I pant. "That was…."

"Amazing."

"Your turn." I get onto my knees, kiss his beautiful body, his gorgeous cock, taking as much of it as I can into my mouth.

"Condom," he mutters. "Now." Then he's on top of me, his hair falling on my face, his green eyes seeking mine.

"This is even better than going fishing with you," he says.

I laugh as he pumps into me. Laugh, as my defenses come down, each rock from his hips delivering a powerful blow.

How am I going to survive this man? Who makes me feel adventurous, alive. Who makes me laugh. Who makes me *feel.*

"More," I plead. "Don't stop." I want every second to last, every sensation.

His chest crushes me. I tighten my body, my thighs steering him deeper.

He comes, groaning in my ear, and then scoops me up into the tightest hug. "You're the best."

He falls back onto the bed, his chest rising and falling.

I wait until a few minutes pass before whispering, "I bought a gun."

"What?" Brady rolls over to face me. "Is this your idea of pillow talk?"

My mouth twists in a strangled laugh.

"Start talking, Bec."

Out of habit, I glance at the window and exit doors, but there's not enough light to make anything out. Then I look at Brady, shadows cutting across his cheekbones, and weigh how much I should tell him. "I think someone's following me."

He grabs my hand. "Walk me through it. Every detail."

Can I trust him? If I can trust him with my body, and my heart, I should be able to trust him with my secrets. Brady may be able to help figure out who's following me.

"It's a long story." I pull my hair off my sweaty forehead. *I can't keep doing this, bottling it inside. I'm about to crack.* "It might be connected to what happened in Alaska."

"I'm listening."

And so, while my daughter plays with her frenemy, I lie naked in bed with her head of school and spill my guts, starting from the very beginning, each bad decision I made. It all comes out: Théo's diagnosis; his refusal of treatment and purchasing the Nembutal; our horrible arguments debating his right to die; waking up and finding his dead body; lying to Willow, to Yolanthe, to the police.

"If I tell you more, you have to promise to take it to your grave. It's not just myself I have to protect, it's Willow."

"I promise," he says solemnly.

The darkness makes it easier to confess.

"Honesty always," I whisper, just like when I was little with my mother.

"Hey, what was that? I couldn't hear you."

Clenching the sheets, I say what I cannot unsay. "It was my fault," I blurt out. "My husband's death was my fault."

"What do you mean?"

"I hadn't slept for three days. I was on suicide watch…."

Brady tightens his fingers around my hand.

"We had a deal. The Nembutal was supposed to be kept in a locked box. Importing an illicit drug across national borders, having a lethal dose in the house with my daughter…carries severe penalties. Legally, it's assisted suicide. I'm complicit."

"What happened?"

"I took it out of the box. I didn't want him to die. I took the key from where he hid it and switched the Nembutal into another blue Ziploc bag, replacing the original bag with icing sugar." A sob threatens to erupt.

"And then?"

"I hid the Nembutal in the top shelf of my linen closet." The rain forces me to speak louder. "But one night, he was awfully ill, and we'd had a bad fight. He was downstairs watching a movie, and I took it out. I lay in bed, going over and over the different options, how each would play out, agonizing about whether I should put it back in the box. Whether he had the right to make such a decision. Then…I fell asleep with the drug in my fists." Hiding my face against Brady's neck, I cry into his arms, my body heaving against his.

"You didn't mean to." His steady voice is a salve. "You were doing what you thought was right. That's what matters. That's what I tell myself."

Only part of me registers what Brady just said. "If I hadn't switched the Nembutal, if I hadn't fallen asleep and left my eleven-year-old daughter in charge of my suicidal husband, he would've lived."

"So, Théo found the drug in your hands?"

*No, no—I can't.*

He squints at me. "Bec?"

Each second that passes, pierces my brain.

"Bec?"

I snatch at my neck, where my locket used to be, hysteria building in my chest. To divert Brady from asking more questions, I jump forward in the story. "To protect Théo's decision, and to keep it from his parents, I had to lie to the police—to the insurance company—which is fraud. As in, jail time fraud. As in, losing Willow fraud."

"You took the money. That's behind you."

"Ever since, someone's following me. Waiting to catch me out." Using my left hand, I scratch the rash on my inner left wrist. "Luckily, there wasn't an autopsy."

"I would've thought an unattended death would be sent to the coroner."

"Not if a terminally ill person dies at home and there were no suspicious circumstances."

"So you think the man following you is from the insurance company?"

"No—that was over a year ago and—and the finances have already been settled. But that's when the feeling of someone watching me started."

"Who else could it be? An ex? A disgruntled client?"

"I have no idea," I say with exasperation. "I've made so many mistakes."

Brady holds me tight. "We all do."

"Says the head of school who wins awards for helping kids."

"I've screwed up too, Bec."

"Like what? Just before, you said, 'You were doing what you thought was right, that's what I tell myself?'—what did you mean?"

His face remains impassive.

"Aren't you going to tell me?"

"I'm sorry, I—I can't."

Nice. I look up into his eyes, hurt searing through me. I guess sharing our shitty pasts isn't two-way. Does he prefer it like this? Broken woman confesses major lapses in judgment while he remains stoic, mysterious. Is it a turn on to see me broken? Exposed. "After everything I told you?"

He leans back against the headboard, arms crossed behind his neck.

The silence is unbearable.

When he finally speaks, he seems flat, distant. "I did something…wrong. Something that would cost me my job, my reputation. If I could go back in time, I would've never done it."

"What did you do?"

He looks away, his mouth a hard line. "A family I can't talk about, a very prominent family. That's all I can say."

Paulita's family—it must be. "Can't you tell me?"

"Sorry, I wish I could."

I'll try to pry the rest of the story out of him another time.

"My point is, we all mess up," he says. "It's called being alive."

*And I want to remain that way.* "Can you shoot?"

"Sure I can."

"Shooting range date?"

"Babe, you're on. Although…"

I finish his sentence, "…we can't be seen together."

Add that to the list of cons.

*Young.*

*Head of school.*

*Can't be seen in public.*

*Has a secret he won't tell me—after I told him mine.*

He runs his hand over my breast. Annoyingly, my body responds, my nipple puckering.

"I'll see what I can do about the shooting range," he says. "What's our plan about the creep following you? What can I do?"

"First, I need evidence I'm being followed. A picture or license plate. Then I can go to the police with something tangible."

"Be careful." He's the second person to say that to me in the past twenty-four hours. "Promise to contact me if you sense anything. I'll drop what I'm doing and be there."

"Okay."

The rain throbbing, I watch the shadows on the wall, Brady's chest pressed behind my back. That's the thing about being alive: you go on living, even when you don't want to, even when your other half is dead.

Brady strums his fingers on my ribs as though he's playing the guitar, reviving me, bringing me from the cemetery to this sacred room.

"You know how guys on death row get a last wish?" I ask, snuggling beside him.

"Of course. I've seen all the capital punishment films. *Dead Man Walking. True Crime. Monster's Ball.*"

"I want mine."

"Morbid," Brady says. "And you're not on death row."

Maybe I am; this could be it, and everything's about to unravel. "Indulge me. Sing for me."

"Nah. And it's a last wish for food, a final meal."

"Please? You said you would."

"Gotta admit, I like it when you beg." His penis hardens against my body. "What song?"

I shift the pillow and adjust it under my neck. "Mmm. Your choice. Something fitting."

As he hums, I try to place the song. He sings about a girl named Janie having a gun, her whole world coming undone....

"Ha! Aerosmith." I knock his arm.

Brady smiles and keeps singing, his voice velvety, his mouth relaxed, the sound natural, not forced. The lyrics wash over my body—how now everyone is on the run, finding out things are untrue. When it comes to the line about asking what her daddy has done, I shiver. I can't help thinking about Willow—is she safe right now?

# Chapter 37

# JUNK DRAWER

–WILLOW–

"How do you sleep in this room with a hundred Justin Biebers watching you?" I ask Stella, raising my voice over the heavy rain. In every direction, Justin Bieber is staring at us. Dancing with a microphone in the poster on the wall. Shirtless. In bright, big hoodies. All the different weirdo hairstyles.

"It used to give me the best dreams, but lately…." Stella nibbles on her last piece of red licorice. "I need more candy. Let's go to the kitchen. I'll show you the craft thing."

"Okay." I climb off her bed.

"I like your perfume," she says.

"It's Sunflowers. Mom took me out and we bought one for her, one for me."

"You should wear it to school tomorrow," she says as we jump down the stairs.

Everything comes back. What happened after lunch today.

Katia cornered me and said I had to stop bitching about the rope climbing thing and getting her in trouble. "I was hazing you," she said, to see if I was tough enough to join KISS one day.

"Just erase the video," I pleaded, unsure whether to believe her.

KISS and the Drew Barrymores came over.

"Willow wants her video deleted," Katia told them. "Look. It's not so bad." She opened her phone.

On the screen—me, twerking. Licking my lips.

Oh, God.

The week before, Katia made me lip-sync to this rap song and reenact the video. It was funny at the time, Katia did it too—but *this edit*—me twerking, then saying the *rudest* thing, "stick it in my ass," which was *one* line of the song.

The rest of the girls giggle as they watch the loop—me twerking, licking my lips, and repeating, "*stick it in my ass.*" The meanest gif.

"Alek is going to love this." Katia grinned.

"Delete it," Stella said to Katia. When she only laughed, Stella called her an asshole—in front of all of KISS. Hella brave.

"If you're gonna talk to me like that, I'll take this." Katia snatched Stella's pendant right off her and passed it to Esrif.

Whatever happens next, I know Stella's my best friend; she proved that today.

"What are you girls doing?" Odelle asks when we enter the kitchen. She's sitting on a stool at the kitchen bench in her fancy gym clothes, her face red—and she smells bad.

"Candy run," Stella says.

Odelle slaps her hand against her forehead. "Did you offer Willow real food?"

Stella sighs. "We've had dinner."

"Where's mine?" She gulps water from her metallic rainbow water bottle.

Stella's mom puts in orders. Like at a restaurant.

"Your steamed Brussel sprouts and other green slimy vegetables are in the fridge," Stella says. "Don't forget to tip or leave a five-star Yelp review."

We giggle. It's actually pretty easy to pretend you're okay when everything is horrible. *Stick it in my ass.* I can't think about it without wanting to cry. Or worse.

The doorbell rings. Stella and I exchange sad looks. Must be my mom already.

"Nobody rush to the door." Odelle rises to answer it.

I wonder if Mom'll be able to tell how upset I am just from looking at me. When I got home from school today and told her I had a headache, she believed that's all it was. She's always thinking about something else lately.

Once Stella collects a bunch of candy, she says, "I'm going to get the extra scissors and the tinfoil for the candy hacks. Grab the pens in the junk drawer."

"Where is it?" I ask.

Stella points to the second drawer on the left.

I walk over and riffle through the drawer. Scotch tape, Band-Aids of all sizes, pencil crayons, measuring tape, magnets, sunscreen, sunglass cases, paper clips, post-it notes, hair bands.... I always thought it was weird: Parents blame us for not keeping our rooms clean. Why can't they ever keep their drawers clean? They even name it the *junk* drawer. How about the *junk* bedroom? What's the difference?

Pictures are in the drawer too. I pick one up. Stella and Katia, probably about eight or nine years old, in the snow, wearing matching pink ski suits. A burning feeling builds in my chest; I get it every time I think about Katia. I take out another picture. Stella and her mom at Disney World hugging Mickey Mouse.

Oh my God.

Another picture. At first, I don't even recognize it. The red bathing suit is what stands out. It's me. The day I was here with KISS and the Drew Barrymores. But, like, the picture focuses on my butt. I have a wedgie, and you can see my butt cheek, and I'm standing with my back to the camera, looking over my shoulder. I laser in on the blubbery fat.

"What is this?" I ask Stella.

"Um...a picture." She doesn't meet my eyes.

"Where's it from?"

She rips off a big piece of tinfoil and folds it in half. "Dunno."

"Where did you find it?"

"My dad's office. In a drawer." She chews on her lip, looking really nervous like when the math teacher suddenly tells you there is a pop quiz.

Why was it there? "Did you ask him about it?"

Stella keeps folding the tinfoil until it's the size of a stamp. "Maybe he printed it for us?"

"It's…I have a wedgie, Stella. It's so embarrassing."

Her eyes flicker, like she has no emotions, she's just a doll in a shop. "Maybe you should get rid of it."

"Why didn't you get rid of it?"

"I don't know. Rip it up now."

She's my only friend, I'll do whatever she wants. I'm just about to tear it in half when my mom comes into the kitchen with Odelle. Even though Mom is drenched and has a poison ivy rash up her left arm, she's glowing. She's wearing colorful shorts and her damp hair is curlier than normal. I hope I'll be as pretty as her one day.

"How was work?" I ask her, tucking the picture into the back pocket of my shorts.

"Finished most of it. Big relief." Two patches of pink color her cheeks and her voice is squeaky.

Then she looks at me, really looks at me. "Willow, are you all right?"

*You mean, besides hating my life and myself?* She has no idea how close I am to doing it. "I'm fine." It's a test, to see if she really cares, or if she just wants to *hear* that everything's all right so she doesn't feel bad.

"Great." She searches through her purse. "Let's get going."

And…that's a fail.

"Stay for a sneaky one?" Odelle asks my mom, already moving to the fridge.

Mom smiles, looking happier than I've seen her since Papa died, and says, "One can't hurt."

# Chapter 38

# SHHH!

Odelle makes a "whoop whoop" party sound as she drops ice cubes into a glass to make Mom's favorite drink. Gin, sliced ginger, and fizzy soda.

"Gin for the lady."

"Thanks." Mom accepts it.

They sit at the kitchen counter while Stella and I do our candy hacks at the table. Although I keep talking to Stella, I'm really listening to what the moms are talking about.

"Gotta say, Becks, you look f-a-n-t-a-s-t-i-c." Odelle's voice drops to a whisper. "The only thing that can make a woman looks so good is some di—"

"Shh. The girls."

"You two, bedroom," Odelle says in her bossy voice. It's the voice she uses when no adults are around. Sometimes she's super fun, though. Depends on her mood. Stella says she takes lots of prescription meds, so that's why she's so up and down.

We gather our stuff and move to Stella's room, but I don't sit beside her on her bed. "I need to go to the bathroom." What I really need is to hear the rest of their conversation.

I sneak downstairs and tiptoe along the hall, standing just outside the kitchen. My breathing is too loud, but I can't make it quieter.

"Tell me, Becks." Odelle laughs. "You were never a good liar and it's written all over your face. I can smell sex on you."

*Gross!* I cover my mouth.

"If you have to know," Mom says. "I have been seeing someone."

"Details, bae."

"He's great with kids, civic-minded, creative, younger…."

In that instant, I know who it is. Mr. Brady! I've seen the way Mom looks when she's talking to him. A few times I heard his voice on her phone, but I thought he was calling about school stuff. Plus, everyone at Aqua Vista knows he has poison ivy. Is it contagious? Did they get it from *doing it* together? Ugh. Did they even think how disgusting it is for me? How could she do that to Papa?

"How much younger?" Odelle asks.

"Oh, just a few years. Anyway, early days. I'll let you know if things get more serious. How's Mr. X?"

"I told you at camp." Odelle sounds irritated, like when Stella leaves wet towels on the floor. "He ended things with me. His wife found out. So now I'm stuck with a husband who should be in jail."

"What?" Mom says.

I step backward. Why does Stella's dad belong in *jail*?

Odelle starts crying.

"It's okay," Mom says softly to her. "You can tell me anything."

Odelle makes hiccupy choking sounds.

"What are you doing?" It's Stella, from behind me. She's smiling weirdly and holding scissors in her hand.

A guilty, sunburned feeling spreads all over my face. Does she know her dad's going to jail?

"Are you spying on them?"

"Um…." Yes. No. I don't know what to say.

The scissors drop from her hands.

"Girls?" A moment later, Odelle rounds the corner. "Everything all right?" She wipes her eyes and picks up the scissors from the ground.

Mom follows, looking equally concerned.

My eyes swing from my mom to Odelle, to Stella.

No one speaks.

What should I say? What's Stella going to say? Am I going to get into trouble for spying on them?

"Ooo-ooh." Stella clutches her stomach and moans, "I feel really sick. I think I'm going to barf. We just ran downstairs."

She's faking it. I can tell.

"Darling!" Odelle fans herself. "You know how much I hate vomit. To the toilet—quick!"

"We better go," my mom says. "Unless you want us to help?"

"No, go."

My mom hugs Odelle goodbye. "We'll talk soon. Thanks for having Willow over."

"No problem. And Becks?"

"Yes?"

"Keep our little conversation to yourself. This sort of thing gets gobbled up like caviar."

My mom nods, and we head to the door, the photograph safely tucked into my pocket.

It's dark and pouring outside.

I follow Mom to the car. She's walking super fast and I'm wheeling my bike so it's hard to keep up.

Nothing makes sense. Why were the moms talking about jail? What did Stella's dad do that was *that* bad? Whenever I'm over, he's really nice. He gives me junk food and asks about cheer and listens and asks me questions when I talk about the environment. Stella's lucky she has a dad. I guess, if he goes to jail, we both won't have one.... Will that make us closer?

Mom parked half a block away, under a streetlight. Once we reach the car, she looks around and checks the backseat.

"Mom, hurry, I'm getting wet."

She lifts my bike into the trunk.

I climb in, buckle my seatbelt, and put my bike helmet on my lap.

My mom starts driving.

As the windshield wipers swoosh, I try to hold back tears. Today was the third-worst day of my entire life, and she can't even tell?

She hums a song—something about Janie having a gun or gum or something, I can't quite hear…about a dad…

I picture Papa ahead of me on the trail. "Keep up, *mon signe*." My legs aching, asking, "How much longer?" He'd always laugh and say something like, "Only 200,523 steps."

Now he's not here to encourage me to keep going.

What would my papa want me to do? Duh! Break her and Mr. Brady up. But how?

I stare at her. My eyes feel like they're going to bulge out of their sockets. She keeps humming the stupid song, pretending she can't feel me looking at her. "Mom, were you really at home working tonight?"

Her hands tighten on the steering wheel. They're all red and scabby from itching them. "Yes," she answers.

"You're lying."

She snaps her head toward me, frowning. When she does that, her wrinkles look bigger, especially the V-shaped one between her eyebrows. Maybe she should get Botox like Paulita and other Aqua Vista moms with their big, shiny foreheads.

"Why would you say that?"

"You're acting differently lately. You smell different."

"Pfft. You and my mother should get a psychic hotline." She smiles, trying to make everything nice when it isn't. "I can't get into any trouble with you smarty-pants around, now can I?"

I don't smile back. "You don't even miss Papa."

"Good grief! What are you talking about?"

"I heard you fighting, Mom. The last few months before he died, when you thought I was sleeping…it seemed like you didn't even like each other anymore."

"Willow, your dad and I loved each other. Yes, we fought sometimes, I'm sorry you heard that. It was a very stressful time."

I face the window. Raindrops slither down the glass.

We pass the Boca Arbor Club and Fort Park, which is halfway between my house and Stella's. It looks spooky in the dark. I wonder what it would be like to sleep there at night with the owls and rats.

I won't tell Mom about the picture. A warm, tingling feeling fills my belly. Mom keeps so many secrets from me. It feels good to keep one from her.

"It's hard to believe someone's turning twelve tomorrow," Mom says—a tactic to distract me.

"Can I still stay home from school?" Papa used to let me on my birthday, even if it was a school day, and we'd have a movie marathon in our pajamas.

Mom nods. "Are you feeling ill, like Stella? You're pale."

"I'm fine." There's just a video out there that can destroy my life.

"Did you eat a lot of candy at Stella's?"

"A bit." Actually, I ate nothing. Which was my plan. My thigh still has fat on it when I pinch it. Every time I eat, I picture Katia beside me saying, *Uh-uh. Fattening.*

"When Stella came over with the brownies, I heard you talking about calories. If there's anything—"

"God, Mom. It's nothing! Just something we joke about."

"Well. You're beautiful and strong, and so is your body."

As she drones on about body image and healthy eating, I fiddle with the strap of my bike helmet. Why do I have to get braces this week? I want to be invisible, not uglier. I'm only pretty with a filter. Filterless me is fugly. I'll never look like the girls on Instagram. Maybe I should do the thing earlier. Then I'll never have to get braces…and if the video comes out, I guess I'll never know.

# Chapter 39

# TOAST & JAM

## –BEC–

Willow woke in a horrendous mood, and she's still in a horrendous mood. Even while I sit beside her on her bed and she opens her birthday presents (a cashmere cardigan from Yolanthe; a gift card from Mom; recycling craft books from me; and a birthday card from Nathaniel, who she's met a few times over the years, with twelve dollars cash enclosed). Even after she talks to her grandmothers on the phone and thanks them for her gifts. Even as I cuddle her tightly, and whisper, "I love you, birthday girl. You know what else I love? These cat-printed sheets."

"They're baby-ish."

"But you picked them." *Just last month.*

"Only because you said I couldn't get the black ones."

"You're not a goth," I try to inject a little humor.

"Says who?"

Every parent's answer: *Me.*

I shift on my hip and rub her arm. "What's this all about?"

"You wouldn't understand." She buries her face into her pillow, her body stiff.

"Try me."

After a few moments, she faces me, eyes panicked. "Mom, it's so bad." She wipes her nose. "It happened yesterday. I did something that I thought was a joke...."

A long pause.

"Go on, honey."

A change comes over her features, a zippering up, as though she's already said too much. She curls onto her side. "Do I really have to get braces on Friday?"

"Oh, Willow." She's holding something back. "What happened yesterday? What joke?"

"I don't want braces."

"They're only temporary." From my experience, it's best not to push; I'll ask her when she seems more receptive. "A little discomfort now will pay off later—and you'll have the most dazzling smile in the room."

"I don't want a dazzling smile."

I outline the downward curve of her mouth. "Fine, the most dazzling frown."

I can tell she's trying her best not to break her stony expression.

"Everything is going to be okay." I rise from her bed. "Okay, birthday girl, what'll it be, pancakes or throw-in-everything smoothies?" We do this on special occasions, tossing in Oreos, chocolate chips, even Doritos once, to her astonishment. I gauge her reaction. From her last calorie comment, I'm on the lookout for any other signs indicating a low body image or different eating habits.

"Whatever," she grumbles. "I need to sleep. Turn off the lights."

"Manners. And don't forget Hannah is coming at 4:00."

"Why do I have to have tutoring on my birthday?"

"She comes every Tuesday. See you in a bit. Love you." I lift my hand in a half-wave, waiting for her to complete the other half of the heart. Instead, she shoves her hand under the pillow and rolls to her other side.

I turn off the lights and shut her bedroom door.

That went well. Add soaring hormones into the mix, repressed grieving, and whatever happened at school yesterday. Plus, her calling me out last night about lying to her when I said I stayed home to work. She said I was acting differently. That I smelled different.

Obviously, I need to be more careful.

A run, yes, that will make me feel better. While changing into my Lululemon jogging outfit, Paulita texts: **Hi Rebecca, can you confirm if ur coming on the girls wknd?**

**Sorry for the delay. Have some conflicting appointments. Can I let you know tomorrow?**

The phone beeps again, but this message is from Brady.

**Can I stop by?**

And…that would be *not* being more careful.

**Willow's home**, I reply. **It's her birthday. PS Don't tell the head of school she's skipping class.**

**I have a day off too. Doing Autism Awesome work. Can u sneak out for 20 mins?**

**What's on offer? :)**

**I'm nearby. Let's meet down the block, corner of Ironwedge & Palm D'Oro. Say ur going for a run.**

I feel a strange frisson. I'm already in my gym clothes, about to go running, and Willow's asleep. Nobody is any the wiser.

**Wow. Covert operations**, I text back. **That's how bad u want to see me?**

**Is that a yes?**

I facepalm myself. Am I really considering this?

**I have another favor. Can u bring toast?**

The man is crazy. **With what on it?**

**Jam, thanks. Didn't have time for breakfast. I'm really hungry.**

**Hungry, huh? What do u know? I feel exactly the same way….**

I jot down a note for Willow that I'm going for a run. *A two-block one, that happens to lead to Brady's lap.*

He's parked in a secluded nook protected by overhanging tree branches.

Looking over my shoulder, I get into his green truck, surprised to see him wearing a suit.

"Hi," I say, with a huge grin, passing him the toast folded in a paper napkin.

"Hey, beautiful." He sets the toast aside and leans in, kissing me sensually. "I've been dying for your lips."

"Oooh, tell me more."

We keep kissing and don't stop, not while I'm unknotting his tie, or he's sliding my pants down my hips, or he's fingering me while nibbling on my ear, and before long, he's driven into the closest alley, I'm on his lap and we're having quick, hot, teenage-style sex.

"Christ Almighty," he says after he orgasms, dropping his forehead onto mine. "What are you doing to me, Bec?"

"Whatever I'm doing to you, you're doing to me too. I feel drugged." And achy in my hips. Truck sex is not meant for women in my age bracket. Nor, usually, daylight sex.

He hooks his hand around my waist. "Guess that means you want another?"

I laugh. "Handing out orgasms like party mints?"

"I figured out what you like."

"Oh, have you now? Can you pass me my undies?"

Once we get dressed, Brady munches on his toast.

"Pretty good," he says. "Next time can you cut off the crusts?"

I whack his arm. "Don't be such a princess."

"Princess?" He sets his toast on the dashboard and tickles me, planting another deep kiss on my mouth.

"Mmm, you taste like strawberries."

After making out some more, I push him away. "As nice as it is to keep smooching, I've got a birthday to plan."

"I'm adding our toast and jam to the best moment of my life list."

"Be serious." I look into his open face.

"I'm deadly serious. You have no idea how amazing you are, do you? I'm in. At your mercy. This is real."

With him, I'm growing stronger, feeling more desirable—and deserving. Happy. I don't want it to stop. I want us to go further, deeper. Willow's starting to get suspicious. At some point, are Brady and I going to stop hiding our relationship? Would he be prepared to face the consequences? Would I? How would Willow feel?

"How long do we need to keep our relationship secret?" I ask. "I don't like lying to my daughter. She's starting to suspect I'm seeing someone."

"It's a tough situation. I'd prefer to keep it from the school, but I agree, you don't want to lie to her. Let's think it through. Talk some more later."

We kiss goodbye and I run back home on jiggly legs, sore in the best way.

I'm only a block away when that primal, hair-standing-up-on-your-arms feeling hits.

Someone's watching me.

I keep running, gaze straight ahead, but I study everything within my periphery.

The shadows in the bushes.

The parked cars.

The bicycle rider on my left.

Stupidly, I left my gun at home.

Asleep at the wheel? Even worse, I was nude in the backseat....

When I near my street, a dark figure in a baseball cap ducks behind a fence.

That's him! The rideshare driver. *Gotcha, asshole.* Next time I'll have my gun.

Running as fast as I can, I make it home and lock the door behind me.

Willow is on the couch, arms crossed. "Took you long enough."

"Sorry."

"How was your *jog*?"

"Good." I bend over to stretch my calves, so she can't see my face. "I better go shower. Then I'm all yours."

# Chapter 40

# HAPPY BIRTHDAY

## –WILLOW–

Mom's picked Flashback Diner for my birthday dinner. Which is nice, because she knows I love fifties diners, but I loved them when I was *eight*.

Stella still hasn't replied to my texts. She was supposed to meet us at the restaurant at 7:00. Nineteen minutes ago.

"Maybe we should go ahead and order?" Mom suggests. "The onion ring tower looks good, don't you think?"

I hate food. Food makes you fat. So why does everyone eat all the time? You can get by on barely any calories.

I check my phone again.

"You can call her if you like," Mom says.

My ears burn, and my thighs stick to the chair. I send Stella another message: **Are u coming??**

Two question marks say a lot. Basically, it's screaming.

A waitress with big, horsy teeth comes over to us. "*Heeeey*, birthday girl, your mom said you're turning twelve!"

I scowl at my mom. Why would she do that? I don't want attention. I shrivel down in my seat. I can imagine Katia fake vomiting, half curled up in a ball, her skinny tanned legs sticking out as she convulses, spluttering, "Your mom's the only one who likes you enough to go to your birthday party. Wait until everyone sees the video."

The waitress asks for our drink order.

"Cranberry juice, please," Mom says. "Willow?"

"Doesn't matter," I mumble.

"She'll have a Coke."

As the minutes pass, I feel Mom watching me. She always watches me these days.

"Something must've come up." She unrolls, then rolls her napkin. "Stella wouldn't let you down like this if she could help it."

"I'm fine. Let's eat." And get home quicker.

When our drinks arrive, I order low-fat things.

By the time I've set my knife and fork down, it's obvious Stella's not coming.

The more Mom talks, the more my head feels like it's going to explode.

I see the candles first. Mom's downward gaze, the noise of the restaurant quiets as everyone turns toward the waitress with the big teeth singing "Happy Birthday."

"I'm sorry," Mom whispers, as the waitress places the cake in front of me. "I got this all wrong."

"Make a wish," an elderly guy booms from the table beside us.

*Leave me alone*, I want to yell.

The flickering candles make me remember of all my birthdays with Papa, all my friends in Anchorage.

*Happy birthday to me,*

*Happy birthday to me,*

*It would be better, if I didn't breathe.*

Leaning forward, I blow out the candle.

"Mmm, looks great." Mom slices me a huge piece of chocolate cake like she's trying to make up for such a bad night.

The chocolate smell…too strong. Since it's my last birthday, it doesn't matter anymore. I'm a pig. Bringing my face close to the plate, I stuff the first bite into my mouth, swallowing without chewing, the thick, butter icing, the layers of chocolate mousse. Another huge bite, shoving more and more down, crumbs falling onto my lap. I'm nearly finished with my second slice when I look up.

Stepping through the restaurant, with an orange box tied in a ribbon….

"I'm so sorry," Stella cries, plopping into the chair beside me.

"What happened?" I wipe the chocolate from my mouth.

Her eyes dart to my mom.

"Excuse me. I need to use the bathroom." My mom pats my arm and rises from the table, but before she leaves, she says to Stella, "How's your mother? I haven't been able to reach her."

"She's fine."

"Tell her to call me, okay?"

When Mom's out of earshot, Stella says, "Katia stopped me from coming."

"Figures."

Stella angles her knees toward mine. "I must've randomly mentioned I was coming here tonight. Katia called me, like, ten minutes before I was about to come, and said she had an emergency. So, I went there. No emergency. And my phone goes missing, so I couldn't call you."

"You could have used her phone."

"No, I couldn't." Stella sucks in her cheeks, deepening her dimples. "Katia's got me."

"What do you mean?"

"She knows everything about me, Willow. Things about my dad. I have to do what she says, or…."

"Or what?"

"I'm dead. She's got videos of me. That's how you get into KISS. Little C—*calories*. Big C—*collateral*. Each year we have to prove our commitment to KISS and do another bad video. Loyalty's everything."

# Chapter 41

# SINGLE

## —BEC—

When Odelle's name flashes on my phone, I immediately put down my camera and press *Accept*.

Ever since I was at her house and she casually dropped into the conversation that her husband should be in jail, she hasn't answered my calls or replied to my texts. "Odelle! You're one hard woman to get a hold of."

"Hard is a good thing," Odelle says, slyly as ever, "depending on who you're doing it with." Her mask of bravado is slipping; I can tell she's hurting underneath.

"How've you been?" Leaving my vegetable display half done, I duck out of my rented room and walk down the hall. I exit the warehouse and step onto the street into a wall of humidity. The glaring sun hits me in the face.

"Musing over a few things. Introspection isn't my strongest skill." She laughs, a dry, hacking sound. "What are you up to?"

"Finishing a shoot for a client."

"And later?"

"Oh, you know, popping a cap at the gun range."

"Really? Who are you planning to kill? How about I put a hit out on Ron?" For a moment, there is dead silence, then she starts cackling.

I don't know how to respond. But it's an in. "What you said to me about Ron…?"

"Forget it."

"If you ever want to talk—"

"I don't. Why the gun range?"

Music from a passing car momentarily steals my attention. Teenagers—speeding—with the false invincibility of youth. "It's just precautionary. I want to know I can protect myself and Willow."

"I don't buy it, Becks. You're keeping things from me."

Talk about female intuition. First my mother, then Willow, now Odelle displaying psychic skills? A bunch of damn witches. Originally, I'd planned to go to the shooting range with Brady, but he canceled because of a meeting he couldn't reschedule.

"Spill, sweet pea," Odelle says. "Why are you really going?"

"What I'm about to tell you stays between you and me."

"Lips sealed."

Another onslaught of itchiness. I wriggle, rubbing my legs together and shaking my hands.

A passing woman looks up from her stroller.

I smile brightly, tempted to mouth, *crabs.*

Even though my rash is still visible—mostly on the side of my neck and knuckles—thankfully I only have occasional bouts of desperately needing to scratch myself.

Once the woman has crossed the road, I say, "I could be wrong, but I think someone's following me." I had told Brady about the rideshare driver following me after our truck romp.

"What?" Odelle's voice booms into my earpiece. "How long has this been going on?"

"Too long. I should've gotten a gun months ago. The night of Paulita's party, my rideshare driver went rogue."

"What happened?"

"He started driving the opposite direction. The doors were locked. Luckily, I was on the phone with my mom, and I gave her my coordinates. Then told the driver I knew we were going the wrong way."

"That's some scary shit. I just read a report that last year one of the biggest rideshare companies, can't remember which one, received two hundred plus reports of rape, and thousands of reports of sexual abuse."

"And they say there's no need for feminism."

A flower truck pulls into the warehouse parking lot. A moment later, a hefty man gets out and starts unloading crates full of plants in plastic pots.

I study him; too big to be the rideshare driver.

"Mmm. I wonder," Odelle says. "What bad things you did in your past to have someone follow you now?"

"Nice, Odelle. Blame the victim." It's becoming her modus operandi. And as for bad things, well, sneaking Brady into my house two nights ago was up there. He left at 3:00 a.m., after shake-me-to-my-core sex. Two rounds, thank you very much. And yesterday, before work, he texted: **I'm out front. Come kiss me for 5 mins.** Which was cute and sexy as hell—but dicey.

"I'm not blaming anyone," Odelle says. "Devil's advocate. You should think about who you've turned on or pissed off."

"There was an artist in New York who tried to sabotage a few of my shows. My mother-in-law has never been a fan. And…." Nathaniel comes to mind. "I have a friend who's had a crush on me for years."

"You're accusing me?" Odelle says playfully.

The driver gets back into his flower truck and pulls out onto the road.

"How's Willow since Tampongate?" Odelle asks.

"Could you not?" Ever since camp, that's how Odelle refers to the rope climbing incident and all the drama surrounding it.

"My bad," Odelle says.

"She's okay." Untrue. But I'm not giving Odelle material to add to the Willow's-a-weird-kid file.

I need to protect my daughter's reputation—a nice, normal girl who nobody has any reason to treat badly or talk about. Nothing to help someone justify their own daughters' cruelty.

The truth? Willow's sleeping more than ever. When she's awake, she doesn't say much. Her appetite is almost nonexistent. And the spark in her eyes? I lie in bed at night, scared shitless, wondering if the darkness she's feeling is the same darkness Théo and Yolanthe struggled with. In Anchorage, my friend Jane's son was diagnosed with an anxiety disorder and given antidepressants. Does Willow need drugs? But the side effects...the potential long-term dependence issues. I've been on the waitlist for her to see a child psychologist, Dr. Ruttenberg, but getting Willow to agree to even go has become another thing to argue about.

Meanwhile, I've been doing what I can. Preparing her favorite meals, watching comedies with her on the couch, strolling the impossibly turquoise Delray Beach. She knows I'm trying. Although she was scheduled to get braces, I cancelled her appointment at the last minute. Given how everything has played out at school, she doesn't need more to feel insecure about.

"What time are you going to the shooting range?" Odelle asks.

"Two."

"Which place?"

"Lock & Load."

"That's in Wynwood, isn't it?"

For some reason, it doesn't surprise me that Odelle is familiar with the location of shooting ranges in Miami. "That's the one." The soonest private booking I could arrange happened to be an hour's drive away.

"I'm coming with," Odelle sings. "And, yes, I'll be wearing fringe and cowboy boots. Don't judge."

I'm glad she's joining me at the shooting range. Afterward, we'll find a dive bar and, over a stiff drink or three, have a sisterly heart-to-heart about what's going on with her husband. "Like being judged has ever stopped you from anything. I admire that about you."

"Aw, shucks."

"I mean it. You're brave and smart and you make everything fun." I figure she needs the boost, and it's true, there's no one else in the world like Odelle Rackark. "Then God broke the mold."

"He broke something, all right."

Once we've said goodbye, I reenter the warehouse, thankful for the AC. At my workstation, I start a different shoot, arranging Brussels sprouts, cabbage, and cauliflower in baskets for a rustic feel. I walk around the bench, studying them from different angles. Cruciferous vegetables of the family Brassicaceae. Mmm, how to come up with something striking from that? Usually, images dance in my mind, but today the magic isn't there.

*Let the vegetables speak for themselves.*

Half an hour later, still frustrated and inexplicably annoyed with the cauliflower, I take a break.

In the small kitchenette, the coffee percolates.

Brady texts: **Good news. I can get out of my meeting today & come to the shooting range.**

Darn. Now I wish I hadn't made arrangements with Odelle. I'm about to text Brady back and let him know my plans have changed—chicks before dicks, as Odelle crudely says—when I receive his next message.

**There's something I need to tell you. It's important.**

I stop pouring milk into my mug. Is it about Willow? Or us? Last night I'd called him after dinner and asked if he wanted to catch up (aka, meet and kiss). He said he was at home and about to head out to band practice. The subtle unease in his voice made me wonder if there was something he wasn't telling me. Perhaps he'd just had a hard day. He got off the phone quickly, and I didn't hear from him again that night.

I'm not the kind of person that can let sleeping dogs lie. I need to know what he has to tell me. Surely it will be easy enough to nudge my catch-up with Odelle until later in the day. She might be annoyed, but she'll get over it.

I give Odelle a quick call and explain it would be better for me if we could skip the gun range and meet for dinner instead.

"Why are you ditching me?"

Trust her not to let it slide. "Dinner will be more fun. How about Yakitori in Boca on Mizner, say, 8:00 p.m.?"

"Fine. If I'm not hanging out with you this afternoon, I guess I'm hanging out with a triple Pilates class—mat, reformer, followed by an infrared sauna."

"Thanks, I appreciate it. Bye."

I resolve to be there for her, whatever she needs. Her callous attitude about Willow's friendship issues could be misdirected pain about whatever's going on with Ron. Grief, as I'm well aware, manifests in confusing ways. A quote comes to mind: *When a friend does something wrong, don't forget all the things they did right.*

Next, I confirm with Brady to meet at Lock & Load in three hours and I arrange private lessons for both of us. We agree we shouldn't risk driving together.

Oh, I know—broccoli and bok choy. Yes, I need more green—vitality—and the baskets have to go. Something more organic? A mound of rich dirt, roots, flower petals. With the image in mind, I hurry back to my workbench.

The rest of the morning passes quickly, and before I know it, it's time to start the drive to Miami to meet Brady.

# Chapter 42

# READY, AIM, LIAR

Picnic lunch? Bike ride? Share a milkshake?

No, our date is somewhere less cliché.

Brady's there first, standing outside Lock & Load in jeans, a V-neck, a baseball cap, and aviator sunglasses.

Behind him, the enormous gray building looks like a kid's activity center, with a thick panel of orange on top and giant silhouettes of James Bond and Laura Croft types painted onto the brick walls. The windows are blacked out and two palm trees frame a metal bench.

"You look lovely." Brady leans in close and whispers into my ear, "Fucking smokeshow."

A rush of desire slams me full force. That man has a damn destabilizing effect.

"Glad you like the outfit." I swing my purse onto my other shoulder. Odelle's idea about dressing western inspired me. After a quick pit stop at home, I went for jeans, a white shirt, a long turquoise-and-silver necklace, a cowboy hat, and boots. The look clearly works for Brady. If we were anywhere else, he'd already be undressing me.

I knock his arm. "You're not so bad yourself." I don't want to give him a big head. Everything about him is already big, his personality, his muscles, and his—

He sneezes and takes a tissue out of his pocket.

"Bless you." His coloring is off and something else I can't put my finger on. Maybe it has to do with the important thing he has to tell me. We only have a few minutes before our classes start, so I'll have to wait to find out until afterward.

He sneezes again. "Sorry. I'm not sure if it's allergies or I'm coming down with something."

"Aw, even though you're not feeling well, you moved mountains to be here." Well, not mountains. Brady had managed to clear a window, but he needed to leave by 2:00 p.m.

Brady smiles. "Nothing stands in the way of a good woman."

"I'm not good, babe." I gesture to the entrance of Lock & Load. "That's why I'm here."

"I've been thinking about you nonstop." He looks behind him before squeezing my hand and quickly stepping away.

Although I'd rather suction myself to his body and kiss the life out of him, I take a step back too. Who knew it would be so hard not to touch? It's the first time we've properly been in public together. I can't tell how he's feeling. He seems relaxed. We're out in the open and need to be careful about how we portray our relationship. Yes, it may look suspicious, but at least we're far from home turf and in the undeniably unromantic setting of a gun range.

"Have you been followed again?" Brady asks.

I shake my head. "Not since I met you for 'my jog.'"

Concern darkens his features.

"Don't worry, I'd call you, as we agreed."

He takes off his sunglasses. "Let's go in and get you prepared just…"

"…in case." *In case the fucker comes for me again.*

The inside of Lock & Load is like a giant café for guns. People milling about, merchandise for sale, and a giant green logo of a mermaid holding two pistols, a mockery of Starbucks. It reads: *I love guns & coffee.*

We approach the first free desk.

"Hi, I've booked a private session for Fournier. Handguns."

"Brady. Automatics. Thanks."

As we fill out the appropriate paperwork, Brady says, "Bec, look," and shows me the services booklet. "They offer different packages. The *007* and *Scarface* package, where you use firearms seen in Hollywood blockbusters."

"That's disturbing."

"Agreed. It glamorizes it."

Florida is where "stand your ground" laws were born: One-third of Floridians carry guns. Like Alaska, it's a way of life.

After paying the fees, which Brady insists on covering, we meet our two buff instructors, who are so top heavy, they look like they could topple over. They hand us safety glasses and earmuffs and give us a tour.

"See you in an hour," Brady says with a wink.

"Hopefully, in one piece," I reply, fighting off a wave of anxiety as I step into the booth beside his.

The next sixty minutes are intense—the volume, the kickback, imagining the rideshare driver chasing Willow through our neighborhood streets, me catching him, and the satisfaction of hitting my target. Now I'm in control. Halfway through, I turn around and catch Brady watching me. He waves before heading back to his stall.

By the time the lesson is finished, I'm more than a little anxious.

"How'd you do?" I ask as we head outside to the parking lot.

"What a rush." He shields his eyes from the fierce sun and sneezes again. "Watching you shoot turned me on."

"That's what they all say. You've got an hour, right? Should we get a drink somewhere?"

"Nah, we need to be alone." His eyes dart to the left. "Where no one can overhear anything."

Well, that doesn't sound good. I hug my arms over my chest. Does he want to break up? Nothing in his body language suggests so; he keeps looking at me like I'm catnip, practically purring. But if we can't be open about our relationship and we can't ask Willow to lie about us having one, what options do we have?

"Let's talk in my truck," he says.

"I'll grab drinks from inside."

Armed with cans of 7UP and salt and vinegar chips, which I know he loves, we walk toward his green pickup truck, which he's parked furthest away from the store entrance, flush to a brick wall.

"I'm so thirsty." After pulling back the tab, I guzzle back a few fizzy mouthfuls. My arms feel wobbly—the aftereffects of the gun's recoil, or because desire runs through me, heady; I'm drunk on it. I'm not sure how I'm going to contain myself once we're in his truck.

When we get in, Brady playfully slaps his head. "Ah, you drive me insane. Thank God we're finally alone and I can have you to myself." He starts the engine, and he puts on the AC and some music. Bluegrass. I guess it fits the mood.

He tosses the chip packet to the side, and we share a look which makes me clench my toes.

"I can't go another second without touching you," he says, eyes half-closed, breathing slow.

The song picks up, a female singer joining the mandolin and steel guitar.

"It was tough, wasn't it?"

"Torture." He flashes a grin. "Get your ass over here."

I laugh and place my can in the drink holder. "You get *your* ass over here."

"Happy to oblige." He leans toward me, then stops. "Before I kiss you, you should know I'm probably contagious."

"We survived poison ivy together, we can survive a cold." But what else can we survive? Our relationship is built on subterfuge and secrets. I don't want to not be able to hold his hand in public or kiss him whenever I feel like it. At some point, we have to stop hiding.

Only…Willow. His career. There are other things to consider.

His lips press against mine.

I focus on each sensation: his stubbly jaw against my cheek, his calloused fingers under my shirt caressing my breasts.

If only there was some way to keep our relationship under wraps until the end of middle school. Huh. I stiffen, an uncanny sense of déjà vu.

Someone else said something similar, hadn't they, about waiting until after middle school…

"You okay?" Brady asks.

"I'd be better if you do that little bite thing on my lower lip."

He chuckles. "Oh, like this?"

The next song is faster. Our bodies move in sync as the windows fog up.

"Didn't you want to tell me something?" I ask between kisses.

"After you ride me, cowgirl," he says in the funniest country drawl, his hands cupping my butt.

I laugh until I realize he's serious. "Here? What if someone sees us?" I glance around the deserted parking lot.

"Let's make that less likely to happen." He takes the large, rectangular, silver sun visor and uses his right hand to hold it against the window, blocking onlookers' view.

"You. Are. Trouble." I lightly smack his cheek.

"On top," he growls.

I shimmy out of my jeans and underwear, as he pulls down his own.

Oh, he's ready for me alright.

Still in my white shirt and cowboy hat, I straddle him.

His eyes gleam. "You're going to have to forgive me, I can only use one hand," he says, slipping a finger down my backside and stopping to outline my—oh my God.

With an electric jolt, I shift my position. Recovering my shock, I say, "I won't deduct points."

All thoughts disappear, heightened sensitivity to skin, touch.

Condom on.

Wet and tight, I clamp down on his erection.

We have fast, hard, naughty sex—my pace, my directions, in tune with the chords of the mandolin.

"Squeeze my breasts," I tell him. It's fun issuing demands and he's very obliging. "A-plus, Mr. Brady. Now kiss my neck. Uh-uh, more to the right." He starts to nibble on my ear, then stops to sneeze. For a brief instant, I become aware of my surroundings. Women my age don't have sex in cars!

(Although, what's the point of all that yoga, if not flexibility?) At what stage in adulting did sex begin to only take place in bed?

"Don't stop," he murmurs.

I grind myself lower, drawing him deep in my center. Arching my body, I throw my arms into the air and reach for—

*Youch!* My elbow knocks the window.

He stops. "You okay, beautiful?" A red mark has already appeared on my forearm, near some poison ivy bumps. He kisses the mark tenderly.

After orgasming—twice for me—I hold the sun visor thing while Brady knots the condom. Then we dress, and I fix myself up, patting down my hair in the car mirror.

"All right, Brady. We shot guns and had sex in the parking lot. Whatever you have to tell me can't be worse."

He raises his eyebrows.

Dammit, it is.

# Chapter 43

# AMBUSH

Waiting in the truck for Brady to tell me the "important thing" is agony, and we only have fifteen minutes left before he has to return to Boca. He ums and ahs, shifts in his car seat, and spends an enormous amount of time fiddling with the tab of his 7UP can.

"Brady, this was your idea."

He rubs his jaw but says nothing.

"Just so you know, I'm trustworthy, and pretty good at keeping secrets." Understatement of the year.

"Alright," he says. "It's about a girl. A student at Boca High when I was still a teacher."

An icy sensation floods my body.

"I oversaw the school rock band. This girl, Gia, showed lots of singing talent. Unique, scratchy voice. I gave her extra lessons, paid her more attention…."

Oh hell no. "*Gia*—as in Giavanna, Paulita's daughter?"

Nodding, he avoids my eyes.

I bury my hands in my lap. I'm not ready for some sick confession involving Brady and Paulita's daughter.

"She was sixteen," he says.

Christ.

"One day, I came to school early, and Gia was in the music room sleeping on the ground. I woke her, and when she saw me, she started shaking and crying. I held her. Anybody would do the same thing."

I shake my head. He wanted to have sex with me first because he knew I'd leave him after he revealed his dirty secret. "Go on," I say, keeping a neutral expression. Giavanna is my friend's daughter and anything he says can, and will be, used against him. I'll press him for every detail, then nail him to the crime.

A man in an Adidas tracksuit, carrying a duffle bag, walks to the car closest to us and climbs inside. He turns to profile—is it him? The rideshare driver? No, the man has two chins.

"Gia said she had a secret that she hadn't told anybody." Brady stares at the foot mat. "I told her if she shared it with me, I wouldn't tell anyone. She said, 'Not even my parents?' I was young, new at teaching, and I made a mistake. I promised her that whatever she told me, would stay between her and me."

Ignoring my queasy stomach, I ask, "What'd she say?"

"She was pregnant. Just a few weeks."

"Who was the father?"

"A drug dealer she met at a party in Miami."

"Oooh." I feel foolish for thinking the worst of Brady, he would never—

"She wanted to get an abortion. But in Florida, you need your parent's approval. The only other option is to go to court and win the right to have an abortion without your parents' knowledge. For Gia, that wouldn't work. Not with her father's dealership, his wealth and fame. Her mother's political circles. A judge would never rule in Gia's favor."

"What'd you do?"

"Her biological father lived in South Dakota, where abortion is legal."

"I didn't know Paulita was married before."

"They don't publicize it. If Gia went to South Dakota, she could discuss it with her dad, and they could decide whether she should have one. I believe women have the right to make those decisions for themselves, although, of course, it's complicated."

Poor Giavanna, not to mention Paulita being left in the dark. Imagine not knowing your daughter was pregnant, not being able to give her counsel and support. "You were trying to help."

"It gets worse." He speaks quickly. "Gia arranged to visit her dad. She came up with a good excuse, bought the plane ticket. She asked to talk to me before she left."

"What did she want?" I ask, anticipation making my chest tight.

"Money."

"For the abortion?"

"I didn't ask. For options." Brady presses his fist against the steering wheel. "Can you imagine what would happen to my career if it got out that I gave money to a student for an abortion?"

The car is claustrophobic. Dry-mouthed, I chug some 7UP. I want to help him, protect him, but—it's smarter to retreat from more drama, more pain.

I think of Willow saying to me, "Mr. Brady knew Katia and those girls did mean things to me and they never got into trouble."

*That's because Paulita had his balls in a vise.*

"I'd never side with a teenager now and tell them I'd keep a secret," Brady says. "Parents need to know what's going on with their kids—and I'd never give money to a student. It's on my conscience forever."

It's a lot to take in. Why would Brady risk so much for Giavanna? I suppose he had firsthand knowledge about what it was like to grow up in a family where your mother didn't want you. His whole life he felt like a mistake, aware his mother resented him. I can see how he wouldn't want the same for Giavanna. "Why are you telling me this now?"

"I want to be transparent with you." He reaches out and holds my hand. "You trusted me enough to tell me your secrets."

"Thank you." I stroke his cheek, feeling as though the parameters of our two bodies are less defined; as though, energetically, we've merged in some unquantifiable way.

"There's more. It's campaigning time. The election is next year. Journalists are digging for dirt about Paulita. I got a phone call a week ago. A journalist wanted to know my thoughts on teenage abortion…and my opinion about the different mayor candidates."

"A coincidence?"

"Not likely. Paulita got the same call. She visited me at the studio, and we had a tense talk. I'm afraid it's going to come out. Blow up in my face."

I suck air through my teeth, unable to reassure him that it won't. "Not a good time to be doing this"—I gesture to the space between us—"with a mom from school, either."

"Right."

"I'm so sorry, Brady"—and fearful—the sense of foreboding is like a giant wave coming our way. "But why did Paulita come straight to you? I thought she didn't know you'd helped Giavanna."

"It turns out Gia told her mom a few years later that when she visited her dad, she had an abortion. Paulita freaked out at her ex, but he said he didn't know anything about it, so Paulita pressed Gia and Gia told her everything, about the drug dealer dad, about me helping her. Paulita and I had a conversation. Although she's Catholic and publicly against abortion, reading between the lines, she was relieved she didn't have a daughter with a teenage pregnancy and drug connections."

"It wouldn't go down well with her constituency." Being anti-drugs is a key component of Paulita's platform.

He kneads his thigh. "Ever since, no matter what their family does—including Katia being cruel to Willow—I have to protect them or else they'll out me. But, at the same time, I have power over them, because if people knew about Gia, Paulita's candidacy would be undermined. It's a mess."

I sit back, digesting what he said. When I next look over at Brady, he's slouched in his seat, a palm over his mouth.

"You're not a bad guy. You've made bad decisions."

He laughs with mirth. "That's what we tell the kids. It's not you, it's your behavior."

"You can make this right. Everyone makes mistakes. Sometimes they have terrible, unforeseeable, ripple effects. I'm on your side," I say, with a fierce surge of protectiveness. "I'm not going anywhere."

"You're not?"

I kiss his mouth. "You're growing on me."

"Bec, there's one other thing I should've told you."

For God's sake. "What is it?"

"Before you came to Boca, I was in a complicated situation where—"

*Knock, knock.* A rapping sound on my side of the car window.

Brady and I both turn our heads.

Holy shit, it's Odelle, in full western gear, and she doesn't look happy.

"Oh, hell no," Brady mutters.

"Don't worry," I say, "I know how to handle her."

He shakes his head. "No one in the world knows how to handle Odelle Wragge."

# Chapter 44

# HOW COULD YOU?

If Odelle had shown up twenty minutes earlier, she would've gotten the show of her life. Thankfully, now at least I have my pants on.

I squeeze Brady's hand. "We better get out."

"God help us all," he murmurs as we swing open the doors of the truck.

Close up, Odelle looks angrier than I've ever seen her. In a flared denim pantsuit and fringed suede vest, her red hair is wild, her eyes even wilder. Psycho, gun-slinging, wild.

"What are you doing…with him?" She points at Brady, who's walked around the truck to join me.

I give her a lopsided smile. "Would you believe me if I said we were discussing Art Synergy?"

My joke falls on deaf ears.

"Huh. How perplexing." Odelle screws up her forehead. "I came here at 2:00 p.m. to support you because I believed your 'someone's following me, I need help' story."

"But—why, Odelle? We made *dinner* plans. And someone is following me. I do need help." I take a few steps toward her. I have no idea why Odelle would drive all the way here. Obviously, there's been a misunderstanding. Maybe I wasn't clear enough on the phone.

"Apparently, you found it," she says with a nasty smirk.

Indignation rises to my cheeks. Who I date is none of her business.

"So, this is why you bailed on me, Becks? After knowing how important it was that we talk."

"I'm sorry."

She cups her ear. "Oh, is that a glitch? I've heard it before."

I go to stand at Brady's side, but he moves slightly behind me, as though I can protect him from the big bad cowgirl.

"Odelle, it's not that big of a deal. I just postponed our talk."

Possibly not my best word choice.

"Not a big deal? Mmm. I wonder what would constitute a big deal?" She plants her hands on her hips. "Would it be a big deal if I was also sleeping with Brady?"

"What?!" Brady shouts.

"It's such a relief." Odelle laughs, eyes gleaming. "Because you didn't know, did you, Becks? That would've been much worse."

Dumbfounded, I can't keep up. "What would be worse?" I don't believe her. Brady wouldn't do that to me.

"Aw, so slow to figure it all out, aren't you?" She speaks in a baby voice as though talking to a toddler. "It would have been worse if you knew you were screwing my boyfriend."

What. The. Fuck.

I stand in between the middle of them.

"I'm n-not dating her," Brady says. "This—this is—*deranged*."

"DERANGED?" Odelle screeches before breaking into tears. "How can you deny our relationship, Brady? I love you. You know how much I fucking love you." She sobs, giant, hiccupy sobs.

At that moment, two men walk out of Lock & Load and look our way. As they pass by, the older of the two says under his breath to Brady, "I don't envy you, buddy. Watch your back. Lots of guns inside."

Under different circumstances, I'd find that funny, but it's as though my insides have been hollowed out.

Odelle clicks her tongue. "Brady doesn't want you to know. We're always together."

"Alright, Bec," Brady says. "Odelle and I, um, have spent some time together outside of school—okay." He drops his car keys on the ground, bends to snatch them. "She was doing pro bono work for Autism Awesome, planning an end-of-year party. We became, er, friendly."

I lean on the truck for support, my feet unsteady on the pavement. This can't be happening.

"Feeling-each-other-up friendly!" Odelle cackles. "It all started on his boat, *Joey Boy*. He took me for a ride and then"—she juts out her breasts, the fringe on her vest, shimmying—"I took him for one."

I cut a glance at Brady, fury rushing to my temples, everything I believed about him, lies. "Not very original. I guess that's where he seduces all the Aqua Vista moms." And here I was thinking what we had was special, that we could possibly have a future together.

"Bec! She's lying."

"We fell deeply in love," Odelle says, clutching her chest. "Everything was perfect."

"Except for the fact you're married," I interject. *And that he's mine. And, God…*I trusted him. My heart feels like it's caving in, my ribs shattering.

"Oh, you don't know anything," Odelle says. "You always act like you're better than me, so proper, the one who does the right thing, but don't jump to fucking conclusions. Ron practically forced me on Brady."

"What—how does a husband force his wife on someone else?" I turn to Brady and ask, "Is that true?" although I don't know why I'm asking him to clarify anything given he left out the small matter of dating my frenemy.

"That's the only thing she's saying that is true."

"Keep talking," I say.

"Ron was all for it." Brady pinches his lips between his thumb and index finger. "We were at the party of a mutual friend and Ron chatted with me throughout the night. At the end of the evening, he said he was leaving for Bangkok for three months—would I keep an eye on Odelle and take her off his hands? Wink, wink."

"How convenient," I snap. "Classy way for your love story to start." I turn on my heel. "I'm too old for this crap."

"No," Brady cries out. "Odelle and I are just friends. Listen." Brady blocks my way. "We are not—we were never—together."

"Liar!" Odelle screams. A bloodcurdling, lock-me-up soprano scream.

My eyes swing to the entrance of Lock & Load. Staff, no doubt, will be outside any minute. A scandal involving me, the head of school, and Odelle Wragge isn't something I need. And I certainly don't need the police showing up asking questions. "Odelle! Keep your voice down!" But she can't hear me because she's weeping uncontrollably.

I glower at Brady. "This? All of it's on you. Taking advantage of vulnerable mothers. Get the hell out of here."

He reaches for my arm, but I shake it away.

"Bec, don't believe a word of this. She's feeding you lies."

"So, you didn't seduce her on *Joey Boy*?"

"She's never been on my boat."

"And you didn't love her?"

"Are you kidding?"

"Have you kissed?"

"Well, it was...." He scrapes a hand through his hair, holds it back, then releases it. "*She* kissed me. I p-pushed her away."

"Right." God. "And you didn't purposely leave that out?"

"Okay, er, I did, b-but you need to understand that—"

"No. All I need to understand is you're a...a...man-whore." Instinctively, I reach for my necklace where my locket used to be.

I'm such an idiot. Emotions—pain, humiliation, defeat—rock me.

"It's n-not true," Brady says.

"Sure about that?" Odelle says with a high-pitched laugh. "Who were you with last night, Brady?"

My eyes seek his. Everything rests on his answer.

"So, I just—stopped by Odelle's house on my way to—"

Odelle wags her finger. "Little louder, Brady, we can't hear you." She whips around to me. "He was at my house when he took a call. I heard him say he couldn't talk because he had band practice. More like sex practice!"

"Bullshit," Brady snarls at Odelle. "Bec! Do not listen to this. Let me explain."

I can't compute. He—he lied to me. I asked him where he was last night, and he said he was at home. Which means every other thing he's said could—is likely to be—false. I'm too angry with him to stick around and hear any more. Too humiliated.

"We're leaving." I hook my arm through Odelle's. "You and I need a drink, am I right?" I'm putting on a brave face, but my nervous system is shot, my hands vibrating, a ringing noise in my skull.

"Desperately," she says. "Margarita. Agave Negro. Anything with tequila."

Brady slumps against his truck, head lowered, muttering words I can't hear. He can't help himself, can he? Everything he does, even Autism Awesome and helping Giavanna when she was sixteen, feeds his ego. The good guy who can't keep his dick in his pants.

With one sorrowful breath, I say, "It's probably stating the obvious, but we're through."

"Make that both of us," Odelle adds. "Motherfucker."

We walk away quickly. I don't look back. Odelle and I get into our cars, and I take North Miami Avenue until we reach the bar. I need a drink.

## Chapter 45

# DISHIN' DIRT

Keeping my own emotions in check, with tequila sunrises in hand, barstools pulled up, I ask the obvious question.

"Was Brady Mr. X?"

"Bingo," Odelle says.

Brady. All the times I lied to Willow on his behalf. All I gave up for him.... How naïve. Stupid. Humiliation washes over me.

Odelle and I both take giant sips of our cocktails.

"But you said he was bald—and married." It's impossible to process everything that's happened. One minute Brady confessed his secret about Giavanna, and the next Odelle and I are here, perimenopausal desperados, the rug pulled from under our cowboy boots.

Odelle wags her finger. "I also said, if you were paying attention, I was using red herrings. As if I'd go around telling people I'm doing the head of school." She catches my eyes. "Surely *you* understand."

A spontaneous snort erupts from my nose. "Not a topic covered at the PTA."

She laughs.

There's something ridiculous about being in western clothes at a western bar with my old best friend, spilling tears over the same guy. "When did our lives turn into a country song?"

"Mine's always been one." Odelle takes the maraschino cherry out of her drink and pops it into her mouth. "Probably a do-si-do."

For some reason, this strikes me as hilarious. I grasp my sides, laughing so hard that the few men seated at the bar look up from their beers to our table in the corner of the room.

"A toast," Odelle says. "Strong women don't need dicks."

Instead of toasting her raised drink, the laughter consumes me, overtaking my body.

Sometimes my reaction to shock is laughter, on-the-edge laughter that can bend me to my knees. The spaces between each choke of laughter grow longer, my throat tight—gulping air.

Odelle jumps up, pats my back. "Becks! Breathe!"

After a few moments, I settle down, left with the weight of my new Bradyless reality. It hurts. Not only was Brady lying to me, so was Odelle. "Did you know he was with us at the same time?"

"I don't share bedfellows. Unless, *purposely*, for the night." Her typical swagger is intact, but her tinny voice gives away her devastation.

"Why did you show up then, guns blazing?"

"I figured it out yesterday. You said you were going shooting, and when Brady was over, he made some offhand remark about the shooting range. Then I remembered you said the new guy you were seeing was charismatic and younger than you. Plus, you ditched me. It wasn't that hard to put it all together."

"Did you confront Brady?"

"Sure did."

I clench my hands. "What'd he say?"

"The same thing every man says when he's caught seeing two women at the same time." She swirls her straw in her Tequila Sunrise.

"Which was?"

"It's a bit terrible. No need to hurt your feelings."

"I'm a big girl. I can take it."

"He said he was sorry, and he still loves me. You were a side thing." She cringes. "A…widow fuck."

My limbs tingle with disbelief. But—that—that can't be right…. Different images storm my mind. Brady, washing me in the bathtub, the soft candlelight. Us in the Everglades under the stars. Him playing the guitar to me in his bedroom. Then I remember Odelle having her meltdowns in public when we were teenagers. She's always been borderline unstable. Where do her motives lie? My relationship with Brady was more than sexual, more than a meeting of the minds, it was spiritual, healing. I wasn't…charity. "He would never say that."

"Of course not, no, that was the gist, that you were sad and gloomy, and he couldn't help wanting to cheer you up. Erm, physically. He has a savior complex. Always helping the heartbroken."

*Sad and gloomy? That's how he saw me?*

I cradle my stomach, taking jagged breaths.

"What the hell does he know?" Odelle rests her elbows on the table. "No man knows anything until they're at least forty."

Why won't my hands stop shaking? My body doesn't feel like it's in this chair. It's as though this is happening to someone else.

Odelle sags into herself, crying silently.

"Oh, honey. It's okay." I scoot closer to her. It's easier to focus on her pain than my own. "I know you feel terrible."

"I do." She bats her tear-coated eyelashes. "I really, *sniff,* feel so, *sniff,* terrible." Her chest heaves, and she drops her head onto the table, her crying building to a crescendo.

"There, there." I pat her back. "You're strong and fun and deserve better than some asshole who lies to you."

She peeks up and whispers, "What if I'm in love, *sniff,* with some asshole who lies to me?"

"Excuse me, lassies."

The bartender slides two shots of tequila onto our table. "Looks like you need some more of the good stuff. On the house." From his back pocket, he pulls out a small tissue packet and hands it to Odelle. "Can't have cowgirls crying in my bar, now, can I?"

"Thanks," Odelle says in a childlike simper.

He smiles at her. "What do ya wanna listen to?"

"Patsy Cline. And keep the tequilas comin'."

At this rate, we'll have to ask Fi to collect the girls from cheer; there's no way we're getting out of this bar sober.

Once the bartender's gone, I broach the other issue. "Are you up to talking about Ron?"

"It's fine," her voice wavers, like at any moment she could break down into an uncontrollable fit. "I overacted."

"Why should he be in jail?"

"Mmm." More toying with the straw.

"Odelle. Talk to me."

"Some things I suspect he's done in Asia…."

"Like what?"

Her tongue protrudes from the corner of her mouth, and I can tell she's thinking about how much to reveal.

"I was on his computer, looking for a receipt, and I…."

"Odelle, you can tell me anything. We've known each other for a hundred years. Since leaving love letters at Jimmy-Kiss-Me-Now-Before-I-Die's doorstep. I'll help you."

"You're a darling." Her eyes glaze over and her lips curve into an exaggerated smile. She starts humming along to the Patsy Cline song, her fingers tapping the melody on the table. "I love this bar. It's so basic."

I knock back my drink.

"Things will be better soon," she says. "I actually feel great…liberated. Did I tell you Lucy's coming home and staying for a few weeks? We're going to some dance performances in Miami. It'll be marvelous." She offers a dazzling smile as if posing for a society page photo. "A few new shops I want to show her too. Nothing like mother and daughter shopping, especially as we're the same size. *Four*. Do you know how much discipline is required to maintain size four?"

"Uh-huh." It seems like Odelle's having a psychological episode. "You were saying, about Ron?"

She sighs. "Not now, Becks. I can't talk about it after Brady, after everything. We'll save it for another time."

“I look forward to meeting Lucy.” I keep my tone light, respecting her wishes. “Is she anything like Stella?”

“No.” Odelle pushes away her empty shot glass. “We need more alcohol.”

As she drowns her sorrows, all I can think about is Brady. How is it possible I miss him already? I was bursting with hope. I was so goddamn happy. I dared to think, one day, we might make a great team. And all along, he was sleeping with both of us. Imagining him touching me, touching her, taking Odelle onto *Joey Boy*, the wind in her red hair as they sailed along the Intracoastal....

Odelle stands, unsteady on her feet. “We have to move tables. Now.”

“Why?”

She nods to the walled-in space. “Because nobody puts Baby in the goddamn corner.”

# Chapter 46

# RUN

"What else do you want me to pick up?" I ask Willow, who's curled on the couch, scrolling on her phone.

A run to the grocery store for movie supplies—popcorn and ice cream—is a hopeful distraction from my increasing-by-the-hour heartache which is more mental than physical, my thoughts a nonstop hamster wheel, making it impossible to eat, sleep, function.

The rain pelts on the roof. I wish someone else could go out into the night for supplies. That's what husbands are for. Sure, I could do a grocery delivery, but at least moving my body is better than sitting in a slump.

Too bad the most recent man in my life has turned out to be a two-timing liar who used me to supplement his fragile ego. Over the last three days, Brady's sent texts and left voicemails about how he needs to tell me his side of the story. It's too late for that. I blocked him from my phone and social media and asked Willow to meet me in the parking lot after school so I didn't bump into him. Today is the last day before the long weekend.

"Willow? What else do you want from the store?"

She looks up from her phone. "Sorry. I'm good."

I wish I could say the same. I miss Brady. He *saw* me. He healed me. Going forward, he needs to figure out how not to be beholden to anyone.

Despite being sickened by his betrayal, part of me recognizes that maybe he served a greater purpose: he helped me breathe again from grief, pulled me up from the bottom of the ocean, gave me CPR, and got me swimming—or at least kicking.

As for Odelle, given everything that's going on with her husband, I've forgiven her for lying to me about Mr. X. Why should Ron be in jail? Odelle said it had something to do with what she found on his computer. Larceny? Pornography? A secret addiction—gambling, debts owed?

"Okay, I'm going." I slip on my rain jacket. "Find something good on Netflix while I'm out."

I'm searching for my keys when I spot it—movement out the rain-splattered window. A—is that a face?—near the shed.

Then it's gone.

I stiffen, alert. It's him—I can feel his presence, almost smell it.

"Willow!" I whisper.

"What?"

"I'm going to ask you a question, but whatever you do, don't look or move your head. Okay?"

"Okay."

"Did you open the curtains?"

"Yeah, when you were in the bathroom. I thought I heard something."

*Oh, Christ. Think!* Whoever's out there could've been watching for a long time.

"Listen, Willow. Something's happening. Something serious."

Her body tenses.

"Stay calm. Do exactly what I tell you. No questions. Keep talking to me. In a second, I'm going to leave the room. No matter what, stay exactly where you are and pretend to keep talking to me." I smile brightly. "Got it? Act normal."

"But, Mom—"

I don't raise my voice, just my intensity. "Fucking listen!"

She jerks her head back. She's only heard me swear when I've had near misses while driving.

Where's my gun? Purse. "Say you're hungry. Now—say it."

"I'm h-hungry, Mom."

"Pasta or pizza," I say loudly, enunciating the syllables.

"Pizza."

As though an accident, I knock my purse to the ground and, out of sight from the window, kick it along the floor to the kitchen.

"Keep talking to me." I walk as naturally as I can to the kitchen, my legs heavy, a strange buzzing noise in my ears. The kitchen curtains are drawn. "As soon as I'm gone, put a timer on your phone. If I'm not back in thirty minutes, call the police."

"Mom!"

"Act normal. Laugh!"

Willow clutches her stomach, guffawing, her dark hair covering her face.

"I'm going now. In two minutes, yawn, act sleepy, then lie down." To block him from seeing her through the window.

In the kitchen, I take the gun out of my purse and—oh, dammit—it nearly slips out of my hands. I tuck it into the back of my pants. Grab my keys.

Plan A: Get a picture of the creep. To protect Willow—and myself. Once I have a picture, the police will know who to catch.

I shove my cell phone into a pocket and look at Willow one last time before slipping out the side door, making sure to lock it behind me.

*Momma Bear's a-coming.*

The minute I step out from the overhang, rain drenches my shoulders. No lights from the Gillaspies' windows next door. The screech of a car breaking in the distance.

I creep along the side of the house.

Adrenaline gives me laser-vision. I'm an animal hunting. All focus on capture.

Get his picture. Then run.

*Picture. Run.*

My heartbeat thrashes in my ears as I reach my backyard, scan left, then right. Where is he?

Not near the shed—the large lawn—the bushes.

It's disorientating, the rain too loud, too wet.

I'm about to move backward when I spot him.

He's standing behind our only tree, facing our living room. Maybe five-foot-eight, wearing a navy rain jacket, hood up. The bottom of his jeans is soaked.

Every part of me stills, except my mind.

*Picture. Run.*

I crouch behind a bush.

In profile, his face is hidden. He's not holding anything. His arms poised at his sides.

Our living room is lit up like a movie screen, everything on display. The artwork on the walls, my pineapple lamp, the back of the couch. My daughter. Willow yawns, stretches her arms, and lies down, disappearing from our sight.

*Good girl.*

Damn, from this angle, I can't get a good picture of him.

Plan A is out.

Plan B.

The pounding rain camouflages my breathing as I rise.

Three steps toward him.

I reach for my gun.

Two steps.

*Please, don't look back.*

One step.

I put the gun to the back of his head. "Who the fuck are you?"

# Chapter 47

# CREEP

"I'm not here to hurt you," he says.

"Who the fuck are you?" I repeat, pressing the barrel of my gun against his skin more firmly, the coaching from the teacher at the gun range coming to me in fragments.

*Keep your grip high and tight.*

I steady my shaking hand.

The man holds his arms away from his body in a gesture of submission. "Put the gun down."

*Get your stance right.*

I adjust my non-dominant foot slightly in front of my other foot. "Why were you looking through my window?"

"Someone paid me to watch you. That's it."

Now my whole body is shaking. "Who?"

"Can't say." I catch a slight accent, European sounding. He didn't sound like that when we were in the rideshare.

*Proper trigger squeeze/press.*

I shove the 9mm lower, right where his skull and spine connect, my fist knuckle joint pressed against the trigger. "You might want to rethink that." Rain splatters on my hand, making it harder to grip the gun.

"I'm a private eye. I don't rat out my clients. I'll stop following you, that's a promise."

"Who paid you?"

"Can't say. But I can prove who I am."

He goes to move his hand.

"Stop! I'll get it. Which pocket?"

"Back right."

I step closer, gun still at his head. He smells of onions, tobacco. I take out the leather wallet. There—a private eye license. I'll google him later.

Moving away, I lower the gun, my finger still firm against the trigger guard, his wallet open in my other hand.

"Turn around."

The instant he faces me, I recognize him—the rideshare driver. Was he the man at Fort Park reading the newspaper? The school janitor with the cap and worker's uniform? I can't tell.

I meet his eyes. Brown. Cold. Nondescript. A regular middle-aged man.

*Be brave for Willow.*

"No more watching me. Following me. Looking at my daughter through the window. Got it?"

"You'll never have a problem with me again."

"I'll make sure of that. Five steps back—hands in the air." He does as I say. "Now, I'm going to take a picture of you and your ID." With my left hand, I place his wallet open-faced on the grass. Still aiming the gun at him, I use my free hand to slide out my iPhone and snap a picture, first of the ID, then him. Rain splatters on the screen. I wipe the screen against my pants and take another shot before kicking the wallet his direction. "The police sure are going to be interested in this."

"They'll be interested in you carrying illegally," he says. "I know a lot of things about you. Best we both stay quiet."

What does he know? "How could you impersonate a rideshare driver?" Maternal rage fills me. Imagine him tricking other women—teenagers. "You can't do that to women."

"*You* got into my car. I wasn't trying to impersonate anyone. I knew there was a fundraising party at the Clarks. It was of interest to my client to find out who you left with."

"But you didn't take me home. You drove the wrong direction."

"When you started talking about personal stuff, I made sure the ride lasted longer."

Personal stuff. What was I taking about? The argument I had with Théo. Nathaniel visiting my mom with quiche Lorraine and not getting the drift I wasn't interested. Willow's cheer schedule.

He looks at me, stone faced. "Sorry you got scared."

I point to the back gate. "Don't ever come here again. Tell whoever's paying you to stop."

"You and your daughter don't need to be afraid. The guy behind this doesn't want you hurt." With that, he disappears into the back alley, movements silent and sure.

I glance back at the living room window. Willow—I shouldn't leave her alone. No other choice. His ID could be fake; I need his license plate.

After counting to sixty in my head, I follow him down the alley, keeping a half a block distance. He turns left at the end of the street. I hug the neighbors' gardens, close to the bushes. A few blocks away, he looks over both shoulders before getting into a gray or silver car that looks like a Honda. I take out my phone and, using one hand to shield it from the rain, press the camera icon, enlarge the screen. *Snap.*

Twenty minutes later, I reenter our house.

Willow runs to hug me, then jumps back. "Mom, you took forever. You're soaking."

I take off my wet jacket, hang it over a chair, my heart still beating erratically.

"What happened? I was so scared."

*Well, I stuck a gun to a man's head, and it went from there....* "Nothing I couldn't sort out." I yank the curtains closed. "I'm sorry I got spooked."

"Are you really doing this again?"

"What?"

"Lying to me?" she yells. "You never treat me like I'm old enough to know anything important!"

"I'm trying to protect you. It's my job."

She indicates the room, us. "It doesn't feel like protection. It feels like… crap. It's my life too."

Is she right?

We blindfold our children. Keep them as far away as possible from the adult world with its dangers, ugliness. We turn off the news so they don't hear about the woman raped and murdered while walking home from the train station, the child kidnapped on their way to school, the terrorist attacks.

We withhold information. Don't let them grow up too fast. But the joke's on us—that happens anyway.

Moms never know when to stop treating their children like babies.

The only way for them to grow up is to make their own mistakes.

I release a slow exhale. "All up, it's been a horrible night. You know what was the worst part?"

She shakes her head, face sullen.

"I never got a chance to buy ice cream."

It takes a moment. Then she says, "Bummer."

I laugh, a strangled snort, and lean against the wall, running a hand over my hair to squeeze off the excess water. "Willow, the world is a shitty place."

"Mom! What?"

Willow's right, she deserves to know. "We were being followed."

She gasps. "Seriously? By who?"

"A private eye. A man paid him to keep tabs on me, what I was up to, who I've been spending time with."

"Who hired him?"

"The million-dollar question. But I know who it was."

The person who asked for my mailing address to send Willow a birthday card.

The person who keeps trying to be with me despite my reluctance.

The person I was talking about when the "rideshare driver" went off course.

"My ex-boyfriend, Nathaniel."

"Why?"

"He's in love with me." When I say it out loud, it sounds stupid. Unreal. "I think he was having me followed to make sure I was safe."

Willow looks thoughtful. "Have I met him before?"

"He visited us in Alaska a few years ago and he was at Papa's funeral. He came to see me recently in Boca."

It all points to him. But what proof do I have?

I review our recent exchanges. Did he make any mistakes? Opening my phone, I scan our text history. Lunch at Oceans 234…oysters…visiting the local vineyards…him suggesting the restaurant, Hinita, adamant that he needed to know when I was coming to New York so he could reserve a table.

On a hunch, I google Hinita's number and place the call.

"No, miss," the woman answers my question. "We don't take bookings. Always first come, first serve."

So. A setup.

"Are you going to tell the police?" Willow asks.

"I'm not sure." Now that I've outed the PI, I don't think he's coming back. But that's wishful thinking. It's tempting to ask Brady what he thinks—but—no. I could call Nathaniel now, confront him. Or maybe book a flight to New York and do it in person.

Willow shivers. "Everything's too weird."

I grab her hand. "If anybody, any man, ever gives you the creeps, you tell me. Got it?" I've talked to her about this many times before, but now it feels more urgent.

Willow says, "Maybe there is something."

My heart sinks. And just after I let him get away. If that motherfucking asshole did something to her, I'll claw his eyeballs out, cut off his cock and feed it to him, and then burn his body. "Oh, really, sweetie? Do you feel like talking about it?"

She avoids looking at me. "I, uh, I guess."

"What happened?"

"So, it's probably nothing, but…"

"Yes?"

Straightening her posture, her expression is unreadable. “Um, this boy at school is a freak. He keeps staring at my chest.”

*Darling, I don’t believe you. What aren’t you telling me?*

# Chapter 48

# NOT MY DAUGHTER

The next night, I stand at the threshold of Willow's bedroom door. She's at Stella's for a sleepover. Ron is away for a work trip and Odelle said Stella would love the company; reading between the lines, she'd love having her daughter occupied so she can focus on herself. Either way, I'm grateful. I feel like I'm coming down with something; my bones ache and even though it's approaching dinnertime, the thought of food makes my stomach churn.

So does thinking about the PI in my backyard. I should've asked him how long he'd been tailing us: Anchorage, New York, Boca? Is he still a danger to us?

Hesitating, I reach for the doorknob, push open Willow's door, and walk to her bed.

Earlier, when I came in to grab laundry, I noticed she'd left her diary face down on her desk with a pen beside it.

Well aware that what I'm doing is wrong, I open her diary. I'm getting plenty of practice at acts of immorality lately, what's one more?

This morning, Brady left a pot of gardenias on my doorstep with a note: *Dear Bec, I'm sorry I've hurt you. Please let me explain what happened. Don't believe Odelle's lies. Please can we talk?*

*Not interested*, I thought, slamming the front door shut—and right now, I have more pressing matters.

I sit on Willow's bed.

Intention is everything and mine is pure. Isn't it a mother's right to cross lines she feels are necessary? To make sure her children are safe, physically and emotionally. Spiritually, even.

I flip open her diary to an early entry, dated from last November....

> **Mom is making me move to Florida!!! I don't want to go! She's so mean. My life is here. My friends are here. Everything is here. Why is she forcing me to go?**

A few pages later:

> **I miss Papa so much. (Secret! He was my favorite.) Whenever I told him that he'd smile and say, "Thanks, but don't tell your mom. It would hurt her feelings and she's the one who does all the hard work." That didn't make sense. HE was the one who shoveled the snow from the driveway. HE drove me to gymnastics and watched the whole time when all the other parents were on their phones. HE never cared if my room was messy. She's obsessed with germs and being neat and wanting us to be normal. Maybe we're not normal.**

*Obsessed? I am not.* Although I do prefer things in their proper place, clean surfaces, empty laundry baskets...okay, maybe I'm a bit obsessed. I'll try to ease off. Did she feel pressured to be normal even then? Another thing to add to the "bad mom" file. Are there moms, anywhere, patting their backs, congratulating themselves, "Did I ever do a good job today!" Maybe for five minutes. Until the next issue crops up and we lose our shit.

I sag against the headboard. My throat, sore. I'm definitely fighting something off. I skip to a more recent entry:

> **Alek Horvat is sooooo hot. He was looking at me in class today and—**

No, reading about her romantic feelings is a further invasion of privacy.

I flick to her account of camp, all of which I was aware of, but to read it in her own words—devastating. Then I scan some more recent entries:

> **I hung out with KISS today at lunch. When no one was looking, I asked Katia to pinch my thigh. She lifted my skirt and pinched it. She said, "Uh-uh, there's still too much fat. You can't come to the movies with us this weekend."**

That—that awful girl. Rage fills me. *Too much fat?* Poor Willow.

When I turn the next page, something falls out of the diary.

I pick it up from the carpet.

A picture of Willow in that red bathing suit, her bottom exposed. I remember the day, KISS were at Odelle's, "Girls Just Want to Have Fun" playing.

Why does Willow keep this in her diary?

I read the corresponding page that the picture fell out of.

> **... going through the junk drawer for candy hack stuff when I found this picture of me in a bathing suit. My bum looked HUGE. Stella said she found the photo in her dad's office! Why did her dad take the picture and keep it in his office? Weird. But I kinda like that he had it. It's nice he wanted something to remind him of me. Whenever I'm over, we talk, sit together, he asks tons of questions.**

An icy sensation comes over me as everything slots into place—Ron filming the girls doing their dance routine. Him secretly taking a picture of my daughter's bum and keeping it in his office. Odelle saying she found something on his computer, that he should be in jail....

He's a pervert! He's into girls, little girls—he's into Willow.

I drop the diary back in place, and run down the stairs, photo in hand. Whoa! I nearly miss the last step. I grab my purse, heavy with my 9mm, and call Odelle while rushing out the front door.

Dammit, her voicemail, but it's probably best to have the conversation in person.

I climb into the driver's seat. The sky is bruised, as though its heart is breaking.

As I gun the engine, I think of the PI, standing in my backyard in his rain jacket, the cuffs of his jeans soaking wet, and it occurs to me.

Maybe the PI only started trailing us when we moved here.

What if *Willow* was the target?

# Chapter 49

# SHOWERHEAD

Driving ten miles over the speed limit, I arrive at Odelle's before I can prepare what to say.

In the twilight, her mansion gleams like the freaking White House.

*Hurry.*

My sandals slap the sidewalk as I run up the walkway and ring the bell, the photograph of Willow in my purse.

I wait a minute, then ring again. Could they have gone out?

If Stella were in the same situation, Odelle would want an open, frank conversation. Of course, Odelle will probably start off being defensive but then—

Footsteps approach.

The door opens and Ron Wragge stands before me in chinos and a Polo shirt.

What. The. Actual. Hell.

"Uh, hi." He was supposed to be traveling; Odelle told me he was away for the next few days. If I hadn't looked through Willow's diary today and found the picture…God—I shudder—Willow would've been with him all night.

"How are you?" Ron asks in a pleasant tone. His eerily pale blue eyes are creepy. How could I have not noticed that before?

"Great." I smile, jutting out a hip like everything's super casual. "Where's Odelle?"

"Yoga."

Meaning the girls were alone with him. For how long? Did he do anything to Willow?

"Um, well, I need to talk to Willow about her homework."

A muscle in his jaw twitches. "I'll get her. Just a moment."

Odd. Why isn't he letting me in the house?

*Willow*, I want to scream. *Get out!*

"I need the bathroom, so I'll just come in if that's okay." I squeeze my legs for effect and say in a singsong voice, "Nature calls."

He gestures inside. "After you."

My nose is suddenly runny. I sniff as we walk down the hall, past the first living room, the movie room, the multipurpose office. My senses are alert for signs of the girls. The only thing I can hear is the news blaring from the TV in the kitchen. Although Willow's stuff isn't anywhere, it looks like they were doing art earlier because one of the tables is covered in paper and felt pens.

In the bathroom, I wait a minute, then flush the toilet.

Time to get my girl out of this house.

When I enter the kitchen, both girls are sitting on stools, talking to Ron.

"Pizza, definitely, with cheesy crusts," Stella says. Her KISS necklace stands out against her white crop top. So it's back on.

"I'm fine with whatever." Willow shrugs.

Ron says, "We're deciding what to order for dinner. It's a tough choice."

My pulse triples. *Oh, that will not be happening.*

"What do you order for Odelle? Steamed kale?" I ask playfully, but it's a segue to the more important question. "Will she be home soon?"

"Any minute."

Oh. In that case, should I talk to her now? No—I'll take Willow home and arrange a coffee with Odelle first thing in the morning when Ron isn't around.

Ron offers me a placid smile. "I always order Odelle dessert. She indulges, and I get to be the bad guy."

*You said it, asshole.*

"Mom loves chocolate pizzas," Stella says. "But not as much as meeee!" She stands in front of Ron, beaming up at him.

"Excuse me," he says. "I have to get my wallet. I think I left it in the car in the garage."

"Why are you here?" Willow asks me once Ron leaves the room.

"Because...." My center of gravity is off, my body weak. It must be the flu. Snot dribbles from my nose. I grab a tissue from the box.

"Hello, peeps." Odelle's voice carries down the hallway. She sees me first, pausing mid-stride, her gym clothes ringed with sweat marks. "Becks?"

Now that she's actually here, my body takes over. I speed-walk to her side and whisper, "Odelle, I need to talk to you privately. Please. It's urgent." I can't sleep tonight without telling my friend what I know.

She raises her eyebrows at the same time as Ron reenters the room, wallet in hand.

"I didn't hear you come in," Ron says to Odelle. "We're just about to order dinner."

"I already had dinner—oxygen—at Bikram yoga." She laughs. "Sorry, darlings, Becks and I need a word about Art Synergy. Mom duties never end. Follow me, Becks."

With a last glance at Willow, I grab another tissue and follow Odelle until we reach her master bathroom, far away from the kitchen in a separate wing.

"Odelle, can you lock the door?"

She gives me a sidelong glance. "So dramatic."

"Why are we in your bathroom?"

"Because I'm sweaty." She locks the door and then peels off her Lycra shorts and a pink T-shirt, flinging her bra and underwear into the laundry hamper.

My jaw hinges open.

"What?" Odelle steps into the shower, her tanned, muscular (and, I can't help noticing, pubic-hair-free) body looking damn fine for a woman who, according to what she told me last week, is perimenopausal. "Talk. I'm multitasking. After this, I have some last-minute calls about a hen's night I'm overseeing tomorrow."

"I'm not talking to you while you wash yourself."

"Picky." She frowns. "You never used to mind."

I blush and take a seat at her vanity area. Fine. There was this one time when we were teenagers, and she taught me to orgasm. Even though, by that stage, I'd had a sexual partner, I never felt enough abandon to have the big O. "It's all about the tools," Odelle had coached me. "If you don't have a beaded rabbit, a showerhead is the way to go." And she'd shown me, parted her legs as the water steamed over her body, angling the showerhead just so, then climaxed before my transfixed eyes.

I rearrange her jars of makeup brushes. "Can you hurry up?"

"I need to leave my conditioner on for at least three minutes."

"Not tonight."

Once she's toweled and dried, we sit together on the edge of her bed.

"What's this all about?" she asks. "Not Brady, I hope?"

"I, uh…." Unable to find the right words, I dig into my purse and take out the photo of Willow in her bathing suit, pushing it into Odelle's hands. "This was taken at your house. Do you remember that day?"

She crinkles her nose.

"The picture was found in a very strange place."

"Where?" she asks, her voice small, fragile.

"Stella told Willow she found it in Ron's office."

Odelle takes a small intake of air. Her hand rises to her bare collarbone, above her towel-wrapped torso.

I look her in the eye. "We're mothers, Odelle. Our number one job is to protect our girls, right?"

Her pupils dilate.

"You said you found something on Ron's computer…." I push on.

She turns away.

"You said he belongs in jail." I grab her limp arms, my fingers pinching into her skin. "Let me help you. Tell me what you know. We can get his computer. We can stop him."

Her eyelids flicker, open, closed, open, closed.

"Odelle?"

Open, closed. Open, closed.

I wave my hand in front of her face.

I'm wondering what to do with her when she stands. "Fucking ridiculous," she barks. "I don't like what you're implying. Lucy is back from school tomorrow and I won't have you wreck everything."

I rise too, desperate to understand. "Did what was on Ron's computer have anything to do with this picture? Is he—"

"Stop!" She faces me, her eyes dark slits.

"Explain what's going on. Please, Odelle. It's my daughter."

"Maybe *you* should explain your accusation to my husband. Let him defend himself." Redness spreads over her décolletage. "Someone else could've taken the picture. Until you have proof, this is defamation. And guess what, my law background still comes in handy when people screw with my family." She opens her wardrobe, her back to me. "See yourself out. It goes without saying, no more playdates for the girls."

# Chapter 50

# I HATE YOU

Downstairs, I maneuver past Ron and Stella and collect Willow from the kitchen, making up an excuse about an emergency at home.

"Mom, why are we leaving?" Willow demands once we're in the car and I'm reversing out of the driveway. "What emergency?"

"It's nothing—I—I needed you to leave that house." Hands aching, I grip the wheel, my thoughts moving so fast that before one finishes, another takes its place. I speed down the night streets, the sky moonless.

Boca is asleep, barely a car on the road.

"Why can't I have a sleepover? You said I could." She's furious. I don't blame her.

"Are you okay, Willow? Did anything happen?"

"I'm fine! Why did I have to leave?"

"It's Stella's dad," I blurt out. "I understand Stella's your best friend, and you don't want to rock the boat but, baby, the ship is sinking."

"What are you talking about? Stella's already really sad. I can't just leave her house. What am I supposed to tell her?"

I screech to a break at the red light.

"Tell Stella—I don't know—there was a gas leak, a small fire."

"You always make me lie." She raises her chin.

"I don't!"

"Did anything happen with Stella's dad? Did he…act strange?"

"No. You're so weird for even saying that."

I begin to ask another question, but she cuts me off. "I'm not talking to you. I'm not telling you anything after you ruined my night. I hate you!"

She crosses her arms.

We're in for a long night. Her silent treatment can last as long as her dad's used to, a family trait.

When I pull into the drive, there, across the street, in his truck: Brady.

What's he doing here?

I glance at Willow; she's hasn't noticed.

We get out of the car. Feeling faint, sicker than I was before I started the drive, I nearly trip on a stone on the walkway. I turn to Willow. There's no point trying to talk to her until she's cooled down. "Honey, go inside, please. I need to do something."

"Do what?"

"I'll talk to you inside."

She stomps up the steps, slams the door.

I walk over to Brady's truck.

He lowers the window.

"This isn't a good time," I say to Brady. Collapsing in bed and sleeping for the next twenty-four hours is all I feel up to.

"I just need five minutes."

"You can have two. Why are you here?" I ask, feverish, my arms, shoulders, and head heavy. Odelle, Ron, now him. I don't know how much more I can take.

"To tell my side of the story. But—are you—you don't look well."

I don't care about his side of the story. I have too much on my goddamn plate to deal with a lost boy disguised as a man.

"Please, Bec. Hear me out. Will you come and talk in the car?"

"No." I remain standing.

"Odelle filled your head with lies." He grimaces. "I never dated her. But I should've come clean about our history."

"You think?" I bite back with sarcasm.

"I'm sorry. I regret it more than anything."

"Why didn't you tell me?" The question comes out lackluster. I don't care. This is the wrong time. My love life—or lack thereof—is nothing compared to what Willow's dealing with.

He steeples his hands, facing me. "I was respecting Odelle's privacy, her family. I figured it was up to her to tell you, and if she didn't, that's because she didn't want anyone to know I rejected her."

I'm only half listening. I need to talk to Willow.

"Odelle claimed she was in love with me. One night, we were planning the Autism Awesome party, and we'd had a few drinks. She kissed me—I told her no. It couldn't happen because I was the head of school."

"So, *that's* the reason? You wanted to go further with her but—"

"No, it was a soft rejection. She didn't get the hint, so later I told her, point blank, I'm not interested."

The streetlights shine on the residential street, manicured walkways, and palm trees.

"Why were you at her house when you told me you were at band practice?"

"Odelle called and said, without me, she, ah, didn't want to live." He looks away with a squeamish expression. "So I checked on her before practice. She often calls, depressed, unable to keep going, begging me to visit."

Was it true? Was Odelle suicidal? Or playing the sympathy card? Either way, I've got bigger problems.

The hum of a neighbor's garage door opening distracts me.

"Odelle told me Ron and she were separated, that they hadn't been a proper couple for years, they were keeping appearances for the sake of the kids. You gotta know, I'd never be with a married woman. Especially not a married mother from my school."

"But you told me Ron practically set up the whole thing between you and Odelle."

"I don't know why he did that."

*Mmm, I do. Distract Odelle so he could focus on his perversions.*

I shove my hands in my pockets. "I have to go in."

"I understand. Bec, please, I'm sorry. We can work it out."

"Don't waste your breath. You and I—we're not important. Nothing that happened between us matters. It was sex, that's all."

He winces, then goes very still. "I get you're hurt, but that's harsh."

"It's the truth. You're a young man making mistakes. I'm a *mom*, making bigger ones with consequences you'll never understand. I'm going."

"Wait, Bec. I'm camping with Paddy next week and I'll be out of range."

"During the school term?"

"He needs me. Can I visit you again when I get back? Talk some more. You might have given up on us, but I haven't."

I turn around, hiding my face so he can't read my hesitation, the small flame of belief that maybe he's telling the truth.

"Goodbye, Brady."

Once inside, I beeline to Willow's bedroom and knock on her door.

No answer.

"C'mon. I need to talk to you."

"Go away," she yells. "I hate you. I'm never talking to you again."

# Chapter 51

# LA PRAIRIE

Even though everything's falling apart, and now Willow and I both have the flu, we need to eat. We've spent most of the day sleeping in our separate rooms. I keep trying to broach the subject of Ron, but only get the silent treatment. Time for the big guns.

I place two bowls of Campbell's chicken noodle soup on the dining room table, dressing it up with sourdough toast on pretty ceramic plates.

"Come on, Willow. Eat up."

Eventually she rolls off the couch and trudges to the table, trailing Théo's blanket over her shoulders like a bridal train.

We're both still in our pajamas.

"Don't spill soup on the blanket, okay?" I mentally scold myself; after all, I'm supposed to be reforming my neat-freak tendencies.

The scent of gardenias pulls my gaze to the pot of flowers on the kitchen counter, and I wonder if what Brady told me about Odelle last night was true. But why should I take the word of a man who already lied to me? I'm through with lies, my lies, telling Willow to lie after Théo's death, Brady's lies. All of it.

"I'm not hungry." Willow sighs from across the table.

After reading her diary, I'm on the lookout for moments like this. Although I've requested an appointment with a psychologist who specialize in body issues and eating disorders, as of now, Willow is still on the waiting list. "You haven't been very hungry lately."

"So? I'm sick."

I swallow the gluggy soup and force myself to continue. "I've noticed you're not eating as much as you normally do. Is there anything you want to tell me?" *Such as your frenemy measuring the fat on your thigh to determine entry into her clique?*

Owning up to invading her privacy and reading her diary is only going to damage our relationship, and I'll avoid it if I can help it.

Willow slurps the soup.

I've texted Paulita twice asking if we could speak on the phone, but she hasn't replied. Her daughter can't keep getting away with such damaging behavior.

"C'mon, you can talk to me."

Willow drops her spoon on the table. "Can I really?" Sarcasm to the max, and our conversation is only going to get worse.

"Why aren't you eating? Is this a calorie thing again? Those messages with Katia?"

She doesn't answer.

A chill sweeps over my body. I wait a few moments until I stop shivering, knowing full well that what I'm about to say could damage our relationship, destroying all trust. "I'm really sorry, Willow, I was tidying your room yesterday, and I knocked over your diary. A picture fell out. A strange one, a closeup of your bum. I put it back in your diary, and I—I saw the name 'Ron.' Darling, I'm sorry, I just read a tiny section."

"You what?" she says, nostrils flared. "It's private! You shouldn't have done that!"

"I know. Please forgive me. I won't do it again. We need to talk about Stella's dad. I didn't realize you'd become close."

Willow lowers her eyes.

"Honey?"

She remains silent.

"If Papa was here now, he'd be asking the same question. We need to know. He'd be worried about you."

Willow traces the wooden grooves of the table with her forefinger.

The clock ticks, too loud, drumming in my ears.

"Stella's dad is just nice to me, Mom."

*Tick tock tick tock.*

"Nice how?"

"…I guess one weird thing happened. Last night just before you came over, Stella was in her room finishing her homework, and he asked me if I wanted to help him with something."

"With what?"

"A present for Odelle. He said he bought her some fancy cream. La Prairie skin caviar. It costs $485 a bottle! He said, 'try it.'"

"Where were you?"

"In his office."

"Were you alone?"

"Mm-hm. He didn't want Stella to blow the surprise."

"And?" My entire body braces.

"He said it would be a good idea for me to lie down so he could show me where to put the cream and do a trial test."

Oh, Jesus. My heart gallops in my throat. She'd already had good touch/bad touch conversations, both at school and at home. Why didn't those lessons stick?

"I lay back and Ron said, 'You place a tiny amount onto your ring finger, and dab the cream under your eyes, like this. Then put the cream onto your face in small dots.' He put it on my face. Then he said, 'Gently massage the cream into your skin using small, upward motions. The apple of your cheeks."

*No, no.* "Keep going, darling."

"He put some cream on my neck and asked how it felt. I said it felt like silk. He said, 'You feel like silk.' Then he asked if he could put it somewhere else on my body. But I said I thought I heard Stella calling me and left the room."

I take her hand. "Why didn't you tell me?" How could I be so in the dark? Of course, in hindsight, she was the perfect victim. Fatherless. Grieving. Insecure. Hungry for male attention.

"Coz he said you'd get mad and adults would never understand our special relationship."

*Oh God. Fuck. Oh Fuck.*

"Mom?"

My temples throb, the room closing in. "Is there anything else about Stella's dad that you haven't told me? Anything he said or did?"

"You know everything."

"I'm going to get my laptop now, and if you can tell me everything again, I'll write it down. I know it's hard but it's important. Stay here, okay?"

Once I'm in my room with the door locked, I place a call to the local police station, and give them an abbreviated version of events. We set up an appointment for the morning, 9:00 a.m.

I return to the table and, as Willow recounts what happened, type it into a Word file.

"You need to understand, it's wrong when male adults go out of their way to befriend young girls." I lean forward and pull a strand of hair off her forehead. "You've done nothing wrong. Ron's intentions weren't good. I hope you understand, you're never going to Stella's house again."

Her eyes glisten with tears. "But Stella stood up for me. She risked everything."

"What do you mean?"

"Stella told Katia to stop being nasty to me—but now they're sending her the meanest messages."

"Like what?"

"Bitch. Slut. Justin Bieber hates fatties. Go hug yourself...with a rope."

"I'm so sorry." My heart breaks for Stella, for Willow, for all the girls who are at the mercy of twenty-four-hour social media, where bullying never stops. "Did you see the messages?"

"Stella recorded them in her notebook, you know, for our homework assignment."

"Did she hand it in to her teacher?"

"She gave one list to the teacher and kept the *real* list for herself."

My head swims. “You poor girls.” I start crying, sniveling over the fat blobs of gray chicken floating in the soup. I’ll have to let Odelle know. “Why don’t you girls tell Katia to go to hell?”

“…she has stuff on us.”

“Stuff?”

“Katia gets us to make videos to prove we’re loyal to KISS.”

“What kind of videos?” Sex tapes? Adolescent porn? God, what?

“Mine was lip-syncing a rap song and twerking.” She cringes, tears falling down her cheeks. “Some of the other girls’ ones are really bad.”

“How bad?” I ask, relieved that Willow’s video only involved twerking.

“I don’t know.”

Willow rises and stands beside me, stroking my hair. Looking at her now, in her unicorn pajamas, innocent and wise, she looks like an angel.

“This isn’t right. I’m supposed to be comforting *you*.” What would Théo say if he could see us now? I’m a failure at the one thing that matters most. Her dad’s dead, I’m all Willow’s got, and I’m utterly useless.

Hiding my face in my hands, I choke back sobs.

“It’s okay. It’s okay,” she repeats softly.

I let the tears come, the hurt from deep inside, erupting.

“Mom?”

Her voice is a dream and I’m back in our Anchorage house, waking up to my worst nightmare.

# Chapter 52

# CHICKEN

*I turn over in our bed and feel for Théo.*

*Where is he?*

*I lift my head, listening for him in the bathroom. No noise except the rain on the roof. Yawning, I pull the comforter closer and snuggle into the pillow.*

*Then it hits me—the Nembutal. It's not in my hands. I jolt up, flick on the lights, search under the comforter, sliding my hands along the sheets. Did I drop it? I get onto my knees, look under the bed. Nothing!*

*"Théo?" I call out, panic tightening my throat. Maybe he's slept in Willow's room. He must be there, sleeping soundly, his arm around her, as he does some nights when he's in a blue mood.*

*I hurry down the hall. It smells like popcorn and music is playing, faintly, a crooning sound. What time is it? Why is music playing? I enter the living room—*

*Théo's sitting on the couch, his eyes open, but even from here, from across the room, it's brutally obvious.*

*No!*

*Please, no!*

*I take two steps forward, pause. Another step.*

*Leonard Cohen is on the iPod. Théo's favorite song.*

*Touch him, Rebecca. Touch his wrist.*

*Cold, his skin feels like flesh, like meat, not like my husband. No pulse….*

*My God.*

*"Théo," I whimper.*

*I put my arms around his shoulders, rest my head on his chest.*

*Let there be a heartbeat.*

*Nothing. No warmth. It's—it's not him anymore.*

*Pain crushes me. I bend over, punched in the stomach. I can barely see through the thick film of tears.*

*Why did he break our pact?*

*When I glance back at Théo, he's smiling, his blank stare…no, I can't look.*

*The music keeps playing, the smell of popcorn, and his dead body.*

*I gently close his eyelids.*

*If only he was sleeping. If only….*

*I grip the coffee table, gravity pulling me to the floor.*

"Mom?" Willow's hands are on either side of my face.

The kitchen lights too bright. The spoon still in my hand. The horrible smell of cold chicken soup.

"Mom, why are you making that scary sound?"

Some area of my brain registers Willow's speaking to me: that my body is in the future and my heart is in the past. I drift back….

*On the coffee table, beside the remote control, the evidence. The blue Ziploc bag. A glass of water. An empty port glass. I remember him telling me alcohol helps the efficacy of Nembutal.*

*I clutch my head, rocking back and forth. Our pact—he promised he wouldn't do it without telling me. How could he betray me?*

*His phone's resting on his lap.*

*Pick it up, Rebecca.*

*I search for his last sent message. There, sent to me at 9:37 p.m. My heart beats so loud it hurts. I open the text:*

***It's not Willow's fault. Pour tous jours.***

*Willow's fault?*

*Our sweet girl, two rooms away—she can't come out. I dig my hands into the thick rug. What am I going to tell her? Her papa's gone. He's never coming back. I retch over and over again.*

*What did he mean—not Willow's fault?*

*Stand, Rebecca. Go to her room.*

*Willow's fast asleep in her bed.*

*Crouching beside her, I give her a gentle nudge. "Honey, wake up." I wait a few moments and try again.*

*She rubs her cheek and slowly opens her eyes.*

*"Did anything happen with Papa before I went to sleep?" I whisper.*

*"Is he okay?"*

*Hysteria rises in my chest. Ludicrous. How far he was from okay. His cold hand, his peaceful smile.*

*"Mom?"*

*"Just tell me every detail about what happened after I went to bed last night. Because, um, Papa said something you told him would, ah, be great for one of his stories. Try to remember everything."*

"Sweat is all over your face," Willow says to me.

I yawn, as though coming out of a spell. Out the kitchen window, the sky is blue. An hour or two left of daylight.

"I think you're really sick. Should we go to a doctor?"

"I need to remember." I need to go back to her bedroom....

*"What happened after I went to bed last night?"*

*"We were watching Mr. Bean," Willow explains. "His tummy hurt. I gave him antacid."*

*"Antacid? What kind?" I ask, crouched at her bedside.*

*"You know how Papa's nurse brings him a big container of that powder?"*

*I nod. "Sodium bicarbonate." It was supposed to have cancer-fighting qualities, and because of his hypogeusia, he didn't mind the taste.*

*"There wasn't any in the container." She sits against the headboard. "Papa told me to look for the blue Ziploc baggies that the nurse made for him for when he travels.*

*But—what? I didn't know she did that.*

*My brain moves slowly, slotting the pieces together.*

*I gasp, shocks of pain...anguish swirling in my stomach. Now it makes sense.*

*"Did I do something wrong?" Willow asks.*

*"No, sweetie." I stroke her forehead, watching her chest rise and fall. Unlike Théo's. Flat, lifeless, a body without breath.*

*The truth is he wanted to die. He got what he wanted. Now it was up to me to get rid of the incriminating evidence. Fingerprints on the Nembutal. Théo's text saying it wasn't Willow's fault.*

*"I'm going to give you something to make you sleepy. When you wake up, you'll feel groggy, but I'm going to be with you, okay?"*

*Once upstairs, I break one of my sleeping pills in half. Return to her room, pass her a glass of water. "Take it."*

*"But—"*

*"Now."*

*I make sure she swallows it. "Okay, lie back down."*

*After a few minutes pass, her head drops to the side. Her eyelids shut. She looks cherubic. Trusting. Her last sleep with two parents.*

*I make a silent promise: I will never let her know she accidentally killed her father.*

*I pull the comforter up under her chin. Her gymnastics clock ticks in the darkness, the legs splitting, second by second, around the balance beam.*

Now, only half aware of what's going on, I let Willow pull me up from the kitchen table. She leads me into my room. I take off my pants and socks, leaving my pajama top and underwear on.

"Get into bed, Momma."

The bed feels like earth, like a lake, like dirt, under the ground where he lays.

"Maybe Papa's blanket will help," Willow says.

Sometime later, she whispers, "Here." Heaviness over my chest.

Then she is gone.

A noise. The room turns black. She slips into bed with me, her body curved against mine, my little spoon, our breathing fills the space, hers calm, mine stifled.

I clutch her hand, reaching for life.

In limbo, time stretches out, suspended. Minutes pass. How long? An hour? Half an hour? My body is drenched in sweat, my ears and eyelids, a furnace. It's like I'm spinning, the bed a magic carpet ride. Odelle, naked in the shower, dances before me. Ron's eerily impassive blue eyes, rubbing cream into the apple of Willow's cheeks. The diary with the silver lock. The smell of onions. Katia pinching Willow's thigh to check for fat.

How dare Paulita ignore my texts.

I sit up in bed. No longer hot, now cold, terribly cold. Yes, I know what I have to do. I check my bedside alarm. With the movement, nausea slams me.

"Sweetie, I forgot, I have to go somewhere."

"Okay," Willow mumbles in her sleep.

Swinging my legs over the bed, I open the door a crack. From the light of the hallway, I get dressed. As I bend to put on my runners, I nearly topple over.

In the kitchen, I grab my purse, aware of the weight of the gun, Katia's face burning in my mind.

Sick or not, it's time for another house call.

# Chapter 53

# GIAVANNA

Once I park in front of Paulita's Le Lac mansion, instead of getting out, I rest my head on the steering wheel, waiting for the dizziness to pass. What is wrong with my car? The whole way here it kept making a metal-on-metal scraping sound and the engine warning lit up on my dashboard.

*Breathe.* I'm bloated and—is there a bag in here I can use in case I vomit?

Paulita's palatial estate is lit up against the night river. I'm hit with second thoughts. Maybe I should have called?

"Hi, it's about your daughter, could we meet?" A café, in public, sharing our gripes over skinny caps.

"Your daughter has given my daughter an eating disorder."

"My daughter?" [Insert look of shocked horror.]

"Yes, your daughter. I blame you for raising such a bitch."

All the café people, the bearded hipster baristas, the university students with their laptops, the nanny with the sleeping baby, looking up, afraid of gunfire. Don't they know there's nothing more brutal than mom warfare? Everything's nice in Mommyland ("Do you want me to pick them up and drive them there? No problem." "Playdate at my house—Wednesday? Perfect!") until your child gets hurt. Left out. Bullied.

No. I heave myself out of the car, the cool evening air tingling on my cheeks. It's better to show up and catch Paulita unaware before she has time to prepare her answers and get a defense strategy in place. The next-door neighbors are watching over Willow for an hour.

I walk to the doorway and press the buzzer.

Anxiety knots my empty stomach.

The unmistakable *click-click-click* of high heels.

The former Miss South Florida answers the door. Giavanna's chestnut hair, straightened, reaches her waist, and her curves are what boys dream about. A Latina Kardashian in rolled-up jeans and a tank top. How old is she, early twenties? Paulita mentioned she was halfway through college. Looking at her now, it's hard to imagine Brady finding her sleeping on the music room floor, all the turmoil she faced at sixteen years of age.

Giavanna gives me a confused look. Oh shoot, am I staring?

"Hi, I'm a friend of your mom's—"

"They're getting everything ready in the living room." She tussles her hair, a practiced move. "Where's your luggage?"

"I—um—don't have any."

As Giavanna leads me down the mega hall, a shrine to herself, it's impossible not to imagine Katia walking down this hall every day, enclosed by photograph after photograph of her older sister. No wonder she has issues. But there's no reason for her to take her issues out on my daughter.

I look down—my outfit is horribly wrong: jogging pants with holes in the knees, striped pajama top, old sneakers. What was I thinking?

As we go further into the house, women's voices grow louder.

Giavanna opens the door to the stately living room. "Mom, your friend is here."

...So is everybody else. Paulita, Deisha, Fi, Odelle.

It takes me a moment to figure out what's happening.

Suitcases lined up by the door, two, open-faced on the coffee table; outfits strewn over the couch, sun hats.

The St. Augustine trip is—this weekend—was it? I'm so confused. The days blending together. I'd forgotten all about it and I guess they'd forgotten all about me.... Why are they leaving so late? It feels like midnight, although it must be closer to 9:00 p.m.

"Um." Paulita steps forward. "Rebecca, hi? What's going on?"

I pull back my greasy, unbrushed hair. "I—uh—I know what this looks like. I don't care about your girls' trip."

Their eyes ping-pong back and forth, sensing trouble.

"No, I really don't care," I say again, which makes it sound like the opposite, as though I'm a psycho mom on the loose, and I've stormed her house to scream: *Don't leave me out! Include me!*

Fi offers a weak smile. "We just thought…since our girls are having a bit of trouble…it might be awkward for you."

"For me?" I snap, a metallic taste in my mouth. "You were worried about me? How kind of you." I fist my hands, self-righteousness raging hotter than my fever.

"Rebecca, you don't look well," Fi says.

"I have the flu."

Fi and Paulita step back, worried my germs will ruin their getaway.

The fountains outside, circling the pool, make an incessant babbling sound. God, how does she live with that? It would drive me crazy.

"What's this all about?" Paulita asks. Her body language is relaxed, but her eyes are warning me to get the hell out of her house. The mayor-to-be doesn't want a scene.

"It's about Willow," I say.

A hush sweeps over the room.

*…and all the other girls who may have been harmed by Ron.*

*…not to mention the horrible messages their daughters are sending Stella.*

I glance at Odelle; awfully quiet, isn't she? Standing there like an innocent onlooker. In fact, I've never seen her so quiet in my goddamn life. Is she going to tell them, or am I?

Deisha, who is sitting on the couch, a bathing suit folded on her lap, makes a disapproving sound.

"Perhaps this isn't the best time," Paulita says, checking her watch. "We have to get going."

"Don't let me hold you up," I scoff. "I mean, I wouldn't want my daughter's mental health to stand in the way of your wine tasting. Wasn't that the plan, ladies? Day one, Michael's Tasting Room; day two, a massage and facials at Casa Monica Spa, followed by heart-to-hearts. But since I'm not there, you can all just talk about me."

Fi's hand flies to her mouth.

"This is uncalled for," Deisha says.

The energy in the room is electric. *The Real Housewives of Boca Raton* playing out before them.

"Like I said," Paulita's eyes swing toward the door, "we have to go. So…."

"Oh, I get it. Sure. Enjoy your holiday. Thanks so much for ignoring my texts."

Paulita makes a scoffing sound.

Fi cautiously approaches, her hand lifted. "Rebecca, you've been under a lot of stress. The so-called man following you, buying a gun—Odelle told us about that—accusing our girls of things they haven't done. Odelle said you're jealous because our daughters are popular."

I see what's going on. Odelle's poisoning them against me, so I don't have a chance to destroy her husband's name. I turn to her, the traitor, the coward. "She speaks. Anything else you wanna share, Odelle? Or is this all about exposing my dirty secrets, not your own…or your family's?"

Odelle pulls back her lips, baring her teeth.

Deisha rises from the couch. "Let's go, ladies. This is trashy. Continue the conversation another time. I won't be there because none of this concerns me."

"It concerns all of you," I yell.

They freeze—staring at me bug-eyed like I'm armed and dangerous.

Ha! I am armed! The gun in my purse. Another wave of heat consumes me. Hunching over, I start laughing, my body damp with perspiration, my laughter sounding strange even to me. The laughter turns to choking. I hack into my elbow, leaning my other arm onto the couch for support. I'm too unwell to be out warring, to be fighting battles that can't be won. To protect their daughters, should I tell them about Ron? No, too cruel, too public. I'll inform the police in the morning about which girls have spent time at Odelle's.

Their voices blur in the background,

"The driver's already here...."

"...extremely irrational."

"Should we call someone?"

"...but if we do that...

"...medicated?"

"Shut up." Did I say that out loud or in my head? "Here's an update. Willow's not eating. She thinks she needs to lose weight. Why?"

They stand there, silent.

"Ask me why." I clench my teeth so hard my jaw hurts.

It's Fi who speaks. "Okay, Rebecca, why isn't she eating?"

"Because Katia told her to pinch her thigh. Katia said if there was fat on her thigh, she couldn't spend time with the girls. And now my daughter's stopped eating."

"Willow needs professional help," Deisha says. "We're all responsible for our own behavior."

I stand squarely in front of Paulita. "*Katia* needs help. There are videos of Willow—that your daughter—is keeping as collateral. That's what Katia does to prove the girls' loyalty. Collects videos of all the girls. It's sick."

Paulita says, "I'm sure it's just a joke. There are two sides to every story."

"No, there's one side. A mother protecting her daughter." I look Paulita in the eye. "I'm sure *you* know all about that."

She frowns. I've hit a nerve.

Paulita jabs her finger at me. "I won't have you going around bad-mouthing Katia."

"More like you're worried about getting bad-mouthed yourself," I shoot back. "Not great press having an anorexia-pushing bully for a daughter and a...."

On my lips: *A teen pregnancy with a drug dealer dad for another.*

"Go!" Paulita flicks her hand toward the door.

I grip the strap of my purse, the weight of the gun knocking against my thigh. I tried doing this the proper way. I tried talking. Being transparent. It's not working with the KISS mothers because they're too busy protecting themselves and their precious daughters.

Slowly, I size up each of them, these women who used to be my friends. "The truth is, you're all to blame. If you look the other way and don't interfere, you're saying it's okay to treat girls like shit. Do you know what your girls have done?" I yell. "The awful messages they're sending Stella? It has to stop. It has to fucking stop. It's not like when we were kids, an argument in the schoolground; no, these girls are getting bullied constantly. When they wake up, when they eat dinner, when they bathe. Horrible, nasty messages!"

"You're not making any sense," Paulita says.

Fi clasps her hands. "She needs to be at home resting."

"Or a mental hospital," Odelle mutters.

"Nice! Pathologize the woman. Can't you think of something more original?" I head toward the hall, then turn back. "Wait until it's one of your girls. Just fucking wait! Then you won't be off, sipping merlot on a girls' trip, will you?"

By blasting them like this, Willow and I are both firmly cemented on the wrong side of the gated community. But I don't care.

"Bye, Becks." Odelle lifts her hand in a dismissive wave. "Are you going to have sex with Mr. Brady now?"

*Gasps*! The moms all breathe in at exactly the same time.

As though hit by a bullet, I lift a hand to my chest. "I…I…."

The moms squint at me, waiting for my comeback, my big, awful confession to verify how messed up I am, and by association how messed up my daughter is, so they can justify what their daughters did.

"You know what?" I say to Odelle. "He's all yours since you claim you two were so in love." *Have him and your pedophile husband.*

Fi looks from me to Odelle, her blue eyes wide. "Let me get this straight, you were both seeing Mr. Brady?"

"*Hijo de puta*!" Paulita swears in Spanish. "Disgraceful. I'm going to see that he's fired and pushed out of Boca."

Someone breaks into a heaving sob.

We all turn toward the door.

It's Giavanna, shoulders curled over her chest, tears sliding down her angular cheekbones.

"What's wrong with your daughter?" Fi asks Paulita.

"Nothing. She's perfect," she snaps as Giavanna rushes toward the door.

I'm not listening to anything they're saying. I need to go to bed.

# Chapter 54

# WAIT FOR ME

"Willow?" I walk inside and drop my leather portfolio case onto the entrance side table.

Hearing nothing, I kick off my high heels. Wearing a tight camel-brown dress, belted, with four-inch heels all day in back-to-back meetings is not my idea of fun, but at least I'm not sick anymore. After the blowout at Paulita's and speaking to the police about Ron the following day, for the last few days, I've kept my head down and concentrated on work and Willow. Even Brady, who's back from camping in Orlando and left another note and a pot of flowers at my door, hasn't distracted me.

The police recorded my account of everything that Willow told me. That afternoon, I took Willow to the local Child Advocacy Center, and a social worker trained in child forensic interviewing spoke to her for about an hour, while the detective, via CCTV, viewed from another room. Afterward, I was told not to discuss the case with anyone. As for the next steps, they said, given the other information they had, swift action would be taken.

"Hello?" I call as I walk down the hall. I didn't expect to be home so late, but there were a few hiccups. Namely, getting my car serviced turned into them needing my car for a few days. "Willow? Hannah? Anyone home?"

Willow's English tutor, Hannah, had offered to pick Willow up from school and take her home for an hour of tutoring.

The house is a mess. The kitchen counter covered in dirty plates, a jar of peanut butter uncapped, half-finished glasses of orange juice. In the living room, I spy discarded items from Willow's dress-up box: a felt pig's head, tattered butterfly wings, beads from an Egyptian belly dancer costume.

Why on earth did they leave the house like this?

Willow's homework is on the kitchen table. A story she's written in pencil, the tutor's corrections in red. I read the first paragraph. It's set in Anchorage, a tale of a black bear and her cubs catching salmon at Bear Lake. Oh, Willow.

Where are they? Maybe they went to the corner store. Or Willow's asleep upstairs. She's been sleeping all the time lately. My little optimist has turned into someone who spends most of her time in her bed, lost in her dreams. After finally getting a psychologist's appointment, Dr. Ruttenberg took me aside and said he thinks she has depression and it's time to consider antidepressants to break the negative thinking cycle.

*Théo? What would you do? Follow medical advice and medicate our baby or take her on one of your Alaskan treks and help her find herself in the Arctic tundra?*

I start putting everything away: dishes into the dishwasher, clothes sorted into piles, her work into her schoolbag.

Willow's iPad is tucked into the arm of the couch.

Sitting down, I take it onto my lap. I stretch my toes, the pads under the soles of my feet tender from wearing high heels all day.

I run my hand over the iPad leather casing.

*How are you, sweet one?*

Ever since spotting the emojis, I have the occasional peek—if she's not talking to me, how else am I supposed to know what's happening in her life? The experts counsel parents to be on top of their children's online activity. Willow's diary, however, has gone missing, or she's hidden it from me.

With a nervous breath, I open her iPad. It asks for her password when before she never had one. How, I wonder, did she set this up? I touch the screen and tap the password she uses for her bank account: her father's birthday. July 14th. It unlocks. Then I search the recent history.

The headings appear.

**Tying bedsheets into rope**

Mmm. Something to do with arts and crafts?

**Rope for hanging**

**Sheets to hang yourself**

Blinking, I have to read it twice. My eyes fly down the list.

**Hanging methods**

**How to kill yourself**

Rigid fear shoots through me. For a moment, I can't move, like I'm trapped in someone else's body. I drop the iPad onto the couch. "Willow!" I yell as I run upstairs.

Stair, stair, stair, chest thudding.

No response.

*Please. Please be okay.*

Her bedroom door is open. More clothes all over the floor. Her bed, torn apart—comforter off, sheets off—the same cat-printed sheets we fought about last week. I bite my hand to stop from screaming. *Sheets to hang yourself.* The fitted sheet is on the floor—the flat one?—I bend down, search under the bed. Fuck, it's missing!

"Willow!"

My feet move before my brain catches up. I hurry downstairs, grabbing my cell from my purse.

Quick. Quick. Dial Willow's number.

Waiting....

Her phone's turned off.

*Willow, where are you?*

The Fort Park! That's where she always goes when she's sad.

First, check the house.

*Cutting...bathtub.*

I run to the upstairs bathroom.

Bathtub empty—thank God.

*Poison?*

I fling open the medicine cabinet, check to see if anything is out of place. Canisters smash onto the ground, Tylenol, vitamins, the *clang* of nail clippers hitting the tiles.

Call the tutor.

I scroll for Hannah's number. Press *Call.*

*Ring…ring…ring….*

Taking too long.

*Answer. Tell me she's with you….*

Dammit, it rings out.

*What else? Could Willow have jumped off something?*

I head downstairs, out the side door. Dusk. The yard looks undisturbed. I search the garage, the shed.

Back in the kitchen, I examine the knives. None seem to be missing….

Get to the park!

Today, of all days, not to have my car.

House keys? I strap my purse over my body, jam my feet into sneakers, rush out the door.

*Go!* I sprint. How many blocks to get there? Five? Six?

"Willow!" I call her name, scanning left, right, the backseat of cars—everywhere possible for a sign.

I hitch my skirt so I can move more freely. The fabric tears, ripping to my thigh.

The sky is turning purple, making it harder to see. *Go faster, before it's too dark.* I pound the pavement, hoping with every cell in my body she's okay.

"Willow!" I scream as loudly as my voice will carry. "Willow!"

An elderly man comes out of his front door, a yappy brown dog trailing him. He smiles and says over the barking, "Good time for an after-dinner stroll."

"Have you seen a girl—walking by herself? Dark hair. Twelve years old." I hold a hand to my chest. "This high."

He shakes his head and starts to say something, but I keep running.

*I'm coming, baby. Don't do anything. Wait for me.*

"Willow!" My voice is hoarse from yelling. Halfway there now. Lungs feel like they're going to stop working, sweat in my eyes, waves of blinding adrenaline.

I keep sprinting.

*Please don't let this happen. I'll do anything.*

Then, a peek of the playground.

The wooden castle in the distance surrounded by grass.

I lunge forward, muscles aching, biggest strides. The swings come into view. Nearby, someone starts their engine. It sounds like a meat grinder buzzing in my ears. Birds squawk. I shout over the noise, calling her name.

"Willow! Willow! Willow!"

I'm running so fast that when I see it, I skid to a stop.

"No!" A roaring sound comes out of my mouth.

On the castle platform—oh God—Willow's hanging from her neck.

Her back is to me. Body swaying slightly. Dressed in her favorite black-and-white dress that Théo bought her for a party.

My eyes move higher. The cat-printed sheet.

"Help me!" I try to scream but no sound comes out.

Gulping, I suck in air and try again as I run to the platform. "Help my daughter, she's—"

My body flies backward.

Head knocking against something hard.

*Uggh—*

Clouds above me….

I'm—I'm flat on my back. What happened? I sit up, my knee twisted underneath me. Blood gushing down my leg. Must've run into the corner of the play equipment.

"Help!" I scream. "Help!"

*Up. Need to lift Willow up. Get her off the sheet.*

I stand, but my lame leg can't take the weight. Hobbling, I move as fast as I can.

As I get closer, her neck. It's—God—bent at a horrible angle.

*No, baby. I'm too late.*

How could this happen? How can she be dead?

Tears blur my vision. From behind, I reach for my beautiful girl, put my arms around her torso, and lift her so the sheet stops pulling at her neck.

*I'm sorry, baby. For all the lies, for making you cover up my mistakes.*

Her perfume, Sunflowers, that we bought together, scents of honey and peaches and rosewood, fills my nostrils.

I hear her voice…coming from far away.

The sheet is knotted around the top of the climbing bar. How can I hold her up and untie the knots at the same time?

Again, I hear her voice. No, that doesn't make sense…. I can make it out clearly, Willow's voice, loud, alive.

Did I pass out? A grief hallucination.

I need to wake up and get Willow off the fucking sheet.

"Stella! Stella!" The voice is closer now.

At that moment, I spot a girl on the other side of the park. She's running along the path in a bridal gown, the white dress billowing, screaming, "Stella! Stella!"

She looks exactly like Willow.

*What's happening to me?*

Now two people are running. Odelle behind Willow—both running toward me, screaming Stella's name.

—the girl in my arms—it's not Willow! It's Stella!

I motion them over. "Help me get her off!"

They run up to the platform.

Odelle is bone white.

Together, Odelle and I lift Stella, shouldering her weight.

I turn to Willow, overwhelmed with gratitude that it wasn't her. Guilt brims at my mouth; my triumph is Odelle's loss. "Call the ambulance—now."

"I can't." Tears drip down Willow's cheeks. "My battery died."

"Take mine. In my purse."

Odelle groans. Her face is as broken as Stella's neck.

We work in unison. Willow takes out my cell and speaks to the 911 dispatcher. Odelle lifts Stella and, with the sheets slackened, I can finally untie the knots.

"Why isn't she breathing?" Willow screams.

Odelle's mouth quivers, her teeth making a terrible knocking sound. "She is breathing," she says nonsensically. "She's fine. She's fine."

We gently bring Stella down to the ground and lay her on her back. Her face, awfully pale. Wooden planks under her lifeless body, the satin black-and-white dress. Her neck rolls in an unnatural direction.

"Is she dead, Mom? Is she dead?"

Stella's moon cheeks are translucent in the fading light, a contrast to the ring of purple around her narrow neck. Her KISS necklace glints, as though it's winking. Odelle checks Stella's pulse, brings her ear to Stella's lips. She starts CPR.

Thirty chest compressions.

Two breaths.

"Odelle, no." I shake my head. Stella's neck is too twisted, each compression makes it worse.

But Odelle keeps pumping, counting out loud, pushing hard and fast, centering on her sternum.

A horrid cracking sound.

"*Stop!*" I pull Odelle off Stella. "Listen, Odelle. It's too late. I'm sorry. She's…gone."

Odelle lets out a moan like an animal being slaughtered. Sinking to the ground, she whispers, "Stella, Stella, Stella," over and over again, an incantation, as if the words could bring her back to life.

I kneel beside her. "Odelle, I'm here. I'm here with you."

She can't hear me. She's crumpled in a ball, weeping for her baby.

Willow hyperventilates and babbles to herself. Her costume wedding dress is ripped, muddy along the hem. She takes Stella's hand into her own, and says, "I'm sorry. I didn't mean what I said, it was just a dumb fight. You're my best friend."

What is Willow sorry for? What fight?

After a few minutes, I pull Willow off her.

Odelle's wailing fills the park, the neighborhood, all of Boca, until we hear the sirens.

Part 3

# AFTER HER FUNERAL

# Chapter 55

# SUNSHINE STATE

The schoolgirls in the church are already crying. Willow, beside me, has shut down; a comatose doll in her black dress, who I had to lift out of bed, push into the car, buckle her seatbelt, and drive to her best friend's funeral.

We're sitting a few rows back from the front of the crowded church. A blue and purple stained glass window, gold in the center, runs all the way to the steeple. I shift my position, leg straight, as it hurts to bend my bandaged knee. How is it possible that only last week Stella was with us, and now….

*Twelve years old.* Ever since it happened, I keep repeating her age in my mind, a horrible mantra.

Music is playing—Justin Bieber, I presume. Stella loved him. Her iPad casing was a picture of him blowing a kiss; she always hummed his songs and stood up for him when people called him a douche. As the church fills to capacity, the chorus slowly builds, the singer acknowledging that he let someone down and wondering if his apology came too late.

I glance at the white coffin at the front of the room. Yes, Justin Bieber, it's far too late.

People take their seats or stand in somber lines at the back of the church.

Teachers are among the crowd: Ms. Naseer and a few others, the school counselor Jan Boroskwi, and Mrs. Fun.

Odelle stands with her back to the congregation, near the front pew. She's wearing a black suit and looks like a stick figure, her hair somehow redder in contrast to all the dark colors in the room. Poor Odelle. *Twelve years old.*

The scent of flowers. The smell of an old person's funeral. Lilies and carnations. Flowers of death.

Odelle's father and mother and a young woman who must be Lucy surround Odelle. Lucy resembles Stella, dark and curvy, although a much smaller frame. No Ron. How could he not attend his daughter's funeral? Will he show up before the service starts? Unless, of course, it's because of what I told the police. It's possible they've brought him in for questioning.

I shiver, my eyes returning to the white coffin.

*Stella, did you do it because of your dad? Did he hurt you too? Or did you somehow hear about what I accused him of?* Was I partly responsible?

Swallowing, I look for the other KISS parents. Deisha and Wendell are sitting with Fi and Erik to the right, Paulita and John with Giavanna in the pew ahead of us.

Paulita, head bent, appears to be praying. She lifts her hand and wipes her eyes.

"Are you okay?" I whisper to Willow. Stupid question. All I seem to ask her lately are stupid questions. *Would you like to get some fresh air? Can I make you something to eat? Darling, will you talk to me?*

Willow stares at the back of the pew. That's okay, I understand. She's still in shock—we all are.

Where's Brady? I can't spot him anywhere. Given the KISS moms know he was seeing both Odelle and me, surely the rest of Boca will have heard by now.

Brady called the night of Stella's death. It was an unknown number, so I'd answered. I don't know how he found out so quickly, but he wanted to check and see how Willow and I were coping. I told him about Katia and the girls sending Stella those awful texts, and that Stella recorded them in her school notebook, one list for the teacher, the *real* list for herself. Then I passed on what Willow had said about Katia collecting video collateral. He thanked me and said he'd follow protocol with the information. When he brought up our personal issues, I said I had to get off the phone.

I open the funeral program.

*In loving memory*

*of*

*Stella Wragge*

*Church on the Hill, 251 SW Fourth Avenue, Boca Raton*

*October 12th*

*2 o'clock*

*Beloved daughter, sister, granddaughter, & friend*

*The service concludes with the burial attended by members of Stella's family.*

*Stella's family would like to thank everyone for attending today. You are welcome to come to the Wragge's family home for food and refreshments at 3:30 p.m.*

*If any students require counseling, please speak to Jan Boroskwi, Aqua Vista Academy school counselor.*

On the corresponding page, there's a picture of Stella, capturing her dreamy brown eyes and dimpled cheeks, her mouth turned up as though she had just been laughing.

Sweet Stella. Making silly Instagram poses with Willow, playing volleyball in the pool, standing at our door with homemade brownies, weaving through the restaurant with the orange wrapped present, the only guest at Willow's birthday party. Of course, there were other memories too. Her excluding Willow. Her mothering Odelle, the little house chef. Purple bruises around her neck.

A strong Irish accent fills the room. "Thank you for coming today," the celebrant says from the podium. I squeeze Willow's hand and fix my gaze on the older man with a neat white beard and a well-cut suit. "I'm Daniel Moore, and I'll be overseeing our service to celebrate the life of Stella Wragge."

Everyone silences.

As the celebrant gives a blessing, I drift back and forth, from sitting here in the church to arriving at Fort Park, screaming for Willow, running to the platform, realizing it was Stella and trying to untie the bedsheets, to Théo's funeral, the snow falling outside, the endless religious hymns, the strangeness, even then, of not having Théo beside me, and realizing I never would again.

Unlike Théo's funeral, everyone here is young.

KISS, I can see them now, are sitting together in the second row, not with their families but with their "found" school family. Katia in the middle, protected on either side by Issy and Sherice. The three of them together, without Stella, is the starkest reminder of her not being here. KISS, lighter by its kindest member—that final S. I guess they're KIS now.... Katia doesn't deserve to be here.

The church choir take their places at the altar. They sing, "May the Road Rise to Meet You," their halting voices fill the room, reaching every heart.

*Twelve years old.*

I replay the events leading to Stella's death.

From what Willow told me, that afternoon Stella had dropped by as Willow was finishing her tutoring. Stella used Willow's iPad for the remaining time Hannah was there. Then they tried on Halloween costumes, Stella picking Willow's black and white dress; Willow, a bridal outfit. Stella borrowed Willow's Sunflowers perfume, spritzing over her wrists. Stella asked Willow where she went when she was sad, and Willow said Fort Park. Willow asked Stella why she was sad.

Because in standing up for Willow, KISS and the Drew Barrymores turned on her, blowing up her iPhone with cruel, nasty messages.

Because Katia was threatening to use the collateral and send a topless picture of Stella to the entire class.

Because Stella loved her dad and overheard a conversation about him between Lucy and her mom that she refused to tell Willow about.

And because when Stella told Willow that, Willow admitted that Ron had rubbed Odelle's La Prairie cream over her cheeks and that sometimes he made her feel weird.

They'd fought, Stella cried. She told Willow she wanted to wash her face and do her makeup. Afterwards, Willow went into the bathroom and was putting away the makeup, but she got distracted. By the time she got back to her room, her bed was trashed, and Stella was gone.

Worried, Willow rang Stella, but she didn't answer. Willow thought Stella might have gone back home, so she went there and found Odelle. Together, they ran to Fort Park.

All of this, I reported back to Odelle, yesterday, in a dreadful phone call.

The choir finishes singing, and the celebrant asks if anyone would like to speak.

I glance at Odelle. Her face, in profile, is waxen; she doesn't move a muscle.

The girls' cheer coach rises and talks to Stella's quiet determination and friendly nature. She's followed by Lucy, Stella's older sister, who tells a few stories about Stella's kindness, even in the face of sibling rivalry.

Odelle's dad, Judge Rackark, is next. Still formidable after all these years, coifed hair and barrel-chested, with a ruddy expression that would make you think, inaccurately, he's jollier than he is. He says Stella was the cutest baby he'd ever seen. That he was there the day she took her first step and nearly tumbled into the bayou. How he got her hooked on red licorice: he was sitting in his favorite leather seat, reviewing a case, and enjoying his stash of licorice, when he felt Stella's hand dart out and snatch it from him. He talks about how much he misses her, her jokes and cuddles, and the devastation of people dying before their time.

Then a boy stands and shuffles self-consciously to the podium. He's blond and bulky, wearing a green shirt with the collar up.

Beside me, Willow exhales.

I catch her smile. It's the first time she's looked happy since we found Stella at Fort Park.

"Who's that?" I whisper.

"Maxwell Zimmermann. Stella's been in love with him since forever."

Standing in front of the stained glass, Maxwell clears his throat and begins to read from a piece of paper. "We are all here today because of our classmate…." He stops and glances down. After what seems like a minute passes, he shoves the paper in his pocket and lifts his head. "Look, I've known Stella since kindergarten. She hogged all the toys in the sandpit and once the teacher called my mom because when I went for her sand bucket, Stella hit me on the head with a plastic shovel. Anyway, um…yeah. She's always fun and cool to hang around with and"—he shrugs, his face red—"over the years, she sent me notes. Like, in first grade, she sent a note saying, 'You know you're going to marry me one day.'"

People laugh and I feel wetness on my cheeks.

"It's sad," Maxwell says. "She's never going to marry anyone now."

Someone breaks into a guttural sob.

It's Issy, her blonde hair in her face, shoulders shaking. She keeps crying, the pitch rising, turning my stomach. The sound of pain, of the world being broken and never being right again.

Maxwell Zimmermann walks back to his seat and sits beside a bunch of boys, and the celebrant asks if anyone else would like to speak.

Will Odelle share some words? She remains frozen, as though she has an eye mask on and headphones, protecting her from seeing or hearing too much.

Glancing around, Ron is still nowhere in sight.

Willow cries, sniffling, snot trailing down her face.

I dig some tissues out of my purse and pass them to her when I hear his voice from the front of the room—

"I'm Clint Brady, the head of school at Aqua Vista Academy."

I sit up straighter. It's a shock to see him after so long. He looks formal, but unkempt, like he hasn't been taking care of himself. He's wearing a brown suit, hair windblown, dark stubble on his cheeks. Thinner.

There's a murmur around the room. The back of my neck prickles and, I swear, people are looking at me, gauging my reaction: the rumor mill at work.

"Stella Wragge," Brady says. "There are a lot of things we all know about her. She loved candy and often stopped by to grab some jellybeans. Her favorite was watermelon. She liked to socialize and hang out with friends and being with you all was what she lived for." He swallows, his expression harrowed. "What you might not know about Stella is she wrote songs."

A few people look back and forth at each other.

"So, while you watch a video montage of some of the family's favorite pictures, I'm going to play one for you. We'd talked about her performing it at assembly or with the school band, but she was shy—not shy about much, our Stella, but she was shy about her singing–songwriting." He gazes out at the congregation. "Before I play it, please, hear me out. If you're feeling not great about life, know it's normal. It's hard to grow up. It's hard to go to middle school. Problems with other kids, schoolwork, family, a boyfriend or girlfriend, teachers, feels terrible at the time. And people think, 'it's not going to get better.'"

Willow and I press our bodies closer to each other, both crying now.

"Even for adults, life can be tough, we make mistakes, and don't feel brave enough to face up to them." For a moment it feels like Brady's speaking directly to me.

"But you have to give the people you love the heads-up if you're not feeling okay. You can always talk to me, any of you. Because if we're talking to each other—honestly—about anything, then we're not feeling alone. I'm truly"—his voice breaks—"I'm truly sorry, Stella, that you felt alone."

Brady walks over to an open laptop and types something before swiping the mouse a few times.

Simultaneously, the lights dim, and a screen lowers from the ceiling.

Suddenly, Stella's voice, as though she's here in the room, fills the space.

"Is it on?" she asks. "I don't want you to record it. No way, Mr. Brady."

Murmurs from the crowd. Willow trembles beside me. Girls crying like mewling cats.

Brady's recorded voice replies, "Stella, let me tape it once and play it back to you. Then you can hear how awesome it sounds. It's a great song."

"Mmm, maybe it's an okay song," she says before laughing. "Okay, start the guitar."

A melody begins, and the acoustic sound vibrates through the church.

On the screen, images appear. Stella as a chubby baby, in a yellow bathing suit, kicking her legs while Odelle held her out over their pool. In a highchair spitting out broccoli. Her and Lucy sitting beneath a Christmas tree, presents on their laps.

Then Stella's sings.

*I tried to let you know, I tried to hold it in, I promise, I tried everything*

Doing a cartwheel in her cheer uniform.

*Throw a little party for me*

KISS dressed up as witches for Halloween.

*I've got somewhere else to be*

Stella at the beach, arms open, leaping toward the camera.

*Don't worry about me. Don't worry about me. I'm free*

There are no pictures of Ron, as if he was never part of their family, as if he didn't exist at all.

Out of the corner of my eye, I spot someone in the crowd.

Why is Nathaniel here?

## Chapter 56

# B FOR BULLY

"It never should've happened. All of this." Fi gestures to Odelle's open-plan kitchen, now filled with mourners. Kids dressed in black.

"A tragedy," Mrs. Fun says to Fi and me.

Wordless, I nod, my mind still partly on the confrontation I had with Nathaniel outside of the church.

"What the hell are you doing?" I'd said crossly. His face had fallen, obviously not the reaction he was going for, and he'd said, "I read about it in the news. I want to be here for you, Rebecca. When times are tough, when times are good." I'd put my hand up and said, "Stop," before he blurted out what seemed to be a goddamn marriage proposal. Then I accused him of hiring a PI and having me followed. "Never. I love you," he said. I'd stared him in the eye, and said, "Find someone else to love." In the middle of all that, I caught Brady watching the exchange a few yards away.

"…and I told them to send the flowers there," Mrs. Fun says, drawing me back to our conversation. She pats down her hair. "Excuse me, bladder calls." With that, Mrs. Fun shuffles away.

A server walks past, and Fi seizes two glasses of white wine, handing one to me, which I gratefully gulp. We're still not speaking like close friends, more small talk than anything else, but now is not the time for grudges.

The same scent of lilies permeates Odelle's house, thickening the air, which is already full of women's perfume and trite pleasantries. Lilies are in vases everywhere, on bookshelves, windowsills, and amongst the appetizers where guests stand in groups, nibbling on sandwiches and pastries. Being here without Stella may be worse than the funeral.

The kitchen is open to the garden and pool, and small tables covered in pink tablecloths and sparkling silver butterflies have been placed on the patio. The KISS girls and Willow, Esrif, and Natalie, are outside, sitting at the edge of the pool, dangling their legs into the water. Standing to their right, Sherice and "Head of School Angus" are holding hands. That's sweet. Above them, yellow streamers have been hung in the trees like a child's birthday party. Lucy must have been in charge of the decorating as well as flowers; Fi told me that Lucy oversaw all of the funeral details because Odelle was incapable.

My gaze turns to my old friend.

"She looks terrible, doesn't she?" Fi says from beside me.

Armored by her father, Odelle sits in a single armchair beside the fireplace, hands knotted on her lap, with the vacant stare of someone who barely resides in their body.

She has put her house up for sale and is planning to return to Jacksonville to live near her family. I understand; it would be too hard here without Stella. After Théo was gone, being in the house, especially when Willow wasn't home, was a constant reminder of his absence.

"Excuse me," Fi says. "I have to give something to Issy."

I nod and take another sip of wine, wishing it was gin, wishing I could go back to the afternoon of Stella's death and intervene.

But we can't rewind time. Every minute, every breath, is borrowed.

Oh is that…? Yes—Stella's father, Jimmy-Kiss-Me-Now-Before-I-Die. He's balancing a handful of crackers with a mountain of brie on them.

Well, look at that. He's still got it—hair, a shoulder-length mane, which at his age is an accomplishment in itself—and that bad-boy attraction. In a blazer and tight jeans, he stands out in a sea of upper-middle-class men whose wives stopped having sex with them regularly a long time ago. Jimmy's face, I can see now more clearly, is puffy from crying. Odelle had said he'd been far from an involved dad, and now his youngest daughter is gone.

"Rebecca."

It's Brady. The hair on my arms stands up. I turn.

His eyes are bloodshot, shirt rumpled. Part of me wants to envelop him in a hug, to call a truce, just for today, but, of course, that's not possible.

"You coping okay?" he asks.

"Not really," I reply with a curt tone, aware of the eyes of the room upon us. I haven't told anyone I found Stella at Fort Park. I don't want the attention, to be the person people ask to hear "the real story." No. Only Odelle, Willow, the police, and the emergency people know I was ever there. And maybe Stella…if her spirit hung around her body, maybe she watched us crying, begging her to come back.

Brady's arms flounder at his sides. "Bec, I've been worried about you. I feel terrible about everything. When I was in Orlando with Paddy—"

"This isn't the place." I give him a fiery look.

"But, you have to understand, I—"

"Stop. Why are you even here? To make Odelle more miserable? You should leave."

His shoulders drop. "You've got it wrong. I've been trying to tell you that. We all need to heal. Especially after Stella, our community—"

Across the room, Odelle makes eye contact. There's a flash, I can see it, of her presence. She's momentarily back in her body.

I hurry over, slowing my pace as I approach where she's seated. "Odelle? Honey?"

Paul Rackark puts a protective hand on Odelle's shoulder.

"It's okay, Daddy," she says in a croaky whisper. "Need to talk to her."

"If you're sure." The light catches the crucifix around his neck on a thick, gold chain. "I'll be back in a few minutes."

I pull up a seat beside Odelle, unsure what to say. At Théo's wake, every well-meaning sentiment shared made each moment worse, more final. "How are you holding up?"

There's no recognition on her face that she's heard me. It seems like she's watching something far away.

"Odelle?" I gently touch her leg. "Odelle, you said you needed to talk to me?"

She drops her head. I expect her to say something, but she keeps blinking.

"Odelle? It's me, Becks." Has she lost her mind? Can she hear me?

The blinks continue.

I'm about to give up when Odelle grips my hand. "Listen."

"I'm listening."

She points to her Gucci purse on the floor. "In—that pocket."

Bending, I slide my hand into the right pocket, feeling something hard and small, an unusual shape.

I take it out. Ah, a KISS necklace. I pass it to Odelle.

"Get Willow," Odelle breathes.

I go to the backyard. She's not with the group at the pool. It takes me a few moments, but I find Willow sitting cross-legged with Katia in the garden, just the two of them, a mound of flower petals between them.

"What are you doing?" Jesus. For her to be with Katia, of all people.

"Nothing," Katia says, with a blush.

She should blush. She should have a scarlet letter, *B* for bully.

*How do you feel, little girl? Your taunting, your collateral, look what you did to Stella.*

I'm surprised Katia was allowed to attend the wake.

I look at my daughter, sitting in the grass—my living, grieving daughter.

"Come with me please, Willow. Odelle has something she wants to tell you."

# Chapter 57

# DOUBLE CROSS

"What were you doing in the garden with Katia?" I ask Willow as we walk toward the living room.

"Just leaving a few things for Stella."

"What do you mean?"

"It's silly," she says. "When Katia and Stella were in elementary school, they used to play fairy garden. They'd make petal beds and flower cup couches and stuff." Her lips turn up in a half smile. "Katia told me about it, and we thought maybe if Stella is a spirit now, or energy, or something, she could have a little fairy house in the backyard to come and visit."

I squeeze her hand. "That's really nice, Willow. But Katia—she's a vile girl. I don't want you spending time with her. How can you forgive her?"

"Katia's so sad, Mom. She wishes she didn't send the texts and make the videos. But it's not like Stella hasn't done the same thing. A few months ago, when Stella was mad at Katia, she sent texts that were way worse than what Katia sent. It's just how these girls fight…but now…I guess everyone realizes that's not how friends treat each other."

I spot Brady beside Mrs. Fun, carrying her plate and drink.

Hopefully, if he retrieves Stella's notebook, there may be an investigation.

When we reach Odelle's side, she appears worse than before: her head bent so low it appears she's lost any inclination to hold it up, her lipstick smudged, hands fisted on her lap.

I keep saying her name, softly, and tapping her leg, but it's no use.

"Are you listening, honey? Come back to us." I sit beside her.

Odelle takes a sudden breath, slowly turning her gaze to Willow. She hands the KISS necklace to her. "I talked to Stella this morning; she wants you to have it."

This morning? Odelle hasn't processed what's happened. She still believes Stella's with the living.

"Oh?" Willow's eyes double in size and I'm not sure whether she wants to take the necklace or not. Her manners kick in. "Thank you." She stares at it for a moment before lifting the chain around her neck. The pendant falls over her dress, red on black.

Odelle makes a tiny gasp, then jerks her head toward the garden. "Butterflies," she mutters. "No. No. No."

I look out at the tree branches, the flowering bushes, too beautiful and lush for such a tragic occasion, and then turn back to Odelle. "Do you see some in the garden? What's wrong?" I gently nudge Willow away; she doesn't need to witness Odelle in this state.

When Odelle doesn't answer, I say, "Everything must feel too painful to bear. All these people are here because we love you, and we love Stella."

A tear drips down Odelle's cheek. First one, then a steady, slow stream, falling off her chin onto her lap.

Using a clean tissue from my purse, I wipe them and carefully dab the corner of her mouth to remove the lipstick. "You'll get through it. Hour by hour. Whatever you need, just say the word."

"You're a good friend." I'm about to reply when she says, "I'm sorry."

Does she mean for telling the KISS moms I'd been with Brady?

She locks eyes with me. "For lying about Brady."

I squint in confusion.

Odelle tucks her elbows into her sides. "Brady was never with us at the same time. I never went on his boat."

"But you said—"

"I lied." Odelle swallows, as though it's laborious to talk, to have to use her mouth, oxygen, to communicate.

"Why?" I picture her in her cowgirl outfit knocking on Brady's truck window, her telling me he said I was a widow fuck, us drowning our sorrows together at the bar while listening to Patsy Cline.

She lifts one small shoulder, mirth on her face. "Love. I was in love with him. I wanted him for myself."

What have I done? Tossed away a fun, growing relationship, because of what? Odelle's desire to sabotage us? Did Brady do anything wrong at all? He should have told me they had history, but he'd explained why he didn't.

"Instead of facing what was going on in my marriage," Odelle says, "or focusing on…on Stella, I…." She crumples and weeps.

People around the room turn toward us.

"Here, drink some water." I take her glass from the ledge and bring it to her lips, making sure she has a few sips. Given her frame of mind, she might be hospitalized or taken to Jax under the care of her parents. But despite her fragile state, she needs all the information possible. Legally, it may be important. "Odelle, about Ron, Willow told me he'd been befriending her, and he—"

"I know."

"You know…about…?"

"I had suspicions over the years, nothing solid," Odelle says. "Last year, I found porn on his computer, the girls—they were very young. That's why I said that he belonged in jail." She coughs, tightening her hands on her lap. "That night you showed me the picture of Willow, I knew I had to do something."

"What'd you do?" My body seizes up. Is that why he isn't here? Did Odelle—

A heavy hand lands on my shoulder.

Paul Rackark's judge-gaze burns into my skull. "That's quite enough," he says to me. "Odelle, deep breaths. Can you settle or shall we bring you upstairs?"

Her eyes flick upward.

"Very well." He extends his hand to her.

It occurs to me, then, that Odelle finally has what she always craved: her father's attention.

Odelle stands and reaches for her father's arm, but as she does, a look of horror flashes across her face, and all I can see is the white of her eyes, followed by her body crashing to the ground.

Then a rush of blue—two police officers.

# Chapter 58

# GARAGE

In the seconds that follow, I take it all in.

—The apologetic looks on the two police officers' faces, who obviously had no idea they were walking into a wake.

—Odelle semiconscious on the ground.

—Her parents and the two police officers hurrying to attend to her. One officer is young, the other older, with a gray buzzcut.

—Jimmy-Kiss-Me-Now-Before-I-Die also dashing to Odelle's side, bending to his knee, and lifting his hand to her cheek in a gallant gesture.

—Everyone in the room whispering, focused on the scene.

I scan for Willow. At precisely the same time I spot her, talking to Angus and Sherice in the backyard, Brady nearly runs into me.

"Sorry," he says, brushing past. Midstride, he keeps moving.

I grab his arm. "Do you know what's happening?"

He nods gravely. "Everything's going to hell."

"What is?" I can feel people staring at us, adding fuel to the drama playing out before them.

"Ah…it's gonna have to be somewhere private."

"There's no need to be alarmed," the older of the police officers addresses the room. A hush follows. "Please go about your business. Our condolences."

"The garage," I suggest to Brady. With a quick glance at Odelle, who is now sitting up and speaking with the younger police officer, I say, "Will you give me a minute? I'll meet you there."

Outside, Willow and her friends are congregated in a circle. I tell her where I'll be if she needs me.

When I reach the spotless, mega car garage, I pass Ron's yellow Porsche, the scent of car wax, leather cleaner, and oil dominates the space.

"I want to hear everything," I say to Brady.

"You sure about that?" He unfolds two outdoor chairs, setting them to face each other. We sit down. "So." He sighs. "The day after Stella took her life, Giavanna showed up at my house. Crying. Freaked out."

"Okay?"

"She told me she'd been in therapy. Reviewing her life. How her experiences when she was sixteen triggered reckless behavior afterward." He wipes his hair away from his eye. "She'd gotten into binge drinking, promiscuous behavior. Even when she was wearing the South Florida crown, behind closed doors she was a mess."

"Poor kid."

"She wanted to thank me." He knots his hands, the fluorescent lights above giving his skin a yellow pallor. "For helping her when she was sixteen. She said she could never have had the baby. It would've been the end of her because of the baby's father."

"A drug dealer from Miami, right?"

He shakes his head. "Worse."

"Who?"

He looks at me, his expression pained. "Ron Wragge."

"But—but—*what*?" I try to link it together. Odelle had said her eldest daughter, Lucy, and Paulita's, Giavanna, had been best friends.

*...Her best friend's stepdad.*

I clutch my stomach, sick with the realization of how much Giavanna had to endure. And Willow, God, she could've been next!

"Sweetheart, are you okay?" Brady asks. "I know it's a lot." I nod and he carries on speaking. "Giavanna said it went on for years. Ron threatened that if she told her parents, he'd ruin their careers." Brady's fists are white as he speaks. "From my little knowledge about pedophiles, I assumed they stuck to an age preference. Wouldn't have thought Giavanna, as a teenager, would still be a target. I suppose it was a case of familiarity and opportunity." Brady's face contorts with disgust.

"He's evil," I whisper.

"Ron initiated things with Giavanna less after she got her period, but if he was drinking.... She suspects the condom broke—that's how she got pregnant, because he was careful about contraception. She was in love with him, Bec, like Stockholm Syndrome. But when she got pregnant, Ron didn't want anything to do with her, said she had to get rid of the baby."

"Jesus. I'm sorry."

"If only I'd known who the father was then, I could've helped put Ron behind bars. Then maybe Stella wouldn't have...." He looks at me from under his eyebrows and whispers, "How do we know Ron didn't do it to other girls?"

"We can't."

He punches his fist into his open hand. "The mistake I made, keeping Giavanna's pregnancy secret—the ramifications are a million times worse than I could've ever imagined."

"You were operating on what Giavanna told you. She came to thank you for what you did. Don't forget that." I touch his gaunt cheek, an instinctive gesture that feels too intimate. "You haven't explained why the police are here."

"Stella's death was a catalyst."

"How so?"

"When Lucy came home from college recently, the two friends had a heart-to-heart. Giavanna told Lucy what Ron did to her when she was young."

I nod, waiting for him to continue.

"Then, apparently, Lucy has an argument with Odelle about it, which Stella overheard. Not too long after, Stella committed—I mean suicided. You're not supposed to say committed suicide."

"Why?"

"The word 'commit' has criminal associations; it implies sin or crime."

I touch my temples, stunned by how interwoven all the players were; a sick web, too dark to fathom.

"Giavanna panicked," Brady says. "She thought the reason Stella took her own life was because of what she told Lucy. She worried Ron might've harmed Stella too. Giavanna decided she'd tell the police about Ron, testify, do anything to stop him. Show them the cards he'd written her. But she was scared and thought back to the guy who helped her when she was sixteen."

"So, she came to you for help again?"

"Right. I convinced her we had to tell her parents because, hell, look what a mess we got into last time." His voice is jittery. "Giavanna thought her parents would want to shut it down. It would ruin their careers, all the bad publicity."

"And then?"

"Giavanna wanted me to go with her. We went to her parents' house, sat in the living room with Paulita and John. She told them what Ron had done."

"How'd they react?"

"Mortified. Paulita said we shouldn't go public. It should be settled privately."

I clasp my hands. "So, Giavanna was right: her mom couldn't face the bad publicity."

"Paulita went into crisis mode. The political implications. Thankfully, John talked some sense into her. He lashed out. Told her the dealership and the election didn't matter. They couldn't protect her political career at the expense of their child."

"And Ron? Why would the police show up at Stella's wake?"

"Turns out, the cops knew all about Ron Wragge. They'd been tracking his movements for months based on some intel about his activities in Bangkok."

"Christ!"

"They suspected he was part of a child porn ring. I suppose Giavanna's testimony was all they needed."

"Plus mine," I say, thinking out loud.

"Yours?" His chair scrapes on the cement as he turns to me.

"Willow. He was grooming her." My eyelids pool with tears.

"Oh, Bec. I'm sorry." He strokes my back, his touch expressing more than words could. "I guess they had both your testimonies, plus all the shit Ron was looking at online. Lucy told Giavanna he was arrested the following night."

"I see."

"From what I heard, they've already searched the house, but then Ron fessed up that he had more USBs stored in the basement. I think that's why the cops are here now. Guess they didn't know it was Stella's wake."

"Bad timing."

"Everything about it is bad." Brady rubs his knuckles over his unshaven face.

All the people affected—Stella, Lucy, Odelle, Giavanna, Paulita, John, Katia, Brady…and Willow. Plus the unknowns.

Brady touches my arm. "Bec, I know it's not the best time to talk about us, but—"

The garage door hinges open.

"Mom?"

Willow stands at the threshold, looking more tired than annoyed. "I wanna go."

"Of course, darling."

Brady and I rise.

He nods and says to Willow, "I'm sorry about Stella. It must be very tough for you."

She keeps her eyes fixed on the floor.

"From what I hear, she stood up for you. She was a good friend."

"A great one," Willow whispers.

"I guess that might be a way to honor her," Brady says. "To continue being a great friend to the people you love."

"Yeah."

With that, I take Willow's hand and we head home.

# Chapter 59

# PINKIE SWEAR

Willow has fallen asleep on the couch in her funeral dress. It's 5:30 p.m., too late to nap; she'll have trouble going to bed tonight.

I'm in the kitchen unpacking the dishwasher when she starts whimpering, "Papa, Papa…."

Another night terror; they're back with a vengeance.

I walk over and give her shoulders a gentle shake.

Her eyes pop open. "What are you doing?" she snaps. Ever since Stella's death, her mood swings are volatile—anger on top of anger. At me, at the world, at Stella. Then, uncontrollable sobbing.

"You were having a bad dream."

"I was with Papa again, our last night together."

"It's all right, sweetie."

She glares and sits up. "No, it's not. You treat me like such a baby. You think I know nothing!"

"That's not true. What's this all about?"

"You're such an idiot," she screams, jumping off the couch.

"Don't talk to me like that."

"I know about Mr. Brady! *Disgusting.*"

A wave of shock renders me speechless.

I stare at the carpet. I'm the one who's supposed to be teaching her wrong from right, not the other way around.

"Why didn't you tell me?" she yells.

"Willow, I'm sorry. I have been dating him, but I wanted to make sure it was going to be a longer-term relationship before involving you. Can you understand?"

"I wish I was the one that was dead."

"No. Willow. Don't say that. Come here, honey." I pull her back onto the couch and take her into my arms.

"Oh, Mom…I miss Stella. I miss her so much. She's the only one I told."

"Told what?"

"That I…I killed Papa." She starts shaking, huge, terrible sounds erupting from her mouth. "I didn't mean to, Mom. I never meant to hurt him."

"Of course not, sweetheart. You would never want to hurt him."

"You think I don't know what I did? You think I didn't figure it out! I'm not that stupid. At first, it didn't make sense. But then I put it together."

"No, Willow, you don't need to say any more."

Tears flood her eyes. "Papa and I were watching a Mr. Bean movie and eating popcorn. Then Papa started moaning, and I asked if he was okay, and he said he was, but he didn't laugh at all the funny parts of the movie. I needed to pee, so he paused the movie."

"Stop."

"I ran to the bathroom. Papa called out that he wanted me to bring him some antacid. He said it was in a blue Ziploc bag with powder in it, but to make sure—something or other—I wasn't really listening because I was thinking about how I kept messing up the dismount of my final double flip at my last meet."

She frowns, lips trembling. "Nothing looked like that on the sink or in the medicine cabinet. He said if it wasn't in the bathroom, to look in his room and then put it in a glass with water."

"You don't have to go on."

"I went into your room. You were sleeping on the bed. The lamp was on, and you were wearing all your clothes, even your snow boots. There was mascara on your face like you'd been crying. The blue Ziploc bag was in your hands. I took it and ran to the kitchen."

"Shhh, Willow, that's enough."

"I mixed the drink for him. When I went back to the living room, I gave him the drink and he put the movie back on."

My heart breaks for her, for what must follow next.

She speaks quickly. "He took a sip of the drink. He said, 'It's not fizzing.' I didn't know what he meant. He asked where I got the bag, and I said you fell asleep holding it, and he said, 'It's important you listen to me.'"

"And then?" I no longer wish for her to stop. I'm desperate to hear his last words.

"He said, 'Thank you. Now I can go to a peaceful place. I'll see you there one day. A green field, with a lake. I'll be fishing.'

"I was like, 'Is this one of your stories?' You know how sometimes he lets me name the characters or pick the setting."

"He said, 'Yes…a story,' then he kissed me on the forehead and told me to go to bed. The movie was only halfway through, but he said, 'Mom won't want you up late. Be good for your mom.'"

Swallowing, I take her hand in mine.

"I walked away, but something made me look back. He finished the rest of his drink and started texting someone.

"I said goodnight and told him I loved him. He said, 'I love you too, *Mon Chéri*. Never forget that. Always fly.'"

"Oh, sweetie." I allow the tears to come, sickened by the burden Willow has been carrying. I thought I was protecting her from figuring it out. If she knew…she wouldn't want to live herself. The guilt would've crushed her. Terminal illness or not, what girl would want to know her actions killed her father?

"It was my fault," she says.

"No, Willow, it was mine." I hold her tightly in my arms, forehead to forehead, her shoulders shaking, the sound of our weeping, merged.

"It's hard to understand, but you gave your papa what he wanted. He bought medicine that people who are very unwell take and don't want to be in pain anymore. I didn't think he should take it—but *I* was selfish. I took the medicine from where he hid it, I was trying to figure out whether

I could give him my blessing, but I fell asleep with it in my hands. That's why it's my fault. Do you understand?"

She nods.

"People have the right—your dad had the right not to suffer. What you did, giving him that powder, was granting his wish."

"It made him go away forever."

I cup her chin, so she's looking right into my eyes. "It was magical. It let him sleep, have no pain, and be at peace."

She cries as I rock her in my arms.

All this time, I thought I was protecting her—overprotecting her, maybe—but instead, all she saw were my lies. "Willow, I'm sorry. I wish I hadn't kept everything from you. We all make mistakes."

She lowers her eyes. "Maybe I don't want you be with Mr. Brady… because then you'll forget Papa."

"Never. Could. Happen." I dab a tear off her nose. "We have hundreds of memories of our family, of Papa. But we can't stop living. When someone we love dies, we have to honor them by appreciating our life." I swallow. "If I do decide to date Brady again, are you going to be okay with that?"

She toys with her bracelet. "No."

"Well, whatever I decide, let's make a pact." I link her pinkie finger with mine. "Honesty always. No matter what."

"Honesty always," she says.

I kiss her soft cheek. "I have a surprise for you."

"What is it?"

"A special visitor is coming in two days."

She smiles and we lie on either side of the couch, our legs twisted like a pretzel, Théo's blanket over us.

*Théo? I'll always love you, and I miss you, but I'm going to stop talking to you, I think. It feels like it's time. I'll take care of our little girl—she's not so little anymore. Au revoir, darling.*

*Pour tous jours.*

# Chapter 60

# MOTHERS & DAUGHTERS

"Oh, Jane, that's the doorbell," I say into the phone. "I better go."

"It was great talking to you," Jane says. "Come and visit us in Anchorage soon. Miss you."

After saying goodbye to my dear friend, who I vow to call more regularly, I walk swiftly down the hallway.

Yolanthe is dressed impeccably: a cream suit, tan purse, and loafers, delicate gold jewelry. She looks older, fragile, as though she's shrunk a size.

"It's good to see you, Yolanthe. How was your flight?"

"Decent enough."

"Please, come inside."

"Where's Willow?"

"She'll be home from her friend, Issy's, soon." According to Willow, KISS has all but disbanded. Sherice is glued at the hip with Angus. The Drew Barrymores have sought other friendship groups. As soon as the heat was on Katia about the texts she sent Stella and the collateral videos, Katia jumped ship—her mom, Paulita, whisking her away on a last-minute shopping trip to Milan. Now only Willow and Issy spend time together, which suits me. "Coffee?"

"Tea."

After I make a pot, we sit at the dining room table, casually chatting until the small talk becomes unbearable.

"How's Gérard?" I inhale the scent of gardenias, Brady's flowers, the aroma filling the whole house.

"No improvement."

"Something sweet?" I gesture to the kitchen.

Yolanthe nods. "Thank you."

I get up, pass her a slice of key lime pie, then sit.

"I figured it out," I say.

"Figured what out?"

"There's been someone following me. I made him stop by putting a gun to his head."

She clears her throat. "How terrible."

"Quite."

I watch her carefully as she cuts into the corner of the pie using the edge of the fork and takes a small bite. "An unusual flavor," she says. "I'm picking up a touch of almond in the crust."

"I forgive you, Yolanthe."

"Forgive me?"

"We don't need to play this game. I understand."

Folding her hands on her lap, she says, "It was a mistake coming. I thought we could have a cordial conversation and I could spend some time with my only grandchild, who you told me is going through a very difficult time." She rises. "I've booked myself in at the Waldorf Astoria. Tell Willow to call me directly. There's no need for us to have to communicate anymore."

"It was you, wasn't it?" I follow her down the hall.

She picks up her pace, her back to me, a stiff gait.

"You suspected I was having an affair and that's why I left Anchorage—"

"Goodbye, Rebecca." She opens the door. "I'm not listening to this garbage."

"Yes, you are." I step in front of her and slam the door shut.

She flinches. "*Mon Dieu*!"

"You hired a PI." I get right up in her face. "Congratulations, he was pretty good. I barely noticed him lurking in the bushes, following my car, and watching me and your twelve-year-old-granddaughter through the windows at night. Oh, and I can't forget, locking me in his car and driving the wrong way. What. A. Blast."

Yolanthe holds her Chanel purse against her like a shield.

"At first, I fell for what he said. His hint that his client was a guy who wanted to make sure I was all right. Very clever. He was trying to get me off your scent."

"May I sit?" Her voice is frail.

We move back to the kitchen table, our breathing loud.

"The facts about Théo's death didn't add up." She takes a hanky from her purse, wipes her nose. "The emotional text he sent me, you making me take Willow out for breakfast when her father was dead in the other room, adamant she didn't talk to the police. Very odd."

It circles back to me.

"Your flirtations with the ex-boyfriend. All the visits to different cities to spend time with men."

"To spend time with *chefs*. For work."

"The money, of course. When Gérard and I pass, Willow will inherit a substantial sum. I was worried you'd find a way to get your hands on it."

I grit my teeth. "I would never steal money from my daughter or"—the first crime she punished me for—"steal your son from you. If you knew me, you'd never suspect me of those things."

She hugs her arms around her delicate frame. "When I was in my twenties, my sister tricked me out of an enormous amount of money." This I know. The sister had a much bigger role in Yolanthe's father's textile manufacturing company, and before he passed, the sister got Yolanthe to sign a contract that she didn't get checked out by a lawyer. "Ever since, I assume the worst about people."

"I get that. It must've been awful for you, the betrayal."

"Yes."

"I wish you would've given me a shot. I can't believe you resorted to a PI."

She twists her hands. "I'm sorry."

Words I thought I'd never hear. "Thank you."

"The truth is I liked getting the updates, all the pictures. Picnics. Willow at school. It made me feel…connected, I suppose. And maybe I needed someone to blame. I didn't feel like I could trust you."

I look out the window at the swaying palm trees. Perhaps, given what I've kept from her, I'm not trustworthy. There are many sides to me, more since I've moved to Boca.

I'm Mom—stable, orderly, compassionate. Albeit too concerned with normality, fitting in.

I'm Rebecca—business owner, photographer, artist. Théo's wife. Who will always grieve for him.

I'm Becks, too, the younger me, full of confidence and sexual power.

And I'm Bec, the woman who Brady met, a combination of all my different sides. The woman I want to be.

I face my husband's mother. The new me isn't lying to anybody. If Yolanthe can't handle the truth, that's on her.

"You were right. I did lie to you about Théo's death."

Her eyebrow quirks. "I knew it."

"He didn't want the fate of his uncle, or to be like Gérard, always dependent on someone."

She sniffs, acknowledging this with a curt nod.

"Théo wanted to leave this world. He knew, you being Catholic, and loving him so very much, wouldn't let him die. Eternal damnation. He purchased Nembutal. He made me promise not to tell you. I'm sorry."

She clutches her elbows.

"Here." I serve her some more tea.

After a few seconds pass, she takes a cautious sip, carefully bringing the porcelain rim to her mouth. To calm her, I ask some questions about the charity she's long been involved with, *La Fondation de l'Hopital de Montréal Pour Enfants*, and as she answers them, the color slowly returns to her cheeks.

At the *click* of the front door, we turn.

"Is Grand-mère here yet?"

Her voice first, then Willow runs into the room.

"*Mon Cherie*!" Yolanthe rises and they embrace. "I've missed you. Look at you. So grown-up."

"So shorn!" Her beautiful long hair has been chopped into an uneven bob with crooked bangs. "What happened?"

"I wanted it short," Willow says matter-of-factly. "Issy cut it."

"But you might get teased at school."

"I don't care, I'll be fine. I'm not like.... I'm not like Stella. I'm going to do what I want."

"You look so much like Théo," Yolanthe says.

"Same stubborn nature too," I mutter under my breath.

Yolanthe makes a noise that suspiciously sounds like laughter.

Willow glances back and forth at us. "You guys seem like you're getting along?"

A sad smile appears on Yolanthe's mouth. For a moment, our eyes meet, and maybe I imagine it, but it seems like understanding is there, that in finally knowing what happened to her son, she also realizes she misjudged me all these years.

Our high spirits carry on later that night. Yolanthe treats us to a fancy three-course dinner and champagne at the Waldorf Astoria. The table is beautifully set with pink roses and white candles.

We toast our first glass.

"To three generations," Yolanthe says.

"If Théo could see us now, he'd be so very happy." I raise my glass. "To making mistakes and being woman enough to own them."

"To India!" Willow holds up her glass of Coke.

Yolanthe's forehead creases. "I feel as though I'm being left out of another secret."

"Mom said we could go on a trek—like Papa! For a whole month, around India! Then she wants to do her own photography thing for a few weeks."

"And leave you? Really." The harsh look is back on Yolanthe's face, the one I know all too well. "Who's going to look after you?"

Willow grins. "So-ooo, now that you're here, Grand-mère, we have a question for you.... Can I stay with you and Grand-père?"

It's a loose plan. After the next semester of school finishes, just as Théo used to go on hero's journeys throughout Alaska, we want to go on a trekking and photography intensive in India. My travel companion? My number one love: Willow. Time for adventure—time to heal.

# Chapter 61

# TREK

## Two weeks later

I approach *Joey Boy*, the wind in my hair, and raise my arm in a wave.

Brady stands and greets me. "Hi," he says with a warm smile.

"Morning, Clint Eastwood."

"Ah, man. I never should've told you that." He offers me his hand and I step onto the boat.

"Thanks."

He pours us pineapple juice into his "head of school" mugs, and we sit facing the Intracoastal.

A few days after the funeral, I called Brady to let him know Odelle had fessed up to me that she'd lied about them ever having a relationship. Going forward, I told him I thought it best for us to remain platonic. Yeah, that lasted a few days. A dinner at his request turned into another one, which ended up with us back in his bedroom. Within seconds of skin-to-skin contact, I was a goner.

"So, what's happening with the investigation about Katia?" I ask.

"Everything's up to the Board of eE. Katia's temporarily suspended while the Board reviews the case. She has to be accountable."

"Agreed. The whole family needs counseling. Katia's a product of her environment." I stare out at the boats moored on the dock, the tranquil water camouflaging the monsters beneath.

"Hungry?" he asks.

"Depends on if you're serving more than potato chips."

"Aw, you know me so well."

I close my eyes, breathing in the salty air.

"Come here," Brady says. He leads me to the bow and looks at me with the goofiest expression.

"What is it?" I ask, suddenly self-conscious.

"This is the moment I knew you were going to rock my world. You were standing right here. The sun in your eyes—"

"You mean when I stripped?"

He laughs. "When you stripped your *walls*. Your defenses."

We smile at each other, and I blush, remembering how forward I'd been.

Brady says, "I thought you should know I've resigned. I'm going to focus on Autism Awesome."

"You what?" I reach out and take his hand. "The kids at Aqua Vista need you.... Because of Paulita, or the reporter, or gossip about us?"

"All of it. I should've stood up to Paulita's family a long time ago. I'm sorry I let you down. I can't help seeking peoples' approval."

"A hang-up from when you were a kid?" I ask gently.

He glances at the deck. "Could be, doc."

I rub his arm. "You're not all that bad."

"No?"

"I, for one, find you very likable."

"Likable's pretty good."

I step a little closer. "Very forgivable."

"Better." He nods.

I get onto my tippy toes. "Very kissable"—whatever else I was planning to say gets lost.

After a few moments, he draws back. "So, is it time for us to take our relationship out into the open in Boca?"

"Think bigger. How about out of the country?"

His eyes sparkle. "What are you thinking? Some epic, multi-country movie quest? *Mission Impossible*. Classic *Indiana Jones and the Last Crusade*."

"You got the India part right. Willow and I are spending a month traveling around India. Afterward, she's staying with her grandmother in Montréal for a few weeks, and I'm planning my own trek. Not sure where yet."

He gives me a shy glance. "Is that an invitation?"

"I mean, if you don't have anything better to do."

I stare into his gorgeous face. A second chance at romance so soon was unexpected. Théo wouldn't want me to spend too long grieving; he was the one who always pushed me into life. *How can you make art if you don't feel it?*

"Are you sure?" Brady asks. "I don't want to step on Willow's toes."

"Don't worry. Turns out you've got her tentative stamp of approval." Last week Willow told me she'd changed her mind and if I wanted to date Brady it was okay by her.

"Huh." He shakes his head. "I did not see that coming. Guess I'm not your 'weekend only' friend anymore?"

"Nope," I reply. "A Monday friend. A Tuesday friend. A Wednesday friend…an every day—and *night*—one."

## The End

According to the American Justice Department, one out of every four children is a victim of bullying, and at least two children are bullied every seven minutes. In the United States, there has been an unprecedented number of child suicides attributed to bullying, including that of a six-year-old in Oregon. Stand for the Silent is an organization started by the parents of a son who suicided due to bullying. It has quickly become one of the leading and most effective anti-bullying organizations.

To donate, please see:

https://standforthesilent.org/donation/

The National Center for Missing and Exploited Children reports that at least 100,000 American children a year are victimized through child sexual exploitation. That is more children than the number of people who die from car accidents and illegal drugs combined.

To learn more, see: The Demand Project: Fighting to Eradicate Sex Trafficking and the Sexual Exploitation of Children.

https://www.thedemandproject.org/Donate

# Acknowledgments

To my husband, Stephen Turner. Sexy. Smart. And forgiving.

To my children, Cohen and Matisse, for leaving me alone…until dinnertime.

To my mother, Gwenda Ellwood, for her completely unbiased belief in me.

To my class act agent, Jill Marsal. I could be in no better hands.

To my acquiring editor, Adriana Senior, for her vision.

To the team at Post Hill Press.

To my brilliant partner-in-crime in all things literary, Andrea Barton.

To my critique partners, beta readers, and writing groups. Our work is truly collaborative.

—Oh, almost forgot, to my hairdresser, Nadia Sabatino, who while getting my roots done, brainstormed with me the scene on page 310.

*Thank you*

# About the Author

**Dr. Bella Ellwood-Clayton** is an award-winning author. She has a BA from Concordia University in Montréal and a PhD from the University of Melbourne in sexual anthropology—and, yes, that makes for interesting dinner party conversations. Her nonfiction book, *Sex Drive: In Pursuit of Female Desire*, was published by Allen & Unwin in 2012. Bella has published short stories, poetry, and written for publications such as *Huffington Post* and *Daily Life*. She frequently appears on TV and gives talks, including a TEDx talk, about relationships. Her work has been featured in a *National Geographic* documentary. Married, she is a mom of two spirited tweens and a mini Maltese who truly believes he's a pit bull.

www.drbella.com.au
Twitter: @BEllwoodClayton
Insta: @BellaEllwoodClayton
Join Bella's Monthly Memo newsletter: https://bit.ly/X3s6c

Made in the USA
Las Vegas, NV
19 November 2023